**Praise for the Novels
of Raymond Khoury**

The Templar Salvation

"[A] sublime narrative. The result is a full-throttle action-adventure thriller wrapped in a political cautionary tale with a gratifyingly eloquent center." —*Library Journal*

"[A] well-constructed blend of historical mystery and present-day thriller.... There's no denying he's got the storytelling chops." —*Booklist*

"The constant suspense, ever-mounting body count, and interesting historical lore will keep readers turning the pages." —*Publishers Weekly*

"Raymond has not lost his touch of creating powerful suspense." —Bookreporter.com

The Sign

"A rapid-paced adventure that delivers equal quantities of story and lesson, neither one suffering in the process. [Khoury] is especially adept at action scenes. His expertly chosen verbs cause the scenes to leap from the page. You can literally feel the blows as they're landed, wince as the bullets find their marks. He has an intense brand of storytelling all his own. *The Sign* is a prize to be savored."
—Steve Berry, *New York Times* bestselling author of *The Emperor's Tomb*

"A real humdinger that taps into some of our deepest fears over the state of the planet."
—*The Evening Telegraph* (Peterborough, UK)

continued ...

"[*The Sanctuary*] may be the most ambitious fictional work of 2007 . . . enough adventure, excitement, and speculation to fill three books."   —Bookreporter.com

The Last Templar

"Like *The Da Vinci Code*, Khoury's novel features age-old mysteries that play out in a modern setting."
—*The New York Times*

"Fast-paced . . . the perfect read for those for whom Dan Brown was the start but not the finish."
—*Sunday Express* (UK)

"[Will] satisfy your historical thriller craving."
—*Glamour*

"Short, quick scenes and cinematic action sequences . . . keep things moving at an absorbingly brisk pace."
—*San Francisco Chronicle*

"For those who think Dan Brown doesn't write fast enough."
—*The Louisville Courier-Journal*

"*Da Vinci*–style thriller flourishes."   —*Publishers Weekly*

"One of the most gripping opening scenes among recent thrillers. . . . Khoury is a screenwriter, and his story is nothing if not cinematic, as it skips across three continents and climaxes with a storm at sea of biblical proportions. A nice twist at the end spins the Christian history everyone's been chasing."   —*Booklist*

ALSO BY RAYMOND KHOURY

THE
TEMPLAR
SALVATION

Raymond
Khoury

A SIGNET BOOK

SIGNET
Published by New American Library, a division of
Penguin Group (USA) Inc., 375 Hudson Street,
New York, New York 10014, USA
Penguin Group (Canada), 90 Eglinton Avenue East, Suite 700, Toronto,
Ontario M4P 2Y3, Canada (a division of Pearson Penguin Canada Inc.)
Penguin Books Ltd., 80 Strand, London WC2R 0RL, England
Penguin Ireland, 25 St. Stephen's Green, Dublin 2,
Ireland (a division of Penguin Books Ltd.)
Penguin Group (Australia), 250 Camberwell Road, Camberwell, Victoria 3124,
Australia (a division of Pearson Australia Group Pty. Ltd.)
Penguin Books India Pvt. Ltd., 11 Community Centre, Panchsheel Park,
New Delhi - 110 017, India
Penguin Group (NZ), 67 Apollo Drive, Rosedale, North Shore 0632,
New Zealand (a division of Pearson New Zealand Ltd.)
Penguin Books (South Africa) (Pty.) Ltd., 24 Sturdee Avenue,
Rosebank, Johannesburg 2196, South Africa

Penguin Books Ltd., Registered Offices:
80 Strand, London WC2R 0RL, England

Published by Signet, an imprint of New American Library, a division of Penguin
Group (USA) Inc. Previously published in a Dutton edition.

Signet International Edition, July 2011
10 9 8 7 6 5 4 3 2 1

To the memory of my father,
Kamal Khoury (1932–2011),
the kindest soul I ever met.

Prologue

✠

"Stay low, and keep quiet," the grizzled man whispered as he helped the knight clamber onto the walkway. "The ramparts are swarming with guards, and this siege has them on edge."

Everard of Tyre glanced left and right, scanning the darkness for any sign of a threat. There was no one around. The towers to either side were distant, the flickering torches of the night watches manning them barely visible in the moonless night. The Keeper had chosen their entry point well. If they acted fast, there was a reasonable chance they could scale the rest of the fortifications and make their way into the city unnoticed.

Making it back out safely—that was a different matter.

He yanked on the rope three times to signal the five knight-brothers who waited below, in the shadows of the great outer wall. One by one, they climbed up the knotted rope, the last one of them pulling it up behind him. With their swords now unsheathed and clenched tightly in their calloused hands, they slithered across the rampart in a silent single file, following their host. The rope was unwound, this time down the side of the inner wall. Minutes later, they'd all touched solid ground and were trailing a man none of them had ever met, advancing into a city in which they'd never set foot.

They crouched low, uncertain of where the Keeper was leading them, wary of being spotted. They wore black surcoats over dark tunics instead of their traditional white mantles, the ones bearing the distinctive red, splayed cross. There was no need for them to announce their true identity. Not when traveling through enemy territory, and even less when sneaking into a city that was under siege by Pope Innocent's crusaders. After all, *they* were crusaders. To the people of Constantinople, the Templars were the pope's men. They were the enemy. And Everard was fully aware of the grisly fate that awaited knights who were captured behind enemy lines.

But the warrior-monk didn't consider the Byzantines the enemy, and he wasn't here at the pope's behest.

Far from it.

Christian against Christian, he thought as they slipped past a church that was closed for the night. *Is there no end to this insanity?*

Their journey had been long, and arduous. They had ridden with only the briefest of pauses for days, exhausting their horses to near-death. The message that had come from the Keepers, deep inside the Byzantine capital, was unexpected—and alarming. The city of Zara, on the Dalmatian coast, had been inexplicably sacked by the pope's army—inexplicably, given that it was a Christian city, and not just a Christian city, but a *Catholic* one at that. The Venetian fleet ferrying the rapacious men of the Fourth Crusade was on the move again. Constantinople was their next target, ostensibly to restore its deposed and blinded emperor, and his son, to the throne. And given that the Byzantine capital wasn't even Catholic, but Greek Orthodox—and given the massacre that had taken place there a couple of decades earlier—the portents for the city didn't look promising.

And so Everard and his brother-knights had left the Templar stronghold at Tortosa in a great rush. They had ridden north all the way up the coast, then west, crossing through unfriendly Cilician Armenian and Muslim Seljuk territory, navigating across the arid moonscapes of Cappadocia, steering clear from any settlements and towns, doing their best to avoid confrontation. By the time they reached the environs of Constantinople, the crusader fleet—more than two hundred galleys and horse transports under the command of the formidable Doge of Venice himself—was well entrenched in the waters surrounding the greatest city of its time.

The siege was on.

Time was running out.

They sheltered in the shadows while a patrol of footmen trudged past; then they followed the Keeper through a small cemetery to a thicket of trees where a horse-drawn wagon awaited them. Another graying man, one whose solemn expression couldn't mask a deep unease, waited alongside it, holding the reins. *The second of three*, Everard thought as he gave him a small nod, while his men climbed into the back. They were soon advancing deep into the city, affording the burly knight an occasional glance through the narrow slit in the wagon's canvas cover.

He had never seen such a place.

Even in the near-darkness, he could make out the hulking silhouettes of the soaring churches and monumental palaces that were of a scale he hadn't imagined possible. The sheer number of them was astounding. Rome, Paris, Venice . . . he'd had the good fortune to visit them all, years earlier, while accompanying his grand master on a trip to the Paris Temple. They all paled by comparison. The New Rome was indeed the greatest city of them all. And when the wagon finally reached its destination, the sight that greeted him was no less awe-inspiring: a magnificent structure fronted by a soaring Corinthian colonnade, its pediment disappearing high overhead in the near-darkness.

The third Keeper, the eldest among them, was waiting for them at the top of the edifice's grand stairs.

"What is this place?" Everard asked him.

"The imperial library." The man nodded.

Everard's expression flagged his surprise. The *imperial* library?

The Keeper caught it and his face lightened up with the merest hint of a grin. "Where best to hide something than in plain sight?" He turned and headed in. "Follow me. We don't have much time."

The older men escorted the knights up the flight of steps, through the entrance vestibule, and deep into the cavernous building. The halls were deserted. The hour was late, but it was more than that. The tension in the city was palpable. The humid night air was heavy with fear, a fear that was stoked by the uncertainty and confusion that only got worse with every new day.

They pressed on by torchlight, passing the vast scriptoriums that held most of the knowledge of the ancient world, shelves upon shelves of scrolls and codices that included texts salvaged from the long-lost library of Alexandria. They went down a spiral stairway at the very back of the building and through a labyrinth of narrow passages and more stairs, their shadows creeping along the speckled limestone walls, until they reached an unlit corridor that was lined with a series of heavy doors. One of the hosts unlocked the door at the farthest end of the passage and led them inside. It was a large storeroom, one of many, Everard imagined. It was cluttered with crates, its walls lined with cobwebbed shelves that housed scrolls and leather-bound codices. The air was musty and stale, but cool. Whoever built this place had known that humidity had to be kept at bay if the parchment and vellum manuscripts were going to survive. And they had—for centuries.

Which was why Everard and his men were there.

"The news isn't good," the eldest of the Keepers told them. "The usurper Alexius lacks the courage to take on the enemy. He rode out with forty divisions yesterday, but didn't dare engage the Franks and the Venetians. He couldn't get back inside the gates fast enough." The old man paused, his eyes despondent. "I fear the worst. The city is as good as lost, and once it falls . . ."

Everard could already imagine the vengeance that

would be taken out on the city's nervous inhabitants if the Latins ever breached their defenses.

It had been only twenty years or so since the Latins of Constantinople had been massacred. Men, women, children ... no one had been spared. Thousands upon thousands of them, wiped out in a murderous frenzy the likes of which hadn't been seen since the taking of Jerusalem in the First Crusade. Venetian, Genoese, and Pisan merchants and their families who had long settled in Constantinople and who controlled its seafaring trade and its finances—the entire Roman Catholic population of the city—had been slaughtered in a sudden upwelling of anger and resentment by the envious local population. Their quarters had been reduced to ash, their graves upturned, any survivors sold off as slaves to the Turks. The city's Catholic clergy didn't fare better at the hands of their Greek Orthodox enemies: Their churches were burned, and the pope's representative was publicly beheaded before his head was tied to a dog's tail and dragged through the city's blood-soaked streets in front of a jubilant crowd.

The old man turned and led the knights deeper into the storeroom, to a second door, which was partially hidden by some heavily laden shelves. "The Franks and the Latins talk about taking back Jerusalem, but you and I both know that they'll never get that far," he said as he fidgeted with the door's locks. "And in any case, they're not really out to reclaim the Holy Sepulchre. Not anymore. The only thing they care about now is lining their pockets. And the pope would like nothing more than to see this empire fall and have its church brought under the authority of Rome." He turned, his expression darkening. "It's been long said that only the angels in Heaven know the date of the ending of our great city. I fear they're not the only ones to know it now. The pope's men will take Constantinople," he told the knights. "And when they do, I have little doubt that there'll be a small contingent of them whose sole task will be to lay their hands on these."

He swung the door open and led them in. The room was bare, save for three large wooden chests.

Everard's heartbeat spiked. As one of the chosen few

within the highest echelons of the Order, he knew what lay within the simple, unadorned trunks. He also knew what he now had to do.

"You'll need the wagon and the horses, and Theophilus will help you again," the old man continued, glancing to acknowledge the youngest of the three Keepers, the one who had helped Everard and his men sneak into the city. "But we'll need to be quick. Things could change at any moment. There's even talk of the emperor fleeing the city. You need to be on your way by first light."

"'You' . . . ?" Everard was surprised by the man's words. "What about you? You're all coming with us, aren't you?"

The elder exchanged a mournful look with his cohorts, then shook his head. "No. We need to cover your trail. Let the pope's men think that what they were after is still here long enough to make sure you're clear of any danger."

Everard wanted to object, but he could see that the Keepers wouldn't be swayed. They'd always known that a time like this might happen. They'd been prepared for it, as had every generation of Keepers before them.

The knights lugged the chests onto the wagon, one at a time, four of them hefting each heavy load while two others stood guard. By the time they had set off, the first hints of dawn were seeping into the night sky.

The gate that the Keepers had chosen, the Gate of the Spring, was one of the more remote entries into the city. It was flanked by two towers but also had a smaller postern to one side of the main gates, which was where they were headed.

As the heavily laden wagon driven by two cloaked figures clattered toward it, three footmen converged to block its path, eyeing it curiously.

One of them raised his hand in a blocking gesture and asked, "Who goes there?"

Theophilus, who was at the reins, let out a pained cough before mumbling a low reply, saying they urgently needed to get to the Zoodochos monastery that was just beyond the gates. Seated next to him, Everard watched in silence as the Keeper's words did the trick and seemed to intrigue the guard, who moved closer and spat out another question.

From under the cowl of his dark tunic, the Templar watched the man approaching them and waited until he was close enough before launching himself onto him and plunging his dagger deep into the guard's neck. In the same instant, three knights rushed out of the back of the wagon and silenced the other guards before they could sound the alert.

"Go," Everard hissed as his brothers rushed to the gatehouse, while he and two of the knights crouched down and scanned the towers overhead. He motioned for Theophilus to sneak away into cover, as they had agreed. The old man's work was done, and this was no place for him; Everard knew all hell could break loose at any second—which it did when two more guards emerged from the gatehouse just as the knights had pulled off the first of the crossbars.

The Templars recovered their swords and cut the guards down with stunning efficiency, but not before one of them had yelped out loudly enough to alert his companions in the towers. Within seconds, lanterns and torches were moving frenetically on the ramparts as alerts were sounded. Everard darted a look at the gate and saw that his brothers were still working on loosening the last of the crossbars—just as arrows bit into the parched ground next to him and by the hooves of the wagon's horses, narrowly missing one of them. There was no time to lose. If one of the horses were to be felled, their escape would be scuttled.

"We have to move," he roared as he loosed a bolt from his crossbow, hitting a backlit archer high above and sending him tumbling down from the rampart. Everard and the two knights alongside him reloaded and fired again, spewing bolts upward, keeping the sentries at bay, until one of the knights yelled and the gates creaked open.

"Let's go," Everard shouted as he waved his men on—and as they scrambled to get back on the wagon, a bolt slammed into the knight by his side, thudding downward into his right shoulder and lodging itself deep into his chest cavity. The man—Odo of Ridefort, an ox of a man—crumbled to the ground, blood spurting out of him.

Everard darted over to him and helped him back onto his feet, calling out to the others. Within seconds, they were all over their wounded brother-knight, three of them firing upward defensively while the others helped him into the back of the wagon. With the archers covering him, Everard sprinted to the front, and as he climbed onto the bench seat, he turned to shoot a parting nod of gratitude to Theophilus—but the Keeper wasn't where he'd last seen him. Then he spotted him—a short distance away, down on the ground, motionless, an arrow through his neck. He glanced at him for no more than a solitary heartbeat, but it was still long enough for the sight to brand itself permanently into his consciousness—then he leapt onto the wagon and whipped the horses to life.

The other knights clambered on board as the wagon charged through the gates and out of the city under a deluge of arrows. As Everard guided it up a hillock before turning north, he cast his eye over the glistening sea below and the war galleys that were gliding past the city's walls, banners and pennants flying from their sterncastles, shields uncovered, bulwarks garnished, ladders and mangonels raised threateningly.

Insanity, he thought again with a pained heart as he left behind the sublime city and the great catastrophe that would soon be upon it.

THE ROAD BACK WAS SLOWER. They'd recovered their horses, but the cumbersome wagon and its heavy payload were holding them back. Avoiding towns and any human contact was more difficult than when they were just on horses and could roam away from the well-trodden trails. Worse still was that Odo was losing a lot of blood, and there was little they could do to stop the bleeding while charging ahead. Worst of all was the fact that they weren't traveling incognito anymore: Their exit from the besieged city hadn't been as discreet as their entry. Armed men—ones from outside the city walls this time—would be coming after them.

And sure enough, before the first day's sun had set, they did.

Everard had sent two knights ahead of the wagon and two others behind, early-warning scouts for any threats.

That first evening, his prescience paid off. The convoy's rear guard spotted a company of Frankish knights, thundering in from the west, hot on their tail. Everard sent a rider ahead to bring back the forward scouts before cutting away from the more obvious, and well-trodden, southeasterly route the crusaders would expect them to take and heading farther east, into the mountains.

It was summer, and although the snows had melted, the bleak landscape was still tough to navigate. Lush, rolling hills soon gave way to steep, craggy mountains. The few trails that the wagon could take were narrow and perilous, some of them barely wider than the track of its wooden wheels and skirting the edges of dizzying ravines. And with every new day, Odo's condition worsened. The onset of heavy rain turned an already terrible situation into an accursed one, but with no other options, Everard kept his men to the high ground whenever he could and trudged on, slowly, eating whatever they could forage or kill, filling up their gourds in the downpours, forced to stop when the light faded, spending the miserable nights without shelter, always tense in the knowledge that their pursuers were still out there, looking for them.

We have to make it back, he thought, ruing the wretched upheaval that had been heaped upon him and his brothers without warning. *We cannot fail. Not when so much is at stake.*

It was easier willed than done.

After several days of sluggish progress, Odo's condition was desperate. They'd managed to remove the arrow and stem the bleeding, but a fever had set in, the result of his infected wound. Everard knew they'd have to stop and find a way to keep him immobile and dry for a few days if he were to have any chance of making it back to their stronghold alive. But with the scouts confirming that their stalkers hadn't yet given up, they had to soldier on through the hostile terrain and hope for a miracle.

Which was what they found on the sixth day, in the shape of a small, isolated hermitage.

They would have missed it entirely, had it not been for a

pair of hooded crows that were circling above it and drew the ravenous eyes of one of the forward scouts. A tight cluster of rooms carved out of the rock face, the monastery was virtually undetectable and perfectly camouflaged, high up in the mountains, tucked into the crook of the cliff that towered protectively above it.

The knights rode as close as they could, then left the horses and the wagon and climbed the rest of the way up the rock-strewn incline. Everard marveled at the dedication of the men who had built the monastery in such a remote and treacherous location—from the looks of it, many centuries ago—and wondered how it had survived in the region, given the roaming bands of Seljuk warriors.

They approached it with caution, swords drawn, although they doubted anyone could possibly be living in such an inhospitable spot. To their amazement, they were greeted by a dozen or so monks, weathered old men and younger disciples who quickly recognized them as fellow followers of the Cross and offered them food and shelter.

The monastery was small, but well stocked for a place that was so far removed from the nearest settlement. Odo was comfortably settled into a dry cot, some hot food and drink helping rekindle his body's worn defenses. Everard and his men then lugged the three chests up the hill and placed them in a small windowless room. Next door to it was an impressive scriptorium that housed a large collection of bound manuscripts. A handful of scribes were busy at their desks, concentrating on their work, barely looking up to acknowledge their visitors.

The monks—Basilian, as the knights soon found out—were stunned by the news the knights brought with them. The idea of the pope's army besieging fellow Christians and sacking Christian cities, even given the great schism, was hard to fathom. Isolated as they were, the monks hadn't been aware of the loss of Jerusalem to Saladin, or of the failed Third Crusade. Their hearts sank and their brows furrowed under the repeated blows of new information.

Throughout their conversation, Everard had carefully glossed over one tricky issue: what he and his fellow Templars were doing in Constantinople, and what their role had been in the siege of the great city. He was aware that, in the eyes of these Orthodox monks, he and his men could easily be seen as part of the Latin forces that were poised at the gates of their capital. And related to that was an even trickier issue, which the monastery's *hegumen*—its abbot, Father Philippicus—finally chose to address.

"What is it you carry in those chests?"

Everard could see that the monks had eyed the crates curiously, and he wasn't sure what to reply. After a moment's hesitation, he said, "Your guess is as good as mine. I was simply ordered to transport them from Constantinople to Antioch."

The abbot held his gaze, mulling over his reply. After an uncomfortable moment, he nodded respectfully and rose to his feet. "It's time for vespers, and then we should retire. We can speak more in the morning."

The knights were offered more bread, cheese, and cups of aniseed in boiled water; then the monastery fell silent for the night, save for the uninterrupted drumming of a patch of rain against the windows. The light staccato must have helped smother Everard's unease, as he soon drifted off into a deep sleep.

He woke up to harsh sunlight assaulting his senses. He sat up, but felt groggy, his eyelids heavy, his throat uncomfortably dry. He looked around—the two knights who'd been sharing the room with him weren't there.

He tried to get up, but faltered, his limbs wobbly and weak. A jar of water and a small bowl sat invitingly by the door. He pushed himself to his feet and shuffled over, raised the jar and drained its contents, feeling better for the drink. Wiping his mouth with his sleeve, he straightened up and headed for the refectory—but quickly sensed something wrong.

Where are the others?

His nerves now on edge, he crept barefoot across the cold flagstones, past a couple of cells and the refectory, all of which were empty. He heard some noise coming from the direction of the scriptorium and headed that way, his body feeling unusually weak, his legs shaking uncontrollably. As he passed the entry to the room where they'd placed the chests, a thought struck him. He paused, then crept into the room, his senses tingling wildly now—a sense of dread now confirmed by what he saw.

The chests had been pried open, their locks yanked out of their mountings.

The monks knew what was in them.

A wave of nausea rocked him, and he leaned against the wall to steady himself. He summoned any energy he could draw on and pushed himself back out of the room and into the scriptorium.

The sight that swam through his distorted vision froze him in place.

His brothers were strewn across the floor of the large room, lying in awkward, unnatural poses, immobile, their faces rigid with the icy pallor of death. There was no blood, no signs of violence. It was as if they had simply stopped living, as if life had been calmly siphoned out of them. The monks stood behind them in a macabre semicircle, staring at Everard blankly through hooded eyes, with the abbot, Father Philippicus, at their center.

And as Everard's legs shook under him, he understood.

"What have you done?" he asked, the words sticking in his throat. "What have you given me?"

He lashed out at the abbot, but fell to his knees before he had even taken a step. He propped himself up with his arms and concentrated hard, trying to make sense of what had happened. He realized they must have all been drugged the night before. The aniseed drink—that had to be it. Drugged, to allow the monks some undisturbed time to explore the contents of the chests. Then in the morning—the water. It had to have been poisoned, Everard knew, as he clenched his belly, reeling from spasms of pain. His vision was tunneling, his fingers shivering uncontrollably. He felt as if his gut had been garroted and set aflame.

"What have you done?" the Templar hissed again, his words slurred, his tongue feeling leaden now inside his parched mouth.

Father Philippicus came forward and just stood there,

towering over the fallen knight, his face locked tight with resolve. "The Lord's will," he answered simply as he raised his hand and moved it slowly, first up and down, then sideways, his limp fingers tracing the sign of the cross in the blurry air between them.

It was the last thing Everard of Tyre ever saw.

Chapter 1

✠

"*Salam*, Professor. *Ayah vaght darid keh ba man sohbat bo konid?*"

Behrouz Sharafi stopped and turned, surprised. The stranger who'd called out to him—a darkly handsome, elegant man, mid to late thirties, tall and slim, black gelled-back hair, charcoal roll-neck under a dark suit—was leaning against a parked car. The man flicked him a small wave from a folded newspaper in his hand, confirming the professor's uncertain gaze. Behrouz adjusted his glasses and regarded the man. He was pretty sure he'd never met him, but the stranger was clearly a fellow Iranian—his Farsi accent was perfect. Which was unexpected. Behrouz hadn't met a lot of Iranians since arriving in Istanbul just over a year ago.

The professor hesitated, then, egged on by the stranger's expectant and inviting look, took a few steps toward him. It was a mild early evening, and the square outside the university was winding down from its daily bustle.

"I'm sorry. Have we—"

"No, we haven't met," the stranger confirmed as he extended an inviting arm out, shepherding the professor to the passenger car door he'd just opened for him.

Behrouz stopped, tense with a sudden, crippling unease. Being in Istanbul had been, up to that very instant, a liberating experience. With each passing day, the looking-over-your-shoulder, worrying-about-what-you-said tensions of daily life as a Sufi professor at Tehran University had withered away. Far from the political struggles that were strangling academia in Iran, the forty-seven-year-old historian had been enjoying his new life in a country that was less insular and less dangerous, a country that was hoping to join the European Union. A stranger in a dark suit inviting him to take a ride had obliterated that little pipe dream in a heartbeat.

The professor raised his hands, open-palmed. "I'm sorry. I don't know who you are and this—"

Again, the stranger interrupted him with the same courteous, nonthreatening tone. "Please, Professor. I apologize for this rather sudden approach, but I do need to have a word with you. It's about your wife and your daughter. They could be in danger."

Behrouz felt twin spikes of fear and anger inside him. "My wife and— What about them? What are you talking about?"

"Please," the man said without a trace of alarm in his voice. "Everything will be fine. But we really need to talk."

Behrouz glanced left and right, not quite able to focus. Apart from the bloodcurdling conversation he was having, everything else seemed normal. A normality that, he knew, would be banished from his life from here on.

He climbed into the car. Even though it was a new, top-of-the-line BMW, it had an odd, unpleasant smell that immediately pricked his nostrils. He couldn't quite place it as the stranger got in behind the wheel and pulled out into the sparse traffic.

Behrouz couldn't contain himself. "What's happened? What do you mean, they might be in danger? What kind of danger?"

The stranger kept his gaze straight. "Actually, it's not just them. It's all three of you."

The even, unflustered way he said it made it sound even more unnerving.

The stranger slid a sideways glance at him. "It has to do with your work. Or more specifically, with something you recently found."

"Something I found?" Behrouz's mind skidded for a beat, then latched onto what the man meant. "The letter?"

The stranger nodded. "You've been trying to understand what it refers to, but so far, without success."

It was a statement, not a question, and said with a firm assurance that made it all the more ominous. The stranger not only knew about it; he seemed to know about the walls Behrouz was hitting in his research.

Behrouz fidgeted with his glasses. "How do you know about that?"

"Please, Professor. I make it my business to know everything about anything that piques my curiosity. And your find has piqued my curiosity. A lot. And in the same way that you're meticulous about your work and your research—admirably so, I must add—I'm just as meticulous about mine. Some might even say fanatical. So, yes, I know about what you've been doing. Where you've been. Who you've spoken to. I know what you've been able to deduce, and what still eludes you. And I know a lot more. Peripheral things. Things like Miss Deborah being your little Farnaz's favorite teacher at school. Like knowing your wife's prepared you some *gheimeh bademjan* for dinner." He paused, then added, "Which is really sweet of her, given that you only asked her for it last night. But then, she *was* in a vulnerable position, wasn't she?"

Behrouz felt the last vestiges of life drain from his face as panic flooded through him. *How can he— He's watching us, listening to us? In our bedroom?* It took him a moment to regain control of his body long enough to eke out a few words.

"What do you want from me?"

"The same thing you want, Professor. I want to find it. The trove that the letter refers to. I want it."

Behrouz's mind was drowning in a sinkhole of unreality.

He struggled to sound coherent. "I'm trying to find it, but—it's like you said. I'm having trouble figuring it out."

The stranger turned to face him only briefly, but his hard stare felt like a physical blow. "You have to try harder," he told Behrouz. Facing forward again, he added, "You have to try as if your life depended on it. Which, in this case, it does."

He swerved off the main road and turned into a narrow street that was lined with shuttered storefronts, where he pulled over. Behrouz gave the surroundings a quick scan. There was no one around, and no lights from the buildings above the shops.

The stranger hit the start/stop button to kill the engine and turned to face Behrouz.

"I need you to know that I'm serious about this," he told him, still with the infuriatingly smooth tone. "I need you to understand that it's very, very important to me that you do everything possible—*everything*—to complete your work. I need you to fully grasp how crucial it is to your well-being, and to that of your wife and daughter, that you devote all your time and energy to this matter, that you dig deep into any untapped resources inside you and figure this thing out for me. From this point onward, you should be thinking about nothing else. Nothing."

He paused to let his words sink in. "At the same time," he added, "I also need to make sure you understand that acting on any silly fantasies you might have about going to the police for help would be, frankly, catastrophic. It's vital that you understand this. We could walk into a police station together right now and I guarantee you the only one of us who would suffer any consequences would be you—and they would be, again, catastrophic. I need to convince you of this. I need you to have absolutely no doubt about what I'm prepared to do, what I'm capable of doing, and how far I'm prepared to go, to make sure that you do this for me."

The stranger palmed the key fob and clicked open his door. "Maybe this will do the trick. Come."

He climbed out.

Behrouz followed him, exiting the car on wobbly legs. The stranger walked around to the back of the car. Behrouz glanced upward, looking for any sign of life, wild notions of making a run for it and yelling for help swelling and bursting inside him, but he just joined his tormentor, walking listlessly as if he were in a chain gang.

The stranger hit a button on the key fob. The trunk of the car clicked open and hovered upward.

Behrouz didn't want to look in, but as the stranger reached in, the professor couldn't rein in his eyes. The trunk was mercifully empty, except for a small travel case. The stranger slid it closer to the edge of the trunk, and as he unzipped it, a putrid smell accosted Behrouz's nostrils, causing him to gag and falter back a step. The stranger didn't seem to mind it. He reached into the bag and casually pulled out a mess of hair, skin, and blood that he held up for Behrouz without the merest trace of hesitation or discomfort.

Behrouz felt the contents of his stomach shoot into his throat as he recognized the severed head the stranger was holding up.

Miss Deborah. His daughter's favorite teacher.

Or what was left of her.

Behrouz lost hold of his body, retching violently as his knees buckled. He collapsed to the ground, gagging and spewing and gasping for air, unable to breathe, one hand clamped across his eyes to block out the horror of it.

The stranger didn't allow him any respite. He bent down to his level, grabbed the professor by the hair and yanked his head up so he couldn't avoid being face-to-face with the hideous, bloody lump.

"Find it," he ordered him. "Find this trove. Do whatever you have to do, but find it. Or you, your wife, your daughter, your parents back in Tehran, your sister and her family . . ."

And he left it at that, comfortably certain that the professor had gotten the message.

Chapter 2

✝

VATICAN CITY
TWO MONTHS LATER

As he strode across the San Damaso courtyard, Sean Reilly cast a weary glance at the clusters of wide-eyed tourists exploring the Holy See and wondered if he'd ever get to visit the place with their casual abandon.

This was anything but casual.

He wasn't there to admire the magnificent architecture or the exquisite works of art, nor was he there on any spiritual pilgrimage.

He was there to try to save Tess Chaykin's life.

And if he was in any way wide-eyed, it was an attempt to keep his jet lag and his lack of sleep at bay and stay clear-headed enough to try to make sense of a frantic crisis that had been thrust upon him less than twenty-four hours earlier. A crisis he didn't fully understand—but needed to.

Reilly didn't trust the man walking alongside him—Behrouz Sharafi—but he didn't have much choice. Right now, all he could do was run through yet another mental grind of the information he had, from Tess's desperate phone call to the Iranian professor's harrowing firsthand account during the cab ride in from Fiumicino Airport. He had to make sure he wasn't missing anything—not that he had that much to go on. Some jerkweed was forcing Sharafi to find something for him. He'd chopped off some woman's head to show him how serious he was. And that same psycho was now holding Tess hostage to get Reilly to play ball. Reilly hated being in that position—reactive, not proactive—though as the FBI special agent in charge heading up the New York City field office's Counterterrorism Unit, he had ample training and experience in reacting to crises.

Problem was, they usually didn't involve someone he loved.

Outside the porticoed building, a young priest in a black cassock was waiting for them, sweating under the heat of the midsummer sun. He led them inside, and as they walked down the cool, stone-flagged corridors and climbed up the grand marble staircases, Reilly found it hard to chase away the uncomfortable memories of his previous visit to this hallowed ground, three years earlier, and the disturbing sound bites of a conversation that had never left his consciousness. Those memories came flooding back even more viscerally as the priest pushed through the oversized, intricately carved oak door and brought the two visitors into the presence of his boss, Cardinal Mauro Brugnone, the Vatican's secretary of state. A broad-shouldered man whose imposing physique was more suited to a Calabrian farmer than to a man of the cloth, the pope's second-in-command was Reilly's Vatican connection and, it seemed, the reason behind Tess's abduction.

The cardinal—despite being in his late sixties, he was still as husky and vigorous as Reilly remembered him from his previous visit there—came forward to greet him with outstretched arms.

"I've been looking forward to hearing from you again, Agent Reilly," he said with a bittersweet expression clouding his face. "Though I was hoping it would be under happier circumstances."

Reilly set his hastily packed overnight bag down and shook the cardinal's hand. "Same here, Your Eminence. And thank you for seeing us at such short notice."

Reilly introduced the Iranian professor, and the cardinal did the same for the two other men in the room: Monsignor Francesco Bescondi, the prefect of the Vatican Secret Archives—a slight man with thinning fair hair and a tightly cropped goatee—and Gianni Delpiero, the inspector general of the Corpo della Gendarmeria, the Vatican's police force—a taller, more substantial man with a solid brush of black hair and hard, angular features. Reilly tried not to show any discomfort at the fact that the Vatican's head cop had been asked to join them. He shook the man's hand with a cordial half smile, accepting that he should have expected it, given his urgent request for an audience—and given the bureau for which he worked.

"What can we do for you, Agent Reilly?" the cardinal asked, ushering them into the plush armchairs by the fireplace. "You said you'd explain when you got here."

Reilly hadn't had much time to think about how he would play this, but the one thing he did know was that he couldn't tell them everything. Not if he wanted to make sure they'd agree to his request.

"Before I say anything else, I need you to know I'm not here in any professional capacity. This isn't the FBI sending me out here. It's a personal request. I need to be sure you're okay with that." He'd asked to take a couple of days of personal leave after Tess's call. No one back at Federal Plaza—not Aparo, his partner, or Jansson, their boss— knew he was in Rome. Which, he thought, may have been a mistake, but that was how he'd decided to play it.

Brugnone brushed his caveat away. "What can we do for *you*, Agent Reilly?" he repeated, this time emphasizing the "you."

Reilly nodded gratefully. "I'm in the middle of a delicate situation," he told his host. "I need your help. There's no way around that. But I also need your indulgence in not asking me for more information than I can give you at this moment. All I can tell you is that lives are at stake."

Brugnone exchanged an unsettled look with his Vatican colleagues. "Tell us what you need."

"Professor Sharafi here needs some information. Information that, he believes, he can only find in your records."

The Iranian adjusted his glasses, and nodded.

The cardinal studied Reilly, clearly discomfited by his words. "What kind of information?"

Reilly leaned forward. "We need to consult a specific *fond* in the archive of the Congregation for the Doctrine of the Faith."

The men shifted uncomfortably in their seats. Reilly's request for help was looking less benign by the second. Contrary to popular belief, there was nothing particularly secretive about the Vatican Secret Archives; the word "secret" was only meant in the context of the archives being part of the pope's personal "secretariat," his *private* papers. The archive Reilly needed access to, however, the *Archivio Congregatio pro Doctrina Fidei*—the Archive of the Inquisition—was something else altogether. It held the Vatican archives' most sensitive documents, including all the files related to heresy trials and book bannings. Access to its shelves was carefully restricted, to keep scandalmongers at bay. The events its *fondi* covered—a *fond* being a body of records that dealt with a specific issue—were hardly the papacy's finest hour.

"Which *fond* would that be?" the cardinal asked.

"The *Fondo Scandella*," Reilly answered flatly.

His hosts seemed momentarily baffled, then relaxed at the mention. Domenico Scandella was a relatively insignificant sixteenth-century miller who couldn't keep his mouth shut. His ideas about the origins of the universe were deemed heretical, and he was burned at the stake. What Reilly and the Iranian professor could want from the transcripts of his trial didn't raise any alarms. It was a harmless request.

The cardinal studied him, a perplexed expression lining his face. "That's all you need?"

Reilly nodded. "That's it."

The cardinal glanced at the other two Vatican officials. They shrugged with indifference.

Reilly knew they were in.

Now came the hard part.

BESCONDI AND DELPIERO ACCOMPANIED REILLY and his Iranian companion across the Belvedere Courtyard to the entrance of the Apostolic Library, where the archives were housed.

"I have to admit," the prefect of the archives confessed with a nervous chortle, "I feared you were after something that would be more difficult to . . . *honor*."

"Like what?" Reilly asked, playing along.

Bescondi's face clouded as he searched for the least compromising answer. "Lucia Dos Santos's prophecies, for instance. You're familiar with her, yes? The seer of Fatima?"

"Actually, now that you mention it . . ." Reilly let the words drift, then flashed him a slight grin.

The priest let out a small chuckle and nodded with relief. "Cardinal Brugnone told me you were to be trusted. I don't know what I was worried about."

The words bounced uncomfortably inside Reilly's conscience as they stopped at the entrance of the building. Delpiero, the inspector general, excused himself, given that he didn't seem to be needed.

"Anything I can do to help, Agent Reilly," the cop offered, "just let me know." Reilly thanked him, and Delpiero walked off.

The three halls of the library, resplendent with ornate inlaid paneling and vividly colored frescoes that depicted the donations to the Vatican by various European sovereigns, were unnervingly quiet. Scholars, priests from various nations, and other academics with impeccable credentials glided across its marble floors on their way to or from the tranquillity of its reading rooms. Bescondi led the two outsiders to a grand spiral staircase that burrowed down to the basement level. It was cooler down there, the air-conditioning straining less than aboveground to keep the summer heat at bay. They ambled past a couple of junior archivists, who gave the prefect small, respectful bows, and reached an airy reception area where a Swiss Guard in a sober dark blue uniform and black beret sat behind a counter-type desk and a bank of discreet CCTV monitors. The man signed them in, and five taps into the security keypad later, the inner sliding door of the air lock was whishing shut behind them and they were in the archive's inner sanctum.

"The *fondi* are arranged alphabetically," Bescondi said as he pointed out the small, elegantly scripted nameplates on the shelves and got his bearings. "Let's see. Scandella should be down this way."

Reilly and the Iranian followed him deeper into the large, low-ceilinged crypt. Apart from the sharp clicks of their heels against the stone floor, the only noise in there was the constant, low hum of the air-management system that regulated the room's oxygen level and kept harmful bacteria at bay. The long rows of shelves were packed tight with scrolls and leather-bound codices interspersed with more recent books and cardboard box files. Entire rows of ancient manuscripts were suffocating under blankets of dust, as, in some cases, no one had touched or consulted them for decades—if not centuries.

"Here we are," their host said as he pointed out a box file on a low shelf.

Reilly glanced back, toward the archive's entrance. They were alone. He nodded his appreciation at the priest, then said, "Actually, we really need to see another *fond*."

Bescondi blinked at him, confused. "Another *fond*? I don't understand."

"I'm sorry, Father, but—I couldn't risk you and the cardinal not allowing us down here. And it's imperative that we get access to the information we need."

"But," the archivist stammered, "you didn't mention this before, and ... I'd need His Eminence to authorize showing you any other—"

"Father, please," Reilly interrupted him. "We need to see it."

Bescondi swallowed hard. "Which *fond* is it?"

"The *Fondo Templari*."

The archivist's eyes widened and did a quick dart to the left, farther down the aisle they were standing in, and back. He raised his hands in objection and stumbled back. "I'm sorry. That's not possible, not without getting His Eminence's approval—"

"Father—"

"No, it's not possible. I can't allow it, not before discussing it with—"

He took another step back and edged sideways, in the direction of the entrance.

Reilly had to act.

He reached out, blocking the priest with one arm—

"I'm sorry, Father."

—while the other dove into Reilly's jacket's side pocket and pulled out a small canister of mouth freshener, swung it right up to the archivist's startled face, and pumped a cloud of spray right at him. The man stared at Reilly with wide, terrified eyes as the mist swirled around his head— then he coughed twice before his legs just collapsed under him. Reilly caught him as he fell and set him down gently on the hard floor.

The colorless, odorless liquid wasn't breath freshener.

And if the archivist wasn't going to die from it, Reilly needed to do something else—fast.

He reached into another pocket and pulled out a small ceramic syringe, yanked its cap off, and plunged it into a throbbing vein in the man's forearm. He checked his pulse and waited till he was sure the opioid antagonist had done its job. Without it, the fentanyl—a fast-acting, incapacitating opiate that was part of the Bureau's small and unpublicized arsenal of nonlethal weapons—could send the prefect into a coma, or as in the tragic case of more than a hundred hostages in a Moscow theater a few years back, it could kill him. A quick chaser of naloxone was crucial to make sure the archivist kept breathing—which he now was.

Reilly stayed with him long enough to confirm the drug's effect, countering the caustic discomfort he felt at what he had just done to their unsuspecting host by thinking of Tess and what Sharafi had told him her abductor had done to the schoolteacher. Feeling that the archivist's breathing had stabilized, he nodded. "We're clear."

The Iranian pointed down the aisle. "He looked that way when you mentioned the *fond*. Which fits. 'T' is the next letter."

"We've got around twenty minutes before he wakes up, maybe less," Reilly told him as he stalked down the aisle. "Let's make them count."

Chapter 3

✛

Tess Chaykin's lungs hurt. So did her eyes. And her back. In fact, there wasn't much of her that didn't hurt.

How much longer are they going to keep me like this?

She'd lost all sense of time—all sense of anything, for that matter. She knew her eyes were taped shut. As was her mouth. Her wrists too, behind her back. And her knees and ankles. A twenty-first-century mummy of shiny silver duct tape and—something else too. A soft, thick, padded cocoon, wrapped around her. Like a sleeping bag. She felt it with her fingers. Yes, that's what it was. A sleeping bag. Which explained why she was drenched in sweat.

That was just about all she was sure of.

She didn't know where she was. Not exactly, anyway. She felt like she was in a cramped space. A hot, cramped space. She thought she might be in the back of a van, or in the trunk of a car. She wasn't sure of it, but she could hear the distorted, muffled sounds coming in through the tape around her ears. From outside. The sounds of a busy street. Cars, motorcycles, scooters, rumbling and buzzing past. But something about the sounds jarred her. Something felt out of place, wrong—but she couldn't quite put her finger on it.

She concentrated, trying to ignore the heaviness in her head and break through the fog that was clouding her memory. Vague recollections started to take shape. She

remembered being grabbed at gunpoint on the way into
town from the dig in Petra, Jordan, all three of them—she,
her friend Jed Simmons, and the Iranian historian who'd
sought them out. What was his name? Sharafi. Behrouz
Sharafi, that was it. She remembered being locked into
some grotty, windowless room. Not long after that, her abductor had made her call Reilly, in New York. Then she'd
been drugged, injected with something. She could still feel
the prick in her arm. And that was it, the last thing she
remembered—how long ago was it now? She had no idea.
Hours. A whole day, maybe? More?

No idea.

She hated being in here. It was hot and cramped and
dark and hard and smelled of, well, car trunk. Not like the
trunk of some scuzzy old car that had all kinds of stinky
residue wafting around. This car, if it was one, was clearly
new—but still, unpleasant.

Her spirits sank further the more she thought about her
predicament. If she was in the trunk of a car, and if she
could hear noises outside ... maybe she was on a public
road. A sense of panic swelled up inside her.

What if I've just been dumped here, just left to rot?

What if no one ever realizes I'm in here?

A vein in her neck started throbbing, the duct tape
around her ears turning them into echo chambers. Her
mind raced wildly, spurred by the maddening internal
drumbeat, wondering about how much air there was in
there, how long she could survive without water or food,
whether or not the tape might make her choke. She began
to picture an agonizingly slow and horrific death, shriveling
up from thirst and hunger and heat, just wasting away in a
dark box as if she'd been buried alive.

The fear of it hit her like a bucket of ice water. She had
to do something. She tried twisting around to change position, maybe get some leverage to try to kick up against the
lid of the trunk or whatever the hell it was she was in—
but she couldn't move. Something was holding her down.
She was pinned down, strapped into place by some kind of
restraint that she could now feel was tugging against her
shoulders and her knees.

She couldn't move at all.

She stopped fighting against the ties and settled back, heaving a ragged sigh that echoed in her ears. Tears welled up in her eyes as the notion of death solidified around her. The beaming face of her thirteen-year-old daughter, Kim, broke through her despair and drifted into her consciousness, beckoning her. She imagined her back in Arizona, enjoying the summer at the ranch of Tess's older sister, Hazel. Another face glided into the picture, that of her mother, Eileen, who was also there with them. Then their faces dissipated, and a cold and hollow feeling grew in her gut, the anger and remorse over leaving New York and coming out here, to the Jordanian desert, all those weeks ago, to research her next novel. The summer dig with Simmons, a contact of her old friend Clive Edmondson and one of the leading Templar experts around, seemed like a good idea at the time. Coming out to the desert would allow her to spend time with Clive and give her a chance to expand on all the Templar knowledge that was the backbone of her new career. Equally, if not more important, it would give her the space she needed to think things through on a more personal front.

And now this.

Tess's regrets swooped across all kinds of dark territories as her mind settled on another face: Reilly's. She felt sick with guilt, wondering what she'd led him into by making that call, wondering whether or not he was safe—and whether or not he'd ever find her. The thought triggered a spark of hope. She wanted to believe he would. But the spark died out as quickly as it had appeared. She knew she was kidding herself. He was a couple of continents away. Even if he tried—and she knew he would—he'd be out of his element, a stranger in a strange land. It wasn't going to happen.

I can't believe I'm going to die like this.

A faint noise intruded—like everything else, annoyingly muffled, as if to torture her further. But she could tell that it was a siren. A police car, or an ambulance. It grew louder, raising her hopes with it—then faded away. It rattled her for another reason. It was a distinctive sound—all countries seemed to have their own signature sirens on their emergency vehicles. But something about this siren didn't feel right. She couldn't be sure of it, but she'd heard ambulance and police sirens during her spell in Jordan, and this one sounded different. Very different.

It was a sound she'd definitely heard before, but not in Jordan.

A ripple of fear swept across her.

Where the hell am I?

Chapter 4

✠

ARCHIVE OF THE INQUISITION,
VATICAN CITY

"How much longer do we have?" the Iranian historian asked as he discarded yet another thick leather-bound codex into the pile by his feet.

Reilly glanced at his watch and frowned. "It's not a perfect science. He could wake up any second now."

The man nodded nervously, droplets of sweat blooming all over his forehead. "Just one more shelf to go." He adjusted his glasses and pulled out another bound set of folios, then, moving fast, untied the leather strap that held it shut.

"It's got to be here, right?" Reilly was craning his head back for another look in the direction of the fallen priest and the air lock into the archive. Apart from the constant hum of the climate control system, all was quiet—for now.

"That's what Simmons said. He was sure of it. It's here somewhere." He put down the ream of bound folios and picked up another volume.

The Templar *fond* occupied three entire shelves at the far end of the archive, eclipsing the *fondi* around it. Which wasn't surprising. The affair had been the biggest political and religious scandal of its time. Various papal commissions and a small army of inquisitors had been assigned to look into the Order, from before the arrest warrants were issued in the fall of 1307 to the ultimate dissolution of the Order in 1312 and the burning of the last Grand Master in 1314. Although the Templars' own archive had been lost—it was last known to have been in Cyprus, where it had been moved from Acre following the fall of the city in 1291—the Vatican had, over the course of its investigation, built up an extensive record of its own. Reports from roving inquisitors, transcripts of interrogations and confessions, witness statements, minutes of papal deliberations, lists of holdings and confiscated paperwork from Templar houses across Europe—it was all here, an exhaustive forensic account of the warrior-monks' infamous end.

And, it seemed, it still had secrets lurking within its fading pages.

As if to confirm it, the historian turned, his face alight with excitement. "This is it."

Reilly stepped in for a closer look. The Iranian was cradling a thick, leather-bound volume. It was heavy and cumbersome, the size of a large photo album. Its covers were tattered and brittle, the hardwood boards inside the tooled leather bindings peeking out from the corners. He had it open, exposing its first page. It was bare, except for a large, brown-and-purple stain in its bottom right corner—the result of a bacterial attack—and a title in its center: *Registrum Pauperes Commilitones Christi Templique Salomonis.*

The Registry of the Templars.

"This is the one," the professor insisted, turning the pages with careful strokes. Most of its linen-based paper leaves seemed to be covered with blocks of prose, written in a cursive black letter script. A few had crude maps on them, while on others were lists of names, places, dates, and other information Reilly couldn't decipher.

"You're sure?" Reilly asked. "We won't get a second crack at this."

"I think so. Simmons never actually saw it, but it's just as he described it. I'm sure of it."

Reilly took one last glance at the remaining volumes

on the shelf and knew he had to trust Sharafi's judgment. Precious seconds were flitting away. "Okay. Let's get out of here."

Just then, a low groan echoed down the aisle from them. Reilly froze. The Vatican archivist was coming to. Keeping a vigilant eye out for any CCTV cameras he hadn't spotted on his way in, Reilly sprinted down the narrow passageway and reached him just as he was straightening himself up. Bescondi leaned back against a shelf, mopping his face with his hands. Reilly bent down, closer to his face.

The archivist looked at him through confused, jittery eyes. "What . . . what happened?"

"I'm not sure." Reilly put a comforting hand on the man's shoulder. "You just blacked out there for a second. We were about to call for help." He wasn't enjoying the lie.

Bescondi looked lost, visibly trying to make sense of the situation. Reilly knew he wouldn't remember anything—not yet, anyway. But he would. And soon.

"Stay there," Reilly told him. "We'll go get help."

The archivist nodded.

Reilly shot Sharafi a "let's-go" flick of the head, his eyes darting discreetly to the codex he was carrying.

The Iranian got the message. He tucked the bulky book under his arm, away from the archivist, as he sidestepped around him and followed Reilly.

They reached the air lock. The two sets of sliding doors seemed to mock them as they plodded through their slow, synchronized two-step—then the outer doors finally parted and Reilly and the Iranian professor were in the reception area. The guard was already on his feet and alert, his brow furrowed, clearly reading the urgent tension in their movement and wondering why the archivist wasn't with them.

"Monsignor Bescondi—something happened to him. He just fainted," Reilly blurted, pointing at the archive while doing his best to shield Sharafi from the guard's sight line. "He needs a doctor."

The guard reached for his radio with one hand while holding his arm out, the heel of his palm in Reilly's and the Iranian's faces, signaling them to stay put. "One moment," he ordered.

Reilly didn't let up. "He needs a doctor—do you understand? He needs one now," he insisted, his finger still jabbing the air, trying to spur the guard into going through the
air lock.

The guard hesitated, mindful about leaving the two
visitors unattended but needing to check on the archivist,
while—

—INSIDE THE ARCHIVE, THE ARCHIVIST had just started to feel
some glimmers of clarity and cast his gaze down the aisle
to his right, then over to his left—and saw the messy stacks
of codices and box files cluttering the floor.

The significance of their location speared through his
dulled senses with the ferocity of a defibrillator. Dumbstruck, gasping with shock, he clambered to his feet and
stumbled over to the air lock, reaching it in time to see
Agent Reilly and his Iranian colleague in heated debate
with the guard. The groggy archivist hit the doors' command button, then started slamming his hands repeatedly
against the air lock's inner door while waiting for it to slide
open, his cries for help bouncing off the reinforced glass
and echoing deafeningly around him, and—

—EERILY MUTED FROM THE RECEPTION AREA by the air lock,
the surreal sight snagged the guard's attention.

The guard's reflexes were quick—his stance went all
tense and feral as he reached for the handgun in his holster while bringing up his mike to sound the alert, two actions that Reilly had to stop in their tracks if he and Sharafi
were going to make it out of there. And though the guard
was, like all the other members of the smallest army in the
world, a soldier who'd been trained in the Swiss Army, he
was a split second slower than Reilly, who launched himself
at him, thrusting his left arm out to ward off his gun while
using his other hand to wrench the radio from his opponent
and fling it out of reach. The guard swung his free arm back
at Reilly, the uppercut aimed at his head. Reilly avoided
it by leaning back and countered with one of his own that
slammed into the guard's rib cage and winded him. The
guard's right hand slackened under the blow—enough for

Reilly to wrest his handgun from him while ramming his body weight into him and shoving him back onto his desk. Reilly watched the gun skitter across the hard floor, away from the guard, who looked groggy from his collision with the desk—and turned and grabbed Sharafi.

"Move," Reilly yelled as he dragged him forward and bolted for the stairs.

Chapter 5

✟

They burst onto the ground floor and flew across the palatial halls unchallenged, though Reilly knew it wouldn't last. Sure enough, within seconds, whistles and heavy footfalls were chasing after them—the Swiss Guard from below had recovered, and he wasn't alone anymore—while up ahead, at the far end of the third chamber, four carabinieri were charging their way with raised handguns.

Not going according to plan, Reilly chided himself as he skidded to a stop and cut left, flicking a glance back at Sharafi to make sure he was still behind him. The archivist had woken up too soon. Reilly knew it could happen. The dose of incapacitant that he'd given Bescondi was intentionally on the mild side. He couldn't risk killing the man or putting him in a coma, and had had to play it safe. Too safe, evidently. And right now, Reilly had to figure out another way out of the holy city, as there was no way they were going to make it back to the driver who was waiting for them by the Apostolic Palace—and even if they did, they weren't about to be chauffeured out of there, not with a posse of Vatican cops chasing after them.

"This way," he yelled to the Iranian professor as they flew through another opulent room and into the contemporary halls of the new wing of the Chiaramonti Museum. There were many more visitors around, turning the vast space into an obstacle course of people of all sizes that Reilly and his accomplice had to slalom through, leaving a trail of startled screams and indignant outbursts behind them, knowing that any collision would be disastrous. Behind, their pursuers had merged into one frantic pack and were cutting through the crowd, hot on their heels.

Reilly saw a main entrance looming on the right and veered toward it—only to stumble to a halt when three other cops stormed in through its big glass doors. He glanced left—there was another exit on the other side of the hall, directly opposite it. He scrambled toward it, with the Iranian tucked in right behind him, and blew out of its doors and onto an open-air terracelike landing that was at the top of a pair of ceremonial, mirror-image flights of stairs.

The summer heat hit him like the exhaust of a transit bus. Sucking in big gulps of air, Reilly turned to Sharafi, hands beckoning. "Give me the book—it's slowing you down."

The Iranian was disconcertingly composed as he shook his head and clenched the book tight. "I'm fine with it. Which way?"

"No idea, but we can't stay here," Reilly answered before bounding down the stairs, his feet landing hard on every third step.

He heard the squawk of a two-way radio, and glancing over the marble balustrade, he glimpsed the caps of a couple more carabinieri who were surging up the lower flight of steps, aiming to box them in. In a second or so, they'd be face-to-face with the Italian cops on the landing—not ideal.

Screw that.

He steeled himself and banked off and hurdled the handrail, clearing it and landing heavily on top of the cops, knocking them down while clearing a path for the professor.

"Keep going," he yelled to Sharafi as the downed carabinieri flailed around him, lashing out and grabbing at his arms and legs—but he managed to free himself from their grip and was soon hurtling down after the professor.

They were side by side as they sprinted across the manicured lawn of the central courtyard before ducking into a barrel-vaulted passageway that cut through the building and led back out onto the open ground of the Stradone dei Giardini and the long row of parked cars on either side of it. Reilly paused, allowing a handful of precious seconds to flit by, scrutinizing the vicinity, searching for someone getting in or out of a car, a motorcycle, anything, just willing an opportunity to present itself, a chance to jack something with wheels to get them the hell out of there. But they were out of luck—there was no movement anywhere, no chirps of a remote control deactivating a car alarm, no obvious target for him—and then another clutch of carabinieri appeared, charging at them from the far end of the road, maybe a hundred yards away.

He racked his brain, trying to get a lock on his bearings and compare it to the map of the Vatican that he hadn't had enough time to study properly before setting off on this ill-fated incursion. He knew where they were—roughly—but the holy city was haphazardly laid out, a maze of intersecting buildings and winding paths that would stump even the most orientationally gifted. No escape route epiphanies popped up, and his survival instinct took over again, spurring his legs forward and propelling him away from the oncoming danger.

He led the professor across the bank of parked cars and up a long, narrow street that opened onto a wide patch of lawn split by two intersecting pathways, the Giardino Quadrato, which fronted another museum—only to realize they'd boxed themselves in. Vatican cops and Swiss Guards seemed to be coming at them from all sides. They'd be on them within seconds—the two men were in open ground with no clear routes to any buildings to duck into for cover. Reilly spun around, scanning the periphery, refusing to accept the inevitable—and then it struck him. His mind cleared long enough to realize where they were and what was lurking nearby, tantalizingly within reach.

"This way," Reilly spurred the professor, pointing at the far end of the ceremonial garden—and a tall concrete wall with no openings in it.

"Are you insane? There's nothing there but a wall."

"Just follow me," Reilly shot back.

The Iranian tore after him—and just before they reached the wall, the ground opened up before them in the shape of a wide concrete ramp that sloped down and led into some kind of underground structure.

"What's down there?" the Iranian wheezed.

"The Carriage Museum," Reilly said, breathing hard. "Come on."

Chapter 6

✛

Reilly and the Iranian professor reached the bottom of the ramp and just kept running.

The Carriage Museum, the most recent addition to the museums of the Vatican, was a vast underground showcase that looked like it tunneled on forever—which suited Reilly. He slowed right down as he entered the first exhibition hall, giving his mental MapQuest a second to kick in. The space around him was sleek and modern, in stark contrast to the gaudy displays that it housed: from sumptuous sedan chairs to nineteenth-century horse-drawn carriages of gold, velvet, and damask, an astounding collection of twenty-four-carat masterpieces on stilts and wheels.

His accomplice looked around, confused. "Why are we down here? It's a dead end, and—I don't think these are going to get us anywhere, not without horses."

"We're not here for the carriages," he replied, before leading Sharafi deeper into the museum.

The gilded carriages gave way to an array of motorcars. They stalked past a trio of hulking black limousines from the 1930s that were straight out of an Al Capone movie, their hand-built coachwork, drum headlights, and flowing fenders harking back to a more elegant age.

"You're kidding me, right?" Sharafi allowed himself a mild chortle.

Before Reilly could answer, he heard some commotion behind them, by the entrance. A clutch of carabinieri and Swiss Guards were bursting into the exhibition hall, storming past startled tourists. One of the cops had spotted Reilly and the Iranian through the clusters of tourists and was pointing at them and shouting frantically.

Reilly frowned. "Have faith," he told Sharafi as he got moving again. He drew the Iranian past a white three-wheeled rickshaw—complete with papal crest on its canvas doors—and into the farthest section of the museum, where more recent Popemobiles were housed. Heading for the very back of the museum, they blew past a Mercedes 600 landaulet, a Lincoln Continental four-door convertible, and a Chrysler Imperial, all from the 1960s and gleaming like black obsidian.

Sharafi glanced back. The posse was closing in. "How are you going to get us out of here? Can you hot-wire one of these cars?"

"I'm hoping I won't have to," Reilly replied as he spotted what he was looking for: a doorway next to a wide roller shutter, tucked into the rear wall and painted to match. "There." He pointed as he took off toward it.

The professor followed in his wake.

As they reached it, the door swung open and two maintenance technicians in white overalls came through, oblivious to the mayhem. Reilly shoved them aside as he swooped past them, catching the door before it slammed shut. As angry shouts echoed behind him, he ushered Sharafi through the door and followed him into a tunnel that was wide enough for a car to get through. He sped up, his lungs and thigh muscles burning, glancing over his shoulder to make sure the professor was keeping up—which, to Reilly's surprise and relief, he was. The tunnel ferried them to a large garage where three mechanics were working on the current Popemobiles: an open-top Mercedes G500 SUV, which the pope used locally, and a couple of modified Mercedes ML430 "Popequarium" SUVs with the elevated bulletproof glass boxes out back, for when he traveled abroad, all finished in what the German manufacturer called "Vatican-mystic white." Another ramp led away from the garage, in the opposite direction to the way they'd come in.

A way out.

Maybe.

Reilly did a split-second triage in his mind and beelined for the ML that was being worked on. It was facing the wrong way, its back to the exit ramp, but trumping that was the fact that it had its hood propped up—and its engine running. The startled mechanics did a double take and moved to confront them, but Reilly was overflowing with adrenaline and out of time. He didn't break step. He just strode straight up to the first mechanic, grabbed him by the arm, twisted it around, and used it to fling him at his colleague, sending them both toppling back into a set of tool trays. The third mechanic hesitated and faltered back, reached into a tool tray and pulled out a big wrench, and started moving forward again.

"Get in," Reilly barked to Sharafi, yanking the hood's support arm out of its cradle and slamming it shut before scrambling into the driver's seat.

He watched as Sharafi hustled around the back of the car, losing sight of him behind the big glass box—then spotted the mechanic with the wrench rounding the passenger side of the car and heading straight for him. He hesitated, unsure about whether or not to jump out and help the professor, then glimpsed him in the side mirror of the car—and was stunned to see the Iranian dispatch the mechanic with a surgically efficient and vicious pair of kicks to the knee and face.

Sharafi climbed in next to him, breathing hard but looking unruffled, his hands still clutching the heavy book. Their eyes met—a split-second, unspoken acknowledgment of the Iranian's efficient handling of his challenge—then the carabinieri burst into the garage from the museum side, yelling at them and waving handguns. A deep whir coming from behind snagged Reilly's attention. He spun back to see the roller shutter at the far end of the exit ramp gliding down. One of the mechanics had recovered and stood by the wall, his hand on the shutter's control button, his face locked in a self-satisfied grin.

"Hang on," Reilly roared as he slammed the car into

reverse and floored the pedal. The four-ton vehicle lurched backward, its tires squealing loudly on the acrylic floor. Reilly guided the SUV through the tunnel and up the short ramp—trying to avoid bouncing off the side walls, eyeing the shutter as it inched its way down—and just managed to slip through under it, the edge of the glass box scraping harshly against the lip of the shutter, metal biting into toughened safety glass—then they burst into daylight, at the far end of the road he and Sharafi had cut across only minutes earlier.

He spun the wheel to turn the big SUV around, wrenched the gear lever into drive, and charged forward. The road was narrow and lined with parked cars, hugging the long façade of the Apostolic Library.

"Nice move on that mechanic back there," Reilly remarked as he slid a sideways glance at the Iranian professor.

"My country's been more or less constantly at war ever since I was born." He shrugged. "Like everyone else, I had to do my time in the army." Glancing around, he asked, "You know where we are?"

"More or less. The gate's on the other side of this building," he said, pointing at the library rushing past them on the left. "If I've got it right, there should be a passage into the courtyard with the parked cars just about here—"

He had it right—and swerved into the narrow tunnel that led into the Belvedere Courtyard.

He slewed the car around the parked cars, startled visitors scrambling out of the way of the lumbering Popequarium bearing the license plate SCV 1—for *Stato della Città del Vaticano*, meaning Vatican City State, though most Romans joked that it really stood for *Se Cristo Vedesse*, meaning "If only Christ could see this," a jab at how, over the centuries, the popes had completely overturned Jesus's original message of possession-free preaching. Another vaulted passage on the opposite side of the courtyard led them out on the other side of the library complex—and onto a clear run down the Via del Belvedere to the Porta Sant'Anna and out of the city.

"We can't stay in this thing," Sharafi said. "It's like a beacon."

"We're not out of here yet." Reilly was staring dead ahead.

Two carabinieri cars—sleek, dark blue Alfa Romeos with menacing, sharklike grilles, spinning blue lights on their roofs, and shrill sirens—burst out of a side street between them and the gate and were rushing toward them.

Definitely not going according to plan, Reilly thought, scowling at the prospect of playing chicken with the Italian police in a stolen Popemobile. But he was doing it. And they were coming right at him, and didn't look like they were about to blink first. And in that moment, Tess's face burst into his consciousness—his mind picturing her in some vile lockdown, chained to some radiator, helpless, the psycho lurking nearby. He couldn't back down, nor could he not get them out of there with the book. He had to make it—for her.

He kept his foot down.

"Agent Reilly—" Sharafi tensed up, his right arm clamping down on the armrest.

Reilly didn't blink.

He was a nanosecond away from slamming head-on into his pursers when the road opened up into a wide piazza outside the Tower of Nicholas V, a massive round fortification that was part of the original Vatican walls. Reilly jerked the wheel to the right—swerving off his arrowlike path just as the two black police cars shot past—then left again to get back on track. He glanced into his mirror to see the two Alfas do some synchronized hand-brake turns that lit up their tires and spun them around before they resumed the chase.

The road ahead was all clear, the gate less than a hundred yards away now. It was the way Reilly had been driven into the Vatican, twice now, a grand entrance with twin marble columns topped by a solemn stone eagle on either side of the heavy wrought iron gates—gates that some Swiss Guards were now rushing to close.

Not good.

Reilly kept the pedal jammed down, feeling a hardening in his gut. With the two Alfas close behind, he cannoned past a few cars that were waiting to be ushered out of the gate onto the main road, ramping the SUV's left wheels over the curb to squeeze by, before blasting through the gates and obliterating them in a deafening frenzy of twisted iron and steel—instantly followed by an eruption of glass as the Popequarium's tall viewing box slammed into the intricate overthrow that spanned the top of the gate and burst into smithereens.

Pedestrians on the busy street outside the Vatican wall scattered frantically, leaping out of the way as Reilly pulled a screaming left and tore up the Via di Porta Angelica. Sharafi looked back as the first Alfa burst out of the gate and hooked a screaming left to follow the SUV—and just then, a massive explosion rocked the street, its shock wave jolting Reilly forward off his seat.

What the—?

Reilly instinctively ducked with the blast, controlling the Popemobile as it swerved from the shock wave before slamming on the brakes and bringing it to a screeching halt. His ears deafened, his head dazed, his body rigid with shock, he glanced across at Sharafi in stunned, confused silence. Sharafi met his gaze, looking surprisingly cool and unruffled, as if nothing had happened. Reilly's mind was too busy slowing down and trying to make sense of the surreal sight around him to process it, but the Iranian's inscrutable look still registered inside him somewhere as he craned around for a better look.

The street outside the gates was apocalyptic, like something out of downtown Baghdad. Thick black smoke was billowing out of the flaming hulk of a car, a parked car that must have had a bomb in it. It must have exploded just as the lead Alfa was passing alongside it, as the cops' car was plastered against the Vatican's outer wall, thrown into it sideways. What looked like the second Alfa was also in the wreckage, piled into some parked cars. Debris was everywhere, clumps of concrete and metal still raining down around them. Shell-shocked people were limping around, dazed, looking for loved ones or just standing stiff in disbelief. There had to be deaths—Reilly was sure of it—and lots of wounded.

"We've got to go," the Iranian said.

Reilly looked at him askance, still groggy from the blast.

"Get us out of here now," the man insisted. "You need to think about Tess."

Reilly glanced back—a couple of carabinieri were coming out of the smoke cloud, running toward them, weapons drawn—then they started firing. Bullets clipped the back of the wrecked SUV.

"Move," the Iranian rasped.

Reilly ripped his gaze away from the pandemonium and hit the gas. And as the armored SUV stormed through the narrow streets without a specific destination in mind, a sudden realization stormed out of Reilly's snarled mind—a realization that shot a piercing sensation through his chest.

Random observations clicked into place. The way the Iranian looked when they were on the run, like he was out for a jog while Reilly was gasping for breath. The way he took out the mechanic with the efficiency of a ninja. The way he didn't even flinch when the bomb went off. The fact that mangled bodies didn't seem to register with him.

Oh fuck.

He turned to the man sitting beside him. "Who the hell are you?"

Chapter 7

✠

Reilly's heart froze. The man sitting in the passenger seat was glancing at him without a trace of emotion. Not a taunting grin. Not a demented scowl. Nothing. Just an even, level gaze. You'd think he was just out on a Sunday drive, watching the scenery drift by while sharing chitchat with his driver.

His words, however, had a completely different ring to them.

"If you want her to live," he told Reilly, "just keep driving."

A frenzy of visual and audio snippets from every minute that had passed since Tess's phone call rushed across Reilly's mind. The clips all confirmed the same thing: He'd been played by the bastard sitting next to him.

His fingers choked the steering wheel, his nails biting into its padded leather. "The bomb . . . that was you."

"Insurance," the man confirmed, pulling a cell phone from his pocket and holding it up with his right hand, away from Reilly. "And as it turns out, one we needed."

Reilly understood. The phone had triggered the bomb. His veins were boiling—he just wanted to reach over and rip the guy's heart out and shove it down his throat and watch him choke on it. "And the real Sharafi?"

"My guess is he's dead." The man gave him a small shrug. "He was in the trunk of that car."

Not a flutter of emotion in his voice.

The next question was bouncing inside Reilly's head, kicking and screaming to get out. He didn't want to let it loose. He knew the answer he was about to get—but his mouth voiced the words anyway. "And Tess?"

The man's eyes hardened a touch. "There's another car back there. With another bomb." He held up the phone for Reilly again, to press the point home. "Tess is in it."

A firestorm ignited inside Reilly's chest as the cityscape flying past him went fuzzy, a blur of parked cars and gray walls. "What? You're saying she's here? In Rome?"

"Yes. And closer than you think."

He'd assumed she was still in Jordan, which was where she was when she'd called him. When she'd been kidnapped by the sick bastard sitting next to him. Reilly's heart was now pounding away, far beyond its red line, deafening him and flooding him with adrenaline and bile, the urgency of getting to Tess eclipsing all other thoughts. He zipped through dozens of potential moves at the same time, evaluating them, looking for an advantage, refusing to accept the notion that the son of a bitch next to him could walk away from this.

"Alive?" He had to ask, even though he had no way of knowing if the answer he'd get was the truth or not. All he could do was look into the guy's eyes and see if he could spot any tell as to what the truth was.

The man's face was maddeningly inscrutable. "Alive."

Reilly was too busy processing it to think of slowing down as the battered SUV blasted past the flower market and charged across a major crossroads at the Circonvallazione Trionfale as if it were on rails, causing oncoming cars to slam on their brakes and triggering a flurry of collisions.

"Keep going straight, and stay focused," the bomber ordered. "You won't do Tess much good if you get us both killed. I don't know how long she'll be able to breathe in that trunk."

Reilly didn't know what to believe. He blinked, gnashing his teeth raw, finding it hard to resist just pummeling the guy. Instead, he scowled at the road ahead and took it out on the gas pedal, mashing it harder. The Merc's engine strained as it propelled the armored SUV faster, and the Via Trionfale bent right and left gently before the rows of low apartment buildings on either side gave way to greenery and the road climbed up a forested hill.

Reilly had the pedal floored, the big 4.3-liter engine growling as the trees whipped past. They were charging up what felt like a small forest in the middle of Rome but was actually a lush small park of fifteen acres that led to the Cavalieri Hilton at the top of the hill. Reilly's eyes had darted sideways, noting that the man was gripping his armrest tightly to avoid sliding around, when a sharp left-hand hairpin came out of the blue, surprising him. He fought the wheel for control, struggling to keep the heavy SUV on the road, its tires screaming for grip. The car fishtailed out of the turn and roared up the hill—where another hairpin, a right-hander this time, loomed ahead.

"I said easy, damn it," his passenger barked.

Fuck you, Reilly seethed inwardly—and saw it, a small, landscaped clearing that was mercifully deserted and sat there, calling out to him in the glorious sunshine, at the end of a small pathway just before the turn.

He lifted off, feigning a slowdown for the turn, then blipped the throttle and threw the car in the opposite direction. It flew off the road and rumbled down the gravel path, slewing all over the place before Reilly jerked the wheel hard to the left and yanked the hand brake. The car spun around angrily, the tires pushing hard against the mounds of gravel that built up against them—and Reilly used its sideways momentum to launch himself onto the bomber, lifting up his elbow, jacking it in place, and aiming it right at his target's face as he flew out of his seat.

The man was lightning quick—raising the big, heavy codex up as a shield to block him. It took the brunt of Reilly's weight, deflecting the hit. Reilly still had some advantage as he crushed the bomber against his car door. The man's hand lashed out and flicked the door open. Reilly put one arm around the book and used the other to throw a punch at him. The man bent away to avoid it, leaning precariously

far out of the car now—which Reilly was quick to capi-
talize on, wrenching the book out of his grasp just as he
shoved him out.

The bomber tumbled to the ground. Reilly clambered
right out of the car after him, but the man recovered fast
and scurried back, putting a margin of ten yards or so between him and the FBI agent. Time slowed to a crawl as
they stood there in silence, facing off under the hot Roman
sun, taking stock of each other in the empty clearing. It was
eerily quiet, especially after the pandemonium they'd been
through, with only choruses of cicadas and the occasional
tweet of a starling cutting the silence.

"Settle down," the bomber told Reilly, holding up his
cell phone with one hand while his other wagged a stern,
warning finger. "One twitch from me and she's gone."

Reilly glared at him, clutching the book tight.

They studied each other as they tentatively inched sideways, moving in unison, keeping the same buffer between
them.

"Where is she?" Reilly asked.

"Everything in its time."

"You're not walking away from this." Reilly's eyes were
locked on him, his senses alert, processing every morsel of
information at hand, looking for an edge.

"I disagree," the bomber countered. "We've established
that you care a great deal for this woman. You wouldn't
have flown halfway across the world and taken me into
the Vatican if you didn't. Which means you won't stop me
from walking away from here if that gets her killed. Which
it would. Unquestionably."

"But then again, I've got this book. And we've established that it's pretty important to you, right?"

The man conceded Reilly's remark with a small nod.

"So here's what we'll do," Reilly said. "You want the
book. I want Tess. In one piece. So we trade. Take me to her,
show me she's alive and well, and you can have the book."

The bomber shook his head, a mock apology on his
face. "Can't do that. I'm not sure it's safe for me to go
down there right now, you know what I mean? No, you'll
have to go get her yourself. So how about this instead. The

book, for her location. And my word that she's safe and healthy."

His word. Reilly mashed his teeth. He knew he had no choice. "And that phone you're holding," he added.

The bomber thought about it for a brief moment, then shrugged. "Sounds fair."

The sick fuck's talking about fair, Reilly bristled. He fought to keep his fury in check and see this through.

"Okay, here's how we'll play this," Reilly said. "You put the phone down on the ground and tell me what car she's in and where it's parked. I'll put the book down too. Then we'll each move sideways, one step at a time, as if we're going around an imaginary circle. Slowly. You get the book, I get the phone."

"And then?"

"Then maybe you get away—for a while. But sooner or later, make no mistake, your ass is mine." Reilly's concentration was lasered on him, memorizing every pore, every wrinkle, every detail about him.

The bomber watched him, as if putting his plan through a final stress test. "She's in a BMW."

Reilly's pulse spiked.

The man held up some car keys and dangled them, taunting Reilly. They were like a bloodred rag to a rabid bull. "A five series. Dark blue. Brindisi plates. It's parked by the Petriano entrance."

Which made sense, Reilly thought. Insurance—to use the bomber's callous word—in case they exited the Vatican from its other gate.

The man held the keys there for a moment; then he turned and tossed them behind him, slightly off to one side. They landed in a small stretch of lawn. He eyed Reilly, an icy smirk just cracking the surface of the hermetic expression on his face. "You're going to want this too," he added as he held up his phone—before turning around and tossing it too.

Reilly's chest seized up as he watched the phone spin in the air several times before it landed on the same grassy patch, by a couple of benches. He just froze there, every muscle in his body knotted to the breaking point, his ears cranked up to eleven, dreading a telltale, distant boom—but he heard nothing.

"Drop the book and go get them," the man barked, pointing an angry finger toward the lawn.

Reilly hesitated, his feet nailed to the ground—he couldn't hang on to the heavy book and go around the bomber to retrieve the phone. The man would have no trouble tackling him. His legs twitched, getting conflicting signals about staying put or sprinting off—then he made his move. He turned and hurled the codex as far as he could, shot-putting it behind him, away from the bomber, then tore off toward the phone.

The bomber sprang forward at the same instant. The two men raced for their prizes, eyeing each other while angling away for safety as they rushed past each other, with Reilly harnessing all of his willpower to resist veering off his trajectory and taking the man down—which he couldn't. He couldn't risk it—failure meant condemning Tess to a certain death. So he stuck to his heading and was on the grassy patch within seconds. He spotted the phone and plucked it off the ground, staring at it in disbelief, hoping the fact that he hadn't heard an explosion in the city below meant that it hadn't triggered one. His pulse was throbbing wildly as he spun around.

The bomber was gone.

As was the book.

Chapter 8

✝

Reilly moved with androidlike purpose, as if he weren't in control of his body anymore. He had to do one thing, and one thing only—and nothing could be allowed to interfere.

He stormed up the hill and cut across the hotel's grounds, shocking its refined guests with his haggard appearance. He didn't even notice them. He just sprinted across to the hotel's entrance, zeroed in on a taxi that was picking up an elegantly dressed couple, charged past them, and stormed into it.

"The Vatican, Petriano entrance," Reilly ordered him. The man, incensed by Reilly's move, started to mouth off in Italian, but he barely got a few words out before Reilly shoved his FBI ID in the man's face and, with his other hand pointing ahead angrily, roared, "*Vaticano*. Now. Move."

They got as far as maybe half a mile from St. Peter's Square before the traffic ground to a halt.

The whole area was crippled by pandemonium as a result of the blast. Police cordons were spreading out protectively on the roads leading up to the Vatican, while hordes of frightened tourists were being herded away from the site. On the roads, taxis and convoys of tour buses were fighting their way out of the snarl under a pall of black smoke that hovered over the cathedral's dome.

Reilly exited the taxi and battled his way through the onslaught of cars and people. He spotted a sign for the "*Cancello Petriano*" that directed him to a narrow street that was choked by fleeing tourists. He hugged the façade of a building that fronted the street and fought his way through the human torrent, heading toward the back of the curved colonnade of St. Peter's Square. Through the swarm of people, he spotted another sign for the gate, this one pointing left.

He cleared the building and turned left, breathing hard as he emerged from the throng. The gate was less than a hundred yards ahead of him now, with a parking area for a few dozen cars leading up to it. Reilly's pulse sped.

A dark blue BMW with Brindisi plates.

It had to be here somewhere.

He had started toward the parked cars when a cop who was shepherding the evacuation cut across him and tried to block him. The cop was rambling something incomprehensible in Italian, his sweaty face bristling with stress. Reilly brushed him aside without breaking pace and kept moving. The cop recovered and caught back up to him and grabbed him by the arm, hard this time, yelling at him, his other hand waving a steel baton angrily and gesturing with it for Reilly to turn around and join the exodus. Reilly reached into his pocket for his creds—then remembered he couldn't use them, not there. He was probably on their most-wanted list right now. He met the cop's gaze, and the cop seemed to read his hesitation.

No choice.

Reilly raised his hands defensively with a sheepish half grin—"*Prego, signore*" (Please, sir)—then decided this would take too long and just sucker punched the cop in the gut, then followed through with another to the jaw.

The cop dropped.

Reilly was on the move again, his eyes scanning the rows of cars, desperately looking for the BMW. He thought of using the remote control to trigger the door locks and let the alarm's beeps announce the car's location to him, but he didn't want to risk it, worried that the bomber might have booby-trapped the car with just that in mind.

A whistle broke through his concentration. The punched cop was pushing himself back to his feet and calling in backup. Within seconds, cops were rushing at Reilly, converging at him from the gate and from behind—and just as the first of them reached him, he spotted it: navy blue, white plates with the BR provincial code that had to stand for Brindisi.

A cop was yelling "*Alt*"—Stop—at Reilly and moved in to block him. Reilly shoved him aside and kept going, now only a few feet from the car. Another cop joined in, the two of them now screaming furiously, arms spread and weapons drawn, ordering him to stop moving. Reilly spread his arms wide with evident frustration, motioning for them to stay calm—while still inching his way closer to the BMW.

"The car," he fired back, his voice hoarse with tension. "There's a woman in that BMW." He was jabbing his finger toward it, his face contorted with rage. "In the goddamn car," he repeated. "She's in there." He put his wrists together, miming someone with tied hands.

The cops' faced clouded with confusion as they moved with him, their arms wide, trying to corral him, but he stared them down and kept moving until he got to the BMW.

He gestured again to them, using his hands and the desperate expression on his face to implore them to give him a second as he eyed the back of the car, his mind buzzing with questions.

Is Tess in there? Is she still alive? Is there a bomb in there with her? Is the bomber watching from somewhere nearby, waiting to take them all out any second now with a second remote trigger? Or does he even need to? What if that sick son of a bitch has booby-trapped the trunk lid?

The carabinieri soon cut short his torment. One of them lunged to hit him with his steel baton—setting Reilly off. He grabbed the cop's hand with both of his own, blocking the hit and twisting the man's arm to wrest the stick from his grip before spinning him around and shoving him back onto his colleague. Now armed with the baton, he dashed around to the driver's side of the car and tried the door. It was locked. He swung the baton and smashed the window, and the car's alarm started blaring just as the cops reached

Reilly. They couldn't stop him from leaning in, and with a silent prayer flashing across his mind, his instincts taking over, hoping as hard as he could that he wasn't making a gargantuan mistake, he reached down to the base of the driver's seat and tugged the trunk's release lever. He spun around, willing away the explosion that would rip him to shreds, and glimpsed the trunk lid pop open and glide upward harmlessly just as the cops slammed him against the car—hard—winding him as more cops piled in to join them.

He yelled at them as they pinned him down, pressing his face against the roof of the car, crushing his cheek and ear, Reilly fighting back, desperate to lift his head up and see what was inside the trunk of the car. And then he heard it—a cop who'd moved back for a look went ballistic and started shouting wildly.

Tess.

Reilly stiffened as fear and hope ripped through him, his mind scrambling to understand what the man was blurting out. "English," he shouted. "Say it in English, damn it. Is she in there? Is she okay?"

He read the panic in the cops' eyes and heard the word "*Bomba*" blurted repeatedly, its meaning glaringly obvious. Then he heard another word, "*Donna*," over and over—the word shredding his heart. *Donna*—woman. But—alive? Or—

He drew on reserves of strength he didn't know he possessed and heaved back, shoving the cops off of him, then fought his way to the back of the car and looked in.

She was there.

Wrapped up inside a sleeping bag, strapped down to the base of the trunk, silver duct tape across her eyes and mouth, her nose and two strips of her cheeks the only visible skin on display.

She wasn't moving.

And next to her, in the right corner of the trunk, a jumble of gray Semtex packs, wires, and a digital detonator with a small red LED indicating that it was armed.

Reilly didn't give it a second glance. He reached in and settled his hands softly against Tess's neck, his thumb brushing against her cheek, looking for a pulse.

Her head twitched sideways.

His face flooded with relief. He glanced at the cops next to him, who were watching in silence, dumbstruck. He carefully peeled the tape off Tess's face, first the strip across her mouth, then the one around her ears and eyes.

She looked up at him, her eyes brimming with tears of fear and joy, her upper lip trembling.

It was the most beautiful thing he'd ever seen.

Chapter 9

✠

Mansoor Zahed glanced into his rearview mirror one last time before he pulled into the driveway. He didn't spot anything that gave him cause for concern. The house that the agency had rented for him was on a quiet residential street. Curious eyes weren't a problem, especially given that the small driveway was shielded from the street by tall metal gates.

He wasn't planning on sticking around too long. Now that what he'd come for was lying in the foot well of the passenger seat, he thought he was probably done with Rome. The American historian, Simmons, would soon confirm whether or not that was the case. In doing that, Zahed hoped, the man would also figure out what their next destination would be. Zahed's instincts told him he'd be on the move again soon, leaving the Eternal City behind as just another blood-soaked entry in his infamous—if anonymous—résumé.

He reflected back on his day and felt reasonably satisfied. Things hadn't gone as smoothly as he'd hoped, but all that mattered was that he was here, he was safe, and he had the codex with him. *Mission accomplished*, he thought with a small smirk—he just loved that expression and its recently minted, delicious irony. But as he replayed the day's events in his mind's eye, his mind kept latching onto the actions of the FBI agent, and he felt a murmur of unease about him. Which wasn't something Mansoor Zahed was used to. Nor was it something he tolerated.

The agent had been easy to manipulate. Zahed had managed to lure him to Rome. He'd fooled him into believing he was the spineless scholar Sharafi. He'd pushed enough buttons to get the agent to take him into the deepest recesses of his religion's inner sanctum. Sean Reilly hadn't flinched then, and he hadn't flinched in all that followed. He'd done what was needed of him without hesitation. He'd turned himself into a criminal and ridden roughshod across the very epicenter of his faith without worrying about the consequences.

And that unsettled Zahed.

He wasn't used to seeing such commitment, not in these soft Westerners. Not that he'd taken the man lightly. Even though he hadn't had much to go on before meeting him, what he had managed to dig up on Reilly had suggested that the man wasn't a lightweight, nor was he particularly concerned with sticking to the rule book. Which had pleased Zahed. Their joint venture needed someone with a reinforced-concrete spine. But there was a tipping point at which the very qualities he needed the man to have would turn him into a pain in the ass.

They were already way past that tipping point.

He wondered whether he'd made a mistake by letting Reilly live, and frowned at the thought. He'd had his chance. He could have made his move when Reilly ran for the phone, when they'd rushed past each other, but in the heat of the moment, he'd felt a stab of doubt, unsure about whether or not he could take the man in hand-to-hand combat. He'd pulled back. He'd seen something in Reilly, a blaze of determination and self-belief that had made Zahed second-guess his own considerable skills. Which, again, wasn't something he was used to. Or tolerated.

Mansoor Zahed chided himself at his momentary lapse. He should have taken him down, there and then, and walked away without the worry that was now dogging him: that this FBI agent could well become a *serious* pain in the ass for him.

If we should cross paths again, it'll be more his misfortune than mine, Zahed decided before vaulting the thought and focusing on more immediate matters.

He waited for the gates to swing back shut before getting out of the car, a rented Fiat Croma. It was a common family sedan that wouldn't attract attention. He'd left it in the Trastevere area, not far from the riverbanks of the Tiber, before taxiing to the airport to meet Reilly. He'd then recovered it once he had the codex in his grips, which was when he'd had to improvise—rushing back down the hill, pulling a hapless teenager off his Piaggio scooter and using it to get back to his car. He wasn't worried about being tracked. Not in Rome. If he had been in London, things would have been different. That city had unashamedly embraced an Orwellian vision and sported CCTV cameras on every block. Rome was different. Old-world. Low-tech. Which suited Zahed—and the Cosa Nostra, who had influence over most City Council decisions—just fine.

He made his way into the house. It had the musty, dank smell of somewhere that hadn't been lived in for months. The few pieces of furniture that were in there were covered up with old sheets and blankets that Zahed hadn't bothered removing. He double-locked the door behind him and stepped into the hall, pausing at the mirror in the entrance foyer. He studied the figure that was staring back at him with cool disdain. The plucked-back hairline, the cheap glasses, the drab clothes—they were all necessary for the deception. He was happy to revert to a character in whose skin he felt more comfortable, something he could now do.

He took the stairs down to the basement and unlocked the door to a storeroom. He stepped inside and flicked on the light switch. Simmons was—as expected—just where he'd left him: on the floor of the windowless room, his back to the wall, his mouth taped shut, his right wrist tied to a radiator pipe with nylon cuffs.

JED SIMMONS HEARD THE DOOR squeal open just before the bare lightbulb that dangled from a cord in the middle of the room came on. He glanced up the stone staircase. After the darkness of the last few hours, even the pale glare was painful. Beyond that, just raising his eyelids felt like an Olympian effort. He didn't recognize himself in this pathetic state—so weak that he could barely move his limbs, his breathing labored, his confused mind adrift in a foggy swell with no ports in sight.

A brief, cruel moment of hope—that it was a rescuer, that somehow, someone had figured out what was happening and was here to end his nightmare—was quickly extinguished as the now familiar silhouette of his abductor came into view.

A spurt of adrenaline shot through him as his anger flared. He felt outraged at being held like this, by someone whose name and intent he knew nothing about. His abductor had been maddeningly disciplined about following his need-to-know code. Simmons didn't know anything beyond the bare basics: that he was there to help the man recover whatever it was some small band of Templars had whisked out of Constantinople. Beyond that, who the man was, who he was working for, why he was after it—none of that was forthcoming.

He wondered if he'd die without knowing. The thought angered him even more.

A shiver rippled through Simmons as he spotted the codex the man had brought with him. He watched helplessly as the man got down on his haunches in front of him and, with one quick flick, ripped the duct tape off his mouth.

"Good news," he told Simmons as he set it down on the tiles in front of him. "I have it. Which means that you're still useful to me."

"Tess . . . Where is she? Is she okay?" The words were coming out weak and slurred.

"She's just fine, Jed. She's perfectly all right. She helped me, and so she's free. You see? I'll do the same for you if you just do what I ask and help me find what I'm looking for. How does that sound?"

Simmons stared at him, a caustic hatred burning his gut. He wanted to believe the man, wanted to believe Tess was all right, but somehow, he doubted it was true.

"What about Sharafi?"

The man smiled. "He's fine too. I don't need him anymore, so he was free to go. It's that simple." He reached out and gave Simmons's cheeks a patronizing squeeze. "Now ... how about we get you nice and comfortable—and awake—so you can get to work?"

The man's hand slipped down into his pocket and came back up with a syringe in it. His other hand brought out a small bottle of medication from another pocket. He plunged the needle through the rubber cap of the bottle and sucked the clear liquid up into the syringe, then held it up for the obligatory squirt to clear out any air holes.

The archaeologist stared at the needle and didn't say anything. He just nodded, his tenebrous gaze dropping down to the ancient book, silently ruing the day that he'd first heard about it and wishing he'd never mentioned the damn thing.

Chapter 10

✠

Tucked away in the Palace of the Tribunal behind St. Peter's Cathedral, the Central Office of the Vatican Gendarmeria was in meltdown. Urgent footfalls were stampeding up and down the medieval building's cavernous hallways, phones were ringing all over the place, questions and updates were being shouted out across rooms and through doorways, the whole discordant chaos drilling into Tess Chaykin's ears and echoing painfully inside her skull.

Reilly and some carabinieri had brought her here, away from the rigged car, and settled her on a couch in a waiting room. A couple of paramedics had been drafted in to check her over. She was dehydrated, weak from hunger—but otherwise unharmed. They'd given her some rehydrating drinks, some Gatorade, and someone was dispatched to rustle up some clean clothes and some food for her. The whole thing had gone by in a blur, except for one question that was firmly anchored in her mind:

Rome?

How the hell did I get to Rome?

She glanced up at Reilly, who was talking to the paramedics. He must have sensed her look, as he turned and smiled at her. She watched him thank the paramedics; then he joined her.

"How are you feeling?"

"Much better now that I'm not in that damn coffin." She had a million questions for him, but still felt groggy and was having trouble ordering her thoughts.

"I'll get you out of here as soon as I can. They're going to find you a room and a bed."

"Thanks." Her voice was still weak, her throat felt rough, and her eyes still hadn't lost their haunted veneer. "I need to get to a phone," she told him. "I need to call Kim, and Mom."

He handed her his BlackBerry. "You know the lock code."

"Yeah," she answered, a faint smile warming up her face. A voice from the doorway cut in. "Reilly."

Reilly turned.

Doug Tilden, the FBI legal attaché in Rome, was standing there. A tall man with combed-back graying hair and sleek, frameless glasses, he looked like he was having his own meltdown. "We need you in here."

Reilly acknowledged him with a slight nod, then turned back to Tess and cupped her cheek in one hand, softly. "I'll be next door if you need anything."

"Go. I'm fine just sitting here with my stash," she said, holding up her bottles and his phone, her face clouded but still managing a pained smile.

He rose to his feet, but Tess caught his arm in her grip and stopped him. She pulled him back down, drawing his face right up to hers. "I'm sorry. I had no idea it would—"

Reilly cut her off with a slight shake of his head. "Don't worry about it. Okay?"

She held his gaze, then pulled him closer and planted a soft kiss on his lips. "Thanks," she whispered. "For finding me."

He smiled, his eyes clearly telegraphing that the relief was mutual, then headed out with Tilden.

"THAT'S ONE HELL OF A shitstorm you've got us in," Tilden told him as they made their way to the inspector general's office. "Why didn't you say anything beforehand? We could have helped."

Tilden was a career federal agent, and as the Bureau's

legal attaché in Rome, he was responsible for FBI operations in Italy as well as liaising with law enforcement organizations in southern Europe, the Middle East, and non-French-speaking Africa. He was undoubtedly used to dealing with crises, but this one had clearly blown out the fuses of his shitstorm-o-meter. His being around wasn't making things any easier for Reilly, who had met him before, years earlier, when they'd both been on a joint task force working alongside the DEA. It had been a painful assignment that had ended in tragedy, just as today had. Innocent bystanders had died on both occasions, although back then, Reilly had pulled the fatal trigger himself. The shooting had never stopped haunting him, and it was something he would have preferred not to have Tilden's presence dredge up, especially not today, of all days.

"You know how these things sometimes go down, Doug," Reilly told him.

"Plus it was Tess, right?"

Reilly gave him a "what do you think?" look.

Tilden nodded grudgingly. "Well, I'm just glad you told them you were here on personal business. Takes a bit of the sting off my ass."

"It was my call all the way."

Tilden slid him a grave sideways glance. "All right," he grumbled. "Just do me a favor and don't make things worse in there."

"Do I need to get myself a lawyer?"

"Probably," Tilden replied tersely. "Assuming they let you walk out of here alive."

Judging from the looks that Delpiero and the two other men in the room shot him as he walked in, Reilly knew that wasn't a given.

Delpiero, the Vatican's head cop, rushed through an introduction of the two men to Reilly—one was from the State Police's antiterrorist unit, the other from the country's intelligence service—then opened out his hands in an incensed "what the hell?" gesture. "Barely an hour ago, I left you with Monsignor Bescondi and your professor and told you I was there for you if you needed anything. This is how you reward our generosity?"

Reilly didn't have an easy answer for him. Instead, he asked, "The second bomb. Is it safe?"

"It's been defused."

Now for the harder one. "And the first bomb? How bad is it?"

Delpiero's expression hardened. "Three dead. Over forty wounded, two of them critical. That's what we know so far."

Reilly scowled, processing the terrible news. He felt his veins petrify with anger and remorse. After a moment, he said, "There was a man in the trunk of the first car."

Delpiero turned to one of his colleagues and rattled off a question in Italian. They had a brief and intense exchange that told Reilly his statement was news to them.

"How do you know this?" Delpiero asked.

"The guy who was with me told me."

"The man in the trunk—do you know who he was?"

"Behrouz Sharafi," Reilly informed him. "The real one."

"So the man who was with you—"

"He was an impostor." The thought welled up some bile in Reilly's throat. He saw that Delpiero and the others were lost.

Delpiero's tone rose with anger and confusion. "So you brought this—this terrorist here, to the Vatican, without even knowing who he really was?"

"It's not that simple," Reilly fired back, trying to keep his fury—at the bomber and, even more, at himself—in check. "I was told I had to get him into the archives or that woman sitting out there would be killed," he said, thrusting an angry finger in the direction of the door. "That bastard, whoever he is—he played his role perfectly, and you can be damn sure that given the level of resources he seems to have at his disposal, he would have had no trouble flashing me a fake ID with Sharafi's name on it had I asked for one." He shook his head bitterly. "Look, he tricked me, all right? I never expected anything like this. I was just trying to save a friend's life."

"And in doing that, you got three people killed and dozens injured," Delpiero countered.

The comment pierced Reilly's chest, and any angry

words he wanted to blurt out just shriveled up in his throat. People had died, others had been hurt, and he felt responsible. He'd been played by that son of a bitch, whoever he was—played and bested. Almost. Reilly tried to console himself with the thought that he could have easily ended up dead himself. If he'd given the bomber half a chance once they were out of the Vatican, there was little doubt in Reilly's mind that the man would have killed him. Which would have meant that Tess would have probably died too. At least he'd managed to turn that part of it around. He didn't give a rat's ass about any book or about wrecking the pope's wheels. He'd saved Tess's life, which was what he'd set out to do. But not like this. That wasn't part of the bargain. People had died, innocent people whom he had no right to draw into his drama, and nothing would ever make up for that.

Tilden read the torment on Reilly's face and stepped in. "With all due respect, *Ispettore*. I think we need to hear all the facts before any of us says something we might regret."

"I agree," a voice chimed in from behind them.

Cardinal Brugnone had walked into the room. Monsignor Bescondi, the prefect of the Vatican Secret Archives, was with him, seemingly recovered from the injection Reilly had given him. They weren't smiling.

Reilly found it hard to look them in the eye.

"We need to know all the facts about why this outrage was allowed to take place," Brugnone grumbled. "Agent Reilly—why don't you tell us what you should have told us when you first arrived here?"

Reilly felt the onset of a massive headache. "I'll tell you what I know, but I don't even know all the facts myself. We need to hear from Tess—Miss Chaykin, out there—to get the whole picture."

"Why don't we invite her in?" the cardinal suggested.

"I'm not sure she's up to that just yet," Reilly said.

The cardinal fixed him with a grave stare. "Why don't we ask her about that?"

Chapter 11

✠

"It all started in Jordan," Tess told the group in the room.

Right now, it was the last thing she wanted to do. She still felt drained, and dredging up the memory of what had happened was making her shiver. Still, she realized it was important. The men in the room—Reilly, Cardinal Brugnone, Inspector Delpiero, the archivist Bescondi, and the two detectives from the antiterrorist squad—they all needed to know what she'd been through. She had to do everything she could to help them catch the guy who was behind all this, and rescue Simmons, who, she hoped, had to still be alive. For how long, though, was something she didn't really want to think about.

"I was out there with another archaeologist. His name's Jed Simmons. He's got this dig going near Petra, he's got Brown backing him, and—" She stopped, reminding herself to stick to what was relevant and not go off-piste. "Anyway, this Iranian historian showed up, someone who knew someone who knew Jed."

"Behrouz Sharafi," Reilly noted.

Tess nodded. "Yes. A sweet, quiet man. Thoughtful, and extremely well read too." Reilly had told her what had happened to him, and the idea that he was dead made her shivers worse. She steeled herself and pressed on. "Sharafi needed help figuring something out. A contact of his had suggested he talk to Jed about it because—well, although Jed's work in Petra was all about Nabataean cultural history, he's also one of the most knowledgeable people on the planet when it comes to the Templars. That's actually why I was there myself."

She noticed Brugnone stir and slide a glance at Reilly, as if things were starting to fall into place for him.

"Tess—Miss Chaykin—she's an archaeologist," Reilly explained to the room. "A lapsed one, really. She's now a novelist. And her first book was about the Templars."

"It's historical fiction," Tess specified, suddenly feeling the walls tightening in around her.

She glanced around the room and noted Brugnone's reaction. He seemed familiar with what she and Reilly had just mentioned.

"Your book," the cardinal mused, his eyes scrutinizing her. "It was rather well received, if I'm not mistaken."

"It was." Tess nodded, graciously but also somewhat uncomfortably. She knew what he meant. Although her novel, a thriller set during the Crusades, was perceived as nothing more than a work of historical fiction, she knew that Brugnone was well aware that the story within its pages wasn't entirely borne from her imagination. She felt a pang of unease and tried to remind herself that she hadn't done anything wrong. She'd stuck to what she and Reilly had agreed to—keeping it private, not talking about it, not telling anyone, particularly Brugnone and Reilly's boss at the FBI, about what had really happened in that storm and on that Greek island. But that didn't mean she couldn't use what she'd lived through and what she'd discovered about the Templars along the way as the basis of a novel—a pretty successful one, as it turned out, but one that only the most radically conspiracy-minded would ever think was based on real history. It had launched her into a new career and a new life, and it had also proven pleasantly cathartic for her.

Until now.

The cardinal held her gaze for an uncomfortable moment, then said, "Continue, please."

Tess took a sip from her bottle and shifted in her chair.

"Sharafi had found something, in Istanbul, in the National Library. It was in the old Ottoman archives. He came across it by chance. He lived there, in Istanbul. He'd moved there from Tehran and he was teaching at a university, and being an expert on Sufism, he was digging into Sufi history in his spare time. He was a Sufi himself, you know." Her lips still ached from the duct tape, and she was having trouble focusing. "Anyway, it was the perfect place for that line of research since that's where it all started, in thirteenth-century Turkey, with Rumi and his poems."

"And he found something there that was Templar?" Brugnone asked, a gentle prod for her to get to it.

"Sort of. He was rooting around in the old archives— you know they have literally tens of thousands of documents that are just stored there, waiting to be sorted out. All kinds of stuff. The Ottomans were maniacal archivists. Anyway, Sharafi came across a book. A substantial volume, nice tooled leather-bound covers, early fourteenth-century. It held the writings of a Sufi traveler that he hadn't come across before. But it also had something else. Some loose vellum sheets had been tucked in under its bindings. Hidden from view for centuries. Sharafi spotted them, and naturally, he got curious. So without telling anyone or seeking permission, he pried them out. His first surprise was that they weren't written in Arabic, like the book itself. They were in Greek. Medieval Greek. He copied down a few sentences and asked a colleague to translate them for him. The pages turned out to be a letter. Not just a letter . . . a confession. The confession of a monk who lived in a Byzantine Orthodox monastery." She concentrated to recall its name. "The Monastery of Mount Argaeus."

She paused and glanced around, looking for any signs of recognition. No one seemed familiar with it.

Bescondi, the prefect of the archives, leaned in. He seemed confused. "You're saying this man Sharafi found the confession of a monk from a Byzantine monastery. What does that have to do with the Templars?"

Only one word came to Tess's lips.

"Everything."

Chapter 12

✞

"Five hundred hyperpyra? That's ... that's just outrageous," the French bishop blurted.

Conrad of Tripoli wasn't moved. He held the old man's gaze with the serenity of someone who had done this many times before, and shrugged. Not a cold, demeaning shrug. He made sure he maintained an air of congeniality and, above all, respect. "We really shouldn't be haggling over a few pieces of gold, Father. Not when it involves something this sacred."

They were seated at a discreet table, tucked away in a dark corner of a tavern in the district of Galata, a Genoese colony on the north shore of the Golden Horn. Conrad knew the owner of the tavern well and often conducted his business there. He could count on him to give him the privacy he needed and lend a hand if things got messy. Not that Conrad needed much help. He had seen more fighting and spilled more blood than most men could even imagine, but that was part of a long-gone past that he kept to himself.

The gilded box sat squarely on the table. It was a small masterpiece with an embossed, floriated design on its side and a large cross on its lid. Inside, it was lined with frayed velvet cushioning that looked like it was centuries old. When Conrad had first presented the priest with the reliquary, the bones it housed had been wrapped inside a sheet of vellum that bore the markings and seal of the Patriarch of Alexandria. They were now laid out on the padded base of the container, their ancient yellow-gray pallor contrasting vividly against the burgundy padding.

The bishop's thin, long-nailed fingers trembled as he reached out to touch the bones again. From the talus to the metatarsals, they were all there.

"Sacred, indeed. The foot of Saint Philip," he muttered, his eyes brimming with reverence. "The fifth apostle." His fingers cut the air gently as he crossed himself yet again.

"The man who kept preaching right to the bitter end, even while he was crucified upside down," Conrad said. "A true martyr."

"How did you get hold of them?" the priest asked.

"Please, Father. We are not in confession here, are we?" Conrad smiled, teasing him for a moment before leaning in and lowering his tone. "There are many crypts in this city. Under the Chapel of the Holy Virgin of Pharos, inside the walls of the Great Palace, at the church in Pammakaristos . . . if you know where to look, they're there. The holiest of treasures, tucked out of harm's way just before the great sack and now waiting to be unearthed and returned to their rightful glory. And as anyone will tell you, I know these dungeons like the back of my hand." He smiled, raising his right hand. "But I need to know if you want these or not, Father. There are other buyers waiting . . . and I need the funding to continue my work if I'm ever going to lay my hands on the greatest treasure of them all."

The bishop's eyes bulged wide. "What treasure is that?"

Conrad leaned in closer. "The Mandylion," he whispered.

The bishop sucked in a sharp intake of breath and his face lit up. "The Mandylion of Edessa?"

"The very same. And I think I'm close."

The bishop's fingers started twitching greedily. "If you were ever to find it," he said, "I would be very, very interested in acquiring it for our cathedral."

Conrad inclined his head casually. "As would many of my clients. But I'm not sure I'd ever want to part with it. Not when the image of our Lord himself is imprinted on it."

The old priest's lips were quivering visibly now, his wrinkled fingers beseeching the air between them. "Please. You must promise. Let me know when you have it. I'll pay handsomely."

Conrad reached out and brought the man's withered forearms back down on the table. "Let's conclude this matter first, shall we? The rest we can talk about, when the time comes."

The bishop studied him for a beat, then smiled, a thin-lipped, rotted-toothed smile that was a fair match for the bones he was buying. They agreed on a time when they would meet up again for the exchange; then the old man got up and walked off.

Conrad cracked a satisfied grin as he packed up the bones and hollered out an order for a pitcher of beer. He took in the bustle out in the tavern's main room. Merchants, aristocrats, common folk, and whores, wheeling and dealing and getting drunk in a raucous blur of pidgin Italian—the lingua franca of the Galata district—and laughter.

Quite a change from the austerity of his previous life, as a warrior-monk of the Poor Fellow-Soldiers of Christ and of the Temple of Solomon—the Templars.

He smiled. The city had been good to him.

It had taken him in and allowed him to create a new life for himself, which hadn't been easy. Not after all the setbacks and disasters that had befallen him and his brethren, not after they'd all been turned into hunted men. But things were going well for him now. His reputation was growing with every sale. And he particularly enjoyed the fact that he was prospering at the expense of those who had brought about the demise of his Order, fleecing those whose ilk had caused him to end up in Constantinople.

If they only knew, he thought with great relish.

Like his adoptive city, Conrad was rising from the dregs of a Vatican-bred calamity. His troubles had begun with the defeat at Acre in 1291, almost two decades earlier, a disastrous battle that ended with Conrad, his fellow Templars, and the rest of the crusaders losing the last major Christian stronghold in the Holy Land, and resulted in the mass arrests of 1307, which the King of France and the pope had orchestrated to take down the Order. The Queen of Cities had suffered its own catastrophic upheaval around a hundred years earlier, when the pope's army had raped and pillaged it in 1204 after besieging it for close to a year. Blood had flowed, ankle-deep, down the streets. Great fires had ravaged it for days on end, wiping out a third of its buildings. Anything that was left standing had been looted and ransacked beyond recognition. In the aftermath, anyone who could afford to do so had moved away. Once the world's marketplace and the proud home of God's emperor on earth, the New Rome had been turned into a city of ruins.

Its conquerors hadn't had much joy in ruling over it. Its first Latin emperor, Baldwin, was captured by the Bulgarians during a skirmish near Adrianople less than a year into his reign. They chopped his arms and legs off and dumped him in a ravine, where he was said to have survived for three whole days. His successors didn't fare much better. They only managed to hang on to the city for five decades before their infighting and incompetence brought their reign to a humiliating end.

The Byzantine emperor who retook the city in 1261, Michael VIII, saw himself as a new Constantine and set about restoring it to its former glory. Palaces and churches were refurbished, streets repaired, hospitals and schools founded. But reality soon put a cap on these ambitions. For one thing, money was tight. The Byzantine Empire wasn't much of an empire anymore. It was much smaller than it had been, effectively no more than a minor Greek state, which meant that its rulers were only receiving a fraction of the tax and customs revenues they had previously enjoyed. Worse, its eastern flanks were under constant attack. Bands of nomadic Turks were further chipping away at the fractured and shrunken empire. Fleeing refugees from the beleaguered provinces, penniless and desperate, were now crowding the city, living in squalor in overcrowded shantytowns and across its rubbish dumps, further straining its economy. A harsh winter had only made matters worse, a late frost wiping out large tracts of cropland and exacerbating the food shortages.

The chaos and the turmoil suited Conrad. He needed the anonymity that a city in flux could offer. And there was good money to be made if you knew where to find it: the pockets of gullible, visiting clerics from the churches and cathedrals of the wealthy West.

Constantinople may have been stripped of anything of value a hundred years earlier, but it was still an Aladdin's cave of holy relics. Hundreds of them were believed to be scattered around the city, tucked away in its many churches and monasteries, waiting to be pilfered and sold. They were of great value to the priests of Western Europe. A cathedral, a church, or a priory far from the Holy Land would gain tremendously in stature—and, hence, in contributions— once it housed a major relic originating from those distant shores. The faithful wouldn't have to embark on long and expensive pilgrimages and travel across land and sea to see, and perhaps even touch, the bone of a martyr or a splinter from the True Cross. Which was why many clerics came to Constantinople, in search of a trophy they could take back to their home church. Some paid good money; others schemed and stole—whatever it took to secure their prize.

Conrad was there to help.

Even if, far more often than not, the prize wasn't exactly what he claimed it to be.

Like any parlor trick, it was, he knew, all in the presentation. Invest in the right packaging, get the backstory right, and buyers would be lining up for a shard of the Crown of Thorns or a fragment from the robe of the Virgin Mary.

"Another satisfied customer?" the tavern keeper asked as he brought over a fresh pitcher of beer.

"Is there any other kind?"

"Bless you, my son," the barkeep chuckled. He set the pitcher on the table and nodded toward the back of the bar. "There's someone waiting for you out back. A Turk. Said his name was Qassem. Said you'd know who he was."

Conrad poured himself a glass and downed it in one chug, then set it down and wiped his mouth with the back of his hand. "Out back? Now?"

The barkeep nodded.

Conrad shrugged, then pushed the reliquary toward him. "Look after this for me until I get back, will you?"

He found the man waiting by a stack of empty barrels outside the rear entrance to the tavern. He'd met Qassem and his father shortly after arriving in the city a little over a year ago. He'd taken an instant dislike to Qassem, a brooding, muscular young man in his early twenties whose eyes lacked any trace of warmth. The father, Mehmet, was a different story. A tub of fat, hairy flesh, he was a dumpling of a man with a wide forehead, bulging eyes, and a short, thick neck. He was also a consummate trader, one who could sell you something, then buy it right back from you at half price and make you feel like he was doing you a favor.

He also had access to whatever Conrad needed to pull off his scams, and he didn't ask too many questions.

"My father has something he thinks you might be interested in," Qassem told him.

"I'll fetch my horse," Conrad replied, not knowing that the young Turk's mundane announcement was about to upend his life.

HE RECOGNIZED THE BROADSWORDS IMMEDIATELY.

There were six of them, sheathed in their leather scabbards, laid out on a wooden table in Mehmet's small shop. Alongside them were other weapons that only confirmed Conrad's startling realization: four crossbows, a couple of dozen composite horn bows, and an assortment of daggers and bread knives.

Weapons with which he was very familiar.

The broadswords were what interested him most. Though modest in appearance, they were formidable tools of warfare. Brutally efficient, expertly fabricated, perfectly balanced, but with none of the gaudy ornamentation commonly found on the grips and pommels of the swords of the nobility. A Templar's sword was not an ostentatious display of wealth, nor could it be—the warrior-knights lived under vows of strict poverty. It was a weapon of war, pure and simple. A comfortable cruciform hilt crowning a pattern-welded blade, designed to carve through the flesh and bone of any enemy as well as through any chain mail that aspired to protect it.

The swords did, however, have one small distinguishing feature, barely noticeable, but definitely there: the initials of the sword's owner, on either side of a small splayed cross—the *croix pattée* used by the Order—the lot engraved on the upper section of the blade, just below the cross guard.

Initials that Conrad also instantly recognized.

An avalanche of images and feelings rolled over him.

"Where did you get these?"

Mehmet studied him with undisguised curiosity; then his doughy face relaxed into a satisfied grin. "So you like my little collection?"

Conrad tried to keep a lid on the disturbance bubbling inside him, but he knew that the Turkish trader wasn't easily fooled. "I'll take the whole lot off you at the price you ask, but I need to know where you found them."

The Turk eyed him with added curiosity, then asked, "Why?"

"That's my business. Do you want to sell them or not?"

The trader pursed his lips and rubbed his chin with his puffy fingers, then relented. "I bought them from some monks. We came across them at a caravanserai three weeks ago."

"Where?"

"East of here, about a week's ride away."

"Where?" Conrad pressed.

"In Cappadocia. Near the city of Venessa," the trader added, somewhat grudgingly.

Conrad nodded, deep in thought, his mind already racing ahead. He and his two fellow knights had slipped through the surreal landscape of that region on their way to Constantinople. They'd skirted around several caravanserais, huge trading posts that were dotted along the Silk Road, built by Seljuk sultans and grandees to encourage and protect the traders who worked the camel trails between Europe and Persia and farther on to China.

"Is that where their monastery is?"

"No. All they said was that it was up in the mountains somewhere," the trader said. "They were scrounging around for food supplies, selling whatever they could. They've got a drought out there that's killed off anything the frost didn't." He chuckled. "Anyway, it doesn't matter where it is. You can't possibly be thinking of going there."

"Why not?"

"It's dangerous territory, especially for a Frank like you. You'd be crossing half a dozen different *beyliks* to get there and risk coming across ten times as many bands of Ghazis along the way."

Conrad knew he was right. Since the fall of the Seljuk Sultanate of Rum, the entire region east of Constantinople had broken up into a tapestry of independent *beyliks*, emirates ruled by beys. The beys' armies were heaving with mercenary Ghazis, warriors of the faith who were hungry for either victory or for what they referred to as "the honey of martyrdom," with no particular preference either way. They were fierce fighters and kept a tight grip on the lands they controlled. It had been hard enough for him and his brethren to sneak through it unnoticed. It would be an entirely different proposition this time around: out in the open, asking around, trying to locate a monastery that probably didn't want to be found.

"We, on the other hand, would have much less trouble getting through," the trader suggested, settling back, his smug smile multiplying the folds that buttressed his chin. "And it wouldn't be too difficult to disguise you and bring you along as one of us."

Conrad eyed the wily trader. The man had sniffed something of value—that much was obvious.

He'd deal with that when the time came. First things first.

"How much?"

"It all depends on what you're after," the trader said.

"A chat."

It was evidently not what the trader was hoping to hear. Then again, Conrad didn't imagine he really expected him to tell him the whole truth.

The trader shrugged. "In that case, double the price of these fine items," he said as he waved his meaty arm across the array of swords and knives. "Each way."

It was, in the words of the old priest, an outrageous price. But the fake bones would more than cover it.

Besides, it was for a worthy cause.

The worthiest of them all.

"I'll let you know," Conrad said.

Mehmet gave him a contented smile and a small, theatrical bow. "I'm at your service, my friend."

They stuffed the swords and knives into a sack of coarse cloth, which Conrad tied to the pommel of his saddle. He was just trotting away from the store when he came across her.

Qassem's sister, Maysoon. Heading back to her father's shop.

Seeing her threw him into instant disarray.

After all the years of strict celibacy in the fortresses of the Holy Land, he'd become reasonably comfortable around women now that he was living among them. But something about her made his heart gallop. By any standard, she was staggeringly alluring. A tall, graceful young woman with blistering turquoise eyes, flawless honey-colored skin, and a cascade of luscious curves that hinted teasingly from under her dark, flowing robe, she was impossible to ignore.

As she sauntered toward him, he pulled on the reins, slowing his stallion right down to just shy of stopping in its tracks, trying to extend the moment as long as possible. Their eyes met. It wasn't the first time they had, and, as before, she didn't turn away. She just kept an enigmatic gaze locked on him, igniting a bonfire of turmoil within him. In the half dozen times he'd seen her, they hadn't exchanged more than a few polite pleasantries. Her father or her brother was inevitably there, his presence hastening her retreat. Qassem's body language, in particular, projected a fiercely possessive attitude toward her, one that she heeded in silence. Conrad had noticed some bruising around one of her eyes and by the edge of her mouth on one occasion, but he hadn't had the opportunity to find out what had caused them. He was never alone with her, never able to really engage her the way he wanted. He knew this encounter wouldn't be any different, given that they were still within sight of the shop. All he could do was give her a slight nod of acknowledgment and watch helplessly as she glided by, her eyes challenging his as long as they could before tearing away and breezing past.

He resisted turning to watch her drift away, and nudged his horse into a canter. As he rode on, he couldn't think about anything else. He'd faced this inner conflict before and still hadn't figured out how to handle it. Up until recently, his entire adult life had been about sacrifice. He had gifted himself to a strict monastic Order and vowed to obey its Rule without hesitation. Like any monk, he'd committed himself to a rigidly regulated life stripped of any kind of possessions, wife, or family. As a warrior-monk, he had to contend with the added burden of quite possibly having his life cut short by a scimitar or an arrow. That sacrifice had already cost him dearly, as he'd left a part of himself on the blood-soaked soil of Acre, a part he would never get back.

But this was all of the past.

The Order was no more.

He was a civilian now, free from the extreme constraints of his previous life. And yet he still felt caught between both worlds, still found it hard to fully embrace his newfound freedom.

It had been hard enough before he met her.

Thinking about her now, he remembered a particular Templar Rule, one that forbade knights from hunting of any kind—except for lions. An odd rule, given that no lions roamed the lands where Templars lived and fought. Early on, Conrad had been taught that it was an allusion to its scriptural symbolism: "Your adversary, the devil, roams as a roaring lion, looking for someone to devour." He knew it referred to the struggle between man and the beast of desire, a conflict that all knights constantly strove to overcome.

He wasn't sure he'd be able to overcome it much longer. Which caused him even more turmoil, now that the past he thought he'd left behind had reached out and grabbed him by the throat.

He had work to do.

"It's over, Conrad," Hector of Montfort told him. "You know what those bastards have done in Paris. For all we know, the others have been put to the torch as well by now."

They sat cross-legged under a blanket of stars, around a small fire in a room of a dilapidated old mansion that had lost its roof and its owners decades ago. Three former brothers-in-arms, three rugged men who had escaped an unjust arrest warrant and were now reinventing themselves in a foreign land.

Conrad, Hector, and Miguel of Tortosa.

The news they'd heard a few weeks earlier had been devastating. In February, well over six hundred of their brethren who had been arrested in France had changed their minds and recanted their earlier confessions. They'd decided to defend their Order against the king's outlandish accusations. A brave move, but an ill-fated one: By denying their previous confessions, they became lapsed heretics, which carried the penalty of death by burning. That May, fifty-four of them had been burned at the stake in Paris. Other Templars suffered the same fate elsewhere across France.

Hundreds of others now awaited their turn.

"We have to try and save them," Conrad insisted. "We have to try and save our Order."

"There's nothing to save, Conrad," Miguel countered, tossing one of the broadswords back into the pile of scabbards and knives that Conrad had shown them. "Ever since Acre and the loss of the Falcon Temple, our Order has been dead and buried."

"Then we have to bring it back to life," Conrad said, his face blazing with fervor. "Listen to me. If we can recover what Everard and his men lost, we can do it."

Hector glanced at Miguel. They both looked weary, clearly still reeling from what Conrad had told them when he'd showed them the weapons earlier that evening. As one of the master and commander's favorites, Conrad had been invited into the small circle of knights who knew the Order's real history. He had been privy to what Everard of Tyre and his men had been sent out to do back in 1203. Hector and Miguel hadn't. They hadn't been aware of the secrets of the Order. Not until this night.

It was a lot to take in.

"Be realistic, brother," Miguel sighed. "What can three men do against a king and a pope? They'd have us up on those stakes before we managed to utter a single word."

"Not if we have it," Conrad said. "Not if we play it right. Look, it brought them to their knees before. Nine men built a small empire with it. We can do the same. We can rebuild what we had and continue their work."

He studied his fellow knights. They were different now. Older, for one. It had been almost twenty years since they had all fought together at Acre. Older, heavier, slowed by the spoils of an unfettered life. He felt a flutter of doubt and wondered if he believed his own words. What he was asking of them was a tall order, a huge sacrifice for something that carried a far-from-certain outcome.

"We can stay here, turn our backs on our past and live out our lives like this," he told them. "Or we can remember our vows. Our mission. We can remember all those who gave their lives for our cause and try to ensure that they didn't die in vain. I say there is no choice here. We have to try." He reached down and grabbed one of the broadswords. "These swords could have ended up in the hands of any trader in the land. But they didn't. They found me. They found us. We can't ignore that. Our brothers are calling out to us from their graves. Tell me you're not going to turn a deaf ear to their pleas."

He looked at Hector. The Frenchman held his gaze for a long moment, then nodded slowly. Conrad nodded back, then turned to Miguel. The Spaniard glanced at Hector, then shook his head with a slight chortle before giving them a nod that was dripping with reluctance.

THEY RODE OUT FOUR DAYS LATER: Conrad, his two brother-knights, Mehmet and his son, along with four other men that the trader had drafted in as muscle.

Much to the trader's curiosity, Conrad wasn't on horseback. Unlike Hector and Miguel, who were, he was driving an old and rickety open-top horse-drawn wagon.

"You never said anything about a wagon," the trader told him. "This is going to slow us down."

"Which has implications on our agreed price—is that it?"

The trader gave him a toothy, mock-offended smile. "Have I ever been anything less than fair?"

"You're a pillar of virtue," Conrad said. "Now name your new price and let's get moving."

They were soon riding out of the city, heading toward the rising sun. A day later, they left Byzantine territory and crossed into land that was now controlled by the various beys.

Enemy territory.

Following the trader's advice, the knights were dressed in a similar fashion to their escorts: simple dark robes and tunics, linen dolmans and sashes. Their faces were partially hidden under their turbans, and their belts carried scimitars, not swords.

The ruse worked.

Along with Mehmet's verbal skills, it got them safely past a couple of bands of wandering Ghazis, and after eight days of hard riding, they reached the Sari Han, a huge, wide, and low stone edifice with no openings in its outer walls apart from a richly decorated entrance portal.

Once they were inside, finding the monastery proved more challenging. None of the caravaneers, or the han's manager, seemed to know of its existence. They rode on and tried a few more caravanserais, without success. Days drifted by without any hint of promise until their persistence finally paid off when they came across a priest from a local Cappadocian rock church who knew of the monastery.

Despite his vague directions, and several steep crags and dizzying ravines later, they eventually found it: the small cluster of rooms, nestling in the base of a rock face, tucked away from the rest of the world.

Conrad asked Mehmet to join him for a closer look. They left their horses and the wagon with the others and crept up a small ridge, where they took up position behind a large rock, close enough to be able to identify the monks as they ventured in and out of the hermitage.

Mehmet soon spotted one of the monks who'd sold him the swords.

The rest, Conrad needed to do alone.

They rejoined the others. Conrad recovered his horse and led it up to the monastery, on his own.

He was still making his way up the rock-strewn incline when two young acolytes came out, alerted by his struggling horse's whinnies and the clatter of its hooves. By the time he made it up to the hermitage, its entire population was outside, watching him curiously and in silence. Then the abbot, a withered old man by the name of Father Nicodemus, came out and studied him cautiously before inviting him inside.

They sat in the refectory, surrounded by a half dozen other monks. After accepting a drink of water, Conrad didn't waste too much time on any idle banter beyond telling them his name—his real one—and saying he had come from Constantinople, despite the fact that the monks were eager to hear news of the city's current state.

"I'm not here by accident, Father," he told the abbot.

"Oh?"

"I'm here because of something you sold not long ago."

"Sold? And what would that be?"

"Some swords." He paused, eyeing the priest, studying every wrinkle around the man's eyes and at the edge of his mouth before adding, "Templar swords."

The word visibly rattled the monk. It wasn't hard for Conrad to catch the tells—the blinks, the dry lips, the fidgety fingers, the adjustments of position. The monks had spent most of their lives in seclusion, cut off from any kind of social interaction. They weren't well versed in the art of deception. Why the monk was rattled, though, wasn't as obvious.

"You do know what swords I'm talking about, correct?"

The monk hesitated, then stammered out a reply. "Yes, I do."

"I need to know how you came across them."

The monk said nothing for a long second, processing the request, his expression somewhat defensive. An uncomfortable smile crawled out of the corners of his mouth. "Why is that, may I ask?"

Conrad's face remained hard, his eyes unforgiving. "They belonged to brothers of mine."

"Brothers?"

Conrad drew his broadsword slowly and laid it down on the table in front of the abbot. He tapped his finger at the engraving at the top of its blade.

The abbot leaned in for a closer look.

Conrad was indicating the splayed cross.

"Templar knights," Conrad told him. "Like myself."

The creases in the abbot's brow multiplied.

"How did they end up in your possession?" Conrad asked.

"I . . . I'm not sure. They're very old, you know. They've been sitting in one of the storerooms for ages. It's just that with the cold and the drought, we couldn't feed ourselves anymore. We needed to sell something. And, as you can see, there isn't much else that we can sell."

Conrad really didn't like the feeling he was getting from the old monk. "And you don't know how they got here?"

The monk shook his head. "They've been here for a long, long time. From before my time."

Conrad nodded, mulling it slowly, making it clear he wasn't satisfied with the answer and consciously stretching his host's discomfort. "You keep a chronicle here, do you not?" he finally asked.

The question seemed to surprise the abbot. "Of course. Why?"

"I'd like to look at it."

The abbot's blinking intensified. "Our chronicles are . . . they're private documents. I'm sure you understand."

"I do," Conrad said without smiling. "But I still need to see them. Brothers of mine went missing. Their trail ends here, with these swords. In your monastery. I'm sure you understand."

The monk's eyes were nipping away and back to Conrad's face. He couldn't hold the knight's gaze.

"I need to see the entries from the year of our Lord 1203 onward," Conrad added. "That's when they went missing. And I imagine that the day their swords and the rest of their weapons came to be in this place would be an event that would have certainly merited a mention in your records. And yet you're telling me no one here has read of such a thing?" He surveyed the tight expressions of the other monks in the room. They were mostly young and slim, with gaunt faces and pale skin. They were also uniformly staring at him with mouths clasped shut, a few of them giving him slight shakes of the head.

"No one?" Conrad asked again. "Not even your chronicler? Who is the chronicler here?"

One of the monks hesitated, then raised a meek hand and shuffled forward by a step.

Conrad asked, "You don't know of this event?"

The man shook his head. "I do not."

Conrad turned his attention back to the abbot. "It seems we have some reading to do."

The abbot took in a deep breath, then nodded. He ordered the chronicler to take Conrad to see the books. "I'll join you in the scriptorium," he told the knight. "You look tired and pale, Brother Conrad. I'm sure you could use some nourishment after your long journey."

Conrad followed the chronicler into the large, windowless hall. Large candelabras laden with dozens of candles illuminated its desks and its book-lined shelves. The chronicler padded over to a far shelf, studied the spines of the leather-bound codices on it, then pulled out two volumes and carried them back. He set them down on a large, tilted desk and invited Conrad to study them.

Conrad took a seat at the table and started scouring the entries for the right date. He knew that Everard and his men had left Tortosa at the beginning of summer that year. He was still wading carefully through the brittle vellum pages when the abbot reappeared with his entourage of young acolytes. In one hand, the monk was carrying a plate that had some cheese and a chunk of bread loaf on it. In the other, he held a cup.

He placed them on a flat board that extended from the

side of the desk. "It's not much, but I'm afraid it's all I can offer you," the abbot said.

Conrad watched him do it. Oddly, the abbot's hands were trembling, causing the cup to do a little dance before settling down on the board. "It's plenty," Conrad said, a crease forming in his brow. "You have my gratitude, Father."

He picked off a small corner of the bread and popped it in his mouth, then raised the cup. It was filled with a hot, golden-yellow liquid. Conrad brought it close and took a sniff of it. It wasn't a smell he was familiar with.

"Aniseed," the abbot said. "We grow it here. When the frost and the drought permit it."

Conrad shrugged and brought the cup to his mouth.

As its hot edge touched his lips, his eyes settled on the abbot's gaze, and an alarm went off somewhere in the dungeons of his brain. Something was wrong. The man's interest was too intense and all his little tells had accelerated.

Conrad's mind lined up what he knew. And in that instant, he thought the unthinkable.

It's not possible, he thought. *They can't be hiding that.*

And yet it was there. A loud siren blaring away inside his ears. Years of dealing with treachery in the Holy Land had sharpened his senses and taught him to expect betrayal at every corner, and living incognito in a foreign land had only heightened those senses even more. Senses that were now warning him that the unthinkable would actually explain a lot.

He kept the cup poised at his lips and, without taking a sip from it, studied the abbot's face.

He pushed it away a bit, clear from his mouth.

"You know," he told the abbot, "you seem rather pale yourself. Perhaps you need this more than I do." He extended his hand, presenting him with the cup.

"No, no, I'm perfectly content," the abbot said as he pulled back slightly. "Please. We'll eat when the day's work is finished."

Conrad didn't blink. He leaned in and pushed the cup closer to the abbot while placing his other hand very clearly on the hilt of a large dagger he had on his belt. "I insist," he said.

He kept the cup there, hovering inches from the priest's face. Tiny tremors broke out across the old man's face, ruffling up the edges of his mouth, his nostrils, his eyelids.

"Take it," Conrad ordered.

The man did so, his hand shivering.

"Drink," Conrad hissed.

The abbot's hand was quaking noticeably now, almost causing the drink to spill out of the cup as it slowly crept closer to his mouth. It reached his lips. He held it there for a moment, his hand shaking even more, his eyes ablaze with fear and darting from the cup to Conrad and back.

"Drink it, Father," Conrad pushed, his tone calm but potent.

The monk closed his eyes and looked like he was about to take a sip from the cup; then he stopped abruptly and let go of it. It fell from his hands and shattered against the stone floor.

Conrad's eyes bored into the monk as he pulled his dagger out slowly and laid it out on the table. "Now, how about you tell me how those swords really ended up here?"

"WE'LL BE FINE," Conrad told the trader as he handed him the small pouch. "We can handle it from here."

Mehmet took a quick glance at the gold pieces inside the pouch, then pulled its ties tight and tucked it under his belt. "It's a long way back to Constantinople. These are dangerous lands. Plenty of Ghazis out there."

"We'll be fine," he repeated. "We're not going back there."

"Oh?"

Conrad just nodded and struck out his hand, his expression clearly signaling that he wouldn't be saying much more about that. The portly trader frowned, then took his hand and shook it grudgingly.

"Safe travels then," the trader told him.

"And to you."

He stood with Hector and Miguel and watched as the Turks rode off. Conrad had no illusions about what was probably going on in the trader's mind. They had paid him a small fortune to guide them to this place, and they had brought a wagon with them. A wagon to carry something. Something that had to have great value if it was worth the risk and the cost.

Something the trader would instinctively covet.

"I'm guessing you found something," Hector told him.

"That I did," Conrad said, keeping watch as the six riders disappeared down the mountain. His mouth broadened with the hint of a cheeky grin. "That I did."

FATHER NICODEMUS SAT at the chronicler's worktable and felt increasingly nauseous with every line he wrote. The weight of his burden was clouding his mind, turning the selection of each word into a herculean effort. Still, he had to do it. There was no road back. Not from this.

We should have burnt it, he thought. *We should have burnt it all, long ago.* He'd thought about it many times over the years, wondered about doing it, even coming close on a couple of occasions. But like his predecessors, he couldn't bring himself to do it. Like all his predecessors, he didn't dare do it for fear of transgressing and bringing upon himself a wrath not of this earth.

He felt the heavy gaze of his gathered acolytes upon him, but he couldn't look up and face them. He just concentrated on the sheets of vellum under his eyes and tried to keep his hand steady as it moved the quill across it.

I have failed my Church, he wrote. *I have failed our Church and our Lord, and from that failure, there is no possible redemption. I fear that the knight Conrad and his fellow Templars have sealed our fate. They now roam the land, headed to Corycus and from there to shores unknown, laden with the devil's handiwork, written in his hand using poison drawn from the pits of hell, its accursed existence a devastating threat to the rock upon which our world is founded. I would not presume to seek forgiveness or mercy for our failure. All I can offer is this simple act to save our heavenly father from the burden of tending to our miserable souls.*

He gave the sheets another read, his eyes tired and watery. When he was finished, he set the quill down beside them and only then did he dare look up at the monks before him. They were all staring at him in silence, their faces more gaunt and pale than ever, their lips and fingers quavering.

In front of each of them was a simple terra-cotta cup.

The abbot cast his eyes across them, meeting each of their gazes with his own forlorn stare. Then he gave them a collective nod and raised his cup to his lips.

Each of them raised his own.

He nodded again.

Chapter 13

✠

A heavy silence smothered the room.

Tess glanced around, her eyes surveying the faces about her as she tried to gauge whether or not to keep going. Cardinal Brugnone and the prefect of the archives, Monsignor Bescondi, seemed particularly disturbed by what she'd related. Which was understandable. For men of the cloth, the idea of monks—not warrior-monks like the Templars, but gentle, highly pious men who'd retreated from society to devote their lives to prayer and study—the idea of such monks resorting to murder, no matter the reason, was unfathomable.

Reilly also looked puzzled by what was in the monk's confession. "So the first group of Templars had something that the monks were prepared to kill them for? And then, a hundred years later, three Templars pick up the trail of their missing buddies, show up at the monastery, and take back what was theirs, leaving that group of monks so freaked-out about it that they kill themselves?"

"That's what the abbot's letter says," Tess confirmed.

"The impostor who came here with Agent Reilly," Tilden asked. "Who was he?"

"I don't know," she replied. "Sharafi didn't know who he was either. You see, after Sharafi found the confession, he felt he'd stumbled onto something big. He couldn't help but want to look into it some more, but at the same time, it disturbed him. Deeply. I mean, remember what the monk wrote. 'The devil's handiwork, written in his hand using poison drawn from the pits of hell, its accursed existence a devastating threat to the rock upon which our world is founded.' Maybe this was something that shouldn't be found. Still, Sharafi couldn't resist it—but he knew he had to be careful. He knew that something like this could be dangerous. Even more so, perhaps, if it fell into the wrong hands. So he sneaked the letter out of the archives—he stole it, basically—and he just worked on it quietly in his spare time, hoping to figure out what happened to those Templars and what they took with them. He spent a lot of time in the library, looking for more clues. The Sufi traveler hadn't written about the confession he'd hidden in his journal; he hadn't left anything behind that said where he'd found it or what he'd done after he'd found it. Sharafi thought he must have been as spooked by it as he was. Still, the Sufi's journal described his travels in the area, which was a starting point, although Sharafi knew that a lot of the names of places and natural landmarks the traveler used had changed many times over the centuries. So Sharafi had a look in the area the Sufi had roamed, the area around Mount Argaeus, which is now called something else, asking around, trying to find the remains of the monastery. He also looked into any material on the Templars that he could find. But he kept hitting walls. The area he was looking in is sparsely populated, and he couldn't find the monastery—not that he really expected to find anything there, not after all this time. He couldn't find any mention of Conrad either, not in any of the Templar records he had access to. He was ready to give up when a couple of months ago, this guy came up to him outside the university, in Istanbul. He knew all about Sharafi's find. He told Sharafi he wanted him to find the writings that the monk had talked about. And he threatened him and his family."

Tess glanced at Reilly. He nodded his support. She swallowed and felt her body stiffen up. "Sharafi was . . . *terrified*. The man showed Sharafi a severed head. The head of a woman he'd killed, a schoolteacher who was Sharafi's daughter's favorite. He'd cut her head off . . . just to make his point." The air in the room bristled with unease at her words.

"How did this guy know what Sharafi was working on?" Reilly asked. "I asked our impostor that question in the taxi on the way in from the airport, thinking I was asking the real Sharafi, and he said he hadn't told anyone about it."

"We asked him too," Tess replied. "He said it was his research assistant at the university. He was the only person who knew about it apart from his own wife. And when he confronted him about it, the guy didn't deny it. He berated Sharafi for not having reported it himself and said it had been his duty to do that."

"His 'duty'? Who was he?"

"A graduate student. From Iran."

"What about the killer himself? Did Sharafi say anything about where he was from?"

"He said he was also from Iran."

"How sure was he?" Reilly felt a blip in his pulse.

Tess thought about it for a beat. "He just said he was from Iran. He didn't seem to have any doubt about that."

Reilly frowned. It was clearly not the answer he'd been hoping for—but after all that had happened, he'd come to expect it. This was starting to sound suspiciously like the dirty work of an intelligence agency. The intelligence agency of a country that wasn't known to pull its punches. Which didn't bode well at all.

"Anyway, Sharafi got the message," she continued. "He had to get results. And when he couldn't go any further on his own, he decided he needed the help of a Templar expert."

"So he went to Jordan," Tilden added. "To consult your friend Simmons."

Tess nodded. "He was in bad shape. At first, he tried to hide it. He didn't tell us the whole story. He just said he'd been working on something for a paper he was writing, and he was trying to track down a Templar knight called Conrad who'd ended up in Constantinople in 1310."

"But I thought all the Templars were arrested in 1307?" Reilly asked.

"The arrest warrants were served in October of 1307, yes. But some Templars managed to hit the road before King Philip's seneschals swooped in. Many French Templars, for instance, ended up in Spain and Portugal, where the local orders were more or less protected by the local kings. They changed their names to escape detection when the pope's inquisitors turned up looking for them. And in the East, the Templars had lost all their bases in the Holy Land long before that. Acre fell in 1291, right? Their last bastion there was on a small island off the Syrian coast, Arwad. They were kicked out of there in 1303 and the surviving Templars ended up in Cyprus, where they got into trouble for helping the king's brother overthrow him. When the king took back the throne, he had the four Templar ringleaders executed by drowning and exiled the rest, who couldn't really go back to their homelands in Europe, where they faced arrest. We know very little about what happened to them."

"So this Conrad is, presumably, one of those escapees," Reilly speculated.

"That's what Jed thought," Tess said. "He checked his records. He found mention of a knight called Conrad right up to the arrests in Cyprus. After that, the trail went cold. He couldn't find anything beyond that—which isn't surprising. Once they were exiled by the King of Cyprus, Conrad and his buddies weren't about to head back to Europe, not with all the inquisitors there waiting to pounce. Jed thought they'd most likely be living incognito in big cities like Antioch and Constantinople. So that was it. And then Sharafi broke down. He told us what was really going on. And Jed, well, he decided he had to do everything he could to help him. We both did. This wasn't just a trivial academic inquiry. It was clear that Sharafi's guy wouldn't accept failure. Sharafi was freaking out with worry that he might do something to his wife or his daughter to push him harder. We had to find something. And when Jed hit a wall with his own records, he told us about the Registry. He knew about it, he knew it existed, he knew it was kept in the bowels of the Vatican—but he also knew no one was allowed to see it."

Tess paused, hoping someone would pick up that ball.

Reilly did. He turned to Brugnone. "Is that true?"

Brugnone shrugged, his expression still locked in its frown, then nodded. "Yes."

"Why is that?" Reilly pressed.

Brugnone slid a guarded glance at Tess, then directed his attention back at Reilly. "Our archives are full of sensitive documents. A lot of what we have can be easily misinterpreted and twisted around by scandalmongers with less than honorable agendas. We try to limit that."

"And this Registry?"

Brugnone nodded to Bescondi, who stepped in. "It's a complete record of the arrest of the Templars and the dissolution of their Order. Everything the inquisitors found, everyone they spoke to, it was all logged into it. The names of the members of the Order from the grand master right down to the lowliest of squires, what happened to them, where they ended up, who said what, who lived, who died . . . The Order's properties, its holdings across Europe and in the Levant, their livestock, the contents of their libraries . . . Everything."

Reilly processed it. "So Simmons was right. He knew that if there was any trace of what happened to Conrad, it would be in there."

"Yes," Bescondi agreed.

Reilly noticed Bescondi glance pointedly across at the cardinal. A silent exchange seemed to have passed between them as the cardinal answered the archivist with an almost imperceptible nod. The archivist did the same to acknowledge it.

Reilly turned his attention back to Tess. "And . . . that's when you called me."

Tess shook her head ruefully. "I'm sorry. It's just—I thought you were the one person I knew could get Sharafi in to have a look at it. Nothing more. Still, I agonized over whether or not I should ask you to do this. Especially given what we were . . ." Her gaze lingered on Reilly for a long second as she let the words trail off. There was no need for the others to hear about their problems. "I talked it over with Jed first. I wasn't sure. I was still debating it . . . and the next thing I know, this guy shows up outside Jed's office with a gun in his hand, herds us into the back of his van and drives us to some grotty place. I don't know where it was. He throws me and Jed into this room—it must have been a cellar of some kind. He puts these plastic cuffs on our wrists and ankles. Sharafi was already there, tied up like us. And all these horrible images of the teacher's head and the hostages in Beirut and in Iraq started flashing through my mind." Tess was feeling colder now. Talking about it was making her relive the whole nightmare. She looked at Reilly. "He made me call you."

"How did he know about all that?" Reilly asked. "Did you discuss it with anyone else?"

"No, of course not. Maybe he was listening in on what me and Jed were talking about—maybe he had a mike planted in Jed's office or something."

Reilly processed it for a few seconds. "This guy, whoever he is, whoever he's working for—and I think we've got some ideas to think about on that front—he's got some serious resources at his disposal. He shows up in Istanbul and thinks nothing of murdering a woman to motivate Sharafi. He shadows him to Jordan and somehow gets wind of what you and Simmons were talking about privately. He grabs the three of you out in Jordan and manages to whisk at least two of you, if not all three, all the way to Rome, undetected. He has the balls to meet me at the airport and sell me on his story and has me bring him in here to recover this Registry, but not before setting up a couple of rigged cars to use as diversions in case he needs them." He shook his head and exhaled heavily. "This guy's got access to the right intel. He's got resources that allow him to travel around as he likes. He's got access to explosives and detonators and cars and God knows what else. He's as cool under pressure as anyone I've come across." He looked around the room to press his point. "This guy is no lightweight. He's the real deal. And we're going to need some serious resources ourselves if we're going to stand half a chance of taking him down."

Delpiero bristled, his expression indignant. "Oh, we intend to do everything we can to bring this man to justice," the Vatican cop confirmed, his tone laced with mockery. "But equally, I think you have a lot to answer for in this matter. You seem to have forgotten that you were his accomplice in this crime."

"I haven't forgotten that at all," Reilly snapped. "I want this guy more than anyone in this room."

"Perhaps I'm not making myself clear," the inspector said. "We're filing charges against you. You brought this man into the Vatican. If you hadn't done that, he wouldn't have gotten into the archives, he wouldn't have needed to detonate any bombs, and—"

"You think that would have been it?" Reilly fired back. "You think he'd have called it a day and scooted home? Are you kidding me? You saw how he operates. If I hadn't brought him in here, he would have found another way in. He might have, I don't know, found a way to get to Monsignor Bescondi. Maybe with another severed head, to make sure he was taken seriously."

"You drugged the monsignor," Delpiero growled. "You helped the bomber escape."

"That was before I knew he *was* the damn bomber or that he even *had* a bomb," Reilly raged. "I did what I had to do to get him his damn book and save the hostages. You tell me this, all right? What would you have said if I'd told you this guy needed to check out the Templar Registry? Would you have just let him waltz in there and given him access to it? Or would you have needed to know exactly who he was and why he needed to see it?"

Delpiero stumbled for a reply, then looked over at Bescondi and Brugnone. The archivist and the cardinal seemed equally flustered by the question.

"Well?" Reilly insisted, his tone fierce.

Their shrugs answered him.

He mopped his face with his hands and tried to throttle back his anger. "Look," he offered, his voice calmer now, but still resolute. "Maybe you think I was wrong. Maybe you think I should have done things differently. Maybe you're right. But in the heat of the moment, I just didn't see any other option. I'm willing to face the consequences of what I did. Absolutely. You can do anything you want to me—once this is over. After he's in custody or in the morgue. But until that happens, I need to be part of this. I need to help bring him in."

Delpiero met his gaze straight on. "That's very admirable of you, Agent Reilly. But we've discussed this with your superiors, and they agree with us."

Reilly followed the inspector's glance across to Tilden, who gave him a "what the hell did you expect?" shrug. "You weren't here on Bureau business—worse, you withheld informing us about what you were really here for. That hasn't gone down too well with the powers that be back home. Unless I'm missing something, my bet is you should consider yourself suspended," the attaché told him, "pending the Vatican and Italian authorities' investigation."

"You can't sideline me on this," Reilly protested. "This guy suckered me into it. I need to do this." He looked around the room and noticed Brugnone studying him.

Tilden spread his hands open in a resigned, helpless gesture. "I'm sorry, but that's how it has to play out for now."

Reilly shot up to his feet. "This is insane," he railed, his hands cutting the air emphatically. "We have to move fast. We've got a crime scene to process. We've got an unexploded bomb to analyze. We may have prints in the cars and in the archives and vidcaps on CCTV footage. We need to get a BOLO out to all ports of entry. We need to liaise with Interpol." He focused on Delpiero. "Don't cut off your nose to spite your face. I know you're pissed off. So am I. But I can help, and I'm here now. You can use FBI resources on this and you can't afford to wait until they figure out who to send and fly them over. He could be long gone by then."

Delpiero seemed unmoved by Reilly's plea. Three chairs away, however, Brugnone cleared his throat conspicuously, drawing everyone's attention as he rose out of his seat.

"Let's not rush into anything." He slid a glance at Reilly and said, "Agent Reilly. Walk with me to my chambers, won't you?"

Delpiero shot to his feet. "*Eminenza Vostra*"—Your Eminence—"begging your forgiveness, but ... what are you doing? This man should be under arrest."

Brugnone stilled him with a languid flick of his hand that, however understated, carried great authority. "*Predersela con calma*." Calm down.

It was enough to stop Delpiero in his tracks.

Reilly got up, glanced uncertainly at Tilden and at Delpiero, and followed the cardinal out.

Chapter 14

✝

Reilly accompanied the cardinal secretary across the leafy garden square of Piazza Santa Marta. It was past noon by now, and the air around them was scorched. Fifty yards to their left, the rear façade of St. Peter's Cathedral soared high into the sky. Only faint wisps remained of the black cloud from the car bomb, but the square itself, usually lively with cars, buses, and tourists at this time of year, was deserted. Even though the second bomb had been defused and cleared, the Vatican felt like a ghost town, and seeing it like this made Reilly feel even lousier than he had felt in the inspector's office.

The cardinal walked in silence, his hands clasped behind his back. Without turning to look at Reilly, he asked, "We didn't get a chance to speak after your last visit—how long ago was it, three years?"

"That's right," Reilly confirmed.

Brugnone nodded, deep in thought. After a moment, he asked, "It wasn't a pleasant time for you either, was it? The questions you had, the answers you got ... and then, after all that, getting sucked into that catastrophic storm ..."

Memories of that episode of his life came flooding back. Even three years later, he could still taste the salt water in his throat and feel the deep chill from the long hours spent half-dead in the sea, floating on a makeshift raft miles away from the coast of some tiny Greek island. But it was the words he remembered the cardinal saying to him back then that chilled him the most: *I'm afraid the truth is as you fear it.* It reminded Reilly that he hadn't had the closure of a definitive answer to his question. He remembered standing on that cliff top with Tess and watching helplessly as the sheets of parchment fluttered down into the roaring surf, robbing him of the chance to know whether they were the real deal or just an elaborate forgery.

"Today wasn't a cakewalk either," Reilly replied.

The cardinal didn't get it. "A 'cakewalk'?"

"It wasn't an easy day," Reilly clarified. "For some reason, my visits here never seem to be," he lamented.

Brugnone shrugged and brushed the comment away with a flick of his big hand. "This is a seat of great power, Agent Reilly. And where there is power, there is bound to be conflict."

They crossed the road and entered the sacristy, a three-story building that had been tacked onto the south side of the cathedral. Once inside, they turned left and cut through the sumptuous halls of its Treasury Museum. With each step, the acres of rare marble and the bronze busts of past popes weighed heavily on Reilly. Every inch of this place was steeped in history, in the very underpinnings of Western civilization—a history he now knew a lot more about.

The cardinal asked, "You were quite a devout person when we first met. Do you still attend mass?"

"Not really. I help out Father Bragg with the kids' softball on Sunday mornings when I can, but that's about it."

"If I may ask—why is that?"

Reilly weighed his words. The adventure he and Tess had survived three years earlier, and its disturbing revelations, had left their mark on him, but he still held Brugnone in great esteem and didn't want to be in any way disrespectful. "I've read a lot, since we met ... I've thought about it all, and . . . I guess I'm less comfortable with the whole concept of institutionalized religion than I used to be."

Brugnone brooded over his reply, his hooded eyes distant with thought. Neither of them spoke as they reached the end of the frescoed gallery and entered the south transept of the cathedral. Reilly had never been inside the great basilica, and the sight that greeted him was a jaw-dropper. Arguably the most sublime piece of architecture on the planet, its every detail dazzled the eye and lifted the soul. To his left, he glimpsed Bernini's papal altar, the twisted barley-shaped columns and exquisite canopy of the prodigious baldachino dwarfed by the mammoth dome that towered above it. To his right, he could barely make out the distant entrance at the far end of the nave. Shafts of sunlight streamed in through the clerestory windows high overhead, bathing the cathedral in an ethereal glow and rekindling a spark deep within him that had died out over the last few years.

Brugnone seemed to notice the effect it all had on Reilly and paused by the intersection of the transept arms to give him a moment to savor it.

"You've never had the time for a proper visit, have you?"

"No," Reilly replied. "And it's not going to be this time, either." He paused, then asked, "I need to know something, Your Eminence."

Brugnone didn't flinch. "You want to know what's in those trunks."

"Yes. Do you know what he's after?"

"I'm not sure," the cardinal said. "But if it's what I think it might be . . . it would be even worse for us than what that man Vance was after." He paused for a beat, then asked, "After what he did today . . . does it matter?"

Reilly shrugged. It was a fair point. "Not really. But it would help to know. We need to find him."

Brugnone nodded, clearly making a mental note of Reilly's request. He studied Reilly for a spell, then told him, "I heard what you said back there. And while I don't condone what you did or agree with your decision to exclude us from your deliberations, I can appreciate that you

THE TEMPLAR SALVATION ✝ 103

were in a tough position. And the fact is, we are indebted
to you. You did us a great service three years ago, one that
I realize was hard for you to stomach. But you kept true to
your principles, despite your doubts, and you put your life
on the line for us, and that's not something any man would
have done."

Reilly felt a twinge of guilt. What Brugnone was saying was partly true, but the cardinal didn't know the whole
truth. Upon their return from Greece three years ago,
Reilly and Tess had agreed to tell a slightly redacted version
of what had really happened. They'd lied. Big-time. They'd
told the brass at the FBI and the Vatican's representative in
New York that the storm had led to the deaths of everyone
involved—everyone except for the two of them, that is—
and said the wreck of the Falcon Temple had never been
found. They'd promised not to talk about what they'd been
through after the raid at the Metropolitan Museum, when
four horsemen dressed as Templar knights had stormed the
Vatican's big gala and trashed the joint before making off
with an old Templar decoder. And that was that. As far as
the Vatican was concerned, Reilly had fought valiantly right
to the end to defend its cause—which also wasn't strictly
true. And the fact that Reilly and the cardinal were now
standing by the Altar of the Lie—a monumental Adami
mosaic depicting what Reilly recognized was the punishment of a couple who had lied to St. Peter about how much
money they'd been paid for a piece of land and were struck
dead for their deception—wasn't helping.

"We needed your help back then, and despite everything, you agreed to help us," the cardinal told him. "What
I need to know is, how do you feel now? Has anything
changed? Are you still willing to fight for us?"

Reilly sensed an opening. It didn't change his answer.
"My job is to make sure guys like him don't get a chance
to hurt others ever again. Innocent people, like the people who died outside these walls today. I don't really care
what's in those trunks, Your Eminence. I just want to lock
this guy up or put him six feet underground if that's his
preference."

Brugnone held his gaze for a moment; then his internal deliberations seemed to reach a verdict as he nodded to himself, slowly. "Well, then, Agent Reilly . . . I think we need to let you get on with it, don't we?"

After everything that had happened, and with his emotions still frayed, Reilly wasn't sure he'd heard right. "What are you saying? I thought I was under arrest."

Brugnone brushed his comment away. "What happened this morning started here, inside Vatican City. How we deal with it is our business . . . and as you know, we also have some influence in what happens beyond these walls."

"Does your influence extend as far as Federal Plaza? 'Cause I think they want my badge back."

Brugnone gave him a knowing, confident smile. "In this matter, I don't think there are many areas that are outside our sphere of influence." His tone turned firm. "I want you to be part of this investigation, Agent Reilly. I want you to find this man and put an end to his savagery. But I also need to know that you'll be looking out for our interests, that if you were to find whatever it is he's after, you'll bring it to me first, regardless of all other considerations . . . or influences." His last word had an edge to it.

Reilly felt its jab. "What do you mean?"

"Some of your associates—or friends—may have other ideas, in terms of what to do with a find of historic proportions." Again, one word—*friends*—came out more pointedly.

Reilly thought he understood. "You're worried about Tess?"

Brugnone shrugged. "Anyone would be a concern in a situation like this. That's why I need to know that you'll have the Church's interests at heart, above all others. Do I have your word on this, Agent Reilly?"

Reilly pondered the cardinal's words. On the one hand, he felt like he was being blackmailed. On the other, it wasn't like he was being asked to do something he wouldn't have done anyway. And besides, right now, his priority was taking down the man who'd caused the carnage. Whatever was in those trunks was of secondary importance. A distant second.

"You have my word."

Brugnone acknowledged him with a slight nod of his head. "Then you need to get to work. I'll talk to Delpiero and to the officials at the Polizia. And to your superiors. You can take it from there."

"Thank you." Reilly extended his hand graciously, unsure if a handshake was the appropriate move here.

Brugnone cupped it firmly in both of his. "Find him. And stop him."

"It won't be easy. He got what he came for . . . and with that Registry, he's got a head start on us. If it's got any information in it about what happened to this Conrad, then that's where we'll find our bomber. But he's got it and we don't."

Brugnone cracked a ghost of a smile. "I wouldn't go that far." He let the words hang teasingly, then said, "You see, it's been clear to us for quite a while that the archive was becoming far too large to administer using traditional methods. We have over eighty-five linear kilometers of shelves, all of them just heaving with material. So, about eight years ago, we initiated an electronic archiving project. We're almost halfway through scanning the entire collection."

Reilly's face brightened slightly. He already knew what Brugnone would answer, but he said, "I'm hoping you're not doing it alphabetically."

"We're doing it according to perceived relevance," the cardinal replied with a knowing smile. "And the Templars—especially after what happened three years ago—well, they're hardly irrelevant, now, are they?"

Chapter 15

✠

The rest of the afternoon was a chaotic and noisy blur. Reilly and Tess spent it in the offices of the Gendarmeria, where a temporary command post had been set up in a large conference room. The frenzy of activity around them didn't abate for a second as Tess gave a full, detailed statement of everything that had happened to her, and Reilly made sure the local cops weren't missing a trick in trying to find her kidnapper.

Much to Reilly's relief, they seemed to be on the ball. A high-priority BOLO—short for "be on the lookout"—was issued to the country's various law enforcement authorities, and alerts were flashed to all of the country's main ports of entry. Interpol was making sure the request was properly relayed across neighboring countries. The information on it was, however, limited. The bomber, who was assumed to be an Iranian using a forged passport of some other country, had managed to avoid looking directly at any CCTV cameras within the Vatican. The only images they'd been able to pull up of him so far were partly shielded and grainy. Forensic teams had been dispatched to try to recover any fingerprints of his from the archive, the BMW, and the battered Popemobile, in the hope that those would help lead to his identification, while their colleagues at the antiterrorist brigade's labs were examining the defused bomb for anything that would help track its provenance.

They also added Simmons to the alert, given the possibility that, like Tess and Sharafi, he'd also been somehow brought to Rome. An urgent request for his passport info was flashed to the embassy; in the meantime, Tess helped the detectives dig up some photos of him off the Internet.

Reilly liaised with the Bureau's legal attaché in Istanbul, briefing him about the need to locate Sharafi's wife and daughter and inform them of what had happened. He also asked the legat to get the local cops to track down Sharafi's snitch of a research assistant, although he wasn't holding his breath on that one.

While all this was going on, over at the archives, Bescondi instructed as many scholars as he could muster to go through the scans of the Registry in search of any reference to a Templar knight by the name of Conrad.

Reilly did his best to ignore the obvious irritation of Delpiero and the Polizia detectives concerning his continued presence. Brugnone's intercession on his behalf hadn't exactly gone down well. The local cops didn't make any effort to disguise the fact that they thought he ought to be languishing behind bars instead of working alongside them. Reilly faced a couple of tense flare-ups with them, but he restrained himself and avoided making a difficult situation even harder. He also tried to be in their faces as little as possible by spending most of the afternoon burning up the phone lines, getting blasted by his boss for his going solo, before filling in various section chiefs at Federal Plaza, Langley, and Fort Meade in advance of a coordinated conference call once everyone was up to speed.

By sundown, there was little more they could do. Alerts were in place, investigators were scrutinizing immigration records and CCTV footage, lab technicians were plugging away at their high-tech stations, and scholars were poring over medieval writings. The waiting game was on.

TILDEN DROPPED REILLY AND TESS at the Sofitel, a discreet midsized hotel the embassy frequently used for visitors.

They were registered under false names and given two connecting rooms on the top floor. Two plainclothes cops were stationed outside the hotel in an unmarked Lancia on the Via Lombardia. It was a quiet, one-way street, which made their babysitting task a bit easier.

The rooms were spacious and had a great outlook over the lush gardens of the Villa Borghese and the domes of the Church of San Carlo al Corso and, farther to the west, of St. Peter's Basilica. It was a glorious view on any day, and even more so with the sky all aglow from the setting sun, but Tess only managed to enjoy it for all of three seconds before stepping away from the window and collapsing into the comfort of the king-sized bed. To her ravaged muscles and drained mind, it felt like heaven.

She stretched her arms out and let her head sink back deeper into the soft down pillows. "What hotel is it that's always rambling on about how amazing their beds are?"

Reilly appeared in the doorway that connected the two rooms, drying his face with a towel. "Westin."

"Yeah, well . . . they ain't got nothing on this baby." She sank back even more, her arms outstretched toward the edges of the bed, her eyes shut with delight.

Reilly crossed over to the minibar and peeked inside. "You want something to drink?"

Tess didn't look up. "Sure."

"What would you like?"

"Surprise me."

She heard the pleasing sound of a cap being popped off a bottle—twist-off tops, for some reason, weren't yet a staple in Europe—then another. Then the mattress sagged slightly to her left as Reilly sat down on the edge of the bed.

She pushed herself up against the propped-up pillows, and he handed her a cold bottle of Peroni beer.

"Welcome to Rome," he said, a tired and wry expression on his face as they clinked bottles.

"Welcome to Rome," she repeated, her face cloudy with confusion. She still wasn't quite sure how that had happened. Even though they'd been over it all back at the Gendarmeria offices, it still felt surreal to be here. In Rome. In a hotel room. With Reilly by her side.

She took a long, satisfying sip, the cold brew tickling her throat before setting off a nice tingle in her belly, and contemplated his face. He had a couple of small bruises, one on his left cheek, the other more pronounced and scabbed, just above his right eyebrow. She remembered how he'd gotten a lot of those back when they'd first met. But after that, once they'd gotten back to the U.S., once they'd started seeing each other and, soon after, he'd moved into her house, the bruises had disappeared—only to be replaced, she knew, by another kind of hurt. She caught herself thinking that she'd missed seeing him in this guise, all lifesaving superagent with the bruises and the intensity and the urgency, and felt awkward about the thought.

"So here we are again, huh?" she asked.

"Yep." His eyes had a distant, weary tinge to them, like his being there still hadn't settled in with him either.

"Miss me?" she couldn't resist asking, the edges of her mouth curled up in a mischievous smirk.

She watched his eyes roam all over her face—God, she'd missed that look—then he let out a small, playfully derisive chortle before taking another long chug.

"What?" she pressed.

"Hey, I wasn't the one who ran off halfway around the world."

Much to her relief, the way he said it didn't sound resentful at all. "Doesn't mean you can't miss me," she goaded him.

He laughed and shook his head with disbelief. "You're unbelievable, you know that?"

"So is that a yes?" Her beaming grin was in full tractor-beam mode. She knew his shields wouldn't stand a chance.

He held her gaze for a long moment, then said, "Of course I missed you."

She raised her eyebrows with mock surprise. "Well, then how about you stop looking at me like that and—"

She didn't get a chance to finish it. He was already all over her, scooping her head up in his hands and kissing her with an urgent, primeval hunger. The half-empty bottles tumbled off the bed and onto the carpeted floor with muffled thuds as their bodies twisted around each other, frantic hands diving under clothes and seeking out familiar flesh.

"I'm filthy," Tess whispered to him as he yanked her shirt off and devoured his way down to her belly.

He didn't stop. "I know. I like that about you," he said, in between big, wet mouthfuls of her skin.

She laughed, a dreamy, wicked laugh, in between moans of delight. "No, I mean, I'm really filthy—as in, dirty."

He kept going. "Like I said, part of the appeal."

She cupped his head in her hands and closed her eyes and arched her back, her head disappearing between two pillows. "I mean I need a shower, doofus."

"We both do," he mumbled without letting up. "Later."

Chapter 16

✝

Later took a couple of hours to come around. They hadn't seen each other in four months. In fact, they hadn't known when they'd see each other again, if at all, since they hadn't exactly parted on the best of terms. And although a couple of hours of disappearing into each other and shutting the world out wasn't going to make up for the four months of pent-up desire as well as the near-death experiences they'd just been through, it was a good start.

After an extended stint together in the marble-lined shower stall, they were on the bed again, in thick toweling robes this time, digging into a room service dinner of *risotto parmigiano* and *scaloppine al limone*.

Reilly watched Tess as she ate. Despite the insanity of the last twenty-four hours, it felt so natural to be with her. Again. Being with her brought it all bursting back to life, everything that he missed about her. The peridot green eyes that glinted with intellect as well as with mischief. The exquisitely shaped lips and perfect teeth, coconspirators behind her luminous smile. The wild blond curls that framed it all and added to the untamed vibe she radiated. The laugh. The humor. The drive and the energy. The magic that entranced any room she walked into. Watching her now, as she wolfed down her food with the wholehearted delight of someone who ate life up in big, greedy mouthfuls, he couldn't believe he'd actually let her walk out of his life. And yet he had, although the reasons for their split now seemed, well, if not trivial, then certainly mishandled. Which was something that was always easily said in hindsight.

He should have said something back then, he thought. Put a stop to the slow erosion, to the frustrations and the feelings of inadequacy, to the hurt. But there had been no easy solution. They'd leapt into starting a life together. She already had a kid, Kim, a daughter from her ex-husband, a sexual-harassment-lawsuit-in-waiting of a news anchor who'd moved to the West Coast. Reilly, on the other hand, had never been married or fathered a child. Which became a problem when the capriciousness of human reproduction came into play. Reilly wanted to be not just a stepfather to Kim, but also a dad himself, and, as it was with more and more women in their thirties, it hadn't proven to be that simple. The gift of life was proving to be frustratingly elusive. Tests had shown that his body wasn't the one at fault. Years of Tess taking the pill were a probable culprit. And so an undercurrent of melancholy took root as Reilly's primal longing became hers too. The IVF treatments added to the malaise, chipping away at the bond between them. Each failed attempt felt like going through a divorce. By the end of it, Tess needed to get away. The heartache and the feeling of failing him were too profound to face. And he didn't try hard enough to stop her, although at the time, he'd felt as drained and hollow as she had.

Yeah, he should have said something, he thought, as he held her firmly in his sights. He told himself he'd never let her walk out of his life again—but in the same breath, he reminded himself that it wasn't just up to him.

She must have sensed his stare, as she slid a sideways glance at him. "You gonna finish that?" she mumbled between chews, pointing her knife at his plate.

He chuckled and passed her his plate. She scooped up the last piece of veal and gobbled it down. After a pause, he asked, "What just happened here?"

"What?"

He tried to order his thoughts. "This. Us. Here. Dealing with whack jobs and Templars again."

"Maybe it's our lot in life." Tess grinned between mouthfuls.

"I'm serious."

Tess shrugged, then gave him a slightly pointed look. "There's still a lot we don't know about them. Why do you think I went out to see Jed? It's what I tried to explain to you . . . before I left. They deserve to be taken seriously. For decades, they've been this academic no-go zone, just fodder for fantasists and conspiracy theorists. But we know better, don't we? Everything we thought was just myth and nonsense . . . it all turned out to be true."

"Maybe," Reilly argued. "We never got a chance to see if the documents from the Falcon Temple were real, or just forgeries."

"Still . . . they were there, weren't they?"

That part was true, he had to agree—and it supported her view of the Order. "So now that your work and your books are all about them," he asked, "does that mean you're going to be in the line of fire every time some crackpot thinks he's got a lead on one of their secrets?"

"This guy didn't come after me," Tess reminded him. "He came after Jed. I just happened to be there."

"This time," he pointed out.

"Well"—she crept closer to him and gave him a wet, messy kiss—"if it happens again, just promise you'll be there to rescue me?"

He drank it in quietly, then pulled away, a pensive look on his face. "Just so I understand things correctly—if you're grabbed by some murderous psychopath, and only then, your request that I give you some 'space'"—he did some air quotes—"and keep away from you to give you some time to 'figure things out'"—more air quotes—"no longer applies." He paused, mock-thinking it over, then nodded sardonically. "Okay. Works for me."

Her expression clouded at his words, as if an uncomfortable reality were coming back into focus. "Can we . . . can we just enjoy this moment and not talk about us for now?"

"Is there an 'us'?" He kept his tone light and playful, even though deep down, the question was anything but that.

"We've just spent a couple of hours putting practically every pose in the Kama Sutra to the test. I think that kind of has an effect on our status, doesn't it? But can we please just . . . not now, okay?"

"Sure thing." He flashed her a slight grin to defuse the moment and decided to drop the subject for now. What they'd been through wasn't the ideal grounding for a serious chat about where they stood with regard to each other. He didn't think it was fair to Tess, not after her ordeal.

He changed tack. "Tell me something . . . these trunks, the writings the monk's confession refers to. The cardinal didn't seem too keen on giving me a straight answer about what they could be. You must have discussed it with Simmons. Any ideas?"

"Some, but . . . we're just guessing."

"So guess."

She frowned. "'The devil's handiwork, written in his hand using poison drawn from the pits of hell,' and the rest of it. It's got a very creepy ring to it, doesn't it? And it's not something that's commonly associated with the Templars."

"But you know different?"

Tess shrugged. "Sort of. The thing is, you have to understand the context of it, the setting. The events in the diary, Conrad and the monks . . . that all happened in 1310. That's three years *after* the Templars were all arrested. And how that happened, why it happened when it happened, could help explain what it's all about."

"Keep going."

Tess straightened, and her face lit up as it always did when she got excited about something. "Okay. Here's the backstory. Late 1200s, early 1300s. Western Europe's going through tough times. After several centuries of warm weather, the weather's now getting freaky and unpredictable—a lot colder and wetter. Crops are failing. Disease is spreading. This was the start of what's called the 'Little Ice Age' that—weirdly enough—lasted until a hundred and fifty years ago. By the time you hit 1315, it rains almost nonstop for three years and triggers the Great Famine. So the common folk—they're having a really miserable time. Now, on top of that, they've just lost their Holy Land. The pope had told them that the Crusades were willed and blessed by God—and they failed. The crusaders lost Jerusalem and were finally kicked out of the last Christian stronghold, at Acre, in 1291. Now keep in mind, the church had spent decades building up the arrival of the new millennium as this thousand-year milestone and was talking it up as the date of the Parousia, the Second Coming. They were warning people that they had to embrace Christianity and submit to the Church's authority before that date or miss out on their eternal reward. So there was a great resurgence of religious fervor at the time, and when nothing happened, when the new millennium came and went without the Big Event taking place, the Church needed to find something else to distract its people, an excuse almost. And they turned to liberating the Holy Land from the Muslims who had taken it over. The pope dreamt up the Crusades as something that God was waiting for, the crowning achievement of that whole movement, the start of a new triumphant age for Christianity. And the Church had even gone as far as to change its position radically, from preaching about peace and harmony and loving your fellow man, to doing the total opposite—the pope was now actively promoting war and telling his followers, 'God will absolve you of all your previous crimes if you go out and slaughter the heathen in the Holy Land.' So there was a lot riding on getting the Holy Land back. And when that failed, it was a huge blow. Huge. And people were feeling scared. They were wondering if God was angry with them. Or if something powerful and evil was at work, undermining God's efforts. And if that was the case, who were his agents, and what powers did they have?

"Now while this is all happening, something else is brewing at the same time," Tess continued. "People in Western Europe, and I'm talking about the people in power, the priests and the monarchs—the few who could actually read and write—they've recently started taking the dangers of magic and witchcraft seriously again. They hadn't, not for centuries. Those concerns had died out with paganism. Magic and witchcraft were ridiculed as nothing more than the superstitions of delusional old women. But when the Spanish took back the south of Spain from the Moors toward the end of the eleventh century, they discovered a whole new world of writings in places like the library of Toledo, ancient and classical scientific texts that the Arabs had brought with them and had translated from the original Greek into Arabic and then into Latin. So the West rediscovered all these lost writings, the works of great thinkers and scientists that they'd completely forgotten about, like Plato and Hermes and Ptolemy and a whole bunch of others they'd never heard of. Books like the *Picatrix* and the *Cyranides* and the *Secreta Secretorum* that explored philosophy and astronomy as well as magico-religious ideas and potions and spells and necromancy and astromagic and all kinds of ideas these people had never seen before. And what they read scared the hell out of them. Because these texts, regardless of how primitive or misguided we might now consider them, talked about science and understanding how the universe worked and how the stars moved and how our bodies could be healed, and basically, how man could gain power over the elements around him. And that was scary to them. It was early science, and early science was considered magic. And since it undermined the concept of 'God's will,' the priests painted it as 'black magic,' and anything it achieved had to be due to demon worship."

Reilly remembered something from his previous exposure to the warrior-monks and asked, "Weren't the Templars accused of worshipping some demonic head?"

"Of course. The Baphomet. Now there are conflicting theories on that. We still don't know for a fact what it was all about. But that's what I'm talking about. To understand why the Templars were rounded up and accused of all these mostly ridiculous things, you have to understand the mindset in which that happened."

"So we've got people thinking God is angry with them and that the devil's agents are out to destroy them, and priests and kings believing black magic might actually exist."

"Exactly. And against that charged backdrop, you've got these arrogant, wealthy warrior-monks who lost the Holy Land and are now back in Europe, and they don't seem to be too embarrassed by their defeat. They've still got all these vast holdings and they're living it up on the fat of the land while everyone else is starving. And people start asking questions. They start wondering about them, asking themselves how these guys are getting away with it—and pretty soon, they're asking themselves if these guys don't have some kind of evil power, if they're not in league with the devil, if they're not debauched demon-worshipping wizards. This fear of black magic—it was at the root of the Templar trials. Of course, their accuser, the King of France, had plenty of reasons to want to take them down. Greed and envy played a huge role. He owed them a lot of money and he was broke, and he was also incensed by their arrogance and their flagrant disrespect toward him. But beyond that, he genuinely saw himself as the most Christian of kings, the defender of the faith, even more so after the death of his wife in 1307—the same year he ordered the arrests, a time when he'd withdrawn into religious self-absorption, something he never came out of. He saw himself as a man chosen by God to do His divine work here on Earth and protect his people from heresy. He was hoping to set up another crusade. And he and his advisors just couldn't understand how these Templars could possibly be as arrogant and as dismissive of God's chosen one if they weren't getting the help of some kind of demonic power."

Reilly chortled. "They really believed that?"

"Absolutely. If the Templars had made a pact with the devil, if they had knowledge that could transform the world—and take away power from those who held it— they had to be defeated. And it's not as outlandish as it sounds. Knowledge is power, in all kinds of ways, and occult weapons are a common thread in history. Megalomaniacs looking for that extra edge, that divine power, that arcane knowledge that would let them conquer the world. Hitler was obsessed with occultism. The Nazis were totally enthralled by black magic and runes, and not just in *Raiders of the Lost Ark*. Mussolini had a pretty nutty personal occultist called Julius Evola. You'd be amazed by the superstitions and the wacky belief systems that a lot of world leaders take seriously, even today."

Reilly felt heavy-headed. "So these trunks . . . ?"

"'The devil's handiwork, written in his hand using poison drawn from the pits of hell, its accursed existence a devastating threat to the rock upon which our world is founded,'" Tess reminded him. "What's in these books that frightened the monks so much? Could there be any truth to the accusations against the Templars? Were they really occultists that practiced black magic?"

Reilly looked doubtful. "Come on. It could all be just metaphorical." His previous meeting with Brugnone, three years earlier, flashed across his mind. "I can think of other writings that would shake up a monk's world, right?"

"Of course." Tess nodded. "But keep an open mind. I'll give you one example that Jed brought up. You know there were a lot of Templars in Spain and Portugal. Big presence there. Well, at some point in the thirteenth century, they got into trouble and they had to pawn off most of their holdings in Castile. Of all the enclaves they had out there, the only one they kept was an insignificant little church in the middle of nowhere. It didn't make sense. It wasn't in a strategic location. Its land didn't even produce enough revenue to allow its friars to send funds to their brothers in the Holy Land. But it was the one *encomienda*, the one enclave, they decided to keep. What wasn't immediately obvious was that this small church actually did have an interesting feature: its location. They had built it right in the center of Spain, equidistant from its farthest capes. And I mean perfectly equidistant, down to the meter."

"Come on," Reilly questioned, "what do you mean, 'perfectly equidistant'? How could they figure that out, what, seven hundred years ago? Even today, with GPS mapping and—"

"It's bang in the center, Sean," Tess insisted. "North-south, east-west, draw those lines, and where they cross, that's where it is. Jed checked it using GPS coordinates. It's really there. And that location has a major occult significance: controlling the epicenter of a territory was meant to give you magical dominance over it. And there are other geographic peculiarities to that location that have to do with the pilgrims' road to Santiago and other Templar holdings. Now, is it all just a coincidence? Maybe. Or maybe the Templars really believed in that mumbo jumbo. And maybe it's more than mumbo jumbo."

Reilly exhaled heavily. Whatever it was, it was something the man he was after was prepared to kill for. And maybe that really was all he needed to know.

"Bottom line . . . it could be anything," Reilly concluded.

"Yup." Tess nodded as she finished off the last piece of escalope.

Reilly studied her curiously, then shook his head slowly and blew out a small chortle.

Tess eyed him curiously. "What?"

"I know you. You're just thinking about how this is all going to be great fodder for your next book, aren't you?"

She set down her fork and stretched lazily, then sank back into the pillows. She turned on her side to face him. "Can we talk about something else?" She grinned, her expression dreamy. "Or even better, how about we don't talk at all for a while?"

He smiled at her, cleared the plates off the bed and onto the room service table cart in one fell swoop, and sank into her.

THE BUZZ OF A TELEPHONE jolted his senses with the velvet touch of a Taser and yanked him out of a dreamless sleep that had eluded him for hours.

He'd tossed and turned forever. It had been an emotionally devastating day, with highs and lows coming at him fast and furious. The night was harder. Images of the devastation and the carnage at the Vatican were suffocating any elation he felt at being with Tess again. He found himself replaying the events over and over in his mind, trying to rationalize what he had done, but he couldn't escape the haunting feeling that he was responsible for it all and wondered how he was going to live with the burden of guilt that was growing inside him.

He pushed himself to his elbows, feeling dazed. Fine

strands of sunlight were streaming in through small openings in the shutters. It took him a couple of seconds to register where he was. He glanced at the clock radio on the bedside table. It showed that it was just after seven o'clock in the morning.

Tess stirred next to him as he answered the phone.

He listened, then said, "Put him through."

As he grunted one-syllable replies, Tess sat up, all groggy and tousled, and looked him a question.

He cupped the phone's handset. "It's Bescondi," he mouthed. "They've got a hit. In the Registry."

"Already?" Then her eyes lit up. "Conrad?"

"Conrad."

Chapter 17

✛

As he steered the car down the last of the switchbacks and drove up to the gate that stood at the end of the scenic country lane, Mansoor Zahed once again felt pleased with his choice of pilot. The airfield seemed as somnolent as it had been when they'd landed there two days earlier. The pilot he'd hired, a South African by the name of Bennie Steyl, clearly knew what he was doing.

Huddled in a quiet valley in the Abruzzo region of Italy, the small facility was only an hour and a half's drive from Rome. As Zahed approached it, he could see that, as before, there was little discernible activity. Recreational flying was far more expensive in Italy than it was in the rest of Europe due to highly taxed aviation fuel and steep charges for everything from the use of airspace to snow removal and deicing services—a compulsory fee, even in Sicily at the height of summer—and the quiet airfield had gradually fallen into disrepair until an earthquake of 6.3 magnitude struck the region in the spring of 2009. The narrow, winding roads in and out of the area were clogged by fleeing locals, but the fact that the remote, run-down facility was within a stone's throw from the devastated towns and villages made a massive rescue and humanitarian effort possible, which in turn inspired the Italian prime minister to relocate that summer's G8 Summit from Sardinia to the small medieval town of L'Aquila to show solidarity with the earthquake's victims. The airfield had been hastily spruced up in order to receive the leaders of the developed world, before it reverted to its natural, sleepy state.

A state that suited Zahed perfectly.

He pulled up to the small gatehouse. In the distance, he could already see Steyl's plane waiting idly on the tarmac, its white fuselage glinting in the morning sun. The twin-engined Cessna Conquest was parked off to one side, away from the dozen or so smaller, single-engined aircraft of the L'Aquila Aero Club that were lined up alongside the short asphalt runway. The beefy gateman set down his pink-paged *Gazetta dello Sport* newspaper and greeted him with a lethargic wave. Zahed waited as the unkempt, potbellied man pushed himself out of his cratered woven-cane chair and lumbered over to the car. Zahed explained that he needed to drive in to drop off some luggage and other supplies to the plane. The gateman nodded slowly, padded over to the barrier, and settled his meaty arm on its counterweight. The barrier tilted up just enough for Zahed to be able to drive through, which he did, with a courteous wave of gratitude to the perspicacious guard.

The gateman didn't ask him about the drowsy man with the dark sunglasses who was half-asleep on the passenger seat. Zahed hadn't expected him to. In a quiet, out-of-the-way airfield like this—kudos to Steyl, again—security wasn't anywhere near as important as the latest football scores.

Zahed drove up to the plane and pulled up alongside it. Steyl had cleverly positioned it so that its cabin door faced away from the other planes, the flying club's hangar, and, farther afield, the simple yellow-and-blue structure that housed the facility's offices and its modest control tower. The precaution was probably unnecessary. There was no one else around.

The pilot, a tall, sinewy, bearded man with slicked-back

ginger hair and deep-set gray eyes, emerged from the cabin door and helped Zahed with Simmons, who was sedated to the edge of unconsciousness. They guided the archae-ologist up the steps and settled him into one of the wide leather seats. Zahed checked him out. Behind the dark shades, Simmons's eyes were staring blankly ahead, and his mouth was slightly open, a small gob of drool pooled at the edge of his lower lip. The American would probably need a top-up before they landed in Turkey.

"Let's get out of here," Zahed told Steyl.

"We're ready to rumble," the South African replied. His tone was gruff, but Zahed knew that was just the man's way. "Leave the car by the edge of the taxiway so as not to draw attention to it. I'll start the engines."

Zahed did as the pilot suggested and abandoned the rental car by the side of the hangar. The Cessna's turbo-props were whining to life as he headed back to the plane, and just as he reached it, he spotted a man in a white T-shirt, a wide pair of black trousers held up by braces, and big, heavy boots emerge from the tower structure. The trousers seemed to have a reflective stripe going down the side of each leg. He had some papers in his hand and looked like he was in a rush. More than that, his body language was giving off a hint of fluster as he climbed onto an old bicycle and started pedaling, heading their way.

Zahed reached the plane before him and climbed in. He found Steyl in the cockpit, flicking switches as he ran through his preflight checklist. He pointed the man out through the pilot's side window. "Who's this guy?"

The pilot glanced out. "He's a fireman. They have to have them around at all times to justify charging us for them. And since the odds of them actually having to deal with a fire are virtually zero, they usually double as paper pushers and help out the guy in the tower with the paper-work. This guy's a bit of a fusspot, but not too much of a pain as long as you flash the cash."

Zahed tensed up. "What does he want?"

Steyl studied the man curiously. "Damned if I know. I already paid him the landing fee and gave him our flight plan."

They watched as the man pulled up in front of the plane, raised his right hand up, and moved it horizontally in a slicing motion, across his throat—the international marshaling sign for the pilot to kill the engines. Steyl nodded and complied.

"Get rid of him," Zahed said.

Steyl stepped out of the cockpit area. Zahed followed him back to the cabin door.

The fireman, a balding, middle-aged carnival of twitches, climbed onto the retractable steps and peered into the cabin. He stank of cigarettes, and his T-shirt had big sweat stains on it. He looked all hot and bothered and a bit dazed as well, as if someone had roused him by shouting into his ears. In his hand were some documents that he was waving at Steyl.

"*Mi scusi, signore,*" the man wheezed in between gulps of breath. Beads of sweat were trickling down his forehead. "I apologize for the trouble, but," he continued, straining to find the right words, "as you know, there was a big terrorist attack in Rome yesterday. And now we have to check the passports of everyone flying in or out of this airport and fill out these papers."

Steyl eyed him thoughtfully for a second, then slid a sideways glance at Zahed before giving the fireman a wide smile. "It's not a problem, my friend. Not a problem at all." He turned to Zahed. "This gentleman needs to see your passport, sir."

"Of course," Zahed replied politely.

Steyl then pointed toward the cockpit and addressed the fireman slowly and with exaggerated enunciation, as if he were trying to explain something to a Martian infant. "I'll just get my passport from my flight bag, all right?"

The man nodded and wiped his forehead with a handkerchief. "*Grazie mille.*"

Zahed stepped back into the cabin, found his briefcase, and fished out the passports—both fakes. The one he picked out for himself, from a handful of passports of different nationalities, was Saudi. The one he'd had hastily crafted for Simmons had him as a citizen of Montenegro, like the ones he'd had made for Tess Chaykin and for Behrouz Sharafi, courtesy of a boxload of blank passports previously acquired from a corrupt employee of that country's interior ministry. Zahed hadn't needed the documents on the way in. Two days earlier, after landing at the airfield, Steyl had locked up the aircraft, disembarked alone, and casually trudged over to the tower to deal with the landing formalities. He'd then returned to the plane with the rental car later that evening and helped Zahed smuggle his sedated companions under cover of darkness. This was getting more complicated, which Zahed had somewhat expected. And as he glanced at the fireman, he saw that the man's gaze had settled on Simmons, who was just sitting there, facing forward, immobile and expressionless, his eyes hidden behind sunglasses. Zahed felt a twinge of unease, and shielded from Steyl and the fireman by the seat back, he reached into his case, pulled out his lightweight Glock 28 handgun, the one with the expanded nineteen-round magazine that he favored, and tucked it under his belt at the small of his back.

He and Steyl rejoined at the cabin door, passports in hand.

"Your friend—he is okay?" the fireman asked.

"Him? Oh, he's fine." Zahed shrugged as he handed the Italian the passports. He gave him a complicit wink. "A bit too much of your local Montepulciano last night, that's all."

"Ah." The man relaxed as he flicked through the passports.

Zahed eyed him carefully, his muscles taut, his senses on edge.

The harried fireman was struggling to keep Zahed's passport open while he filled out one of the forms on his knee. He completed it, moved it to the back of the pile, opened Simmons's passport, then set it aside as he flicked through the clutch of papers in his hand, evidently looking for something. He looked up at Zahed and Steyl with embarrassment and gave them a sheepish smile, then went back to his sheets—then one of them snagged his attention. He flicked past it, then stopped, did a double take and went back to it. He pulled it out of the pile and studied it curiously. And then he did what he shouldn't have done: He

glanced at Simmons. A glance that wasn't casual or acci-
dental. A furtive glance, one that was loaded with information. A glance that made Zahed reach behind his back and,
in a calm and fluid motion, pull out the handgun and aim it
at the fireman's face.

Zahed moved his other hand to his own face, index
pointed up and tapping softly against his lips, signaling the
fireman to keep quiet. Then he stretched that hand out toward him and gestured for him to hand over the bundle of
papers and the passports that were in his hand. The fireman's face clenched up further and his eyes did a nervous
left-and-right flick, again telegraphing the options he was
thinking about. Zahed gave him a calm "no-no" gesture
with his finger before the man nodded his understanding
and handed him the documents.

Zahed's eyes left the fireman for the briefest of moments as he said to Steyl, "Help our friend into your plane,
won't you?"

Steyl hesitated, then said, "Sure thing." He bent down
and clasped his hand around the man's forearm. The fireman nodded nervously and climbed into the cabin. He
stood there, sweating even more profusely now, fear flooding his face, his puffy body all hunched up by the open
cabin door in the low-ceilinged fuselage.

Zahed flicked through the paperwork and found the
sheet that had caused the problem. It was the all-ports
alert. A picture of Simmons was on it. Interestingly, Zahed
noted, there was no photo of him. He deduced that none
of the vidcaps from the Vatican's CCTV footage had been
clear enough—which was good news. He had to make sure
it stayed that way.

He looked up at the fireman and gestured invitingly
at the seat across the aisle from the one Simmons was in.
"*Prego.*" Please.

The man nodded. As he turned his back to him and
went to sit down, Zahed raised his handgun and slammed
it sideways against the man's head, the hardened steel colliding against the man's skull with a dull crack. The official
crashed heavily into the chair, face-first. Blood was seeping

out onto the hair at the back of his head and oozing down onto the leather seat. He wasn't moving.

"Aw, man." Steyl grimaced, annoyed. "That's gonna make a bitch of a mess."

"Don't worry about it," Zahed told him calmly as he pulled the man off the chair and dumped him on the cabin floor. "Just get us out of here."

"We can't land there with him on board, you know that," Steyl told Zahed.

The Iranian thought about it for no more than a second, then shrugged. "So we won't." He gave the pilot a pointed look.

Steyl nodded his understanding.

The pilot shut the cabin door, took his seat, and restarted the engines. He guided the plane off the runway, and within seconds, they were climbing into the cloudless sky. Zahed was seated facing backward, with Simmons across from him. He looked out his window and waited.

A few moments after takeoff, Steyl slid the right cup of the headset off his ear and leaned back into the cockpit's opening. "We've been cleared to five thousand feet," he informed Zahed.

The view was spectacular, all the more so as Steyl banked the plane in midclimb. The high-country plains around L'Aquila quickly gave way to forest-cloaked mountains. The small aircraft soon crossed over the fortified hill town of Castel del Monte, and within minutes, they were skirting a bold line of jagged peaks, with the snowcapped tip of the Gran Sasso, the highest peak in Italy, to their left.

Steyl leaned back across. "Leveling off at five thousand feet," he told Zahed. "We've got about a minute or so before I have to start climbing again."

Zahed felt the aircraft slow down and knew Steyl was throttling back to an airspeed of a hundred knots. When he sensed they'd stabilized, Zahed pushed himself out of his seat. He took Simmons's shades off, tucked them in his pocket, and gave him a quick check. Simmons was awake, but still heavily tranquilized, his dimmed eyes staring at Zahed from a vegetative face. Zahed tugged on the archaeologist's seat belt to check that it was secure, gave Simmons a patronizing pat on the cheek, and crouched over to the cabin door.

The Conquest's door consisted of two sections that opened like a clam—the upper panel, a third of the height of the opening, was hinged from the top and opened upward; the other, which also contained the stairs, opened downward. Zahed held the latch with both hands and twisted it slowly, then held his breath for a second and nudged the upper part of the door out about an inch. It instantly flung open, the edge of the panel catching the airflow that was rushing away from the fuselage. He released the handle of the bottom panel, and it too flew open.

A blast of cold air rushed in, filling the cabin with a deafening roar. Zahed steadied himself. He had to act fast. Air traffic control would already be giving Steyl the all clear to ascend to his next flight level and would start questioning him if he didn't resume his climb soon after. He stepped over to the fireman, leaned down, slid his hands under his armpits and yanked him up. He grunted under the man's sheer weight and had started pulling him when he felt him stir. The man was groggy, but conscious. His arms flailed around a bit, weakly. Zahed moved with added urgency. He half-lifted, half-dragged the fireman the four feet to the cabin door, keeping to his side, alert for any sudden movement. None came. He got him to the doorway and set him down on the cabin floor, then moved to his feet and started pushing.

The fireman's head went out first. It hit the fierce airflow and twisted sideways violently, wrenching him awake and causing his senses to fire back to life. It was something he would have probably preferred to avoid. His eyes snapped open, and after a brief moment of confusion, what was happening to him clearly hit home as he stared down the back of the aircraft, then strained against the wind and hauled his gaze into the plane, where Zahed had his arms locked around the fireman's legs—and he was still pushing.

Their eyes met for a second, long enough for Zahed to see the absolute terror in the fireman's expression—then he gave him a final shove. The fireman's body tumbled out of the plane and instantly plummeted out of view, trailing the briefest split-second scream. Zahed hung on as the aircraft's nose pitched down violently, its center of gravity shifting forward the instant the fireman flew out, just as Steyl had told him it would. Steyl controlled it and steadied the plane. Zahed glanced toward the cockpit. Steyl glanced back. Zahed nodded. Steyl nodded back and turned to face forward.

Zahed felt the plane yaw slightly to the left, as if it were sitting on a turntable that someone turned counterclockwise. Steyl had the Conquest under crossed controls and was, as planned, forward-slipping the aircraft. It was now plowing ahead at a slight angle away from its fuselage's main axis. The move redirected the airflow around it: It was now curling around the plane's body from the windward side rather than from the front, and hitting the open door panels from behind. Zahed was ready. The wind blew the panels so they were now sticking out almost horizontally, within easy reach. Zahed reached out for the bigger of the two, the lower door, pulled it in, and secured it shut. He then grabbed the upper part of the door and locked it into place. The noise inside the plane went from hurricane roar to lawn mower buzz instantly. Zahed relaxed and inhaled deeply, then turned and saw Steyl's face leaning across the cockpit opening. The pilot give him a thumbs-up. He returned it and took another deep breath.

He settled back in his seat as the small aircraft resumed its climb. He felt the pressurization start to kick in, shut his eyes, and leaned back against the lush headrest, punch-drunk from the wild sensation that was coursing through him. Mansoor Zahed had experienced things most men could never conceive of, but he'd never been through that before. It took a lot to get his pulse racing, and it sure as hell was racing now. He felt electric. He inhaled deeply and allowed the sensation to anchor itself into his memory more intensely. It pleased him no end to realize that, even for someone like him, there were still new experiences to be sought out in this lifetime.

He and Steyl had talked about this, a few years earlier, when the Iranian had first hired the South African for one of his covert jaunts. They'd discussed the possibility that something like this would happen one day. One night, over a few beers, Steyl had told Zahed about his days in the Angola bush wars, where he used to ferry UNITA rebels around in an old Cessna Caravan. He'd told the Iranian how one of the rebels' favorite pastimes was taking a bunch of captured SWAPO men—the Soviet- and Cuban-backed government forces they were fighting—and chucking them out of his plane while whooping it up in drunken frenzies. Zahed had been deeply intrigued by Steyl's story, but up until this moment, he hadn't had a chance to experience it firsthand.

It had been worth the wait.

He opened his eyes slowly as he came out of his reverie, and his gaze found the man sitting facing him. Simmons was awake and conscious, but his eyes were straining wide. Judging by the horror radiating from them, Zahed knew that the archaeologist had witnessed what he had done.

Zahed gave him a thin, humorless smile.

Knowing that Simmons had been watching in a helpless daze made the event even more memorable.

Chapter 18

✜

Reilly spotted Vedat Ertugrul just as the Alitalia Airbus's cabin door swung open. The legal attaché of the Bureau's Istanbul suboffice, a paunchy American of Turkish descent with a trumpet player's jowls and puffy crescents under his eyes, was waiting for them at the edge of the Jetway. They'd met briefly three years earlier, in the southern coastal town of Antalya, when the legat had proven to be very efficient and easygoing. Reilly hoped that was still the case as he stepped out to meet him, with Tess close behind.

A couple of darker-skinned men were standing there alongside Ertugrul, one in a navy blue police officer's uniform with a gold star on each shoulder, the other in a charcoal-colored suit over a white shirt. Both had humorless, dark brown eyes, buzz cuts, and severe mustaches accessorizing the stern expressions on their faces. After quick introductions all around, Ertugrul, the chief of police, and the spook led Reilly and Tess out of the air-conditioned Jetway through a side door and down some stairs to the tarmac. Even though it was late in the afternoon, the air was still stiflingly hot and dry, made worse by the stench of aviation fuel.

Two black Suburbans with tinted windows were waiting

for them by the plane's front landing gear. Moments later, the armored SUVs were being waved through the airport's security gates and storming off toward the Queen of Cities.

Ertugrul, riding in the middle row directly in front of Reilly, twisted around to face him and handed him a holstered handgun and a box of shells. "These are for you."

Reilly took the gun and checked it over. It was a standard issue Glock 22 with a fifteen-round magazine, no scratches on it and freshly oiled. He clipped the holster onto his belt and slipped the gun into it. "Thanks."

"I'll need you to sign for them," Ertugrul said, handing Reilly the forms and a pen. "I spoke to Tilden just as your plane came in," he added, "and, well, it's not looking great."

"Nothing from the prints?" Reilly asked as he signed the forms.

Ertugrul shook his head. "New York's liaising with Langley, the NSA, and the DOD on trying to pin an ID on this guy, but so far, nothing."

"We've got to have him on file somewhere," Reilly grumbled as he handed him back the paperwork. "This guy's no amateur. He's done this kind of thing before."

"Well, if he has, he's been pretty good about ducking the limelight."

Reilly fumed for a beat and looked out at the cloudless sky. Several jets were lined up on final approach, an array of silver dots that stretched as far as he could see. It was peak season in Istanbul, and tourists were flocking in from all over. "What about the border controls here?"

The chief of police, who was seated next to Ertugrul in the middle row, turned and caught his eye.

"He's coming here," Reilly told him. "If he's not here already."

"You're assuming he's already reached the same conclusions as the boys from the Vatican archives," Ertugrul queried.

"I'm sure he has," Reilly insisted. "He's still got Simmons to figure things out for him."

Ertugrul and the cop exchanged a few words in Turkish; then Ertugrul told Reilly, "Our friends have the country on a tight lockdown. Most of the airports here are also military airfields, and given the situation with the Kurds and with everything that's going on in Iraq, the security is usually pretty tight anyway. The thing is, we don't have much to go on for the main perp. We don't even know what kind of passport he's using." He rummaged through his briefcase and pulled out a couple of printouts that he passed back to Reilly. "The only face we can really ask them to look out for is Simmons's."

Reilly perused the all-ports alert. It had parallel paragraphs in both Turkish and English and consisted of the usual bold, urgent lettering and a couple of short, descriptive paragraphs alongside two photographs: one, a grainy, pretty useless one from the Vatican CCTV cameras of the bomber; the other, a clear, smiling, passportlike portrait shot of Simmons, showing a ruggedly handsome man with shoulder-length, wavy hair and probing eyes. A young, ruggedly handsome man.

It was the first time Reilly had seen a picture of the missing archaeologist. He turned to Tess, surprised. She was seated next to him on the rear bench. "*That's* Jed Simmons?"

"Yeah, why?"

Reilly studied her with a bemused look on his face, then shrugged. "Nothing."

"What?"

He saw that Ertugrul and the Turkish officer were having a sidebar, and leaned in a bit closer to Tess. "When you said he was this famous archaeologist and this big Templar expert and all that . . . I kind of pictured someone older. And nerdier." He paused, then threw in, "Maybe uglier too."

Tess let out a small chuckle. "That, he ain't," she teased. "And he's so fit. I mean, my God, you should see him kite-surf. Talk about ripped."

"Professor Jed Simmons, brainbox-slash-hunk. Who knew?" Reilly muttered wryly.

Tess studied him curiously for a beat, then whisper-laughed. "Oh my God. You're actually jealous, aren't you?"

Before he could find an answer to that, Ertugrul turned again to face them.

"We also tracked down Behrouz Sharafi's wife and kid. I went and saw her last night. She's in bad shape, as you can imagine. Our friends here have got them under protective custody."

Reilly frowned. "What are they going to do?"

"It's a tough one. They can't exactly go home to Iran, not given who might be behind all this."

"You talked to our guys?" Reilly asked him.

Ertugrul nodded. "Yeah. The station chief spoke to the ambassador and the consul. Shouldn't be a problem to get them political refugee status. She's got cousins in San Diego, so that's a possibility."

"And the research assistant?"

"There's no sign of him. It looks like he got out of Dodge already. Around the same time Sharafi went to Jordan, it seems." His expression darkened as his mind seemed to latch onto something else. "That poor bastard. I wonder if he was still alive before . . ." His eyes darted hesitantly sideways at Tess, and his voice trailed off. He then remembered something else, causing him to riffle through the paperwork in his hands before passing another sheet back to Reilly.

"On that front, we got something," he told him. "The unexploded bomb, the one that was in the car with you, Miss Chaykin?" He gave her a glance that was somewhat apologetic. "The bomb tech guys' report came in. It was a serious piece of hardware. Twenty pounds of C4 jacked to a cell phone."

Reilly was already scanning the sheet. "No taggants?"

"None."

"What are taggants?" Tess asked.

"Manufacturers of explosives such as C4 and Semtex are bound by international conventions to add unique marker chemicals to their products, to help identify their provenance if needed," Ertugrul explained. "And surprisingly, the system works. You rarely see untagged material. One place we have seen it, though, is in Iraq. In car bombs."

"Car bombs attributed to Iranian-backed insurgents," Reilly added.

Ertugrul turned back to Reilly. "Also, the architecture was identical to devices we've seen there. The way the circuit board was hot-wired. The solder points on the detonator caps. Right down to the wiring itself. Whoever put it together studied under the same jihad master." He gave Reilly a pointed look. "We may not have much, but what we do have all seems to be pointing at Tehran."

Reilly caught a noticeable hardening in the Turkish intelligence officer's jawline at the mention. The Turks and the Iranians weren't exactly BFFs. It wasn't a big secret that the Iranians had been supporting the Kurdish Workers Party separatists inside Turkey for more than two decades, supplying them with weapons and explosives and participating in their drug smuggling operations. The fact that the Kurdish militants had, in the last few years, spread their theater of operations to inside Iran itself was only of little solace to the long-aggrieved Turks. If their quarry— who was already a wanted man in Turkey for the beheading of Sharafi's daughter's teacher—was an Iranian agent, the Turks would want nothing more than to get their hands on him and string him up before an outraged world.

The highway ramped upward as they reached the big Karayolu interchange, opening up a clear view of the city's full majesty. Its seven hills rose and fell gently in the distance, each one of them topped by a monumental mosque, their massive, squat domes and thin, rocketlike minarets giving the imperial city its unique, otherwordly skyline. In the far distance, to their right, was the largest of them all, Hagia Sophia, the Church of the Holy Wisdom, for close to a thousand years the largest cathedral in the world, before it was converted into a mosque after the Ottomans conquered Constantinople in 1453. The city that was once known as "the city of the world's desire," the imperial capital that had endured more sieges and attacks than any other city on earth, was the only city on the planet that straddled two continents. Ever since it was founded more than two thousand years ago, it had been a place where East and West met—and battled. A dual role that it was still, it seemed, destined to play.

"So this piece of info . . . you said you think the target's coming to Istanbul to try and find out where some old monastery is?" Ertugrul asked.

"The Templar at the heart of what's going on is a knight called Conrad. There's very little about him out there, but the guys at the Vatican archives found references to him in the scans of the Registry," Reilly explained. "That's what our target was after. See, Conrad was in Cyprus after the crusaders got kicked out of Acre in 1291. Simmons knew that already. But there was more info in the Registry, about what happened to him after that."

He deferred to Tess. She picked up the baton. "In the months and years after the arrest warrants were issued in 1307," she told Ertugrul, "a small army of inquisitors was sent out to round up any fugitive Templars and confiscate whatever Templar assets they could get their hands on. One of those inquisitors, a priest who'd been dispatched to Cyprus to track down the Templars who'd been exiled from there, had sailed on to the mainland and spent a year roaming the area between Antioch and Constantinople, hunting them down. In his journal, he recorded coming across a derelict monastery tucked away up in the mountains that was strewn with the skeletons of its monks. He then recorded finding the tombs of three Templars in a canyon not far from there. According to the markings he found by the tombs, one of the knights buried there is our man Conrad."

"What mountains was he talking about?"

"Mount Argaeus," Tess said. "It's an old Latin name. You probably know it as Mount Erciyes."

Ertugrul nodded, recognizing the name. "*Erciyes Dağı.* It's an extinct volcano." He gave them a dubious look. "It's big."

"I know," Reilly said somberly.

"It's bang in the middle of the country, in Anatolia. There's a skiing resort there somewhere." Ertugrul thought about it for a moment, then said, "So that's the monastery you want the guys at the Patriarchate to help you locate?"

Reilly nodded. "Right now, Conrad's trail ends with his grave. I think there's a good chance that's where our target's headed, hoping to find some clue to the location of what the knights took back from the monks. But we don't know exactly where those graves are, and he doesn't either. In his journal, the inquisitor only described the location of the canyon *relative to the monastery*—but we don't know where that is."

"Can't we extrapolate his journey by trying to fit it to the terrain around the mountain?"

"The area is riddled with valleys and canyons. Without knowing where the inquisitor set off from, we'd be guessing," Tess told him. "We need to know where the monastery is to use it as a starting point, to know what direction to look in."

"What we do know is that it's a Basilian monastery," Reilly added. "Meaning it's an Orthodox monastery."

"And if there's any record of it, the first place to look would be at the heart of the Orthodox Church," Ertugrul inferred.

"Exactly," Reilly agreed. "If we find the monastery, we can follow the inquisitor's pointers from there to get to the Templars' graves. And if we can get there first, maybe we'll find our bomber—and Simmons—there."

"Well, I spoke to the archbishop's secretary after we spoke," Ertugrul told him. "They're expecting us." He shrugged and added, "Maybe we'll get lucky."

Reilly felt a boil of rage bubble up inside him as he remembered how perfectly the bomber had played his role, from the point he'd met Reilly at the airport in Rome until Reilly had confronted him in the Popemobile. The man didn't seem to leave anything to chance, and Reilly didn't think they ought to be hoping for a lucky break here either. It was going to take more than that to bring him down.

They got off the highway and slipped into the chaotic streets of central Istanbul. Loud diesel belches from old trucks and buses and irate car horns blared around them as they cut through the city, heading toward the defensive walls that lined the calm waters of the Golden Horn. The small convoy navigated through a few turns before veering into a narrow, one-way lane that rose up a gentle hill, skirting a tall wall to its left.

"There's the Phanar," Ertugrul told them, referring to the Patriarchate by its nickname as he pointed out the window.

Reilly and Tess looked out. Beyond the wall lay the

Greek Orthodox Patriarchate, which was to the Orthodox Church what the Vatican was to the Catholics—though nowhere near as grand. The Orthodox Church wasn't a unified movement and didn't have one spiritual leader at its head. It was fragmented and had a different patriarch wherever it had a large body of followers, such as in Russia, Greece, or Cyprus. The ecumenical patriarch of Istanbul, however, was considered its ceremonial leader—the "first among equals"—but his Patriarchate was still nothing more than a humble cluster of unprepossessing buildings.

The compound was built around the Cathedral of St. George, a plain, domeless church that had started off as a convent. The whole church could probably have fit inside the nave of St. Peter's cathedral, with room to spare. Still, it was the spiritual center of Orthodoxy, a beautifully decorated church that housed several treasured relics, including part of the Column of Flagellation to which Jesus was tied and whipped before His crucifixion. The leafy compound also included a monastery, some administrative offices, and—of most interest to Reilly and Tess—the Patriarchate Library.

About seventy yards or so from the compound's entrance, the cars ahead of the armored SUVs slowed to a crawl. The approach road, which rose to the top of the hill before dropping back softly, was lined with parked cars on both sides, and was only wide enough for a single lane of traffic, which was now grinding to a halt. A couple of impatient car horns were quick to challenge the delay. Reilly, frustrated by the holdup, leaned sideways for a better look. Up ahead, about a dozen cars down the lane, a small crowd was clustered around the Patriarchate's main gate. They seemed agitated and were all looking at something inside the compound and pointing up at it. A small tour van and a taxi that were dropping off some visitors were also stalled there, their drivers out of their vehicles and looking up in the same direction.

Reilly followed their gazes across and into the compound, and saw what they were all looking at. A plume of black smoke was rising from the far corner of one of its buildings.

And then he saw something else.

A lone figure, walking out of the compound.

A man with short, dark hair, wearing the black cassock of a priest, walking with a casual gait, maybe a bit hurried, but not in a way that would draw attention.

A burst of blood flushed through Reilly's temples.

"That's him," he blurted, climbing out of his seat as he pointed dead ahead. "That priest, right there. That's our guy. The son of a bitch is right there."

Chapter 19

✠

A mad panic erupted inside the lead SUV as all six of its occupants lasered their attention onto the gathering crowd outside the entrance of the Patriarchate.

"Where?" Ertugrul asked as he craned his neck left and right and scanned ahead. "Where is he?"

"Right there," Reilly growled, now leaning forward so far off his seat that he was almost climbing over the back of the legat. He fought to keep his target in view, but the man in the priest's cassock was moving away and disappearing behind the crowd. "We're going to lose him," he rasped, and seeing that the cars weren't going anywhere, he clambered over the back of the middle row of seats and over Ertugrul, flung the car door open and burst out into the street.

Just as he was exiting the car, he heard the police chief bark something angrily to their driver, spurring the young trooper to do what was probably the worst thing he could have done: slamming his hand down on the horn and leaning out of his window, shouting and gesturing at the driver of the car ahead of him to move out of the way.

Reilly was already charging away from the armored Suburban when he saw the bomber react to the misjudged outburst. Without slowing down, the man spun his gaze around and their eyes met.

Wrong move, Reilly cursed inwardly as he sprinted forward and drew his handgun. *Wrong fucking move.*

ZAHED SAW REILLY STORM OUT of the black SUV and spurred his legs to life. There wasn't a second to lose. Reilly was now rushing toward him, gun drawn, a dozen or so car lengths away. Other men were also pouring out of the black Suburban and from another one just behind it.

All of which took him by surprise.

They're good, Zahed seethed. *No, not they*, he corrected himself. *Reilly. Reilly's good.*

He stowed the concern. There were more pressing matters at hand.

He'd parked his rental car down the hill from the Patriarchate's gates, and he instantly realized he'd have to abandon it there. It was about fifty yards away down the lane, too far to reach safely, and besides, there was no time to coax it out of its tight spot.

He decided on a far more efficient escape route.

Moving with the cool facility of someone who'd practiced the routine a hundred times for the final of a reality show, he banked right and doubled back and headed uphill—cutting through the crowd toward Reilly but, more relevantly, beelining his way to the vehicles that were stopped outside the compound's gate.

From underneath his cassock, he pulled out the big Glock.

And without missing a beat, he started firing.

He loosed his first six shots into the air, just firing into the sky as he yelled, "Get out! Move! Now!" while waving his arms in the air like a madman. The effect was instantaneous—a torrent of screams cascaded outward as the terrified onlookers stampeded for cover, heading away from him and running straight into Reilly's path.

Zahed was still moving briskly and went right up to the driver of the vehicle at the root of the backed-up traffic. The man had been standing by the door of his van and was just rooted there, startled and confused. Zahed squeezed off a round virtually point-blank, and before the man even knew what had hit him, the force of the .45-caliber shell ripped the driver's chest open and flung him backward with a vicious snap. Zahed kept moving. Oblivious to the mayhem around him, he just loped past the driver's open door and raised his handgun again, this time at the taxi that was stopped behind the van. The taxi driver, who was standing next to it, looked at the gun-toting priest in terror and raised his arms, his legs crippled with fear. A dark, wet patch bloomed around his crotch. Zahed held his gaze for a second; then his emotionless eyes swung away from the man in concert with his gun hand until both settled on the car's right front wheel. Zahed pulled the trigger again, and again, then a third time, shredding the tire to bits and causing the car to lurch and drop heavily onto its rim.

He glanced over the hobbled taxi's roof and caught a glimpse of Reilly battling the tide of escaping onlookers. The agent was now less than thirty yards away. He raised his handgun and tried to line Reilly down its sight, but there was too much commotion around the agent and Zahed couldn't get a clean shot.

Time to vamoose.

With his weapon still in his grip, he leapt behind the wheel of the van, slammed it into drive, and floored it.

REILLY HAD LOST SIGHT OF his target for no more than a few intakes of breath before the first shots sent the crowd scurrying in his direction.

They were coming right at him—men and women of all ages and sizes, screaming and yelling and running for their lives. He tried dodging and cutting through the onslaught, but it was hard enough for him just to hold his ground. Precious seconds ticked away as blurred bodies slammed into him and scurried past, seconds during which he heard another shot, then a few more, each one of them whipping his neurons and urging him forward.

He held his gun up close to his face and used his other arm to clear a path through the frenzy, waving and yelling, "Get down," as he fought his way forward—and then he heard the wail of a burdened engine and the squeal of scrubbed tires, and the last of the crowd streamed by to reveal the van tearing down the lane.

Reilly sprinted after the van as fast as he could, then skittered to a stop and lined up a shot and pulled the trigger once, twice, a third time—but it was pointless at that distance. The van was already disappearing from view. He spun around, his instincts doing a lightning-fast assessment of the situation around him. He registered the black smoke now billowing out of a window on an upper floor of one of the compound's buildings, the priests spilling out of the Patriarchate in panic, Ertugrul and the Turkish cops rushing toward him, the shot man sprawled on the ground, another man standing by a taxi with a petrified stare on his face, the taxi's tilt and low stance on the driver's side, the fact that it was blocking all the cars behind it and didn't look like it was going anywhere, not soon enough anyway.

Which meant he had only one option.

To run, as fast as he could, and hope for a miracle.

Chasing after the van that was now disappearing around a bend down the road, he bolted forward, breathing hard, his palms cutting through the still air, his elbows rowing him forward, the soles of his shoes hitting the asphalt hard in a staccato of crisp slaps. He must have covered twenty or so car lengths before he spotted his miracle, a middle-aged woman who was getting into her car, a small burgundy VW Polo.

There was no time for lengthy explanations.

Within seconds, Reilly had blurted out a couple of apologetic words, snatched the keys out of her hand, jumped behind the wheel, and screeched out of the parking spot, leaving the woman's incensed shouts in his wake as he rocketed after his prey.

Chapter 20

✠

Mansoor Zahed scanned the view from the van's wind-shield with heightened concentration.

He was somewhat familiar with Istanbul, a city he'd vis-ited on a number of occasions in the course of various as-signments. But he didn't know its road configuration that well, and he certainly didn't know the narrow streets of the Phanar district well enough to know where he was go-ing. He didn't really care where he ended up. He'd gotten what he wanted from the library of the Patriarchate. All he needed to do now was put a reasonable buffer zone be-tween him and the Orthodox compound while making sure he hadn't been followed, then dump the van and grab a cab to join up with Steyl and their captive archaeologist.

He reached an intersection and turned right, heading to-ward the waterfront and the dual highway that snaked up and down the south bank of the Golden Horn. If he could make it onto it, he was home free. It was a major artery that he could comfortably ride to distance himself from Reilly and his posse. It had to be close to the water, he thought, the tension across his body starting to dissipate. No more than a handful of streets away.

The squeal of a car sliding around a corner brutally guil-lotined his reprieve.

He glanced in his mirror. A dark hatchback had skidded into view and was eating up the road behind him.

A glimpse of the driver was enough to tell him it was Reilly.

"*Madar jendeh*," he swore under his breath as he mashed the gas pedal and tightened his grip on the wheel.

He reached a busy intersection, and punched the brake pedal before hitting the horn and barging through. He scrutinized his rearview mirror for a couple of tense heart-beats before he heard the long dopplery howl of a car horn and spotted the hatchback emerge from the chaos of the intersection and scurry after him like an angry terrier.

He stormed through a couple more intersections, cut-ting past infuriated drivers and using the van's bulk to bully them out of his way as if he were in a demolition derby, and managed to put a few cars between him and Reilly. He dove into another street just ahead of a big truck and motored away, keeping an eye on his side mirror to see how many car lengths he'd gained by the maneuver—and then disaster struck. He'd reached the on-ramp to the coastal road, a dual parkway that consisted of two separate two-lane roads, one heading north and the other south, that ran alongside each other in places and were far apart in others.

The problem was, the access road he was on was blocked by traffic.

He slammed on his brakes and scanned ahead. The road that the ramp was leading to, the one heading north, was totally swamped. Frustratingly, the one heading south was clear, but he couldn't get on it, not with cars and trucks now backed up behind him and two-foot aluminum barriers on either side.

He was boxed in.

Worse, he glanced in his mirror and, about seven car lengths back, spotted a burgundy-colored car door swing-ing open and Reilly bursting out.

He grimaced, impressed and angered in equal measure by the agent's relentlessness, and lunged out of the van.

He sprinted down the access road, clambered over one of the barriers, and cut across a parched grassland to reach the main road. He glanced back and saw Reilly rushing after him, and thought about pulling out his gun and taking a shot, then decided against it. Instead, he kept moving, snaking through the stalled cars, hurdling over another barrier, and tearing across another bit of grassland, then over a farther barrier to reach the south parkway that was flowing with cars.

He looked back. Reilly was closing in. He turned and sized up the oncoming cars. He spotted a white sedan with a single occupant coming toward him, and stepped into the middle of the road, his hands held out high and wide, waving them as if calling out for help. He calculated that the priest's cassock he was wearing would help—which it did, as the car slowed right down and pulled in close to the barrier. A couple of cars slid to a halt behind it, tires and horns shrieking. Zahed ignored them. He just approached the driver with a sheepish, friendly look on his face. The driver, a slight, balding man, started to open his window. It had barely slid down a few inches when Zahed's hand darted in and wrenched the door open; then he reached in and released the hapless driver's seat belt, grabbed him, and yanked him out of his car in one ferocious move. He flung him onto the asphalt as if he were unloading a duffel bag, sending him tumbling across the lane divider and causing an oncoming truck to swerve away to avoid flattening him. Zahed didn't notice. He was already behind the wheel of the human skittle's Ford Mondeo and streaking away down the open road.

REILLY LEAPT OVER THE LAST BARRIER and reached the commotion on the main road with the tailgate of Zahed's stolen car barely still in view. Gasping for breath, he saw the stunned bald man talking animatedly with the drivers of a couple of cars that had stopped. They were blocking one of the lanes and causing a ripple effect of irate shouts and horns behind them.

Can't let him get away. Not again.

He rushed up to the men, pointing at the lead car with manic urgency. "Is this your car?" he asked one of the men. "Is this yours?"

The bald man and one of the others eyed him suspiciously and took a step back, shaking their heads to indicate that it wasn't, but the third, a strong-boned man with a thick neck and craggy, leathery skin, stood his ground and started spitting out a tirade of angry words in Turkish while waving his hands defiantly.

I don't have time for this.

Reilly shrugged, reached behind his back, and pulled out his handgun. He held it up, his other arm also raised, the gun and his palm facing the man appeasingly.

"Calm down, will you?" Reilly ordered them. "You want this guy to get away? Is that what you want?"

The bald man looked like he was about to say something, but the hotheaded bruiser wasn't impressed. He resumed his tirade, clearly berating Reilly and back-slapping the air to show he wasn't impressed by the artillery.

Screw this. Reilly frowned as he brought the gun down and fired three shots at the ground by the man's feet. The man leapt back like he'd just stepped on a snake. "Your keys," Reilly shouted, pointing at the car again and shoving the heated muzzle into Mongo's face. "Give me your goddamn car keys, you understand me?"

The big guy's face crinkled with confusion; then he held out his hand with the car keys in it. Reilly snatched them from him and spat out a grudging "Thank you" as he darted over to the car, a station wagon of nondescript provenance. He slid behind the wheel, avoided gagging from the stench of a mound of stale cigarette butts that clogged an ashtray in the dashboard, and tore off in pursuit of his target.

The first mile or so flew by with barely any other cars to overtake as a result of the choke point Reilly had left behind. He spotted a white dot in the far distance, and the sight energized him further, though there wasn't much more he could wrangle out of the car's engine. He was blowing past an old, overloaded bus when a ring from the inside of his jacket startled him. While he kept one hand gripped on the wheel, his other dove into his pocket and fished the BlackBerry out.

Nick Aparo's ebullient voice boomed down his ear canal, as clear as if he were calling from another car beside him and not from Federal Plaza in lower Manhattan. "Hey, what's going on? Your European vacation getting any better yet, Clark?"

Some vague connection to an old Chevy Chase movie flashed across Reilly's frazzled mind, but he was too focused on reeling in the white tailgate for it to register.

"I can't talk now," he said, breathless, his eyes locked dead ahead.

"You'll want to hear this, Clarkie," Aparo insisted, still oblivious to what his partner was going through. "It's about your mystery man. We got a hit."

Chapter 21

✟

"Later," Reilly fired back. "I need you to call Ertugrul for me, right now. Tell him I'm driving down the waterfront in a station wagon"—he glanced at the steering wheel that, helpfully, had a name and not some obscure logo on it—"a blue Kia, and our target's in a white sedan just ahead of me and we're heading"—he glanced out quickly to get a read of the sun's position and did a quick mental jam to figure out his heading—"south, I think, along the waterfront."

True to form, Aparo's tone went from jovial to dead serious as if a hypnotist had just snapped his fingers. "What target? The bomber?"

"Yes," Reilly blurted. "Just make the damn call, will you?"

Aparo's tone morphed into manic. "Hang on. I'm dialing him on another line. What's the asshole driving?"

"I'm not sure. I didn't get a good look at it. But he won't be hard to spot, not at the speed he's going."

"All right, hang on. It's ringing."

Reilly hit the loudspeaker button and chucked the phone onto the car seat next to him as he shot past the stalled traffic in the opposite direction at a dizzying speed. The road snaked left and right slightly while maintaining a broadly straight heading, and Reilly's pulse spiked as he saw the white sedan swerve far to the left to try to get past a slow-moving and packed *dolmu* share-taxi that had been trundling down the lane divider. He finally managed it, but the lumbering minivan had delayed him, and the son of a bitch was now within reach. Reilly hit his lights and mashed the horn and swept past the *dolmu* without delay, gaining precious ground on the white sedan, which he could now distinguish as a Ford.

His fingers tightened against the wheel, feeling their quarry's neck within their grasp, while up ahead, the first of two bridges across the Golden Horn came into view. Reilly gained more distance on the Mondeo as it slowed slightly to ride a cloverleaf ramp system, and within seconds, he was tailing the bomber across the Atatürk Bridge. It was old, more of a causeway than a bridge really, given that it sat on concrete piers and had two lanes in each direction, with a narrow pedestrian sidewalk on either edge. There was a lot more traffic on it, which slowed the Mondeo down and allowed Reilly to reel him right in and tuck in behind him as the bomber ducked and weaved and bullied his way past the hapless Turkish drivers.

"I'm right behind him now—we're going across a bridge," he yelled, leaning sideways, in the direction of the Black-Berry, as he swerved around a slower car. "I can see an old tower on the other side, to the right, looks like something from an old castle."

"Got it," Aparo's voice squawked back, muffled against the seat now. "Ertugrul's passing it on to some local cop he's with. You stay on him, buddy."

It's happening too fast, Reilly thought. *They're not going to be able to help. I have to do this alone.*

"That's the Galata Tower," Aparo came back, as breathless as his partner. "They've got a handle on where you are. Hang tight."

Reilly kept his foot jammed and charged ahead, now within yards of the Mondeo's tailgate—and kept going, ramming the white car, hard, watching it fishtail left and right before it resumed its straight heading.

He floored the pedal again and went in for another hit.

*   *   *

THE KIA WAS NOW SO CLOSE BEHIND that Mansoor Zahed could actually see the hunger that was blazing in Reilly's eyes.

"Madar jendeh," he cursed again as he watched the blue station wagon eat up his mirror. He mashed the throttle and swerved out of harm's way, squeezing between two slower cars and avoiding another pounding.

He saw Reilly drop back as the cars behind him slowed down and settled back into their lanes.

The American's possessed. He's not going to be easy to shake off. Not now. Not after all this.

Zahed knew the traffic could snarl up again the minute they left the bridge. He had to do something now, quickly, if he was going to avoid another running chase with the bloodhound that was breathing down his neck.

With his hand hard on the Mondeo's horn, he muscled past a few more cars, leading one of them to ride up the low curb of the sidewalk that ran along at the water's edge.

That, and a crowded bus up ahead—an old, 1970s-era Mercedes, its roof stacked with luggage, its exhaust spewing out a thick black cloud of diesel—inspired him.

He raced on until he was almost alongside the bus, then jinked his sedan left and right and rammed it sideways. The bus groaned and bounced off to the right, its windows suddenly crammed with the startled faces of its passengers, suitcases and boxes snapping their ties and tumbling down off its roof and into the path of the cars behind it. Zahed jerked the wheel to keep the Mondeo pressed against the side of the bus, shepherding it off on an angled trajectory and sending it bounding onto the sidewalk and pulverizing the thin metallic railing before flying off the bridge.

Zahed straightened his own car's trajectory and eyed his mirror, where, much to his delight, he saw Reilly do exactly what he'd hoped the agent would do.

REILLY'S FACE CLENCHED as he watched the white Mondeo launch the old bus over the curb and off the bridge.

It just flew off with little fanfare and dove out of view for a nanosecond before a huge white plume erupted out of the estuary. Given the mountain of luggage that had been stacked precariously on its roof, Reilly knew it was probably packed with people—people who he could imagine were about to be dragged underwater.

The car ahead of him slammed on its brakes, and he did the same. Screeching brakes and crunched fenders chased after him. He saw that there was room for him to squeeze past the cars ahead of him, but he couldn't do that. Not with a bunch of people possibly sinking to their deaths.

He had to help.

He scrambled out of the car and ran toward the big gap in the railing. In the distance, he could see the back of the white Ford disappearing down the bridge, and for an instant he imagined the smug face of his quarry. *Motherfucker*, he thought, the anger and the frustration propelling him even faster to the edge of the bridge. A few people from other cars converged to join him, looking down, pointing, talking animatedly.

In the water, the old bus was only partly visible, the back of its roof sticking out like a tiny iceberg. Reilly scanned the surface of the water, but couldn't see anyone floating around. The windows of the bus looked like they were sealed shut, with only a narrow section at the top that slid open and wasn't anywhere near wide enough for anyone to slip through. Reilly watched for an extended second or two, wondering if the doors were hydraulically operated, if they were jammed shut since the electrics had shut down, if the passengers were too shocked to figure out where the emergency exits were. No one was coming out. They were trapped inside. And no one was doing anything about it.

He glanced at the stunned faces around him—a mixed bag of young and old, men and women, all in shock, blabbing and looking down gloomily—and moved.

No more deaths. Not because of me. Not if I can help it.

He kicked off his shoes, yanked off his jacket, and leapt in.

The water around him was littered with pieces of luggage and cardboard boxes, hampering his progress, but he managed to reach the back of the bus and grab on to its roof rail just before it disappeared with a final belch of air.

He hung on as the bus slid under, slowly. Through the murky water, he could see the ghostly, fear-stricken faces of the passengers on the other side of the bus's rear window. They were tugging at the emergency release handle, which wasn't responding, and banging their fists against the glass in desperation. Hanging on with one hand, he reached down to his side holster and pulled out his gun, then waved it at the passengers closest to him, hoping they'd understand. They weren't moving away, but it didn't stop him. He just put the gun against the very top of the glass and angled it right up, aiming it at the underside of the bus's roof— and fired, again and again—five quick shots that punched through the window before dying out in the water inside the bus. The shots weakened the window enough for him to be able to kick and hammer it in with the butt of his handgun, until it finally gave way and blew out with a big whoosh of trapped air that almost made Reilly lose his grip.

One after another, the trapped passengers streamed out in a mad frenzy, a shoal of desperate arms reaching out to Reilly and taking hold of his outstretched hand before kicking away and gliding up toward the light. He hung on as long as his lungs could last; then he finally let go and followed them up to the surface, the elation of knowing all the passengers were safe not quite making up for the bitter frustration that was gnawing at his gut.

Chapter 22

✠

By the time Reilly made it back to the Patriarchate, the compound was one big, chaotic mess. The approach road was choked by fire engines, ambulances, and police cars. Emergency services personnel were swarming around frenetically, doing what they did best.

He'd swum onto one of the support piers and climbed back onto the bridge. A cop had finally made it onto the scene and, after some wrangling, agreed to drive him back to the Phanar. He'd taken off his shirt and slipped on his jacket, which he'd pulled off before jumping into the water, but his trousers were still drenched, which hadn't exactly endeared him to his driver either. Because of the mess and the security lockdown, he'd had to walk the last couple of hundred yards and found Tess standing by the gates. Ertugrul was alongside her, as were a couple of young paramilitary soldiers who looked a bit too trigger-happy for comfort. Frustrated cops were having a hard time keeping reporters and curious bystanders away while a small army of cats—revered in Istanbul as the bearers of good luck—sprawled on the walls and sidewalks around them and calmly observed the proceedings.

Tess's face erupted with relief when she spotted him; then her expression went all curious as his shirtless-and-soggy-pants look came into focus.

She gave him a quick kiss and held his arms. "You've got to get out of those clothes."

"My bag still in the car?" he asked Ertugrul.

"Yeah," the legat answered. "It's parked down the road."

Reilly glanced into the compound, where some paramedics were loading a gurney into an ambulance. The body lying on it was fully covered up by a gray blanket, head included. A gaggle of priests was crowding around it, their expressions forlorn, their shoulders sagging.

Reilly looked a question at Ertugrul.

"Father Alexios. The grand archimandrite of the library. One bullet, right between the eyes."

"They also found the body of a dead priest in an alleyway down the road," Tess added.

"No cassock," Reilly deduced.

Tess nodded.

He expected as much. "And the fire?"

"It's out, but the library's a mess, as you can imagine," Ertugrul said. After a frustrated grunt, he added, "I guess he got what he came for."

"Again," Reilly noted, the word laced with acid.

He stood there, his fists balled with rage, and took in the scene silently for another moment, then said, "I'll be right back," and headed down the road to change.

He was halfway there when he remembered something, and fished out his BlackBerry from his jacket. Aparo picked up on the first ring.

"Fill me in, buddy," his partner urged.

"I lost him. The guy's a fucking lunatic." The sideswipe that catapulted the bus off the bridge flashed in his mind's eye. "You said you had something for me?"

"Yeah," Aparo confirmed. "We finally got a hit from military intel. Talk about pulling teeth. These guys are really cagey about who they share with."

"So who is he?"

"We don't have a name. Just a previous."

"Where?"

"Baghdad, three years ago. You remember that computer expert, the one that was grabbed from the Finance Ministry?"

Reilly knew about it. It had caused quite a furor at the time, back in the summer of 2007. The man, an American, had been plucked out of the technology center of the ministry along with his five bodyguards. The kidnappers had shown up in full Iraqi Republican Guard regalia and just marched in and grabbed the men under the guise of "arresting" them. The specialist had only arrived in Baghdad a day earlier. He was there to install a sophisticated new software system that would keep track of the billions of dollars of international aid money and local oil revenues that were flowing through Iraq's ministries—billions that were going missing almost as fast as they were coming in. Intelligence sources knew that a lot of the missing funds were being diverted to Iran's militia groups in Iraq, courtesy of Iran's cheerleaders who occupied many top Iraqi government posts and who, no doubt, helped themselves to a healthy commission along the way. No one wanted the corruption to stop, or for it to be exposed. The Finance Ministry had been shamelessly resisting the software's implementation for more than two years. And so the man who'd been finally flown in to try to put a stop to the embezzlement was snatched less than twenty-four hours after landing there, right from his keyboard in the very heart of the Finance Ministry.

The kidnapping had been meticulously planned and executed, and was attributed to the Al-Quds force—the word was Arabic for "Jerusalem"—a special unit of Iran's Revolutionary Guard for covert foreign operations. When the American specialist and his bodyguards were found executed a couple of weeks later, the anti-Iranian rhetoric coming from the White House escalated. A half dozen Iranian officials were caught and detained by U.S. forces in the north of the country. Never one to resist stoking the flames of conflict with reckless abandon, Iran's leadership—via a supposedly unaffiliated, rogue militia group called the Asaib Ahl Al-Haq, or the "Righteous League"—proceeded to launch an even more brazen attack, this time on the provincial headquarters in Karbala, during a high-level meeting between U.S. and Iraqi officials. It was even more audacious than the earlier kidnapping. A dozen Al-Quds operatives showed up at the gates of the base in a fleet of black Suburbans that were identical to the ones used there by U.S. military contractors. They were dressed just like the mercenaries and spoke perfect English, so much so that the Iraqis guarding the gates were convinced they were American—and let them in. Once inside, the commandos ran amok. They killed one American soldier and grabbed four others, whom they executed shortly after storming out of the compound. It ended up being the third-deadliest day in Iraq for U.S. troops. Amazingly, no Iraqis had been injured in the raid.

"He was there. Your target. He was one of the guys who hit the base," Aparo told him. "His prints match a print they lifted off one of the cars they left behind. And according to the intel we had, both ops were pulled off by the same team, so it's possible—even probable—that he was also involved in the programmer's kidnapping."

"Do we know anything about him?"

"Nope," Aparo told him. "Nothing at all. The guys behind the raids just vanished. All I can tell you is that it looks like he was there. But it gives us some insight into what the rest of his CV might look like. I mean, who knows what else this asshole's been involved in? It sounds to me like he's their go-to guy when they need something special done."

Reilly frowned. "Lucky us." He knew that if history was anything to go by, this wasn't looking promising at all. In every confrontation between the U.S. and Iran since Khomeini came to power in 1979, Iran had come out on top.

"You've got to nail his ass, Sean. Find him and wipe him off the face of the earth."

A siren startled Reilly. He turned to see one of the ambulances rushing down the road, and stepped aside to let it through.

"Let's find him first," he told Aparo, "and when we do, I'm not exactly planning to split a six-pack with him."

Chapter 23

✜

Given the internal and external political tensions gripping the country, the Turks took matters of national
security very seriously, and this was no exception. Within
an hour of getting back to the Patriarchate, Reilly, along
with Tess and Ertugrul, was seated in a glass-walled conference room in the Turkish National Police's Istanbul headquarters in the city's Aksaray district, trading questions
and answers with a half dozen Turkish security officials.

One question was at the root of Reilly's frustration.
"How did he get into the country?" he asked, still pissed
off by the slipup. "I thought you guys had military-level security at your airports?"

None of his hosts seemed to have an immediate answer
for him.

Suleyman İzzettin, the police captain who was at the airport with Ertugrul, waded into the pregnant silence. "We're
looking into it. But remember," he said, clearly as vexed by
it as Reilly, "our border controls didn't have a clear photo
or a likely alias for him. And besides, maybe he didn't fly
in."

"No way," Reilly countered. "He didn't have time for
a road trip, not from Rome. He flew in. Definitely." He
glanced around the room, speaking a bit slower than usual
and slightly overenunciating to make sure they all under-

stood him. "This guy managed to move his hostages from Jordan to Italy without a problem. Now he's here, and he's still got one of them. We need to figure out how he's just hopping around from one country to another. And finding out which one of your airports he slipped through would be a big help."

The security officers erupted into a brief, heated debate in Turkish. Clearly, they didn't take kindly to being embarrassed in front of a foreign official. İzzettin seemed to call a time-out among them before simply repeating, to Reilly, what he had said before: "We'll look into it."

"Okay. We also need to figure out how he's moving around now that he's here," Reilly pressed on. "If we're going to track him down, we need to know what we're looking for. How did he get to the Patriarchate? Did he have a car parked there somewhere that he abandoned when he saw us arrive? Did he just take a cab? Or was someone waiting for him? Does he have people here helping him out?"

"Also," Ertugrul chimed in, "assuming he's brought Simmons here with him, where did he park him in the meantime?"

"We took control of the area immediately after the shoot-out," İzzettin told him. "I'm pretty sure he didn't have a driver waiting for him. No one drove away from there."

"He could have just abandoned his car and walked off," Reilly countered.

"The research assistant," Tess asked Ertugrul, "the snitch who kick-started this whole mess by selling out Sharafi? You're sure he left the country?"

He nodded. "He's long gone."

"This guy's moving too fast to be doing this alone," Reilly said. "He's got to have some backup. Remember, he didn't know the trail led back to Istanbul until last night, when he got the Registry from the Vatican. It's not like he's had a lot of time to plan this. He's winging it. He's reacting as the information comes in, just like us—but he's one step ahead of us." He turned to Ertugrul. "This monastery . . . Who else can we talk to about finding out where it is?"

"I had a quick word about that with the patriarch's secretary, after the shooting," Ertugrul said. "He wasn't in the clearest state of mind. But he said he'd never heard of it."

"That's not surprising," Tess added. "The inquisitor who came across it said it was abandoned, and that was back in the early 1300s. Seven hundred years, it's probably little more than rubble now, just some ruins in the middle of nowhere."

"The secretary's going to talk to the other priests there," Ertugrul said. "Maybe one of them will know."

Reilly turned to their hosts, frustrated. "You've got to have access to some experts at the university, someone who knows their history."

The police chief shrugged. "It's an Orthodox Church, Agent Reilly. Not just Orthodox, but Greek. And this is a Muslim country. It's not exactly a priority area for our academics. If no one at the Patriarchate knows . . ."

Reilly nodded glumly. He was well aware that there was no love lost between the Greeks and the Turks, not since the dawn of the Seljuks and, subsequently, of the Ottoman Empire. It was a deep-seated animosity that went back more than a thousand years and continued to this day, flaring up over thorny issues such as the divided island of Cyprus. "So right now, all we know is that it's in the Mount Argaeus region, the Erciyes Dağı Mountains. How big an area are we talking about?"

Ertugrul exchanged some words with their hosts, and one of them picked up the phone and mumbled away in Turkish. A moment later, a younger cop brought in a folded map, which was spread out on the table. Ertugrul had another to-and-fro with the local officials, then turned to Reilly.

"Actually, it's not a range. It's just one mountain, over here," he explained, pointing out a wide, darker-shaded area in the center of the country. "It's a dormant volcano."

Reilly checked out the scale at the bottom of the map. "It's about, what, ten miles long and the same across?"

"That's a big haystack," Tess said.

"Huge," Ertugrul agreed. "Also, it's not the easiest area to canvass. It goes up to eleven, twelve thousand feet, and its flanks are heavily wrinkled with valleys and ridges. It's no wonder the monastery managed to survive all those years, even after the Ottomans took over. It could be tucked in any one of those folds. You'd need to trip over it to find it."

Reilly was about to respond when Tess spoke up. "Do you think you could get hold of a detailed map of that whole area?" she asked Ertugrul. "A topographic map, maybe? Like the ones climbers use?"

Ertugrul thought about it, then said, "I imagine we should be able to," his tone somewhat belittling of her request. He explained her request in Turkish to their hosts, and one of them picked up the phone again, presumably to source one for her.

Reilly flicked her a quick quizzical glance, then went back to studying the map. "How far is it?"

"From here? Five hundred miles, give or take."

"So how would he get there from here? Drive? Fly? A small plane, or a helicopter maybe?"

Their hosts exchanged a few words, and shook their heads vigorously. "He could fly," Ertugrul replied. "Kayseri's close by and it's got an airport. There are a couple of flights a day from here. But I don't think he'd need to. Depending on the traffic and on what road you take, it's eleven, twelve hours by car versus under two by plane, but it's less risky, especially now that the airports are on high alert."

Which, presumably, they also were last night, but that didn't stop him, Reilly wanted to say, but he held back.

"There's also a train," the chief of police remembered. "But if he has a hostage with him, it's not really doable."

"Okay, so if he's going to drive there, where'd he get the car?" Reilly asked Ertugrul. "What do we know about the cars he used in Rome? The ones Sharafi and Tess were in?"

Ertugrul flicked through his papers, then found the relevant report. "All they have right now is that they had fake plates. The prelim VIN number check on the one Ms. Chaykin was in says it wasn't reported stolen, but it can take time for a stolen car claim to filter through. And it's too early to tell with the other one—they have to find the VIN tag first."

"It's the same MO of car bombs we've seen in Iraq and

in Lebanon," Reilly noted. "The cars are stolen, or they'll have been bought for cash with fake IDs. Either way, we don't usually find out which one it is until after they've been blown up." He fumed. "We need to know what he's driving now."

"We're going to need a list of all stolen car claims since, well, yesterday," Ertugrul told İzzettin. "And we'll need to have a constant feed of any new reports that come in."

"Okay," the cop answered.

"How many roads are there that lead to that mountain?" Reilly asked him. "Can you put up roadblocks? We know he's heading there."

The chief of police shook his head as he leaned into the map. "Even knowing he's coming from here, there are many different roads he could take to get there. And it depends on what part of the mountain he's going to. There are different approaches from all sides."

"Besides," Ertugrul added, "we'd still have the same problem as the airport guys. We don't have a clear photo or a name to give to the guys at the roadblocks. They can only look for Simmons."

"It's not possible," İzzettin concluded. "The area around the mountain is very popular with tourists. Cappadocia is very busy this time of year. We can't stop everyone."

"Okay." Reilly shrugged, his eyes darkening with frustration.

Tess's voice broke through the gloom. "If you're saying he might be working for the Iranians, wouldn't they have people here helping him?" she asked. "They could get him a car. A safe house. Weapons."

"It's possible," Reilly agreed. It was something he'd been wondering about too, but he knew that it was tricky territory. He asked Ertugrul, "What level of surveillance do we have on their embassy?"

Ertugrul hesitated, then ducked the question. "The embassy isn't here—it's in the capital, in Ankara. They just have a consulate here." He didn't offer more. No intel officer liked to talk in front of his foreign counterparts about who he and his colleagues were or weren't watching, unless he knew he could trust them—which was, basically, never.

"Do we have them under watch?" Reilly pressed.

"You're asking the wrong guy. That's Agency business," the legat said, reminding Reilly that the CIA handled foreign intel gathering.

Reilly understood and dropped it for now. He turned in frustration to one of the Turkish officers at the table, Murat Çelikbilek, from the MIT—the Milli İstihbarat Teşkilatı, otherwise known as the National Intelligence Organization. "What about your people?" he asked him. "You must have some kind of surveillance in place."

Çelikbilek studied him for a beat with the inscrutable concentration of a vulture, then said, "It's not really a question one can answer casually, especially not in front of "— he nodded somewhat dismissively in Tess's direction—"a civilian."

"Look, I don't need to know the sordid details of what you guys are up to," Reilly said, with a disarming half smile. "But if you're keeping tabs on them, particularly on their consulate here, someone might have seen something that can help us." He held Çelikbilek's gaze for a long second; then the intelligence officer's hooded eyes blinked and he gave Reilly a small nod.

"I'll see what we've got," he said.

"That would be great. We need to move fast," Reilly reiterated. "He's already killed three people in your country, and it could get worse. He's probably already on his way to the monastery, and unless we can figure out what he's driving or where he's headed, he's got an open playing field." He paused long enough to make sure his comment sank in, then turned to Ertugrul and, in a lower voice, said, "We're going to need to talk to the Agency boys. Like, right now."

Chapter 24

✠

With the setting sun turning his rearview mirror into a blazing lava lamp, Mansoor Zahed settled into the stream of evening traffic that was leaving the city and he concentrated on the road ahead.

He glanced to his side. Simmons was sitting there, in the passenger seat, his head slightly slumped, the now familiar half-vacant stare in his eyes, the tranquilizer having once again sapped his vibrancy and turned him into a docile, subservient pet. Zahed knew he'd need to keep him sedated for a while. They had a long drive ahead of them, far longer than the one they had completed earlier that day.

Zahed wasn't thrilled to be on the road again. He wasn't one to dawdle, especially not after what he'd done at the Vatican. He would have preferred to fly to Kayseri, just as he'd have preferred to fly straight from Italy to an airfield close to Istanbul. Steyl had kiboshed that idea, though they were both well aware of the fact that the Turkish military kept a tight grip on all the country's airfields. Steyl had reminded Zahed that the risks, after Rome, were too high, and Zahed hadn't questioned his judgment. He knew that when it came to flying in and out of countries without drawing too much attention to whatever illicit cargo he had on board, Steyl knew exactly what was doable, and what wasn't. You could count on him to fly any payload into pretty much anywhere and get it past the airport checks unchallenged—but you could also count on him not to land you in hot water, metaphorically speaking. And so they'd flown slightly north instead, to Bulgaria, and landed in Primorsko, a small resort town on the country's Black Sea coast. It had a small, civilian airfield—not a military one—the kind where exactly who was on what small plane wasn't the first thing on the local officials' minds. It was also less than twenty miles from the Turkish border, making the drive from the airfield to Istanbul a not-too-taxing five-hour stint.

This drive would be more than twice as long, but there was no other option. Zahed hadn't particularly enjoyed negotiating the never-ending traffic nightmare that was evening-rush-hour Istanbul. The chaotic free-for-all had reminded him of the less attractive aspects of Isfahan, his hometown back in Iran, another arena of outstanding architectural beauty that was marred by its drivers' demented jousting. But in contrast to his earlier outing that day, when evading Reilly, he'd exercised careful restraint while driving out of the city and avoided getting into any dick-measuring contests with the aggressive taxi and *dolmu* drivers, allowing them to barge through instead, knowing that the smallest fender bender could have dire consequences given that he was driving a stolen car and transporting a heavily drugged captive.

As the highway snaked through some fast, sweeping bends and rose into a series of gentle hills, Zahed was finding it hard to relax. He'd never seen as many trucks and buses, big, overloaded mastodons that were hurtling down the Istanbul-Ankara *otoyol*, as the six-lane highway was known, oblivious to its often hazardously patchy road surface and ignoring its 120-kilometer-per-hour speed limit. Turkey had one of the worst accident rates in the world, and the car Zahed had been given, a black Land Rover Discovery, while ideal for any off-road sections of his journey, was definitely too tall for cruising comfortably down a highway. Like a light sailboat caught in a storm, it was constantly getting buffeted by the passing heavyweights, forcing Zahed to correct his heading repeatedly by banking into the turbulent air to keep the car facing forward.

As he always did after each step in the course of an assignment, Zahed ran through a quick mental assessment of his mission's status. So far, he had no major quibbles with how it was working out. He'd made it into Turkey undetected. He'd gotten the information he needed from the Patriarchate. He'd evaded Reilly, who, somehow, had managed to track him down with unsettling efficiency. He reeled his attention back to the previous day's events, at the Vatican, triggering a pleasing cascade of images in his mind's eye. A deep-seated feeling of delight swept over him as he relived the rush he'd felt when he'd watched the coverage of his actions on the televised news and all over the day's newspapers. More would follow, no doubt, after his brief visit to the Patiarchate. He thought about his quest and took great solace in the fact that, even if he weren't able to find what Sharafi had unearthed, or if it turned out to be worthless, his venture had already turned out to be more than a worthwhile undertaking. This was better than anything he had achieved in Beirut, or in Iraq. Far better. It had given him the opportunity to attack his enemies at the very heart of their faith. Their news-hungry media would keep milking it for days, searing it into the minds of his target audience. The financial markets were already doing their bit to add to the pain, plummeting as expected, wiping out billions of dollars from the enemies' coffers. No, his act would not be soon forgotten—of that, he was certain. And with a bit of luck it would only be the beginning, he thought, imagining how it could awaken a thousand other warriors and show them what could be done.

His mind wandered back to another beginning, to another time, and the faces of his younger brothers and his sister swam into view. He could hear them running around, playing around the house back in Isfahan, his parents never far from sight. His thoughts migrated to his parents, and he thought of how proud they would have been of him right now—had they been alive to witness it. Memories of that cursed day came raging back and stoked the flames of the fury that had consumed him ever since—memories of that Sunday, the third of July 1988, a torridly humid day, the day on which his family was blown out of the sky, the day on which his fourteen-year-old world was incinerated, the day that sparked his rebirth. *Not even the merest hint of an apology*, he thought, thinking back to the empty caskets they had buried, an upwelling of bile scorching his throat. Nothing. Just some blood money for him and for all the others who had also lost loved ones. And medals, he seethed. Medals—including the Legion of Merit, no less—for the ship's commander and for the rest of the godless perpetrators of that mass murder.

He stifled his anger and took in a deep breath, and let his mind settle. There was no need to lament what had happened or, as his countrymen were fond of telling him, what had been willed to happen. After all, he kept hearing, everything was written. He chortled inwardly at the backward, naïve thought. What he had come to believe, though, was that the lives of his parents and siblings weren't lost in vain. His life, after all, had taken on a far greater purpose than it otherwise would have had. He just needed to make sure he achieved everything he'd set out to do. To do any less would dishonor their memories and was simply not an option.

He thought ahead and knew he'd have to stop in a few hours. He didn't want to be driving through the night, when traffic would be sparse and when police roadblocks might pop up. He couldn't chance staying in any hotels either. A motel would have been doable, but Europe had never embraced the concept or the anonymity such places afforded. No, he and Simmons would be spending the night in the SUV. In a few hundred miles or so, at around the halfway point of his journey, he'd pull into a lay-by, tuck in between some eighteen-wheelers, and, after giving Simmons a knockout dose, wait for morning. Then he'd be on his way again, bright and early, riding the *otoyol* east to Ankara and on to Aksaray before taking the ancient Silk Road toward Kayseri and to the prize he so desperately sought.

Chapter 25

✠

"The thing is, with an area this big," the CIA station chief told Reilly and Ertugrul, "it's going to be tough getting hold of something that'll do the trick."

They were in a windowless room deep inside the U.S. Consulate, a squat concrete bunker of a building that huddled defensively behind fortified walls and security checkpoints. Located twelve miles north of the city, it looked more like a modern prison than a proud emblem of its mother nation. It was a far cry from the stately, old-world elegance of the Palazzo Corpi, the previous consulate that had mingled with the bazaars and mosques in the bustling center of the old city. That consulate, sadly, was part of a long-gone world. The new facility, built on a hill of solid rock shortly after 9/11, looked like a prison for a reason. It had to be impervious to any kind of attack. Which it was, so much so that one of the terrorists who was captured after the bombings of the British Consulate and a British bank there told the Turkish authorities that he and his men had originally intended to attack the U.S. Consulate but had found it to be so well secured that, to quote the terrorist himself, "they don't even let birds fly there."

Three men did try to attack the consulate a few years later. All three were shot dead before they even made it to the gate.

"What do you mean?" Reilly asked.

"Well, we can probably retask a Keyhole satellite to pass over the area within the right time frame, but we won't get real-time video or a constant feed. It'll just show us what's going on during the time that it passes over the area with each orbit. And that's not gonna do it for you."

Reilly shook his head. "Nope. We don't know when he's going to show up."

"Better would be to see if we can wrangle one of our UAVs out of Qatar for a constant grid search, but—"

"—he'll spot it," Reilly interjected, shaking his head, nixing the suggestion of using a remote-controlled, unmanned surveillance drone.

"I'm not talking about Predators. I'm talking about the new kids on the block. RQ-4 Global Hawks. Those babies hang out at forty thousand feet. Your guy doesn't have bionic vision, does he?"

Reilly frowned. He didn't like it. "Even with the high altitude . . . This guy knows what he's doing—he knows what they look like. The skies will probably be clear this time of year. He might spot it. Can't we get one of the big birds?"

Like the station chief, Reilly knew the more widely used surveillance satellites—the Keyhole class popularized in movies and on TV—wouldn't do, not in this case. They were more suited to monitoring a location once every couple hours for, say, the construction of a nuclear plant or the appearance of missile launchers. What they couldn't do was provide live, constant monitoring of a fixed location. For that, Reilly needed something the National Reconnaissance Office tried to keep under the radar, so to speak: a surveillance satellite that could maintain a geosynchronous orbit above a fixed point on the Earth's surface and relay live video back in real time. It was a very hard thing to achieve. Satellites drifted away from their positions due to all kinds of perturbations—variations in the Earth's gravitational field in part due to the moon and the sun, solar wind, radiation pressure. Thrusters and complex "station-keeping" computer programs were needed to keep the satellite over its target for extended periods. And as the birds needed to be deployed at an altitude of twenty-two thousand miles to make this possible, they also needed to have exceptionally advanced imaging technology. Which was why they were bigger than a school bus and were rumored to cost more than two billion dollars each—if, that is, they existed at all. And why there weren't enough of them to go around.

The station chief's face crinkled at the request. "Not a chance. With all that's going on out in that idyllic little part of the world, they're constantly fully tasked. It'd be impossible to get hold of one. Besides, I don't think we could even retask one within the time frame you're talking about."

"We need something," Reilly insisted. "This guy's already done some serious damage, and he's intent on causing more."

The station chief spread out his hands appeasingly. "Trust me on this. An RQ-4 will give you what you need, and then some. Our boys in Iraq and in Afghanistan swear by them. More to the point—they're your only option. So I'd say, embrace it and hope for the best."

The station chief was underplaying the Global Hawk's talents. It was an awesome piece of technology. A big aircraft with a wingspan of more than a hundred feet, the unmanned, remote-controlled drone could travel three thousand miles to its target zone, where it would have "long-dwell"—meaning it could spend many hours watching the same spot—and "broad area coverage" capability. It could carry all kinds of imaging cameras and radars—electro-optical, infrared, synthetic-aperture—and relay back images of the target, day or night, no matter the weather. At a unit cost of thirty-eight million dollars, it was a stunningly powerful and cost-effective way of obtaining IMINT—imagery intelligence—without any risk of ending up with a Francis Gary Powers kind of debacle.

The station chief regarded the map of the mountain again. "Now, assuming we get one, we still have some problems to work out. For one thing, there are too many approach routes to keep under watch. The target area's just too big to have a constant fix at any resolution that's useful. Unless we can narrow it down, we'll need to rotate around it. In which case we might miss our target."

"It's all the information we've got right now," Reilly grumbled.

The station chief mulled it over for a beat, then nodded. "Okay. I'll talk to Langley. See if we can get the guys over at Beale to free one up for us pronto."

"We just need it for a day or two," Reilly told him. "But we need it now. No point in having it otherwise."

"We'll bust some balls and get one lined up," the station chief reaffirmed. "But then, we still don't know what we're looking for, do we?"

"Just give me some eyes," Reilly said. "I'll make sure they have something to look for."

HE FOUND TESS IN AN empty interview room, sitting at a table that was swamped by big maps. She had her laptop open beside her and was deep in thought. She only noticed his presence when he was standing next to her, and she looked up at him.

"So?" she asked. "How did it go?"

Judging by the tone of her questions, his funk was clearly visible.

He shrugged. "We can't get the satellite I want, but I think we'll get a surveillance drone. The target area's too big, though. The coverage window won't be as tight as I'd like it to be."

"What does that mean?"

"It means we might miss something," he said, his tone somber and heavy with fatigue. He pulled out a chair and plopped himself into it.

Tess smiled. "Maybe I can help."

Reilly's brow furrowed; then he managed a small grin. "Not a good time to be taunting me with a back rub."

Tess shot him a look. "I'm serious, doofus." She reached for a map of the whole country, laid it on top of the topographic map of Mount Erciyes, and tapped her finger on Istanbul, in the upper left corner. "Take a look."

He moved closer.

"Okay," she began. "Constantinople's up here. That's where Everard and his merry men, the first Templars to visit the monastery, started their journey."

She glanced at Reilly to make sure she had his attention. He gave her a "go on, I'm all ears" nod.

"They were trying to get back to here," she continued, "to Antioch, the nearest Templar stronghold." She pointed out its location, on the Eastern Mediterranean, in present-day Syria. "But, as we know, they only made it as far as here," she said as her finger arced back to the center of the map, "Mount Argaeus, where the monastery is."

"That's just ... astonishing," he ribbed.

"Look at this mountain, you bonehead. It's round. Round like a dormant volcano should be. They could have easily gone around it, right?" She derisively stretched out the word "round" and twirled her finger around the mountain on the map. "It's not like it's a wall or a barrier that they had to cross. And yet, for some reason, they decided to climb up it."

Reilly thought about it for a second. "Doesn't seem reasonable—unless they were trying to stay out of sight."

She grinned with mock admiration. "God, that Quantico training of yours, the way you just see the most obscure connections ... It just boggles the mind, you know that?"

"Well, unboggle yourself and tell me what you're thinking."

Her tone reverted to serious. "Everard and his troupe *were* trying to stay out of sight. They had to. This all happened in 1203, and back then, the Seljuk Turks had taken over a big chunk of this area." Her fingers circled the middle of the country. "So as far as the Templars were concerned, it was enemy territory, teeming with roving bands of Ghazi fanatics. So if they had half a brain cell between them, our little gang of Templars would have definitely wanted to avoid wide-open spaces. Hence sticking to mountain trails, wherever they could find them. Hence the pit stop at the monastery."

"Hang on, a Christian monastery in Muslim territory?"

"The Seljuks tolerated Christianity. Christians were free to practice their faith openly. They weren't persecuted. But this was before the sultans and the Ottoman Empire. This area was like the Wild West, with all these gangs roaming around, looking for blood—kind of like the gangs of Confederate soldiers after the Civil War. They were dangerous, which is why the churches and the monasteries were tucked away in caves and mountains and not just out in plain sight."

"Okay, but that doesn't really help us," Reilly told her. "Once Everard and his people started climbing, they could have gone clockwise or counterclockwise, right? Which means we still have the whole mountain to watch."

"Maybe. But check this out." Now visibly enthused, she brought the mountain-climbing map back out. "Look at the contour lines, here and here." She was pointing out an area just west of the north side of the mountain, kind of at the volcano's eleven o'clock line. "See how tight they are?"

The contour lines that showed the elevation levels—in this case, at regular intervals of fifty meters—had converged and were virtually on top of one another, meaning that area was very steep. In fact, more than steep—it was a vertical drop.

"It's a cliff," Tess explained. Her eyes were ablaze with excitement. "A pretty big one, in fact. They would have seen it as they started heading up the mountain. And they would have had to go the other way—counterclockwise. Which, as it turns out, is the more direct route for them anyway."

Reilly leaned in for a better look, his interest piqued. "What if their approach was from farther east? They would have hit the mountain on the other side of that cliff and gone around it the other way."

"I doubt that," Tess countered. "Look at the area here, north of the mountain. Kayseri's been around for over five thousand years. It was one of the most important Seljuk cities. If our Templars were looking to go unnoticed, they would have steered clear of it too—and given that they were coming from the northwest, they would have skirted around it from the west, maybe through the valleys of Cappadocia, where they would have found good cover with the Christian communities who'd been sheltering in that area's caves and underground cities since the earliest days of the faith. And I did some more digging around, if you'll pardon the pun. This area right here?" She indicated the north-western flank of the mountain. "Very popular with moun-taineers, year-round. I've got to think that if the ruins of the monastery were there, I would have found some men-tion of it on some Web site. And this side, the north face, is where the skiing resort is. Same thing there. The whole face must have been surveyed to death. Someone would have seen it and made a note of it." She framed Reilly with an assured, adrenaline-charged look. "You want a smaller search area? Forget about the right side of the mountain, Sean. Concentrate on the western half."

Reilly studied the map for a beat, then looked up at Tess. "If you're wrong, we'll miss him."

Tess thought about it for brief moment, then nodded. "We might miss him anyway if we need to monitor the whole mountain. I really think it's the right call."

He held her gaze, enjoying the radiance lighting up her face, feeling her enthusiasm and her confidence infuse him. "Okay," he said. "I'll let them know."

Tess smiled, clearly pleased with his response. As he pushed himself out of his chair, she said, "We should be there, you know. Waiting for him."

Reilly turned and was about to say something when she cut him off.

"Don't."

He looked lost. "What?"

"Don't start. With the spiel."

He was genuinely confused. "What spiel?"

"You know, the spiel where you say you're going out there but I should stay here because it's way too dangerous, and I say, no, you need me there 'cause I understand all the Templar mumbo jumbo, then you insist that's not gonna happen, I counterinsist that without me you might miss the one clue that'll lead you to him, then you play dirty and tell me that I should really be thinking about Kim and be a good mom, I get all peeved at you for bringing it up and insinuating I'm a bad mom . . ." A playful, questioning look spread across her face. "Are we really going to do this? Se-riously? 'Cause you know I'm gonna end up coming along anyway, right? You must know that."

Reilly just stared at her, looking baffled, her verbal fusillade still ricocheting inside his skull. Then, without saying anything, he just raised his hand in defeat, turned, and walked off.

She was still grinning as he left the room.

Chapter 26

✠

Jed Simmons drifted back to consciousness with the dry mouth and the grogginess of a big, boozy night out. The sight that gradually fell into focus, though, quickly dispelled any vague illusions that this was the result of anything even remotely enjoyable. He was in the front passenger seat of some kind of SUV that was driving through unfamiliar terrain—vast, sun-soaked plains that seemed to stretch forever. The sensation from his right wrist confirmed the uncomfortable feeling. It was tied to the door's armrest, a plastic snap-cuff anchoring it in place.

The voice of the man in the driver's seat brought the whole nightmare crashing back.

"Wakey wakey," his abductor said. "There's a bottle of water and some chocolate bars in the bag by your feet. You should have some. I imagine you must be feeling pretty dried out right now."

Simmons was too tired—and too angry—to resist. From all the time he'd spent in the desert in Jordan, he knew how crucial it was to remain properly hydrated, for both mind and body, both of which were currently in a lousy state.

He reached down to the bag with his free arm, and as he leaned over, he felt something uncomfortable around his waist, something he hadn't felt before. He looked down and shifted in his seat, checking it out with his free arm, trying to suss out what it might be. There was something there, under his shirt.

He was moving to pull his shirt up when the man said, "The less you disturb it, the better."

Simmons's arm froze. He raised his gaze at his abductor.

The man was just staring at the road ahead, concentrating on the driving, his face impassive as slate.

"What . . . you did this?"

The man nodded.

Simmons was afraid to ask, but the words spilled out of his consciousness, slowly, as if from beyond his control.

"What is it?"

The driver thought about it for a beat, then turned to Simmons and said, "On second thought, maybe you should have a look."

Simmons eyed him for an uncomfortable beat, unsure about whether or not he really wanted to see it, whatever it was. Then his resistance broke and he pulled his shirt up.

He had something on around his waist, just above his trousers. A belt of some kind, a couple of inches or so wide, made up of tough, shiny material, like sailcloth. It seemed innocuous enough—until he pulled out the shirt some more and spotted the padlock that connected two brass eyelets that had been sewn into it and kept the belt locked tight. Then he saw something even more alarming: a bulge, on the front part of the belt. There was something sewn into it, something hard that felt no bigger than a pack of cards. There was no access to it that he could see, no pocket or zipper or Velcro flap. It was embedded inside the belt.

A stab of dread tore through him.

"What is that?" Simmons asked, his temples suddenly pounding outward. "What have you done?"

"It's a small bomb. Nothing fancy. A bit of Semtex and a detonator. Remote-controlled." He pulled out his phone and held it up for Simmons to see, then slipped it back into his pocket. "Just big enough to blow a hole the size of my hand through your belly." He held up his hand, fingers extended as if they were clasping an imaginary baseball, to graphically drive the point home. "If and when it blows up, the odds are it won't kill you instantly. You could live for a minute, maybe even more, and you'll actually be able to see the crater it will have made. Not very pleasant though," his abductor added. "I wouldn't recommend it."

Simmons felt like he was about to throw up. He shut his eyes and tried to take in some air but found that he was having trouble breathing. He couldn't understand what this thing was doing on him, but a meek "Why?" was all he could manage.

"Motivation."

Simmons just stared at him, his mind strangled with fear.

"Motivation to behave," his abductor told him. "We're going to be doing some sightseeing, and I need to make sure you don't do anything stupid. So I'm hoping that the threat of having your guts blown straight out of your back will be a reliable motivator for you to do as you're told. It usually does the trick." He slid a sideways glance at Simmons, seemingly studying his reaction, then added, "Oh, and don't try to undo the buckle. It's locked shut." He smiled. "Just think of it as a chastity belt. To block out any wild urges you might have."

Simmons slumped back in his seat and looked ahead, drowning in despair. The occasional car trundled past in the opposite direction, but there were few vehicles on the road, which was narrow and uneven.

"Where are we going?" he finally asked, not really sure what difference it would make.

"Up to the mountains. I think the fresh air will do you a world of good," the driver replied, a hint of a grin now breaking through. "You look a bit pale."

A flash of recall sparked inside Simmons's mind. "You know where the monastery is?"

"More or less," the man replied, and left it at that.

THE GUIDE WAS WAITING for them at the designated spot, which, as it turned out, wasn't too hard to find. In-car GPS navigation was a great boon, both for avoiding the main roads through Kayseri, in order to evade any potential roadblocks, and for meeting up with someone Mansoor Zahed had never met, in an obscure location he'd never been to.

The route he'd chosen, a detour that added more than an hour to his journey, bypassed the city and approached the mountain from the west, snaking through a few sleepy towns and cutting through the national park and wildlife preserve of the Sultan Marshes before climbing into the rolling foothills that surrounded the rugged, dormant volcano.

The mountain was an imposing sight. Ever since its distant silhouette had first appeared in his windshield, more than an hour earlier, Zahed had found it hard to take his eyes off it, its majestic, postcard-perfect profile looming ever bigger and beckoning him with every mile. Like Kilimanjaro and other dormant volcanoes, it was a free-standing mountain, an immense, flattened cone of rock that presided triumphantly over the flatlands through which it had arisen. And even though it was the height of summer and the temperature readout on the Discovery's dashboard was showing a scorching ninety-five degrees, a crown of snow still embellished its peaks.

He pulled into the meeting place, a tired gas station on the outskirts of the town of Karakoyunlu. The guide, Suleyman Toprak, was waiting there, standing next to a battered Toyota jeep that had evidently spent many years being thrashed around mountain trails on the kind of bone-jarring, off-road excursions for which it had been designed.

Zahed pulled in behind him. He reached into the back of the car and found a handgun, which he tucked into his jacket's pocket, in full sight of Simmons.

He looked at his captive and gave him a stern, cautioning finger, out of view of the guide, who was now approaching their car. "Don't forget to follow the script. Your life—and his," he warned, pointing at the man, "depend on it."

Simmons's jaw muscles tightened visibly; then he gave him a grudging nod.

Zahed studied him for a beat, then said, "Okay," and stepped out of the car.

Toprak, a gregarious man in his late twenties, looked like he'd ridden Doc's DeLorean straight in from Woodstock. He had a thick mane of long, black hair that was parted in the middle and a geometric goatee that looked like it had been chiseled into place. He was in khaki cargo bermudas, a white, collarless shirt that was open down to his navel, and hiking sandals. An array of leather necklaces lurked beneath a luxuriant field of chest hair.

"Professor Sharafi," he called out to Zahed.

Zahed acknowledged him with a small wave and a nod.

"Suleyman Toprak, but you can call me Sully," the guide said with a big, toothy smile and a quasi-American accent that seemed to owe more to watching American television than to any actual time spent stateside. They shook hands.

"Ali Sharafi," Zahed said, his expert eye giving the locale a quick scan. He didn't spot anything out of place. "I'm so glad you were available at such short notice." He'd chosen him out of several local guides who had Web sites touting their services, and booked him before leaving Istanbul.

"I'm glad you called," Sully replied. "This sounds like fun."

Zahed gestured at Simmons. "This is my colleague, Ted Chaykin." Zahed had chosen names that his captive wouldn't easily forget, as per his training, but it still gave him a perverse internal tickle to watch Simmons's reaction to the ones he'd chosen.

The guide said, "Great to meet you both. I hope you had a good drive."

"No problems, except that Ted's got some stomach problems. We had to stop a few times on the way." Zahed grimaced with mock empathy. "He's usually much bubblier than this."

"It happens sometimes." Sully nodded. "Nothing a strong glass of raki won't fix. And fortunately, I keep a bottle in my car. For when we get back, of course." He flashed that big smile again and gave Simmons a conspiratorial wink, then turned to Zahed. "So this monastery you said you were looking for," he asked. "You said you had more information about where it might be?"

Zahed pulled out a small notepad on which he'd written the information that Father Alexios, the grand archimandrite of the library, had found and translated for him shortly before he'd pumped a bullet through the priest's forehead. "We're still looking for more clues, but at the moment, the best thing we have to go on is the journal of a bishop from Antioch who described visiting the monastery back in the thirteenth century."

"Great, just give me a second." He dove into his car and came back holding a large climbing map, which he spread out on the Toyota's hood. "We're here, and this area here is the mountain," he told his new clients, indicating the places on the map.

"Okay, well . . . what we know is this. The bishop describes how he went north, from Sis, which, at the time, was the capital of the Armenian kingdom of Cilicia." Zahed was talking with great nonchalance and assurance, as if this were all second nature to him. "And Sis, as you probably know, is the old name of the city of Kozan."

A flicker of recognition lit up in the guide's eyes. "Kozan. That's here," he said, indicating its position on the map. "About a hundred kilometers south of here."

"Exactly," Zahed continued. "The bishop then visited the fortress of Baberon before crossing into Seljuk territory through the Cilician Gates."

"That's the Gülek Pass, over here." Sully pointed it out. "It's the only easy way to get across the Taurus Mountains."

"Then he says he headed northeast, toward Mount Argaeus, and, I quote, 'ventured into the mountain, past orchards resplendent with apple, quince, and walnut, across pastures strewn with sheep and goats, then across a steep incline and a small forest of poplar trees. We then climbed past a glorious waterfall before reaching the most pious of monasteries, dedicated to St. Basil.'"

The guide's face clouded. He studied the map, his mind visibly scrolling through all the visuals he had experienced over the years. After a moment, he said, "Well, if he was traveling from Baberon, he probably followed this road. It's been a trading route for centuries." He pointed out the area he was referring to on the map. "And on this side of the mountain, I can think of three, even four spectacular waterfalls that he might have been talking about. Same for the trees; there are several pockets of them in this area." His tone lost its bounce. "You don't have anything more?"

"Well, he describes the sunset over the distant horizon,

which tells us that he was somewhere here, on the west-facing ridges of the mountain. But there is something else, an intriguing reference to something he saw along the way," Zahed told him. "Something he describes with highly reverent terms as being a stone from the vessel of the Lord inscribed with crosses and the sign of Nimrod."

"The sign of Nimrod?"

"A diamond," Zahed explained. "Nimrod. From the Hebrew Bible. Noah's great-grandson, the first king after the great flood."

The guide's face lit up. "A big stone with crosses carved into it. From the Ark."

"You know it?" Zahed asked.

Sully nodded to himself as the cogs in his mind fell into place; then his face widened with a smug grin. "Let's go find this monastery of yours." He folded up the map and trotted off to his car. "Follow me, okay?" he shouted back. "We can drive up the first bit."

"Lead the way," Zahed replied. He watched the guide fire up the Toyota's engine, then glanced at Simmons and gave him a satisfied nod. "Let's go find that monastery, 'Ted.'"

Within minutes, the two 4x4s were trundling up the mountain.

Chapter 27

✠

The waters of the Bosphorus shimmered a mesmeric gold under the morning sun as the small jet banked over Istanbul and whisked Reilly, Tess, and Ertugrul out of Europe and into Asia. The aircraft, a sleek, white Turkish Air Force Cessna Citation VII, was ferrying them to the city of Kayseri, bang in the middle of the country, where a unit of Turkish Special Forces would be waiting to take them up into the mountain.

As the aircraft streaked up to its cruising altitude, Reilly took in the receding panorama of domes and minarets with weary eyes that he could barely keep open. He'd lost count of how many cups of coffee he'd drunk in the last twenty-four hours or so, a number that would have to be multiplied by a factor of two or three to take into account the high potency of Turkish coffee. Still, he needed to get some sleep if he was going to be effective in the field op that was coming up.

All three of them had worked late into the night at the consulate, and they'd ended up not bothering with hotel rooms and crashing there instead. Tess had spent her time trying to get a clearer handle on where Conrad and his gang could have been heading, while Reilly and Ertugrul had spent long hours poring over all the local surveillance intel that had come in from both CIA and Turkish sources, looking for anything out of the ordinary that might suggest complicity with the Vatican bomber. Additionally, calls had had to be made to their superiors in New York City as well as to Langley and to Fort Meade, home of the NSA, where chatter was being analyzed and voice intercepts combed for anything that could help answer the one pressing question: how the bomber was getting from Istanbul to his intended destination.

By the time the sun came up, none of it had borne fruit. All they had to go on was the most recent update from the local *polis* telling them what cars had been stolen in and around Istanbul in the last forty-eight hours. Unsurprisingly, there hadn't been that many, given the short time frame. Fifty-seven vehicles were on the list. Reilly and Ertugrul had been able to eliminate more than half of them on the grounds that they wouldn't be suitable for a ten- to twelve-hour drive. They'd then waited while the data was fed into the police's MOBESE information and security network, linking over a thousand surveillance cameras across the city to a license plate recognition and vehicle tracking center. Several of the cars on the hot list had been picked up on video at various locations, and given that Reilly and Ertugrul knew which direction the bomber was headed, they were able to narrow it down even further, to fourteen vehicles of interest. Then, shortly after dawn, word had come in from Air Combat Command that they'd agreed to let them have one of the Global Hawks. It was on the ground at the Al Udeid Air Base in Qatar, in the Persian Gulf, being readied for its sortie, and was expected to be in position over the target area by midmorning. The list of hot cars had been relayed to the drone's controllers in the 9th Reconnaissance Wing at Beale Air Force Base in California, where computers would analyze the drone's video feed for any matching vehicles.

There was nothing more they could do except wait. And hope. And try not to dwell too much on what had happened so far and what mistakes they thought they might have made.

Reilly swung his gaze to the seat facing him. Tess felt it and looked up from her laptop. Even after a virtually sleepless night in the discomfort of a consulate meeting room, the sparkle in her look and the mischievous curl at the edge of her lips was still there. He had to smile, but it was a weak smile that didn't reach his eyes.

Tess caught it. "What is it?"

He was too tired to go into it. Instead, he deflected the question and asked, "Any verdict yet?"

She studied him for a beat, as if debating whether or not to let it go. Then her eyes flicked down to her screen and she said, "I think so. I'm not sure it's enough to help us find Conrad's grave without knowing on what side of the mountain that monastery is, but it might."

"Show me," he asked, leaning forward.

Tess spun her laptop around so he could see its screen, and pointed at the map on it. "In his dying missive, the monk says they said that Conrad and his men were going to Corycus, which is down here, on the coast." She indicated a small town on the south coast of the country. "It's called Kizkalesi today."

"He could have been wrong," Reilly said. "They could have lied to him."

"Maybe, but I don't think so. I mean, it makes sense—they didn't have too many choices. By 1310, the Order had been abolished. They were wanted men in Western Europe, so they couldn't go there. They couldn't head east, either, since the Muslims had taken back the whole coast and torn down their fortresses."

"So where were they going?"

"The only logical place for them to go: back to Cyprus. Conrad probably still had friends on the island. The pope's men weren't powerful there. He could lay low there in relative safety and plan their next move. Which means that wherever they were on that mountain, they'd have to head south, to one of these passes through the Taurus Mountains, to make it to the coast. The question is, which one?"

Reilly nodded, not really focused on what she was saying.

She studied him for a beat, then said, "You freaked me out back there, you know that?"

His face wrinkled. "What are you talking about?"

"Outside the Patriarchate. The way you charged at the guy, the way you stormed off after him like a one-man army ... jumping in the river." She paused, then added, "It's not your fault, Sean."

"What's not my fault?"

"What happened at the Vatican. The bombs and all that. Hell, I'm more responsible for it than you are." She leaned in closer, and tightened her hand around his. "I know you want him. And I want you to wipe that bastard off the face of the earth even more than you do. But you can't keep going ballistic like that. You need to keep your rage in check or you're going to get hurt. And that scares the life out of me. I don't want that to happen."

He nodded quietly. At some level, he knew she was right. He was letting his anger cloud his judgment. Only problem was, with someone like the bomber, Reilly knew that half measures wouldn't be enough. He had to be reckless if he was going to have a chance at taking him down. It was part of the job description. But it was also something about which he didn't necessarily need to keep reminding Tess.

He half-smiled. "It's no big deal, honest. I have had a bit of training in that kind of thing, you know."

Her expression didn't soften. She wasn't buying it. She pulled her hand back. "I'm serious, Sean. I don't want you dying on me. Not here. Not now. Not ever. We've still got a lot to do together, don't we?"

Her comment took him by surprise and made his mind wander back to what they'd been through months earlier. After a moment, he said, "Don't worry. I'm not going anywhere."

A sadness darkened her face. "But I did. I bailed on you. And I'm sorry. I'm really sorry about that. But you understand, don't you? You understand why I had to go, right?"

Sound bites from their parting conversation echoed faintly in his ears. "Has anything changed?"

Tess took in a deep breath and glanced out the window. It wasn't a question she was keen to think about. "What if it doesn't happen for us?" she finally said. "Will we ever be able to really move beyond it, or will it be a hole in your life that I'll never be able to plug?"

Reilly pondered it for a beat, then shrugged. "Given what we do, what's brought us out here again ... It all makes me wonder whether or not we should have even tried."

Confusion and surprise flooded her face. "You're having second thoughts now? About us having a baby?"

"It's probably a moot point now, isn't it?"

"What if it isn't?"

He thought about it for a moment, and surprised himself by realizing he wasn't so sure anymore. "I don't know. You tell me. I mean, this is what we do, isn't it? You, with your long-lost mysteries that seem to bring all kinds of whackos out of the woodwork. Me, with my job, running down guys who get wet dreams about slamming planes into towers. What kind of parents would we have been?"

Tess waved it off. "What are we gonna do, give it all up and play Scrabble every night while sipping chamomile tea? Like you said, this is who we are. It's what we do. And regardless of that, we'd be great parents. I don't doubt that for a second." She gave him a slight grin and tightened her hand around his again. "Look, don't worry about it. You're a guy. You're not supposed to get these things. Just leave that part of it to me, okay? All I need you to do is tell me we can get past it if it doesn't work out for us on that front ... and make sure you don't make yourself too big a target for that creep in the meantime. Deal?"

An acute sense of tiredness overcame Reilly. He nodded with a faint smile, his eyelids now feeling like they were made of lead. "Deal."

Despite her words and despite his exhaustion, images of the carnage at the Vatican kept swooping through the dark recesses of his mind. He shut his eyes and decided that maybe a nap wouldn't be such a bad thing after all. He leaned back against his headrest. But as much as he needed to sleep, it just wouldn't come, and might not for a while, he knew.

Not until the hunt was over.

Chapter 28

✝

Alpine meadows and vast orchards of vine and fruit gave way to a harsher, rockier terrain as Zahed and Simmons followed the guide's battered SUV up the mountain.

The paved road, its tired asphalt fissured and patchy from the big seasonal swings in temperature, was barely wider than their cars. After a couple of miles, it turned into an even narrower path that mules would have a hard time climbing, but none of that seemed to faze the guide. He kept on going, the Toyota's tired diesel engine straining against the bone-rattling incline, its suspension springs stretching and compressing like four big Slinkys, leading them farther up the desolate mountain, until the trail finally came to an end in a small clearing at the foot of a big rock slide.

Sully glanced up at the midday sun, then checked his watch.

"We'll leave the tents and everything else here for now and travel light," he told Zahed and Simmons. "We'll be able to cover more ground that way. But we'll need to be back down here by sunset, which is in about eight hours' time."

"I hope you managed to pick up some hiking gear for us?" Zahed asked.

"I think I've got everything you need." He retrieved a

big duffel bag from the back of his car and handed it to Zahed. "T-shirts, shorts, fleeces, socks, and shoes. Let's go, gentlemen." He smiled. "The mountain's waiting."

ONCE THEY MADE IT UP the narrow path that snaked along the steep rock face that abutted the clearing, they had a relatively easy trek for the first hour, traversing several *yaylas*, the high-altitude meadows that ringed the volcano in a series of undulating hills. Despite the August sun, the air felt more crisp and dry with each new meter of altitude, a marked difference from the humid furnace at the base of the mountain. Scattered herds of animals—sheep, cattle, and the Angora goats the region was famous for—grazed peacefully in the arid grassland, while overhead, flocks of pink rose finches swooped past for a look before resuming their aerial ballet.

Despite the pastoral serenity surrounding him, Zahed was not at ease. Time was draining away, time in which Reilly and the rest of his enemies could pick up his trail and close in on him, and yet here he was, out on a leisurely hike with sketchy information and little more than a hope that the stranger he'd selected hastily knew what he was doing.

Simmons hadn't said much throughout the climb, which was just as Zahed had instructed him to do. Sully, however, much to Zahed's irritation, more than took up the slack, yapping almost nonstop, clearly suffering from another form of diarrhea.

The terrain soon became more challenging as the slope steepened and the meadows gave way to slippery bowls of scree and coarse volcanic rock. High above, a series of jagged rock spires delineated the valley head. Two hours into the climb, the guide suggested they take a break in the shelter of a thicket of trees. He handed them some water bottles and spicy *sujuk* sandwiches, along with some energy bars, all of which they consumed heartily while taking in the breathtaking view.

The Anatolian Plain stretched out far below them, an infinite, striking golden beige plateau that was punctuated by an array of unusual shadows from the late-afternoon sun. Hot-air balloons drifted slowly by, multicolored gumdrops gliding over the distant valleys and the hidden canyons. Even from this distance, one could make out the distinctive features that made the area one of the most unusual—and spectacular—landscapes on the planet.

More than thirty million years ago, during the Cenozoic Era, the entire area had been smothered by volcanic eruptions from Mount Argaeus and a couple of other volcanoes. They'd dumped lava all over it on and off for tens of thousands of years. Once the eruptions had petered out, stormy weather, rivers, and earthquakes all colluded to churn the deposits and turn them into tufa, a soft, malleable stone made up of lava, mud, and ash. Centuries of erosion then carved the plain into valleys and canyons, and lined them with an astonishing landscape of undulating, sensuous rock formations that looked like mammoth dollops of whipped cream, endless fields of massive cones of rock, and "fairy chimneys," strange spires of bone white tufa that looked like asparagus tips topped by gravity-defying caps of reddish brown basalt stone. And if nature's work wasn't phantasmagoric enough, man had added to it by burrowing into the tufa wherever he could. Small holes poked out of rock formations of all shapes and sizes, windows to the most unlikely of human habitations, entire valleys carved into warrens of underground cities, hermit cells, rock churches, and monasteries.

"Beautiful, isn't it?" Sully asked.

"Very," Zahed replied.

The guide took a swig from his canteen and said, "You're from Iran, right?"

"Originally, yes. But my family left the country when I was seven." He lied with ease. It was a profile he'd used before.

"The name of this whole area, Cappadocia," Sully said, "it's originally Persian, you know. *'Katpatuka.'*"

"'The land of beautiful horses,'" Zahed told him.

Sully nodded. "Long ago, they used to be all over the place. Not anymore, though. But it must have been something, to come across wild horses roaming free in a landscape like this." He let his eyes wander over the outlandish terrain below, sucking in slow, deep breaths, then said, "Have you had a chance to explore the valleys?"

"This trip wasn't really planned in advance, and we have to get back to the university very soon."

"Oh, you've got to find some time to do it while you're here," Sully enthused. "It's not like anything you've seen before. It's another planet down there. And it's all because of this monster here," he said, pointing up at the peak of the extinct volcano that loomed over them.

Zahed shrugged with fake chagrin. "We'll try."

Sully nodded; then a cocky grin spread across his face. "You haven't noticed where we're standing, have you?"

Zahed glanced around, unsure of what Sully was talking about. He caught Simmons's eye—the archaeologist was looking up at the trees.

"Poplars," Simmons said. "They're poplar trees."

"Yep." Sully was enjoying this. "And if you'd care to follow me, there's this rock I'd like to show you."

HALF AN HOUR LATER, THEY REACHED IT.

It was a large, upright, rectangular rock, roughly cut to shape like a massive grave marker, about eight feet tall, tucked away in a narrow hanging valley that separated two ridges. Its front had several crosses carved into it, along with a diamond shape in its bottom right corner. Close to its top, a hole of about seven inches in diameter had somehow been drilled through it.

Zahed studied it curiously. "What is it?"

Simmons was also examining it closely. The sight had injected some life back into him. "There are quite a few of these farther east, near the border with Armenia. Some people think they're drogue stones—anchor stones that ancient mariners used to suspend from the backs of their hulls to slow their boats down and make them more stable in stormy seas. But given that we're far inland . . . they think they're from Noah's Ark. Jettisoned before it settled on Mount Ararat." His tone had a tinge of mockery and pity.

"You don't agree?" Zahed questioned.

Simmons gave him a look of quiet surprise. "You really think I would?" He scoffed. "It's almost as if you don't know me, 'Ali.'" That last word had a bite to it.

Before Zahed could play it down, Sully waded in, oblivious to Simmons's little game. "You don't believe in the Ark?"

The archaeologist sighed. "Of course not. The story of the Ark was never meant to be taken literally. It's in the book of Genesis, for God's sake, and . . ." He shrugged, as if he didn't even know where to begin on that one. "This rock, for example. It's basalt. Volcanic. *Local.* And the Ark—according to the Old Testament—was meant to have set off from Mesopotamia. No volcanoes there. And you'd expect drogue stones to be made out of material from the place the ships set out from, not from where they landed, no?"

Sully asked, "So what do you think they are?"

"Pagan stones, from long before Christianity. There are many of them scattered across Armenia and eastern Turkey. The crosses were carved into them much later, when Christianity took over from paganism. This is where the Christian concept of tombstones with crosses carved into them first started. First with the pagans. Then with Christians."

"And the holes?"

"Just niches for lamps."

Zahed scanned the area, then said, "Okay. What about the waterfall?"

"I think I know which one we need," Sully said. "It's the only one that makes sense, given that he passed this way."

IT DIDN'T TAKE TOO LONG for them to reach the waterfall. And an hour after that, they were exploring the ruins of the monastery.

Not that there was much of it left to explore.

After seven hundred years of abandonment, there was little to show that it was anything more than a series of primitive caves, albeit ones with cuboid shapes and with more or less rectangular openings in their walls. An infestation of wild grass and thick, tall bushes shielded the ruins from view, and when Sully, Zahed, and Simmons did manage to cut their way through the overgrowth and enter the rooms of the monastery, there was nothing there beyond bare, cold walls and the ghosts of long-faded murals depicting, they assumed, Biblical scenes.

Still, it was in no way a disappointment. They weren't there to find anything beyond the monastery itself.

They took a breather and huddled on some boulders on a ridge outside, at the head of the steep rocky incline that led up to the ruins. In the late-afternoon sky overhead, a lone buzzard circled around lazily, hitching a ride on a thermal, while down below, the valleys had shifted to a brooding panorama of purples and grays. Sully was using the fold-out blade of his multitool to cut pieces of pistachio *helva* that he was handing out to his clients. His map was back, spread out beside him. He'd already marked the position of the monastery on it.

"So now you need to follow another set of directions from here?" he asked Zahed in between mouthfuls.

"Yes. The directions of a traveler who passed through here in the fourteenth century." He pulled out a folded piece of notepaper and handed it to Sully. On it were the details of the inquisitor's journey that Simmons had harvested from the Templar Registry. "We need to find the canyon he was talking about."

Sully glanced at the sheet, then looked up at Zahed. "What is this all about anyway?" A cheeky grin broadened across his face, like he was on to them. "Are you guys on some kind of treasure hunt?"

Zahed chortled. "A treasure hunt? Do we look like treasure hunters to you?" He turned to Simmons, pointing mirthfully at Sully, shaking his head and laughing off the suggestion. "You watch too many movies, my friend."

Simmons dredged up a weak laugh that didn't reach his eyes.

"What then?" Sully prodded. "I mean, why the rush?"

"We didn't expect to be here. We're putting the finishing touches to a book about the Crusades, and these graves could prove some knights survived out here longer than we assume, which would contradict things we've said in the book. But as we're on a budget, we can't stay here forever. We're due back at the university in two days."

Sully looked crestfallen. "So there's no treasure?"

Zahed shrugged. "Sorry. But we'll be happy to send you an autographed copy of our book."

"That would be great." Sully smiled, clearly trying not to sound too crestfallen. He then dropped his eyes to the note Zahed had given him and studied it, his gaze flicking across to the map and back, his mind consumed by the challenge.

After a long moment, he seemed to reach a verdict. "The description is a bit vague to be sure of anything, but given what's in here . . . if I had to guess, I'd say they were trying to get to the Gülek Pass, the mountain pass that the bishop also took on his journey north. It was the only way to get across the Taurus Mountains. Which means the canyon he's talking about is south of here, in this area." He circled the area he was referring to on the map. "But there are lots of canyons there. I can't say which one of them it might be, assuming I've got the first part right, without making that journey and following in his footsteps."

Zahed nodded thoughtfully. "Then that's what we need to do. First thing tomorrow." He paused, then grinned and added, "We've got to beat the other treasure hunters to it."

Sully chuckled. "Not a problem," he replied; then his face lit up with an idea. "You know what? Let me call my uncle, Abdülkerim. He's a Byzantinist—he used to be a professor at a university in Ankara. He now works as a tourist guide. You'll like him. He lives down in Yahyali, which is near the canyons I'm talking about. He knows them better than anyone, and if anyone can help us figure it out, he can." He pulled out his cell phone, glanced at it briefly, then seemed to remember something. "Damn, I forgot," he said, holding up his phone with a sheepish look on his face. "There's no signal up here."

Zahed's nerves went as taut as steel cables. He knew where those words would resonate, and glanced across at Simmons.

The eruption in the archaeologist's eyes was all the confirmation he needed.

Chapter 29

✛

No cell phone signal. The comment set Simmons's neurons on fire.

No cell phone signal.

No detonator.

No bomb.

It was now or never—even more so as he saw his abductor's right hand dive into his rucksack, where Simmons knew he'd stashed a handgun.

"He's got a gun," he yelled as he launched himself at Zahed.

He reached him just as the weapon made its appearance and thrust his left hand out at the hand gripping it while bending his right arm and aiming his elbow at his opponent's face. His hand clamped down hard on the Iranian's right wrist and shoved the gun away, flicking it off-target just as a wild round detonated out of it. Its roar exploded in Simmons's eardrums and reverberated up the cliff behind them, but it didn't slow down his right elbow, which connected with the shooter's face a split second later. Zahed's training came into play and he managed to avoid the worst of the blow by lunging backward, but the archaeologist's taut forearm still plowed into the Iranian with a sickening crunch that lit up Simmons's shoulder. The momentum of the collision caused them both to tumble off the boulder,

Simmons hanging on to Zahed's gun hand and fighting him for the weapon, the two of them twisting over each other and sliding backward before hitting the ground.

The Iranian's head slammed back heavily against the loose rocks that littered the top of the incline, causing him to howl with pain—and loosening his fingers' lock on the handgun. Simmons, still half-deaf from the gunshot, saw his opening and took it. With both hands now gripped around Zahed's wrist, he raised it off the ground and pounded it back down, once, twice, again, hammering the back of the Iranian's hand against the shards of rock, blood spurting out from it, until he saw the man's grip weaken—and felt an eruption of pain in his right flank where Zahed's balled fist had just impacted with the force of a pile driver. The blow was staggering. Simmons grunted out loud as he fought to keep control of his hold long enough for one last hit—which he just managed, but in yanking Zahed's wrist too violently, he inadvertently sent the gun flying off and skittering down the rocky slope behind the Iranian.

Simmons's heart stopped as he glimpsed it tumble out of reach, his nails now clawing into Zahed's wrist, pinning it down against the scree, his mind reeling with confusion as to what to do next. He saw Sully's shocked face looming down on him from higher up and yelled out, "Do something. Help me get the g—"

Pain lit up his chest and brought the air in his lungs gushing out as Zahed landed another blow, this time using the heel of his free palm. Simmons jerked back, gasping for breath, his rib cage feeling as if someone had filled it with napalm and torched it. As he toppled back, Zahed rose in tandem, curling upright and lunging at Simmons with a bloodcurdling scream of pure fury. His fingers darted at Simmons's throat like the fangs of a cobra, tightening around it with brutal strength. Simmons twisted his head left and right, trying to escape the Iranian's death grip, his arms flailing wildly and landing insignificant, puppet jabs at the shooter. Zahed had Simmons's head pinned down sideways now, crushing his left eye against the jagged edges of the gravel, squeezing the life out of him. Simmons felt his vision darken as the last vestiges of strength seeped out of him, and in that moment, he figured this was maybe a better way to go than watching his insides drain out of a huge hole in his belly—then something called out to him, something on the ground within reach, a stone, the size of a mango, just sitting there in that sideways angle of vision, offering him salvation. He'd almost lost all feeling in his arms by then, but somehow he managed to swing his arm over to it, coax his fingers to tighten around it, and will his muscles to give him one last swing.

The blow struck Zahed just below his ear, rattling him hard enough to cause his lips to judder out of sync with the rest of his head and send spit and blood spewing to one side. Simmons wheezed, his lungs desperate for air, and he lashed out with both arms, shoving the Iranian off him. Zahed fell back, onto his side, then snorted in a big gulp of air, shaking his head, his eyelids half-shut, his hand coming back from the wound dripping with blood. Then his eyes popped back open and locked on Simmons with a rage so primal, like nothing the archaeologist had ever witnessed before—and he was pushing himself to his feet like he was possessed.

Simmons bolted upright, breathing hard, alarms blaring inside his head and telling him he shouldn't stick around and chance another mano a mano, not with this guy.

Telling him to get the hell out of there while he could.

He scrambled up the boulders to rejoin Sully, who was still standing there, transfixed, his face glistening with an outbreak of sweat, his eyes alight with a combination of horror and confusion. Sully started to mouth, "What are you d—"

But his words dried up as he saw that Simmons wasn't listening. The archaeologist's mind was locked on one thought, his eyes scouring the ground frantically, desperate to find it—and then he spotted it, where he'd last seen it. Still in Sully's hand.

The multitool.

"Give me your knife," he rasped, and without waiting for an answer, he lunged at the guide and snatched it from him. He looked around, getting his bearings, then sensed movement to his side and turned to see Zahed clambering up the boulders to rejoin them.

The Iranian had something in his hand. His handgun. The bastard had managed to retrieve it.

"Run," he yelled to the guide, grabbing him by his collar and yanking him down the rock-strewn incline and away from the monastery.

ZAHED'S HEAD WAS STILL RINGING from the blow, but he knew how to bury the pain until he had completed what he had set out to do. He wasn't about to let some pissant archaeologist mess up his plans. The man would be brought to heel. He'd teach him a lesson in respect and make sure he never forgot it.

But he had to get to him first.

He made it onto the last boulder in time to see the archaeologist scurrying down the slope about a hundred yards away, his feet struggling for purchase in the loose rocks. The guide was close behind him, but less assured in his movement. Something else, too—he was wasting time by looking over his shoulder repeatedly, wary of Zahed coming after them. Unlike Simmons, this was all new to Sully; it had hit him completely unexpectedly, and there was still a slight uncertainty about what was going on, an infinitesimal hesitation inside him, that was holding him back just slightly.

The hesitation was all Zahed needed.

The Iranian snatched his rucksack, shoved his gun into it, and slung it over his shoulder as he barreled after them, his eyes scanning the ground ahead and making sure to select the perfect footings for him as he hurried down the rocky incline. His mind was locked on the immediate essentials of the task at hand—making sure he didn't trip and twist an ankle, keeping his breathing deep and sharp to keep his energy up, assessing his enemies' changing positions and making microadjustments to his heading to gain precious seconds on them.

It was working.

He gained ground with every stride as his quarry scampered across a track of loose gravel before traversing diagonally down a steep hillside to reach a broad, grassy ridge. By now, Sully had fallen behind Simmons by about ten yards or so—and when he twisted around for another glance, Zahed was close enough to see the fear in his eyes. The sight gave him a boost of adrenaline that lit up his legs like an afterburner and soon brought the guide within reach.

He tackled his first target in a steeply angled scree bowl. They rolled down the slope, with Zahed's arms clutched around Sully's neck. He kept them in place until they reached the bottom of the slope, where Zahed adjusted the positions of his hands quickly—grabbing hold of Sully's head with a tight, clawed grip—then twisted them around in one savage wrench to snap the guide's neck. It gave way instantly in a loud crack of bone and cartilage, his head sagging to one side as his lifeless body toppled to the ground.

Zahed didn't waste any time. He gave Sully's pockets a quick frisk, found the guide's phone, and stuffed it in his own pack. He also took the man's keys and his wallet. Then he glanced around, saw an outcropping of rocks a dozen or so yards away, and grabbed hold of the dead man's ankles and dragged him over to a position where he wouldn't be easily spotted. The precious seconds would put more distance between him and Simmons, but he was confident he would still reach him in time, and given that he still had a lot of unfinished business in Turkey, it was best not to leave dead bodies lying too far out in the open.

Then he resumed his chase.

Simmons was a small silhouette in the distance by then, but it was enough. Zahed wasn't in that much of a rush to catch up with him. They were still hours from where they'd left the cars, and the faster they got down there, the better, as far as he was concerned. He just needed to keep Simmons in sight and motivate him to keep going as fast as he could, which he managed to do by stalking him from a safe enough distance.

After about an hour of doing this, Zahed felt it was time to pounce. Simmons had slowed down and was moving awkwardly, and the Iranian guessed what he was up to.

He caught up with him by a narrow scree col at the head of a valley. Simmons saw him appear and stopped running. He was bent over with the tool in his hand, sawing desperately at the bomb belt, trying to cut it off.

Zahed just stood there and watched him from about ten yards away, breathing in deeply, slowing his heart rate back down, wiping his brow.

Simmons looked up, panting. His hand's movements quickened as he sawed more frantically.

It wasn't working. The cloth was too strong.

"I wouldn't bother," Zahed yelled out to him. "It's made of sailcloth. Kevlar sailcloth. You can't cut through it. Not with that, anyway."

Simmons glared over at him, sweat streaking down his face, fear glistening in his eyes. He collapsed onto his knees, his hands working harder still, desperately trying to cut through the fabric.

"Besides," Zahed said as he pulled out his phone and glanced at it, "guess what?" He held the phone face-front at Simmons, knowing the archaeologist was too far away to read its screen, but enjoying the taunt. "I've got a signal again."

Simmons looked at him, breathless, his face contorted in exhaustion and despair.

"It's up to you," Zahed called out. "You want to live? Or are you ready to pack it all in?"

Simmons shut his eyes and didn't move for an agonizing moment. Then, without looking up, he let the knife tumble out of his hand. It clinked against the scree. He didn't move, didn't look up. He just stayed there, immobile, slumped, his head drooped, his chin tucked in against his chest, his arms tightening around his waist, his entire body trembling.

"That's a good boy," Zahed said as he walked right up to him. He stood there, like a bullfighter looming over his downed prize—then he flicked his hand out and gave Simmons a ferocious backhanded slap that lifted the archaeologist off the ground and sent him plowing into the gravel.

Chapter 30

✠

"This is Hawk Command. Pullback will be in just under thirty minutes."

The voice of the drone's controller boomed through Reilly's wireless earpiece with a clarity that belied the fact that the man with the joystick was sitting comfortably several thousand miles away, in the rolling hills of northern California. His words didn't come as a surprise. The drone had been circling overhead throughout the night. Its dwell was long, but it wasn't indefinite—and the bird still had a long flight home.

Reilly frowned. "Copy that," he responded. "Hang on." He pulled his eyes off the two small orange blobs on the screen of his laptop and across to the burly commando huddled a few feet away from him and Ertugrul. "How much longer till we go?" he asked, his voice cautiously low.

Captain Musa Keskin of the Turkish Gendarmerie's Special Forces Unit—the Özel Jandarma Komando Bölüğü—checked his watch and looked up into the night sky. Dawn was close. The sun would have to scale the summit of the big mountain that was facing them before they'd see it, but its glow would suffuse the area long before then. A stocky man, Keskin had a tree stump for a neck and forearms that would have driven Popeye into a jealous tizzy. He gave Reilly an "almost there" nod, then flashed him an open-palmed, five-minute signal before turning and giving his men the same gesture.

Reilly nodded, and looked up into the murky distance. "We're going in five," he told the controller.

"Copy that. And good luck," the voice said. "We'll be watching."

Reilly felt a quiver of anxiety. They were there more out of a lack of other options than out of any certainty that they were in the right place. Before the sun had set several hours ago, the drone had picked up a vehicle that matched the description and color of a car that had been reported stolen in Istanbul a day earlier. Just as important, it hadn't spotted any other vehicle in the target area that matched anything on the list Reilly and Ertugrul were given. Because of the terrain, the drone hadn't been able to get a fix on the car's license plates in order to confirm things either way, but the vehicle, a black Land Rover Discovery, was parked alongside another SUV in the foothills of the volcano, in an area that wasn't usually frequented by climbers and in the quadrant that Tess had thought was most likely to be the right one. It wasn't any kind of confirmation that they had a bead on their target—but it was all they had.

The Vatican bomber—if indeed it was him—had made it tough for them to get a better look. There was no way for a sniper or a spotter to get eyes on whoever was up there. The two SUVs were parked in a small clearing that backed up against a big rock face, which effectively cut off any chance of getting a visual from the back or from most of the sides without risking alerting him to their presence. The only imagery they had to work with was infrared and thermal and coming down to them from thirty thousand feet overhead via the unmanned drone's operators at Beale Air Force Base.

The clearing's location had also made things difficult for them. The only way to reach it was up a narrow, winding, rock-strewn mule path that pretty much nuked any chance of sneaking up unannounced. The engine noise of their vehicles would give them away long before they reached it. Reilly, Ertugrul, and the Turkish paramilitary squad had been forced to leave their vehicles—and Tess—almost a mile down the road and hike the rest of the way up. They were now in the cover of a thicket of basswood saplings and wild bush at the edge of a small *yayla*, a couple of hundred feet and slightly downhill from the clearing.

The two orange blobs on Reilly's screen weren't moving. Judging by their oblong shapes, they seemed to be lying down, asleep, which was hardly surprising, given the time. A long-distance directional microphone wasn't picking up any chitchat or snoring. The question was, who were they? Was one of them the target, or were they just a couple of civilians sleeping under the stars? And if one of them was the bomber, who was the other? Simmons? Or the owner of the second SUV? In which case, where was Simmons?

The plan was to go just before sunrise. Use the advantage of having the right gear, the Hawk circling overhead, while knowing that if things didn't work out as planned, daylight wasn't far off. Reilly glanced around him. The men of the Özel Tim were making their final preparations, checking their weapons and adjusting the straps on their night vision goggles. There were sixteen of them altogether—three down the road with Tess, the others, under Keskin's command, up there with Reilly and Ertugrul. They had all come from the military and were specially trained in antiguerrilla warfare. They were well equipped and heavily armed, and from what Reilly had seen so far, they seemed to know what they were doing.

Reilly tried to release the knot of tension at the back of his neck. He told himself that things were looking up. If his guy was up there, the son of a bitch was cornered, outnumbered, and seriously outgunned. But he might have a hostage. And, Reilly knew, that kind of thing rarely worked out without some kind of wrinkle.

He caught Keskin's eye. The burly man nodded, raised a bullhorn, and aimed it at the two SUVs up ahead.

"*Dikkat, dikkat,*" the captain bellowed. Attention, attention. "You, up there by the cars," he called out in Turkish. "This is the Jandarma. You are surrounded. Come out with your hands where we can see them." He repeated it, then said it again in a heavily accented, broken English.

Reilly peered out into the darkness, then dropped his

eyes back to his screen. The ghostly, orangey shapes on it sprang to life. They moved around by the vehicles, merging into each other and splitting up again like molecules in a petri dish. The veins in his neck hardened as he tried to picture what was going on up there. Seconds turned to a minute; then Keskin raised his bullhorn and sounded out his warning again.

The shapes stayed merged for a tense moment, the better part of another minute. Keskin glanced over at Reilly and Ertugrul, his hard features brimming with confidence.

"If they were just regular civilians up there, they would have shouted back," he told them. "I think it's your man."

"The question is, who's up there with him?" Reilly asked. "Is it Simmons or an accomplice?"

"Either way, he can have us believe it's a hostage," Ertugrul noted. Addressing the captain, he asked, "How do you want to play this?"

"We'll give them another minute or so, no more. Then we'll hit them with stun grenades and go in." He turned to one of his men and fired off some crisp words in Turkish. The man nodded and slipped away quietly, gesturing to his men to get ready.

Reilly turned to his screen. The figures were still one, still in the same position, behind the Discovery. Then they started moving, gliding around the back of the car—then they detached. One of them remained behind the SUV; the other stopped momentarily, then headed out. Into open ground.

Reilly raised his night vision binoculars as clipped shouts burst out around him. He saw a lone figure appear behind the Discovery, a pale green silhouette in a sea of black. He squinted to allow his focus to adjust. The figure now definitely looked like it was a man. He was walking toward them, slowly, his gait reluctant. Reilly flicked a glance down at his screen. The other orange blob was still behind the Discovery, but it had edged to the very back of the car.

"Who is it?" Ertugrul asked as he also tracked the man's approach through infrared binoculars.

"Not sure yet," Reilly replied, his eyes locked on the figure.

The man started down the narrow path that led to them. The lenses' 3.5 magnification range now allowed for a clear ID. His face came into view, the long hair, the athletic build.

"Hold your fire," Reilly hissed. "It's Simmons."

A few brief commands in Turkish bounced down the line of paramilitaries. Simmons was now barely fifty yards away, and Reilly could see him more clearly. He was wearing a Windbreaker and had his arms behind his back, and as he swung around to have a look behind him, Reilly could see that they were heavily tied with duct tape. He also had a side strip of tape around his mouth.

The other blob was still huddled behind the Discovery.

Simmons was about thirty yards away when Keskin barked another order. A half dozen men in camouflage fatigues, black balaclavas, and night vision goggles surged from behind trees and boulders and converged on him. They grabbed hold of him and hustled him back to safety.

Reilly kept his eyes lasered on Simmons. The archaeologist seemed totally distressed, in a panic even, twisting around, shaking his head sideways, struggling against the commandos, a muffled, high-pitched wail coming from behind the tape.

A loud siren started blaring inside Reilly's head.

Why is he struggling like that? Why isn't he jumping for joy?

Then his gaze dropped to the thin Windbreaker Simmons was wearing, how it was zipped all the way up, how it seemed much puffier than he'd have expected it would be on that ripped kitesurfer's torso.

Oh shit.

A rush of blood flooded his brain and he bolted up, waving wildly, shouting out at the top of his lungs, "No, get away from hi—"

And Simmons blew up.

Chapter 31

✠

The night went bright with a flash of searing light that obliterated everything from view a nanosecond before the blast wave hit Reilly. It punched the wind out of him and wrenched him off his feet, flinging him back into the gravel-strewn ground. In the blink of an eye, all of his sensory inputs were shut down and he was plunged into a dark and silent bubble.

It wasn't the small belt charge.

That one would have only killed Simmons and wouldn't have hurt anyone else unless they happened to be lying on top of him.

No, this was entirely different.

This was thirty-odd pounds of plastic explosive strapped around the archaeologist's waist. A proper, full-bore suicide bomber's rig. And the effect was devastating.

As he stirred to consciousness, Reilly felt as if his ears had been turned inside out. He couldn't hear anything apart from his own ragged breathing, and he felt heavy-headed and unbalanced, as if he were lost deep underwater and couldn't tell which way was up. His eyes were having trouble focusing, but from the vague shapes drifting into view, he figured that he was on his back. He tried to move his arms and legs, but they wouldn't respond at first. He gritted his teeth and found the strength to roll slowly onto his right side, wanting to check and make sure none of his limbs were missing, but not wanting to discover that wasn't the case. He lifted his hands and saw that at least they were both still there. His hand settled on the handgun in his holster for a split second before he realized the weapon was burning hot and quickly pulled it back.

He propped himself up on one elbow and looked out.

The mountain had turned into a vision of Hell.

The trees around him were ablaze, spewing acrid black smoke, which stuck uncomfortably in his throat. Screams and moans reverberated around him. Through the haze, he glimpsed strewn body parts littering the scree—an arm, a leg sticking out of a stray boot. Injured commandos were sprawled on the ground, cradling their wounds, calling out for help. The explosion had shredded Simmons's body to bits before ripping through the commandos who were escorting him back to safety. Every bone in his body, even his wristwatch and his belt buckle—it had all been smashed into superheated shrapnel that burst out and sliced through any flesh that stood in its way.

Reilly's eyes roamed around the carnage and the chaos, then fell on a couple of bodies on fire by the trees, the air thickening with the sickly smell of their burning flesh. One of them was still alive, moving slowly in a flaming death-crawl. Then he spotted Ertugrul, closer to him, a dozen yards or so to his left. He was on the ground, sitting up, motionless and soundless, looking over at Reilly with a shocked, confused stare, his right hand on his cheek, his fingers inching their way up toward a big hole in his skull, a shrapnel wound that was spewing blood.

"*Vedat*," Reilly mouthed, but the word caught in his throat and he coughed. He tried to push himself to his feet to help him, faltered, then attempted it again and managed to get up—which was when two things happened.

First, more explosions went off nearby, smaller detonations, but still loud and potent enough to send him reeling backward. He realized they were grenades that the commandos had on them, blowing up as the flames licked them.

Then he heard the distant wail of a car engine. Coming straight at him.

He stumbled forward and turned, his mind still frazzled, not sure what to make of the noise, feeling a trickle of blood now oozing from his left ear and down the side of his neck. Through the smoke, he glimpsed the grille of the Discovery, glinting from the flames, hurtling down the mule path, its engine screaming. He saw a lone commando rush toward the SUV from the driver's side, his weapon raised, unleashing a torrent of bullets on the Discovery—then he saw an arm gripping a handgun dart out of the car's window and heard a trio of sharp gunshots slice the air just as the commando faltered and crashed to the ground, face-first.

The Discovery was bearing down on him, now so close his eyes could fill out the Iranian's features through the dark windshield. Reilly shook his head and tried to breathe in some air, focusing on what he was doing there, on who was in that car, on how much he wanted him dead. He was reaching for his gun when a figure burst out in front of him, the Özel Tim commander, Keskin. The man was covered in blood and limping, with a telltale crater in his thigh and another in his shoulder, but he seemed impervious to the pain, like he was on crack. He had a haunted look in his eye and an automatic in his hand and was lurching right into the path of the onrushing SUV.

Keskin stopped and raised his weapon, adjusting his aim—

Reilly stared in dazed disbelief as the arm darted out again from the car's side window, only this time it was aimed forward—

"No," Reilly yelled out—

—and bolted toward Keskin, feeling the big man's body shudder from the impact of the bullets just as he tackled him from the side and shoved him out of the Discovery's path. The two of them hit the ground hard just as the black SUV plowed through the very spot they'd been standing in and thundered down the mule track and out of view.

Reilly was winded and felt himself teetering on the edge of consciousness. Through foggy eyes, he glanced at Keskin. The man was staring back, his eyes wide-open, blood gurgling out of his mouth. Reilly felt an impotence and a primal rage he'd never experienced before, a cauldron of hate roiling deep within him. He felt any strength remaining inside him drain away, and the thought of passing out and falling into a dark sleep seemed like an attractive one until one word burst through his daze and his fury and reminded him of who was in the bomber's path.

Tess.

TESS HEARD THE EXPLOSION AND JUMPED.

This wasn't part of the game plan. Worse—it was too big, far bigger than anything she imagined the weaponry she'd seen Reilly and the commandos take up with them could sound like. Which meant that it was someone else's doing. And that didn't sound good at all. Not when you considered how handy the man they were chasing was with explosives.

She switched off the flashlight she was using to study the map of the area that she'd brought with her and looked up the mountain. Seconds stretched out torturously; then more explosions followed. Smaller ones, different, more muffled, like thuds—but explosions nonetheless, echoing across the hills. Then came some scattered gunfire, and by now Tess was crippled with fear. It sounded like Iwo Jima up there.

The commandos around her were as startled as she was. They exchanged nervous words in Turkish that she couldn't understand, though their body language said plenty. They didn't know what was going on either. One of them reached for his walkie-talkie and, in a controlled tone, radioed the others. No reply came back. He tried again, this time with more alarm in his voice. Still nothing.

Then came the distant groan of a diesel engine, straining as it fought to slow the heavy SUV down the steep incline. Tess couldn't see any lights coming down the mountain then in the faint glimmer of moonlight, she saw a dark, boxy shape swerve down a hairpin before disappearing from view. The commandos saw it too and went into action mode, readying their weapons and flipping down the lenses of their night vision goggles as they shouted out to one another. One of them grabbed Tess with his free arm and hustled her back to safety, behind a Cobra light-armored vehicle, positioning himself to shield her. The others ducked behind the two Humvees that were also parked there, and waited.

More nerve-racking seconds followed, the engine's growl rising and falling as the SUV snaked down the mountain—then it appeared. A dark shape, heading toward them.

The commandos hesitated, unsure about whether or not to fire—then the car's headlights suddenly came on, high beams, full blast.

Blinding.

They tore their goggles off, but their retinas were already seared, and in the precious seconds it took for them to adjust, they were exposed. Bullets quickly tore into one of the commandos, sending him snapping sideways like he'd been whipped. More rounds punched into the Humvee the other soldier was using for cover, biting into its panels and punching through its canvas cover.

Tess huddled low and covered her ears as the commando protecting her kept leaning out and firing quick bursts from his MP5 machine gun. His rounds took out one of the SUV's headlights and drilled into its front grille, but it kept on coming, turning now so it was headed at the Humvee. It clipped the front left side of the wide jeep and sent it arcing right, slamming into the second soldier and knocking him to the ground. Moving with uncanny speed and precision, Zahed slammed on the brakes, burst out of the SUV and around its back, and pumped two bullets into the downed commando.

A shriek of anguish accompanied each shot, followed by haunting groans of agony. Tess spun her gaze to her guardian, unsure of what to make of it at first; then she understood. The bomber hadn't killed the commando. He was toying with his victim, killing him one piece at a time to goad any remaining opponents and unsettle them. What he didn't know was there was only one man left.

One man, and Tess.

The moans went on for the better part of a minute, then died out. The clearing was quiet now, except for the clicking of the idle diesel engine. Tess looked to her guardian for guidance. He raised a finger to his mouth, then edged sideways for a peek. Tess swallowed hard and pressed back against the cool hull of the armored carrier. She glanced down and suddenly became very conscious of the high ground clearance of the vehicle, and edged closer to the commando, both of them now tucked in behind one of its big, donutlike tires. Her protector was looking out, his brow furrowed with concentration, a lone bead of sweat glistening in the faint light, inching slowly down the side of his face.

He looked as scared as she was—then a metallic snap cut through the silence, followed by the sound of something spinning through the air.

The commando's eyes instantly went wide with recognition. He grabbed Tess and threw her to the ground, throwing his body on top of hers, pressing her down. Whatever flew over them landed in the loose gravel beyond the Cobra and bounced a couple of times with a metallic clinking noise before exploding. The soldier knew what pulling a clip out of a grenade sounded like, but it had been thrown too far to cause them damage. Then Tess saw booted feet rush up to them, felt the commando scramble off her, and heard the bullets slam into him and punch him down to the ground.

The bomber hadn't wanted to kill them with the grenade. He only needed the distraction.

Tess looked up.

He was looming over her, his eyes darting down at her while scanning the surroundings for any remaining threats. Tess knew there weren't any left.

He picked up the dead commando's submachine gun and told her, "Get up."

His voice was as she remembered it. Dry, monotone, devoid of any trace of emotion.

She pushed herself to her feet, her arms and legs trembling at the sight of the same man who'd kidnapped her in Jordan and stuffed her into the trunk of a car alongside a big wad of explosives. And now here she was, in the middle of nowhere, alone with him. At his mercy.

Again.

Hoping he wasn't about to utter the last words she ever wanted to hear from him.

No such luck.

"Let's go," he told her.

She thought of running, thought of lashing out at him for everything she knew he'd done, but she knew it would be pointless. Instead, she let him lead her to the Discovery and watched helplessly as he pumped several rounds into the tires of the Humvees and the Cobra to ground them. She got into the passenger seat beside him, and said nothing as they pulled away from the kill zone and drove off into the Anatolian night.

Chapter 32

✠

Just getting up onto his feet was a titanic effort. Reilly felt like a boxer who'd been knocked down one time too many and could do nothing else but hug the canvas and ride out the count. But he couldn't stay down. Not while Tess was out there.

He managed to push himself upright. All around him, small fires were blazing, lighting up a macabre tableau of suffering. The acrid stench of death shrouded the scorched earth near him. Keskin was still there, by his feet. The beefy commando wasn't moving anymore.

Reilly fought to regain some kind of focus in his mind, to order his frazzled thoughts into some kind of coherent plan. He spotted Ertugrul around thirty yards from him. The legat was flat on his back and wasn't moving either. Beyond him, Reilly could see a couple of commandos who seemed uninjured and were tending to the wounded. He started toward them, hoping they were in radio contact with their comrades down the hill, the ones who had stayed behind with Tess. Then he remembered his own comm set and instinctively brought his hand up to his ear. His wireless headset was gone, no doubt blown away by the blast. He felt his pockets, but his transmitter wasn't there either. He paused and dropped his gaze to the ground, scanning the rough soil for it, but quickly decided that was pointless.

He'd moved around since the first explosion, and there was little hope of spotting the transmitter in the darkness. He staggered across the clearing again, toward the commandos, and stopped when he got to Ertugrul. A large patch of blood had darkened the soil around the legat's head, and it didn't look like he was breathing. He was just staring out into nothing, without blinking. Reilly bent down beside him and put two fingers to his neck. Ertugrul's carotid artery wasn't throbbing. He was gone.

Reilly set his hand on the fallen agent's shoulder and exhaled heavily. He glanced around through seething eyes, the frustration pinning him down. Then he saw it, shimmering in the flames, a few feet behind Ertugrul's body: the legat's earpiece. He got back on his feet and retrieved it, and held it up with trembling fingers that were caked with blood and mud. It seemed intact. He clipped it onto his ear, hoping it was still working, and with a hoarse, faint voice, muttered, "Hawk Command? Come in, Hawk Command."

The controller's voice thundered back. "Jesus Christ, what the hell happened out there? You okay?"

"I'm okay, but Ertugrul's dead," Reilly said. He was back with the legat now, rummaging through his pockets, looking for the dead man's transmitter and feeling like a vulture. "Others too. It's bad. Real bad. We're going to need medevacs. You need to get them here now."

"Copy that. Hang on," the controller said. "I'm handing you over to my CO."

"Wait," Reilly interrupted. "The bird. Is it still here?"

"Affirmative. Pullback is in seven minutes."

Reilly shut his eyes tight, blocking out the carnage around him, trying to keep his mind focused. "The target vehicle. Are you tracking it?"

"Affirmative. It traveled down the mountain just after the blast. What was that?"

Reilly knew the explosion would have registered as a big flash on the drone's infrared sensors, but chose to ignore the question. "And then what? Where did it go?"

"It reached the detachment at the bottom of the hill and

it looks like it crashed into one of the Humvees. One person got out of it. We're assuming that's your target, correct?"

Reilly's insides tightened. "Then what?"

"We're assuming an exchange of gunfire. There was some movement. We're showing three friendlies down."

The tightening turned into a garrote as his mind raced through its cache, trying to remember how many commandos had stayed back with Tess. "Three? You're sure of that?"

"Affirmative. Then two figures got back into the target vehicle and it drove off."

Two figures. Reilly's heart flared. "Where is it now?"

"Hang on." After a brief moment, the voice came back. "It's about four clicks south of your position, heading toward a town called Cayirozu."

"Keep tracking it as long as you can. I think our target's got Tess Chaykin with him and—"

The controller interrupted, his tone distant and robotic. "Pullback's now in under five—"

"Stay on them, do you hear me?" Reilly rasped. "Don't lose them. And get through to the Jandarma's command and give them their position. I'm going after them." His fingers found Ertugrul's transmitter. He pocketed it, took one last look at his dead colleague, then got up again and headed down the hill.

He knew they'd soon lose sight of the Discovery, once the drone had to bail and head back to its base in Qatar before its fuel ran out. No one at Beale was going to authorize trashing a multimillion-dollar piece of top secret wizardry just to track down Reilly's target. And even with the best will in the world, it would take a while to get another drone approved and retasked. By then, the Discovery would be long gone, taking Tess along with it.

Not what he needed to focus on right now.

Not with the endless slog down, in near-darkness, along the rock-strewn trail, on legs that could barely hold him up.

It took him twenty minutes to reach the clearing where he'd left Tess. The first glimmers of daylight were rising from behind the mountain, painting the area in a soft, golden glow. The sight that greeted him, however, was at great odds with its pastoral setting. Three dead commandos. Three crippled vehicles. And no sign of Tess.

He leaned against the Humvee where he'd last seen her standing, and caught his breath. He assumed the Turks would have reinforcements on the way by now, but they'd need time to get there. He had to decide what to do. If he stayed there and waited for them, it was likely that he would get embroiled in a jurisdictional tug-of-war and get sidelined. The Turks wouldn't take kindly to the massacre that had occurred, and they wouldn't necessarily want an outsider to interfere with their manhunt. Plus there was the language barrier to consider. By the time strings were pulled to try to keep him in the game, precious time would have been lost.

More important, he realized that getting Tess back safely wouldn't be the Turkish military's priority. They would be desperate to get their hands on the bomber; that would be their prime objective. Tess's safety was a distant second. If it ever came down to it and getting their man meant sacrificing Tess, Reilly had no illusions that she wouldn't be expendable in their eyes. Hell, he'd be expendable too. Not that he'd been particularly effective at keeping Simmons safe either. No, he couldn't trust anyone else to try to rescue her.

He had to keep going, on his own. Ahead of the troops. Stay on point.

They were more than welcome to follow in his tracks and swoop in. In fact, he'd call in for backup and invite them in—*after* she was out of harm's way.

He found the pack he'd left in the Humvee and recovered it. It still held his BlackBerry and his wallet. Something on the seat beside it caught his eye: a hastily folded map, next to a flashlight. He recognized the map. When he'd left Tess, she had been trying to lay out the inquisitor's journey on it now that they knew where the monastery was.

He opened it up. Sure enough, Tess had marked the monastery's rough position on it, based on the location of the parked SUVs and on the assumption that Simmons and his abductor had actually found it. She'd then marked possible routes and scribbled notes alongside them, using the contours of the terrain to try to follow the inquisitor's notes. The route split up into different branches at a couple of locations, and she'd put several question marks along the way. One route, however, had been marked off more solidly and seemed to stand out. It looked like the one she thought was the right one.

Reilly studied it for a moment, then folded up the map.

"Clever girl," he said under his breath. His depleted reservoir of adrenaline had just gotten a small top-up.

He checked the vehicles, grabbed a canteen full of water, a pair of powerful field binoculars, a handgun, and three full magazines, threw the lot along with his stuff into a field pack, and set off again.

Chapter 33

✠

Tess sat quietly in the passenger seat, crippled with dread, as the Discovery cut through the sleepy town. The roads were deserted at that early hour. There were a few signs of life here and there—an old man on a rickety horse-drawn cart lumbering down the side of the road, another man and his son walking across a vineyard—but none of it was really registering in her mind. All she was thinking about and agonizing over was what had happened farther up the mountain from where she'd been, who might still be alive, and who might have died. She'd seen him kill up close, she knew how effective he was at it, and no matter how hard she tried to console herself and stay hopeful, the thought that Reilly could be lying somewhere up there, bleeding out—or worse—was tearing her up inside.

She saw her abductor check his watch, then look ahead again, his mind clearly planning.

"Are we late for something?" she asked, trying to appear stoic and avoiding the question that was burning inside her.

He didn't react for a moment, then turned to her, sphinx-like as ever, and gave her a humorless smile that reeked of pity and condescension. "Did you miss me?"

She felt her spine tighten up, but made sure nothing in her expression gave it away. She thought of a snappy retort or two that she could hit him with, but she didn't want to engage with him that way, preferring to keep some kind of barrier between them. Instead, she finally succumbed to her desperate need to know and asked, "What happened up there?"

He ignored her for a beat, then said, "I had to improvise."

His smugness was driving her nuts. She felt like grabbing his head and pounding it repeatedly against the steering wheel, and she found a snippet of pleasure in picturing herself doing it. She ran through a couple of wild moves in her mind—yanking the steering wheel from him and forcing the car off the road, waiting for a slow turn and leaping out the door—but decided against them. They wouldn't work. She resigned herself to the idea that she needed to bide her time and hope for a more promising opening to present itself.

She calmed herself and asked, "And Jed?"

He looked at her curiously. "You ask about him, and not about your boyfriend? Despite everything Reilly did to get you back?"

She really didn't want to give him the satisfaction of knowing he could toy with her emotions like that, but she had to know. "Are they still alive?"

He shrugged. "Maybe. Maybe not. It was pretty dark up there. But you shouldn't worry too much about them. Think more about yourself, and about what you can do to stay alive." He paused, then added, "You can start by telling me how they found me."

Tess froze, conflicting thoughts colliding in her mind. She couldn't put off answering for too long, so she said, "I don't know," realizing how unconvincing she sounded even before the words had left her mouth.

Her abductor slid a knowing look her way, then reached into his waistband and pulled out a handgun. He swung it across until it settled against her cheek. "Please. Your boyfriend's leading the charge and you're not exactly a wallflower. So I'll ask you one last time: How did you find me?"

The steel muzzle was pressing uncomfortably against her jaw. "We . . . we guessed." She thought the pause, and his inevitable retort, would buy her time.

"You guessed?"

"Well, an educated guess, really. We looked at the probable route the Templars took from Constantinople, what side of the mountain they'd most likely have been on when they stumbled on the monastery. Then we studied detailed topographic maps of that area and applied the inquisitor's notes from the Registry to them. And we got lucky."

"It's a big mountain," the man pressed. "How did you pinpoint our position?"

"They used a satellite," she lied. "They fed it details of recently stolen cars from the Istanbul police." She hoped he already knew what she had only recently learned from Reilly about the difference between the loitering capabilities of a satellite and a drone. If he did, and if he bought her lie, maybe he wouldn't worry that a drone could still be up there tracking them.

The man pondered her words for a beat, then pulled his gun back and tucked it away. He focused ahead, and at the next curve, he slowed the car and pulled over by a thicket of pine trees.

He parked under the cover of the trees, then took the key out of the ignition. "Wait here," he told her.

She watched him get out and walk to the edge of the shaded area. He then just stood there and looked up into the sky, in the direction of the mountain.

ZAHED SURVEYED THE SKY OVERHEAD, looking for the dark spot that would confirm his suspicions.

She was good; he had to give her that. Able to finesse the truth to try to keep some kind of an advantage. But this was his field of expertise, not hers. And given their requirements and the urgency involved, and the realities of what was quickly achievable, he knew they were far more likely to be using an unmanned surveillance drone than a satellite.

Sure enough, he soon spotted it, a tiny dot hovering silently high up in the virgin dawn sky, keeping track of his movements. It was circling at high altitude, but given that it had the wingspan of a 737, it wasn't exactly invisible. He scowled as he stared at it, studying its trajectory. Evading it would be very tricky—even more so with a prisoner in tow.

Then he saw something he hadn't expected. The drone entered into a long, banking maneuver before gliding away in an easterly direction, back toward the mountain. He tracked it until he couldn't see it anymore, then scanned the rest of the sky, looking for another dot.

He didn't see one.

Zahed smiled inwardly. The drone must have reached the limit of its loiter, and it seemed to him like they hadn't anticipated needing a replacement to continue its mission. He stayed there for another ten minutes, at the edge of the canopy of the trees, scrutinizing the sky, making sure another drone didn't show up. Once he was reasonably confident that there wouldn't be one, he pulled out his cell phone and hit the call button twice, redialing the last number he had called. It was a number he had taken off Sully's phone.

After two rings, a drowsy voice picked up.

Zahed's tone went all gregarious. "Abdülkerim? Good morning. Ali Sharafi here. Suleyman's client. We spoke last night?"

The man he'd called—Abdülkerim, Sully's uncle, the expert the guide had wanted to contact when they were up by the ruins of the monastery—had clearly been asleep. After a quiet moment, Zahed's words seemed to have registered. "Yes, good morning to you," the man blurted into the Iranian's ear. His voice trailed off, obviously surprised by the early call and still foggy-headed.

"I'm sorry to be calling you this early," Zahed continued, "but our plans changed and we got here a bit earlier than expected. I was hoping we could meet sooner than agreed, perhaps in the next hour or so? You know, get an early start. Our time here is unfortunately limited, so the sooner we get going, the better, really."

Abdülkerim cleared his throat audibly and said, "Of course, of course. It's not a problem. Earlier will be better anyway. Less sun."

"That's great," Zahed said. "We'll see you soon. And thanks for being so accommodating."

He took note of where and when they would meet up and ended the call, satisfied with the outcome. He approached the car and glanced through the rear windshield. He could see the silhouette of Tess's head from behind. His mood darkened. There was something else he needed to do.

He opened the Discovery's rear hatch, picked something out of it, and slammed it shut again. Then he went around to Tess's door and swung it open.

"Get out," he told her.

Tess stared at him for a beat, a look of surprise on her face, then climbed out. She stood there in front of him in silence. He just looked at her without saying a word—then, with lightning agility, his hand flew up and struck her with a vicious, backhanded slap.

Her head twisted sideways violently under the impact and she fell to the ground. She stayed down, motionless, her head turned away, saying nothing. After a moment, she pushed herself back onto her feet and, brushing the soil off her hands, turned back to face him. Her eyes were tearful, but defiant. Her cheek was seared red, the imprint of his hand and fingers clearly visible on it.

"Don't lie to me again," he told her. "Understood?"

She didn't react. He raised his hand menacingly again, ready to swing again. She didn't flinch, but this time she nodded faintly.

He lifted up his other hand. In it was a wide canvas belt.

He held it out to her and said, "I'm going to need you to put this on."

Chapter 34

✝

Reilly was moving fast, as fast as his tired legs could carry him. He was finding it a bit easier, now that the steep, uneven trail down the mountain had given way to a flatter and smoother dirt road. Still, he was barely managing to stay on his feet. The nearest town, a small cluster of houses at the base of the volcano, was still half a mile away. He needed to find some kind of transportation that would give his muscles a rest if he didn't want his body to shut down in protest at the appalling treatment it was getting. And he had to do it fast.

The drone, he knew, was long gone.

Every second counted.

He cleared a low ridge and spotted something moving a couple of hundred yards ahead. Someone, riding something. The sight gave him a small boost. As he closed in on it, Reilly saw that it was an old man sitting astride a haggard-looking horse. The scrawny animal had two huge straw baskets slung on either side of its rump and was trudging ahead lazily, oblivious to the fleet of flies that was circling it.

Reilly picked up his pace and shouted, "Hey," waving his arms frantically. He saw the man turn his head nonchalantly, without slowing down. "Hey," he shouted again, and again, and this time, the man pulled on the reins and the horse stopped.

"Your horse," Reilly told him, pointing and gesturing wildly, his panting making him sound even more incoherent to the confused local. "I need your horse."

The man's weathered face suddenly tensed up as his eyes fell on the weapon in Reilly's waistband. But instead of going all fearful and panicky, he started shouting at Reilly, seemingly berating him for his affront. Young or old, strong or frail, the men Reilly was encountering didn't seem to be easily cowed. Reilly shook his head and spread his arms out calmingly, doing his best to get the man to ease back.

"Please, just listen to me. It's not like that. I need your help, okay? I need your horse," he told him, making all kinds of gestures that he thought could signal humility and respect.

The man was still eyeing him suspiciously, but after a moment he calmed down a touch.

Reilly remembered something and reached into an inside pocket. He pulled out his wallet.

"Here," he told him as he fished out all the cash he had in it. It wasn't much—but it was still more than he suspected the tired old horse was worth. He held it out to the man. "Please. Take it. Come on. Don't make me reach for the gun." He knew the man wouldn't understand that last bit.

The man studied him curiously for a beat, then muttered something and relented. He climbed off the horse with surprising ease and handed Reilly the reins.

Reilly smiled at him, the gratitude on his face clearly coming through. The man's expression softened up. Reilly looked into the baskets. They were filled with grapes.

"Here, you keep these," he told him as he loosened the ties that held them in place and helped the old man set them down by the side of the road. He then climbed on the tattered blankets that were there in lieu of a saddle, pulled out Tess's map, and studied it.

He thought of asking the old man to confirm his heading, but he knew the Jandarma's backup would soon be crawling all over the mountain and he didn't want to give them a head start. Instead, he used the sun's position to orient himself. The road from his location to the target area Tess had marked up, somewhere called the Ihlara Valley, was a circuitous one. That would be the road the bomber would be taking. A more direct route across open terrain, as the proverbial crow would fly, was far shorter and didn't seem to be intersected by any major obstructions such as a river or a mountain range. And given that his steed wasn't exactly a Thoroughbred, Reilly decided that any gain in distance that needed to be covered was a gift he couldn't turn down.

He put the map away, gave the man a parting nod and wave, and spurred the horse forward, leading it off the road and into a wide-open field, and hoping the poor animal wouldn't die on him before he got to where he needed to be.

Chapter 35

✝

The miles blew by as the Discovery traveled south along the winding, pockmarked road. The barren landscape only added to the numbness that Tess felt, both in body and soul, a numbness that was only pierced by the painful questions that remained unanswered.

She looked across at her captor. He felt her gaze and glanced over at her.

"We should be at the rendezvous in about ten minutes," he told her, then filled her in on the cover story they'd be using, the same one he'd used on Sully—the one that had him posing as a university professor called Ali Sharafi.

Tess's face tightened at his casual use of the dead Iranian historian's name. "You have no shame, do you," she said. "Using his name like that. After what you did to him."

She wasn't asking, and he didn't react.

"Why am I here anyway?" she pressed. "What do you need me for? The Turks aren't going to bargain with you just because you have me. Not after everything you've done."

He shrugged. "You're not here as a hostage, Tess. You're here because of your expertise. I can't do this by myself. And since I had to give up your dear friend Jed, I need you to step into his shoes."

She wasn't sure what that meant, whether or not Simmons was now safe. Somehow, given the precedents in Rome, she doubted it. The thought sent a shot of bile up her throat. "And what is it exactly that you can't do by yourself?"

He glanced sideways at her, looking amused. "Come now, Tess. You read the monk's confession. You saw the terms he used to describe this . . . *trove*. These monks, these gentle, pious servants of God—they actually resorted to murder to keep it hidden. So you tell me, Tess . . . What do you think I'm after?"

There was no point in playing coy. "The devil's handiwork? Something that could shake the very rock upon which our world is founded?"

He smiled. "It's worth finding, don't you think?"

"Not this way," she grumbled. "Who are you? What do you want with it?"

He didn't say anything and just kept his eyes dead ahead. After a moment, he said, "My country and yours . . . we've been fighting a dirty, undeclared war for over fifty years. I'm just a patriot trying to help my side win."

"Your side being Iran," she ventured.

He glanced at her and smiled enigmatically.

"We're not at war with you," she told him. "And whatever your problems are, we're not the reason for them."

That raised a dubious eyebrow on him. "Aren't you?"

"Hey, we're not the ones funding terrorists and threatening to wipe other countries off the face of the earth."

Her words didn't seem to cause any flutter inside him. Instead, he just coolly asked her, "Do you know about Operation Ajax, Tess?"

She'd never heard of it. "No."

"I didn't think so. That's part of your problem, you see. You people have no appreciation for history. You only have time for tweets and Facebook and who Tiger Woods is fucking. And when it comes to the big stories, to wars that can kill thousands and ruin millions of lives, you never bother to look behind the headlines. You don't take the time to read about why things are the way they are and look for the truth behind the spin of your politicians or the hysteria of those talking heads on your TV screens."

Tess scoffed. "That's just great. I'm being lectured on the subtleties of history and the great failings of our democracy by a man who cut off an innocent woman's head just to prove a point. There's so much we can learn from you guys, isn't there?"

He turned to face her again, only this time there was something deeply unsettling in his look. Something very dark and sinister had been prodded awake. His hand slid sideways and settled on her thigh. It sent a jolt of dread through her. He just let it sit there for a few interminable seconds, saying nothing. Then he squeezed her thigh slightly before giving it a patronizing little tap.

"You're a very attractive woman, Tess. Attractive, and clever too. But you really need to brush up on your history," he told her, looking at her while keeping an eye on the road. "Look up Operation Ajax. It's an important milestone in the history of our two countries. And while you're at it, find out what happened on the morning of the third of July in 1988. What *really* happened that day." His face darkened further. The mention of the date seemed to stir up a cauldron of hatred deep in his soul. He held her gaze for a beat, then turned his attention back to the road ahead.

Tess's heart was thudding against her rib cage like an alien wanting out. She fought to keep her composure as she racked her brain for any insight into what he was talking about, and was frustrated at coming up blank. She hated not knowing what he was referring to, and hated not being able to throw his smug assumptions back in his face.

"I think this is it," he finally announced, then pointed ahead. "And that's got to be our man. Let's hope he knows his stuff."

Tess followed his gaze. Up the road, by a dusty three-way intersection, she saw a ramshackle fruit and vegetable stall next to a small gas station. A man was standing there, by a parked mustard-colored Jeep Cherokee. He seemed to be in his late fifties and looked somewhat incongruous in his cargo pants, denim shirt, and khaki boonie hat. He had to be their contact, Abdülkerim, Sully's Byzantinist uncle. Confirming it, the man waved as he saw them approach.

The Iranian slowed down, and as he pulled over, he gave

Tess a stern look. "This doesn't have to end badly for you. You understand that, don't you?"

"Sure." She nodded, making sure the word was clearly seeping sarcasm, not fear.

ABDÜLKERIM DEFINITELY KNEW HIS STUFF.

The pointers mentioned in the inquisitor's journal had been sketchy, referring to natural landmarks that time—more than seven hundred years' worth—could well have eroded, if not erased altogether. But the man was not only intimately familiar with the region and with its unique geographic features; he also had a thorough understanding of its history. This allowed him to put the writings in their proper historical context—what the main towns were at the time, where the trading routes were, which valleys were populated and which ones weren't—and stay on the inquisitor's trail.

They were advancing off-road, all three of them riding in Abdülkerim's Jeep. The Byzantinist's suggestion to that effect had suited Zahed perfectly, allowing him to ditch the stolen, flagged Discovery, which he tucked away out of sight behind the gas station. The early start had allowed them to cover a lot of ground and still have plenty of daylight left, and Abdülkerim was really putting the Cherokee through its paces. They bounced across plateaus and climbed up and down ridges on the trail of their seven-hundred-year-old ghost, stopping at a couple of locations and hiking around to confirm their bearings before piling back into the Jeep and continuing on.

The sun was almost at its zenith in the perfect, unblemished sky when Abdülkerim pulled over by a steep ridge and switched off the Jeep's engine. They all downed some mineral water and *lahmacun* flat bread; then he led Tess and Zahed down a long, narrow trail that ran through some oddly shaped rock spires and led to the valley floor—the beginning of the canyon that, the Byzantinist suspected, held the Templars' tombs.

The canyon widened and narrowed as it undulated south. On either side of them, the cliff face rose more than two hundred feet, a drama of soft, bleached stone carved

out of the earth by long-gone rivers. The canyon floor itself
was dry and dusty given the time of year, but tufts of green
bushes and rich clusters of poplars and willows helped
soften its barren, rugged feel.

"These valley weren't populated the way the ones further north were," Abdülkerim explained. He had a peculiar way of talking; he spoke English fluently, considering it
wasn't his mother tongue, except for one little quirk: he had
this peculiar habit of often, and quite randomly, forgetting
to add an "s" to plurals. "They're too far south, too close to
the mountain passes that Muslim raiding party were using.
You won't find lots of rock church or underground cities
here—which is why you don't get many tourist trekking
around. They're all up around Göreme and Zelve, which
are also, without a doubt, much more dramatic to look at."

"So we've heard," Zahed said, surveying the savagely
beautiful landscape surrounding him. "But if the Templars
were trying to reach the coast without getting spotted by
Ghazi raiders, it made sense for them to stick to these
canyons?"

"Absolutely. Some of these canyon are over ten miles
long. That's a lot of miles of great cover—but they're also a
great place for an ambush."

They split up, Zahed sticking with Tess, Abdülkerim on
the opposite side of the canyon from them, and moved
slowly, combing both rock faces, looking for the markings
the inquisitor had referred to. The sun was baking now, its
heat weighing heavily on them and making each step more
of a chore. They took turns working the shaded side of the
canyon when there was any shade to be had, but even that
wasn't much of a respite from the heat.

After a couple of hours, the going got easier as the sun
dropped out of view and the canyon was plunged into
shade. Over the next mile or two, they came across a couple of small rock chapels—single cells that had been carved
out of the soft volcanic tufa centuries ago, the simple frescoes painted directly on their walls and ceilings barely visible now—but little else. Until the Byzantinist called out
to them.

"Over here," he bellowed across the canyon.

Tess and Zahed rushed over to join him.

He was bent down, scrutinizing the rock face at the base of the cliff, brushing it softly with a gloved hand. At first, what had snagged his interest wasn't obvious—then it came into view: faint markings, chiseled into the smooth rock, their rough edges eroded by the passage of centuries.

The carving Abdülkerim was dusting off was about ten inches square. Though crudely executed, it was still easily recognizable as a cross, which wasn't surprising, given the huge Christian presence in the region in the first thousand years or so of the faith. Crosses were scattered across the landscape in abundance. But its location was unusual—at the base of the cliff, with no rock church in sight—as was its shape. This wasn't just any cross. Its arms were wider at their extremities than at their base, a distinctive feature of the *croix pattée* that was used by several groups throughout history—including the Templars.

"This could be it," the historian said, visibly excited by the possibility. He kept brushing the surface around and below the cross. More carvings appeared, barely discernible at first, but clearer with every stroke of his glove.

They were letters. Nothing intricate, not the work of a master craftsman. They looked like they'd been fashioned hastily, using whatever tools were available. But they were there, and they were legible.

Tess leaned down beside the historian, her eyes locked on the rock face. Her skin quivered with anticipation as the letters bloomed into clarity. And as she read out the words they formed—there were three of them, arranged one underneath the other—her mind raced ahead, churning over their significance.

"Hector . . . Miguel . . . and"—she looked up at her abductor—"Conrad."

Chapter 36

✜

The Iranian nodded, his brow knotted with concentration as he stared at the carvings. "So," he finally said, "our Templar is buried here."

Abdülkerim's face was beaming with excitement. "Not just one. Three of them. They could all be buried here, under our feet." He took a couple of steps back and dropped his gaze, studying the soil at the base of the cliff. There was a slight rise in the ground that was otherwise pretty uniformly flat. He glanced up and down the valley, then looked up at the sheer bluff face towering protectively over them. "This is marvelous. We could be standing over the tomb of three Templar knight, here, in an area where there's never been any record of a Templar presence."

Tess wasn't paying attention to him. She was busy processing what their find meant, and a furtive glance at the Iranian told her he was doing the same thing.

The Byzantinist's expression changed to one of bewilderment at the lack of euphoria—and the evident tension—coming back at him from his clients. "This is what you were looking for, isn't it?"

She ignored him. "If he's buried here," she told her abductor, "then that's the end of the trail, isn't it?" She hesitated, not sure if her conclusion boded well for her and the Turk, then added, "We're done, aren't we?"

The Iranian didn't seem convinced. "Who buried them? We know three knights left the monastery. They had it with them. What happened to them here? How did they die? And who buried them? Who carved their names out?"

"Does it matter?" Tess replied.

"Of course it does. Because that's where the trail continues. Someone walked away from whatever took place here. We need to find out who that was."

Abdülkerim was clearly confused. "What do you mean, they had 'it' with them? What are you talking about? I thought we were just looking for these tomb. What more do you know about these knight?"

Tess ignored him again and stayed on her abductor. "How can we possibly do that? They died seven hundred years ago. All we have are the markings on this wall. That's it. There isn't anything more to go on. Not in the Templar Registry, not in the inquisitor's journal. It's the end of the road."

The Iranian scowled, mulling her conclusion. "It's not the end of the road. We don't know what's buried here. And until we do, we haven't taken this search to its limit." He fixed her with a resolute stare and said, "We need to dig them up. For all we know, it could be buried here with them."

Tess's heart sank at the suggestion. The man wasn't giving up.

The Byzantinist's eyes went wide too. "'Dig them up'? Us?"

Zahed turned to him. "You have a problem with that?"

The hard stare threw the Turk. "No, of course not. It'll have to be done. But there's a procedure to follow. We'll need to apply for permission from the ministry. It's a very complicated process and I'm not even sure they'll—"

"Forget about getting permission," the Iranian interrupted. "We're going to do it ourselves. Right now."

Abdülkerim's jaw dropped an inch. "Now? You want to . . . You can't do that. We have very strict laws in this area. You can't just dig things up."

Zahed shrugged, nonchalantly reached into his rucksack, and pulled out a graphite gray automatic. He chambered a round and swung his arm out so the weapon was leveled right at the Byzantinist's face. "I won't say anything if you don't."

He held the gun barrel there, hovering millimeters from Abdülkerim's eyes. Droplets of sweat multiplied on the Turk's forehead like someone had turned on a sprinkler inside his skull. He raised his hands to his sides instinctively and took a tentative step back, but the Iranian inched forward and jammed the gun barrel against the man's forehead.

"We dig. We have a look. We leave. No harm done. Okay?" Zahed told him, his tone easy and calm.

Abdülkerim nodded nervously.

"Good," the Iranian said, pulling back. "Now, the sooner we start, the sooner we can all get out of here." He tucked the gun into his waistband, reached into his pack, and pulled out a dark green canvas cover. He flipped it open and took out a compact, folding camping tool that had a shovel on one side and a pick on the other.

He extended the tool's handle and snapped its heads into position, then held it out to Tess. "You're the expert, right?"

She scowled at him; then, grudgingly, she took it. "This could take a while," she said, giving the small tool a sardonic glance.

"Not necessarily. You've got an able assistant just dying to help you out." Zahed smiled. He turned to the Byzantinist and opened his palm out in an inviting gesture. Abdülkerim nodded and joined Tess.

They got down on their knees and stared at the ground as the inevitability of their task settled in; then they got to work.

TESS USED THE PICK to loosen the top layer of soil, which was dry and compacted. Abdülkerim cleared the clumps of dried mud she was breaking off, chucking them into a pile away from the wall. It didn't take that long for them to clear an area around six feet square; then Tess started to dig deeper.

The pick struck stone—nothing too big, just a bowling

ball–sized rock. She cleared the soil around it and Abdülkerim helped her pull it out. There were other rocks tucked
in around it, and more underneath, two tightly packed layers of them blanketing whatever was buried below.

"These rocks weren't here naturally," Tess said. "Look
at how they're arranged. Someone put them there." She
hesitated, then added, "To keep wild animals from getting
at the bodies."

Zahed nodded. "Good. Then the bones should still be
in one place."

He gave her a look that prodded her on, and she got
back to work, prying the stones loose and handing them
to Abdülkerim, who would then throw them clear behind
them. They worked in tandem, moving in parallel, and got
a good rhythm going until something interrupted the flow.

A look, from the Turk—a questioning, worried look.

He'd noticed the bomb belt and its padlock under Tess's
loose shirt.

She flashed him an intense, staying look, with a barely
perceptible shake of the head, signaling him not to ask
about it and unsure about whether or not their captor had
spotted the Turk's reaction. If he had noticed it, he didn't
say anything. She saw Abdülkerim's jawbone tighten as he
gave her a tiny nod back before carrying on.

Before long, the rocks were gone and her pick was biting into loose soil again, less than two feet from the surface.
And then the first bone appeared. A femur. Smaller bones,
phalanges from what appeared to be a left hand, lay scattered around it.

She was using her fingers now, clearing the soil carefully.
The rest of the skeleton soon came into view.

Its bones were a sickly brown, infused with the earth it
had been lying in for centuries. And even though the soil
of the region didn't suffer from high acidity, Tess hadn't expected to find much else. There wasn't a lot that could survive seven hundred years of burial. Armies of maggots and
worms would see to that. Her fingers stumbled upon some
copper-alloy buckles, the only remnants of a belt and some
boots whose leather had long been eaten away, but she saw
nothing else. It wasn't immediately obvious whether she

was staring at the remains of a man or a woman, but judging from the length and the girth of the main leg and arm bones, she thought it was more than likely that it had been a man.

"There's nothing here to tell us who this was," she remarked as she stood up and wiped her forehead with her sleeve. She was exhausted, the arduous effort having drained what little strength she'd had left after the sleepless night at the mountain stakeout. Adding to her discomfort, the bomb belt had been straining against her ribs and digging into her with every move, bruising the edge of her rib cage, but she knew there wasn't anything she could do about that.

The Iranian stood next to her, eyeing the remains. He checked his watch, then said, "Okay, good work. Let's keep going."

Tess shook her head with disdain and despair, and drank some water from the canteen Abdülkerim had given her. Then she got back down on her knees and kept going.

An hour or so later, she and the Byzantinist had uncovered the remains of one more corpse.

One more—not two.

Tess dug small exploratory holes on either side of the communal grave, but came up blank. There were no layers of rocks there either, confirming that no one else had been buried there, not close to the two skeletons anyway.

Which meant the trail wasn't dead.

Which also meant her ordeal wasn't over.

She got up, drenched in sweat, and leaned back against the rock face, taking in deep breaths to slow her heart rate down. Abdülkerim rummaged in his backpack and shared the last of his honey cakes with her. She chewed on the soft, gooey pastry slowly, relishing the taste, feeling their effect suffuse her body, and tried to give her mind a break from wondering what their find meant.

"Two bodies, not three . . . And yet, there are three names on the grave," the Iranian announced, clearly pleased with the outcome. "Which raises so many questions, wouldn't you say?"

He fixed her with a curious, slightly amused gaze.

She was too worn out to play games—but she had to try something. She replied, "Such as, which two are they, right? Well, hey, you want to play *CSI* and come up with an answer for that one, be my guest."

He kept staring at her with the same bemused smirk on his face. "Really, Tess? That's the best you can do?"

Abdülkerim spoke up, stepping in to defend Tess. "They're seven-hundred-year-old skeletons. How can we possibly know who they were?"

The Iranian gave her a dubious "come, now" look. "Tess?"

He said it like he knew already. A spasm of dread shot through Tess as she considered the consequences of being found out—again.

She relented, wondering how much Jed had told the Iranian. "I don't think either of these is Conrad."

"Why not?" Abdülkerim asked.

She looked at the Iranian. He nodded his approval. "These skeletons . . . they're complete. Both of them."

The Byzantinist seemed lost. "And . . . ?"

"Conrad was hurt at the battle of Acre. Badly." A sense of doom flooded her face, her spirits drowning at the thought of not finding closure in the grave she'd just opened up. "This isn't him."

Chapter 37

✠

CAPPADOCIA
MAY 1310

They spent the first night in a narrow valley down the mountain from the monastery, camped out around a tall, rectangular rock that had crosses and other markings chiseled into it. They rode out early the next morning, spread out from one another with Hector riding point, Conrad farther back in the heavily laden wagon, and Miguel trailing far behind to watch their backs, all three of them acutely aware of the dangers they might encounter and keen to get to the relatively safer territory farther south as quickly as possible.

Conrad still wasn't sure what their best move would be. It had all happened too fast, and it wasn't something that he'd ever thought he'd be doing. He had some important decisions to make. The first of which was where to stash their consignment. Once that was settled, he'd need to figure out how to go about using it to get the pope to release his brethren and rescind the charges against their Order.

He thought of taking the consignment to France. The pope, a Frenchman, was now based there, in Avignon. Conrad's imprisoned brothers were also in France, as was their nemesis, King Philip. Any approach to the pope and any monitoring of its results would need to happen there. But France was dangerous. The king's seneschals were everywhere. It would be difficult to travel around with a conspicuous cargo in tow, and Conrad didn't know whom he could still trust there. The other option was Cyprus. He had friends there, and there was little Frankish presence on the island. They could hide their trove there; he could leave Hector and Miguel in place to guard it and venture alone to France to make his play. Either way, they had to get to a port first, the one they'd landed in when they'd left Cyprus: Corycus. Heading there made sense in another way: Once they got across the Taurus Mountains, they'd be in the Armenian kingdom of Cilicia, which was Christian territory.

The problem was, the going was slow. The old wagon was lumbering along, its twin horses straining from the heavy load under its canvas cover. Harder still was that the knights had to avoid the easy route. The last thing they wanted was to meet up with some roaming Ghazi warriors, which meant they needed to keep away from any well-trodden trails. Instead, they were trudging up rocky, less stable terrain and cutting through dense forests, which was delaying their progress even more.

By the end of the next day, they'd reached a wide plain that stretched all the way to the distant mountain range they needed to cross. The open ground ahead of them provided little in terms of cover, which made Conrad uncomfortable. His only other choice was just as unattractive: the long, narrow canyons that snaked across the plain, cut into the flatlands as if gouged out by a set of gargantuan claws. Given the load they were carrying and their lack of chain mail and battle weaponry, coming across a horde of bandits in one of the canyons would lead to a certain defeat. The odds of encountering one, though, had to be less likely than being spotted out in the open. After a short debate, they opted to take the canyon route and camped out on a ridge at the mouth of the one they thought would be their best bet, using some unusual rock spires for cover.

Their reasoning was sound—except that the threat came from elsewhere.

The first arrows struck the next morning, a couple of

hours after they had set off. Hector was on point, leading the small convoy through the twists and turns of the
canyon, when one of the bolts slammed into his chest, far
enough under his right shoulder to cut into his lung. Two
others buried themselves into his horse, one of them hitting
it in its foreleg and causing its leg to collapse under it. Hector hung on as his mare neighed in agony and came down
in a messy cloud of blood and dust.

Conrad spotted two archers at the top of the canyon,
ahead of them, and pulled hard on the reins of his steed
to spin it around, anticipating what was coming up behind
them and hoping he was wrong.

He was right.

Four riders were charging at them, riders that he recognized.

The trader, his son, and two of the men they'd brought
with them.

He felt a flush of acid in the pit of his stomach. He knew
the trader was greedy, but they'd been careful about covering their tracks and had Miguel making sure they hadn't
been followed.

Clearly, they hadn't been careful enough.

Twenty years earlier, in the heat of battle, Conrad
wouldn't have batted an eyelid about engaging them. With
a helmet and chain mail, a lance, broadsword, and mace,
and a well-shielded horse, any Templar knight would have
thought nothing of taking on four enemy fighters.

This was different.

This wasn't twenty years ago. It was now. After Acre.

After the defeat that had cost him his hand.

He'd lost it in the heat of battle to a Mameluke scimitar,
sheared right off at the wrist, a clean cut that came close
to costing him his life. He had never experienced pain like
what he felt when the infirmarer had fought to sear his
wound shut with a red-hot blade. He'd lost a bucketload
of blood, and as he and his surviving brethren sailed away
from the fallen city, he hovered at the precipice of death
for days on end, until a gust of life somehow found him
and dragged him back from it. During his long recovery in
Cyprus, he tried to find some comfort in the fact that it had

THE TEMPLAR SALVATION ✦ 241

been his left hand and not the hand with which he held his sword, but that didn't cheer him much. He knew he would never be the formidable warrior he had once been. Then he found a talented Cypriot blacksmith who said he could help and made him a copper prosthesis, a false hand that fit snugly onto the stump of his forearm with leather straps to hold it in place. It was beautifully crafted and had five fixed fingers that were a reasonable rendition of what he had lost and were fixed in a bent position that allowed him to do certain key tasks such as holding on to his horse's reins, lifting a jug of water, carrying a shield, or punching the jaw off anyone who crossed him.

Still, given his handicap, he knew the odds weren't favoring him and Miguel. The odds shrank to four-to-one an instant later when another arrow thudded into the Spaniard's back and threw him off his horse.

Conrad drew his scimitar and struggled to control his rearing horse as Mehmet and his men thundered in. The two hired riders were at full gallop and streaked past him, one on either side, right up against the wagon. He whipped his blade across in a wide, upward arc and caught one of them across the face, opening up a wide gash under the man's ear and flinging a wake of blood through the air behind it, but the other rider cut him in the thigh as he threw himself onto him and knocked him off his perch.

He fell heavily to the ground, his arms breaking the fall but losing the scimitar in the process. He pushed himself to his feet, surveying the situation through hazy eyes. All three of them were now down: Hector, trapped under his wounded horse, blood gurgling out of his mouth, gasping for breath; Miguel, back on his feet now, but staggering like a drunkard from his injury; and Conrad, limping now, blood flooding down his leg, straightening up in time to see the trader and his son riding in for the kill.

Qassem was bearing down on him, fast. Conrad's eyes scanned the ground around him, looking for something, anything he could use as a weapon. There was nothing within reach, no time to think of anything fancy. His body reacted instinctively and he just leapt up at the Turk as he blew past, leading with his metal hand and letting it take the brunt of the blade's strike while grabbing the man's belt with the other hand and pulling him off his horse.

They fell in a heap of flesh and bone and a frenzy of elbows and fists, but it was a fight Conrad knew he'd lose. A kick to the gash in his thigh sent a shock of pain through him and brought him to his knees. An elbow to the cheekbone floored him. He squirmed on the hot canyon bed, a metallic taste of blood back in his mouth, a sensory blast to a long-gone era, one that had also ended in defeat.

He looked up. The trader had dismounted and was sauntering over to join his son, who loomed proudly over his vanquished opponent. Behind them, Conrad saw Miguel, lying dead at the feet of the two riders who had rushed him, and, farther away, he saw the prone body of Hector.

"I told you these lands weren't safe," the trader chortled. "You should have listened to me."

Conrad sat up and spat some blood out, hitting the son's boots. Qassem pulled his leg back and was about to launch a kick at the knight's face when his father's shout stilled him.

"Stop," Mehmet ordered. "I need him awake." He scowled at his son for a moment, then turned his attention at something up the canyon and smiled contentedly.

Conrad followed his gaze. The archers had climbed down from their ambush positions and were bringing the wagon back.

The trader waved them over. "So this is how you treat your partners?" he told Conrad. "You call on me to help you with all your little swindles. Then, when a big deal shows up, you decide to keep it to yourself and brush me away like some pustular servant?"

"This doesn't concern you," Conrad hissed back.

"If it's worth something, it concerns me," the trader replied as he stepped away to examine the packhorses' cargo. "And I have a feeling it's worth quite a lot."

He climbed onto the body of the wagon and nodded to the men. They loosened the clasp around the first of the chests and opened it up.

The trader looked inside it, then turned to Conrad, his face crinkled with confusion. "What is this?"

"It doesn't concern you," the knight repeated.

Mehmet blurted out some orders while waving his hands manically, clearly displeased. His men moved furiously, unlocking and opening the other two chests.

His expression only darkened further as he looked inside each one.

He jumped off the wagon, stormed over to Conrad, and shoved him back onto the ground with a vicious flick of his leg. He then drew a dagger from under his belt and dropped down to face him, pulling the knight's hair to yank his head back and pushing the dagger's blade right up against his neck. "What is the meaning of this travesty?" he rasped. "What kind of a treasure is this?"

"It's of no value to you."

Mehmet pushed the blade harder. "Tell me what these are. Tell me why you wanted them this badly."

"Go to hell," the knight replied and lunged up like an uncoiled spring, shoving the trader's dagger away with one hand while landing a crushing blow from his metal hand with the other.

The trader shrieked as he flew off him and hit the ground, an airborne rivulet of blood trailing out of his mouth and nose. Conrad threw himself after him, but Qassem jumped in and pulled him off his father before he and his hired hands pummeled Conrad into subservience.

Barely conscious, Conrad looked on helplessly through veiled vision as the trader's son, dagger in hand, came in for what looked like the final blow. He braced himself for it, but it wasn't what he expected. Qassem didn't gut him or slit his throat. Instead, he bent down and set one knee firmly against Conrad's chest to hold him in place, then used the blade to cut the leather straps of Conrad's copper prosthesis and yank it off. He held it up, gloating, staring at it like some kind of prize scalp before holding it up proudly to the others.

The trader pushed himself to his feet and faltered before steadying himself against his son, spitting blood, his eyes bloodshot with rage. "You always were a stubborn bastard, weren't you?"

Qassem held his dagger up and hunched down over Conrad. "I'll make the infidel talk."

The trader shot his arm out and stopped his son. "No," he said, still glaring down at the fallen knight. "I don't trust what he'd tell us. Besides, we don't need him. What's in these trunks is clearly of great value. And I'm sure we can find someone in Konya who can tell that it is."

"What about him?" Qassem asked.

The trader frowned and looked around, casting his eye about the deserted canyon. It was quiet, apart from the groans of the fallen horse. The sun had risen well clear of the canyon's walls and was now beating down on them with all its midsummer might.

Conrad saw the trader glance up at the sky. Three griffon vultures were circling high above them, attracted by the dead and the dying. He watched as the trader then dropped his gaze to the bloodied horse, turned to his son, and managed what was clearly a painful half grin.

He pictured the fate that now awaited him, and wished that an arrow had found him too.

THE HEAT WAS STIFLING, and it wasn't just because of the sun.

It was because of the horse.

The one he'd been sewn into.

They'd taken Hector's dying horse and sliced it open, pulled most of its innards out, then stuffed Conrad inside it, back to front, before suturing it shut around him. They had him on his back, with his head sticking out of what had been the animal's anus. His arms and legs were also protruding, out of holes they'd cut into the stallion's hide, and except for the stump of his left arm, his limbs were securely tied to wooden stakes that had been driven into the hard ground.

They'd left him like that, crucified against the canyon floor, before trotting off with the horses and the wagon and everything they'd been carrying.

It was unbearably hot in there. Worse than the heat, though, was the smell. And the insects. Putrescent flesh and gelling blood littered the ground around him, rotting in the sun. With the trader and his men still in view and receding down the canyon, flies and wasps were already swarming over him and over his dead brethren's corpses, feasting on the abundance of spoils, buzzing and landing and nibbling away at the open cuts on his lips and across the rest of his face.

That would just be the start of it.

The real agony would come courtesy of the three vultures that were hovering overhead. They'd swoop in, sink their claws into the horse's carcass and tear away at it with their sharp beaks. Eventually, they'd break through the horse's skin and start feasting on Conrad's body, morsel by morsel, pulling the flesh off him before moving on to his internal organs.

He knew death wouldn't come quickly.

He'd heard of this form of scaphism before—the name was derived from the Greek word *skaphe*, which meant "vessels," as the original method involved sealing the victim inside back-to-back canoelike rowboats. Some victims were covered with honey and made to drink milk and honey until they could no longer hold their bowels; then they were set afloat on stagnant ponds—hence the boats. The feces made sure the insects showed up. Other victims were left under the sun, in a hollowed-out tree or an animal's carcass. Conrad had heard how the Turks and the Persians were fond of scaphism, heard how horrific the remains looked when they were ultimately found, but he'd never witnessed it himself. In a way, he was lucky the buzzards were there. In areas where there were only insects to feed on the victim, death could take days. Conrad had heard of a Greek priest who had survived them breeding inside him along with gangrene fermenting across his body for seventeen days before his body finally gave in.

It was a particularly vile way to die, he thought as he stared up at the circling vultures, knowing they wouldn't be circling much longer.

They didn't.

Two of them came down in quick succession and landed heavily on the horse, with the third settling for the Spanish knight's corpse. They began tearing away at the exposed flesh, their beaks and claws working in a ravenous frenzy, like they hadn't eaten for weeks. Conrad spasmed left and right to try to shake them off, but his frantic moves were strictly limited by his ties and he didn't make any impression on the birds. They just ignored him and kept on digging away, ripping and pulling and chewing and flinging bits of flesh off the carcass and splattering Conrad with dripping wet morsels. Then the one closest to his head spun around, eyed him for a beat, and dove its beak in for a taste. Conrad flicked his head from side to side and yelled fiercely, but the buzzard knew what it was doing and kept going, undeterred. Conrad buried his head as far into the carcass as he could, but he couldn't get in far enough, and he was staring straight into the bird's wide-open beak as it darted in for a bite, when something thudded into it and slammed it clear off him, too fast for him to see what it was, too sudden for his dulled senses to process what had happened.

He heard the predator's wings do a little death-swat against the ground, out of view, behind the carcass. The second vulture didn't flinch. It just sidestepped across the horse's hide to take its dead friend's place, but something slammed into it too and flung it to the ground, this time closer to Conrad, giving him a clear view of what had happened:

The vulture had an arrow through it.

He spun his head around, his heart pumping wildly, his senses frazzled, straining to see who was there, wondering who had saved his life—and he saw her, sprinting over to him, a crossbow in her hands.

Maysoon.

Elation crackled through him.

He watched her charging in and saw her let go of her crossbow and pull out a big dagger just as he felt a sudden beating of air around him and something bristly brush up against his face. The third vulture thudded heavily on his chest, its claws biting into the horse hide, and just as it dove in for a taste, Maysoon was already in midair, pouncing onto it like a panther, grabbing its neck with one hand and slitting it open with the other.

She tossed the vulture aside and turned to face him, breathing heavily, her face dripping with sweat, her eyes fierce with determination. She swatted the air a few times to disperse the swarm of insects, then bent down and cut the ties off his hand and feet before getting to work on freeing him from his gruesome coffin.

He watched her slicing away at the sutures. Her eyes found his and she held his gaze without blinking as her hands kept moving, working expertly, her face locked in concentration. In his groggy, dehydrated state, he still couldn't quite believe she was actually there, couldn't believe he was still alive, even as she helped him out of the carcass and onto his feet.

He just stood there, hunched, breathing hard, dripping with blood and guts, staring at her with a mix of awe and confusion. "How . . . What are you doing here?"

The edge of her mouth curled upward with a cheeky grin. "Saving your life."

He shook his head, still bewildered. "Besides that." He smiled. It hurt his bruised lips. "How did you get here?"

"I followed you. You, my brother, my father. I followed you all the way from Constantinople."

His thoughts were taking a moment longer than normal to formulate themselves. "Why?"

"I heard them talking. They suspected you were after something big. They had a feeling you wouldn't be splitting it with them. So they decided they'd take it all for themselves. I wanted to warn you, but I couldn't get away. You know how they are with me."

"But they're . . . your father? Your brother?"

She shrugged. "They're bad men. I knew you wouldn't give up whatever it was you were after without a fight. I knew what they'd do to you to take it."

"So you followed them . . . for me?"

She kept her eyes firmly locked on his, and nodded. "You would have done the same for me, wouldn't you?"

The simple honesty of her reply sank in with startling clarity. Of course, he would have. He didn't doubt that for a second. There was an unspoken connection between them, an attraction that had built up over weeks and months of frustrating encounters. He was well aware of that. But for her to risk her life like this was beyond anything he'd imagined.

She handed him a leather wineskin. "You need water. Drink."

He uncorked it and took a long chug from it.

"What's this all about?" she asked as she watched him. "What did you want from that monastery?"

He handed it back to her, studied her for a beat, then led her to some shade under an outcropping in the canyon wall and told her everything.

From the very beginning.

The whole truth and nothing but the truth.

The origin of the Order. What the Keepers set out to do. How it all went well. How it all went wrong. Everard and his men in Constantinople. The defeat at Acre. The disappearance of the Falcon Temple. The lost years in Cyprus. The King of France's move against the Order. Friday the thirteenth. His rebirth in Constantinople. Meeting her. The swords. The monastery. The texts. The ambush.

It was the least she deserved.

Throughout, she listened intently, not interrupting more than a couple of times, for some clarification. And when he was done, they just sat there in silence for a long moment, she letting the information sink in, he assessing his current situation and trying to decide what his next move should be.

She watched him rub the stump of his forearm and nodded to indicate it. "Did they take it?"

He nodded back. "Yes."

She watched him silently for a long second, then said, "I know what you're thinking."

He exhaled heavily. "I have to try and get it back."

"There's six of them and two of us."

He held his stump up and gave her a self-deprecating grin. "One and a half." He frowned. "One more thing I need to get back. Your father said they'd take it to Konya. Do you know where that is?"

"Of course. It's where we're from—it's where I grew up."

"How far is it?"

She thought about it for a beat. "Four days' ride? Maybe three at a good gallop."

"They're weighed down by the wagon and what it's carrying. We'll be much faster than them. And they'll have to find somewhere sheltered to stop for the night, out of view. Less easy when you've got all those horses." He let his thoughts sink in, looked around, and made a decision. "I need you to help me with something first."

"What?"

"I need to bury my friends."

"We'll have to do it fast. We don't want to give them too much of a head start."

"'We'?"

She gave him a knowing, sardonic glance. "I saved your life, remember?"

"They're your family."

She frowned. It was evidently not easy on her. "You don't know enough about me."

"And if I did?"

"You'd understand better." Her tone was level and clear, and didn't leave much room for debate. "Let's not waste time. We can talk on the way." She smiled. "But you'll need to ride downwind of me until you bathe."

"They took our horses. I can't be downwind of you if we're sharing a saddle."

She shot him a look. "I brought two horses. In case one of them got hurt. It's a long way from Constantinople."

Conrad nodded, then glanced over at Hector's corpse. "Hector's more or less my size. I'll take his garments. Until we find a stream to wash in."

They used her dagger and their bare hands to open up a rectangular hole in the ground, at the base of the rock face. They placed Hector and Miguel's bodies in it, side by side, before covering them with stones to protect them from any more buzzards and other scavengers that roamed the valleys, and topping it all off with a layer of soil. Conrad used the dagger to scrape their names into the rocky wall behind the grave, then added a *croix pattée* above them.

He stood up and stared at the flattened earth and the carving in the rock. It wasn't as fitting a grave for his fallen brethren as he would have liked, but it was the best he could do.

Maysoon read the grief etched into his face. "'*It may look like the end*,'" she said. "'*It may seem like a sunset, but in reality it's a dawn. For when the grave locks you in is when your soul is freed.'"*

He looked a question at her.

"Rumi," she said.

He still didn't understand.

"I'll explain later," she said. "We need to go."

"Very well." He contemplated the grave for a final moment, but before turning away, he decided to do something else.

He carved his own name as well. Below theirs.

It was Maysoon's turn to look a question at him.

"Just in case anyone else should ever come looking for me," he said.

Then they rode off, thundering down to the end of the canyon before emerging into open flatlands and following the trail the Turk and his outfit had left behind.

They didn't get too far on that first day. The sun was already sinking fast by the time they reached a small stream that wove its way through some forested, rolling hills. It was a good, safe place to spend the night. They'd catch up with their quarry the next day.

Conrad cleaned himself in the stream, relishing the feel of the cool water on his wounds. As he did, he thought about the past few days, about the abrupt disruption to his life, about the trapdoor that fate had conjured up and dropped him into. He didn't have much time to think about it. The sight of Maysoon stepping out of her robes and joining him in the stream yanked his thoughts to a far better place. And right there and then, he decided he would suffer no more dilemmas about long-dead oaths and self-denying rules.

He pulled her toward him and kissed her with a feverish hunger. And then he buried himself inside her, and with it, he buried the last vestiges of his life as a warrior-monk.

From here on, the monk part of his life was definitely over.

He was just a warrior now.

Chapter 38

✝

"The hands. They're all here, all four of them," Tess grumbled. "Neither one of these is Conrad. He didn't die here."

Abdülkerim stared at her with utter confusion. "So why is his name carved into that wall?"

Tess ignored the question and slid down onto her haunches, cupping her face in her hands and blocking the world out for a moment. She wanted it all to go away, all of it. She just wanted to be back home, in New York, with Kim and her mom close by, spending her days filling her laptop's blank screen with words and her nights curled up with a cool glass of sauvignon blanc, Corinne Bailey Rae's dreamy swoons in the background, and Reilly by her side. The mundane never felt so attractive, or out of reach, and she wondered if she'd ever enjoy such simple times again.

"Tess? Our friend asked you a question."

The Iranian's eerily dispassionate voice yanked her back to the bleakness of the canyon.

She looked up, half-dazed, struggling to order her thoughts. They were both still there, of course, the Iranian looming over her impatiently and the Byzantinist sitting on a wide boulder opposite her.

"Why is Conrad's name on this wall?" she asked, her

tone reeking with exasperation. "How the hell should I know?"

"Think," the Iranian insisted drily.

Tess felt the walls of the canyon creeping in on her. She wondered if it was better for her to remain useful to him, very much doubting that he'd actually just let her go if his quest did hit a brick wall, but her brain wasn't playing ball. No epiphanies were forthcoming.

"I don't know."

"Think harder." The Iranian's words had an unsettling finality to them.

"I don't know," she shot back angrily. "I don't know any more than you do. I mean, God knows what happened here. We don't even know if these skeletons are really those of the other Templars."

"Well, let's look at both possibilities. What if they are?"

She shrugged. "If they're really the bones of the knights who went to the monastery with Conrad, then he's the only one of them left. And if that's the case, then I'd expect that he was the one who buried his buddies here and carved the names on the wall—including his own."

"Why would he do that?"

An answer quickly formed in Tess's mind, and much as she didn't want to voice it, she didn't have much of a choice. "To buy himself some peace. To put off anyone who was on his trail."

"Which makes sense if he's carrying something important. Something he wants to protect."

"Maybe," Tess fumed. "It's not here, is it? But if he didn't die here, he could be anywhere . . . Though I can't imagine that a one-handed man alone in enemy territory could get too far, even if he was a Templar knight."

"Unless he found refuge with one of the Christian communities just north of here," the Iranian speculated.

Just then, something caught her eye. A reaction, small but perceptible, in the Byzantinist's expression.

The Iranian caught it too. "What?" he asked.

"Me? No, it's nothing," Abdülkerim muttered, not very convincingly.

The Iranian's hand flew out so fast neither Tess nor the Turk saw it coming. The slap hammered the Byzantinist's jaw, rocking it sideways and sending him flying off his perch and crashing onto the ground in a heavy thud and a plume of dust.

"I won't ask you again," the Iranian told him.

Abdülkerim stayed down, trembling. After a moment, he raised his eyes to the Iranian. He looked pulverized by fear. "There might be something," he stammered. "Not far from here." He turned to Tess. "Do you know which hand Conrad was missing?"

"The left one. Why?"

Abdülkerim frowned, like he wasn't sure he should be saying this. "There's a fresco, in the rock church, in the Zelve Valley. The church is in ruins, like all the other, but ... the painting is still there. It shows a man, a warrior. Someone the villager there thought highly of. A protector."

"What does that have to do with Conrad?" the Iranian asked.

"The warrior was referred to on the mural as 'the one true hand,' fighting off the heathen. One of his hand is visible while the other is missing—the left one. I always assumed it was a metaphor, you know, one of those crazy legend from the times of the Crusade." He paused, then pointedly added, "The man in the fresco is buried in the church's crypt. I think it could be your Conrad."

"'The one true hand,'" the Iranian repeated. He gave Tess a satisfied, "this sounds promising" look. "I think I'd like to see that church."

REILLY'S HORSE SLOWED as it reached the ridge that bordered the *yayla* he had traversed. Patches of wild lavender and wormwood scrub covered the slope, beyond which was a wide plain that spread south all the way to distant mountains. He paused there to get his bearings, his back and thighs aching from the long, saddleless ride. The horse, panting heavily after the uninterrupted journey, was also in bad need of a breather.

The air was still, the valley silent. Reilly sensed movement down his left flank and looked across. An old woman was standing underneath a thicket of almond trees, beating the branches of one of them with her walking stick. Fresh leaves were falling to the ground, where a small flock of sheep were feasting on them. The trees were all stunted after centuries of being struck that way. The old woman felt Reilly's attention and looked over. She eyed him with little interest, then turned away and carried on with what she was doing.

Reilly pulled out his map and compared it to the landscape laid out before him. The valley was a beige canvas bordered by softly undulating rock formations and dotted by pockets of pine trees, apricot orchards, and vineyards. He focused on the left side of the valley, his eyes roaming across the area that Tess had circled on the map. He could make out the dark cracks of several canyons that had been cleaved into the valley bed, but he saw no signs of life. Just undisturbed nature, stretching for miles—

—then he noticed something.

A disturbance.

A spot of movement, half a mile away, at the edge of one of the canyons.

He pulled out his binoculars.

They were distant, but there was no mistaking the familiar silhouettes. It was them. Tess, the Iranian, and someone else, someone he hadn't seen before.

He felt like his heart had been released from a bear trap. The sight of her blasted a wave of relief through him. She wasn't free, or safe—but at least he'd caught up with her.

The three tiny figures reached a thicket of trees where Reilly saw a parked vehicle, a beige SUV that he recognized as a Jeep Cherokee, the smaller, boxy one from a couple of generations back. He turned his attention to the third figure, wondering if it was friend or foe, then watched as all three of them climbed into the car. The new guy was behind the wheel, with Tess next to him and the Iranian in the back. There was nothing in the arrangement that indicated whether the driver was an ally of the Iranian or someone else, maybe someone he was using to drive them around or some kind of local guide. For the time being,

Reilly had to assume the man was an enemy. Not that it really mattered just yet. His gut was already twisting at the thought of what was happening.

Sure enough, they were now driving off, away from him—and he was half a mile away and sitting on a half-dead horse.

He spurred the horse on, kicking and yelling and slapping its rump to get it moving. The tired animal lurched forward hesitantly, clearly reluctant to head down the slope.

"Come on, damn it, let's go," Reilly yelled as he tried coaxing it on by squeezing his thighs together and nudging the back of each of the animal's front legs as it came toward him. The horse grudgingly picked up a bit of speed, whinnying in protest and kicking up dust as it finally clambered down the hill. Reilly tried to keep track of the Jeep's movements while guiding his ride onward, and saw the SUV bouncing across the plain, heading west. He steered his mount to the right as soon as it hit level ground, putting it on a diagonal trajectory to the Jeep's motion, but he was still a few hundred yards away from the SUV. Then he saw it reach a small road and turn onto it. It was now heading directly away from him, and his heart shriveled up as he realized there wasn't much he could do to catch up with it.

Still, he kept the pressure on, summoning his inner cowboy and urging the horse on as best he could. The SUV had disappeared from view by the time he reached the road. He guided the horse onto the cracked asphalt, but he knew it was moving too slowly to have any chance of catching up with Tess. He had to find another way to keep going. A car, a truck, a motorcycle, anything motorized—even an old, beat-up pickup truck creaking under the strain of a mountain of watermelons, which was what he got, trundling up the road and honking for him to move aside.

He had little choice.

He steered the horse into the road, then tugged on the reins, forcing it to stop sideways and block the way. The pickup truck slid to a halt just a few feet short of him. Two men were in its cab, the driver jabbing his horn angrily, his passenger leaning out the window, both men yelling and waving for Reilly to get out of the way.

It didn't take long.

A wave of the handgun did the trick with ruthless efficiency, and a few frantic seconds later, Reilly was on the road again, hurtling after the long-gone Jeep with a truckful of watermelons in tow.

Chapter 39

✠

With every leaden step, reality receded further and further from Tess's mind as she followed Zahed and Abdülkerim across the alien terrain.

She wasn't sure where she was anymore. Her eyes were having a hard time focusing, and her feet felt like they were made of lead. The relentless strain of the last few days, compounded with the heat and the lack of sleep, was debilitating. Worst of all was the haunting mirage that was Reilly. It wouldn't leave her. She was desperate to know that he was all right, that he hadn't died on that mountain, but she knew she wasn't about to find out soon, and possibly never would. The uncertainty was crippling and added to the sense of disorientation that she felt, a feeling that was heightened even more by the bewildering landscape around her.

The valley they were hiking through was very different from the canyon where they'd found the Templars' grave. In fact, it was unlike anything she'd ever seen before. It was broader and edged by bizarre clusters of huge pinkish white stone cones and turrets. Fields of fairy chimneys dotted the plain haphazardly, mushroomlike spires twenty or more feet tall that were topped by caps of rust red basalt. Framing the whole surreal spectacle were gentle slopes that rose up to a crowning cornice of vertical tufa. And while the valley may have looked disconcertingly like a behemoth meringue tray, it was the canyon within it, the one that they were now traversing, that threw Tess the most. Everywhere she looked, dark openings in the rock formations peeked out at her. It was one of three parallel canyons that held the ancient—and now deserted—village of Zelve and its walls were riddled with living quarters, hermitages, churches, and monasteries that had been excavated out of the most unlikely of places. From the narrowest of fairy chimneys to the soaring rock walls that lined the ravines, there didn't seem to be a patch of smooth rock that wasn't studded with a small window. Hundreds of rock-hewn sanctuaries were scattered across the region, tucked away in its valleys and hidden ravines, their walls covered with a veritable trove of Byzantine art.

From the earliest days of the faith, Cappadocia was an important cradle of Orthodox Christianity, second only to Constantinople. Paul of Tarsus—St. Paul—preached throughout the area just twenty years after the Crucifixion. Cappadocia soon became a refuge for the first followers of the Cross who were fleeing Roman persecution, its mazelike landscape providing a natural shelter from danger. In the fourth century, Basil the Great, the bishop of nearby Kayseri and one of the so-called "Cappadocian Fathers" of the faith, witnessed monasticism on a trip to Egypt and brought the concept back with him. Monks started colonizing the area like moles, building anything from individual prayer cells in ten-foot-wide spires to rock-cut churches of surprising grandeur and multilevel monasteries that reached high into the cliffs.

The burrowing didn't only extend aboveground. With the Mongol and Muslim conquests under way, it expanded below the surface. Dozens of underground cities—some whose origins dated back to the Hittites—riddled the area, and many of them hadn't yet been fully explored. Some of them extended as much as a dozen levels below the surface, perhaps even more, vast labyrinths of tunnels, living quarters, and storage rooms. With their ingeniously designed air shafts and one-ton "millstone" trapdoors to keep enemies out, they served as sanctuaries for entire communities whenever invading hordes were running rampant aboveground and helped the Orthodox Christian population cling to the valleys and ride out the centuries of Seljuk and Ottoman rule pretty much unscathed.

Ironically, it wasn't until 1923, in the dawn of the secular Turkish Republic, that the Christians were finally expelled from the region. Under the forced repatriation agreement between Turkey and Greece that followed the four-year war between the two countries, the local Orthodox population was resettled in Greece while Muslim Turks moved into the valleys in its place. Following the exodus, most of the churches and monasteries there gradually fell into disrepair, through neglect and vandalism, a sad end to the last surviving link to the glory of Byzantium that had started over one and a half thousand years earlier.

As they moved through a cluster of thirty-foot-tall rock cones, Tess was finding it hard to keep in mind that the canyon had been colonized by humans. In her exhausted, weary state, it looked more like something trolls would inhabit, and her mind kept dredging up disturbing images of Morlocks and sand people creeping out of the dark recesses and dragging her away.

Zahed's voice broke through her daze.

"Where are all the tourists?" he asked Abdülkerim. "This place is like a ghost town."

Although the valley was a national park, they hadn't encountered more than a half dozen groups of hikers, each with no more than a handful of individuals in it.

"This canyon and the two on either side of it were deemed unsafe back in the fifties," the Byzantinist explained. "The caves were crumbling on their occupant. All the villager were relocated to a new town a few kilometers away, and nowadays, tour group prefer to stick to safe areas, like Göreme."

"The less, the merrier," Zahed said, his eyes surveying the trail ahead. "How much farther?"

"Almost there."

Moments later, they had cleared the cone village and paused by a featureless rock face. The sun was much lower now, its shifting angle bathing the moonscape around them in a striking mix of pinks and blues.

"This is it," the Byzantinist announced.

It didn't look like much until the man pointed upward. Tess followed his direction. There was a gaping, square-cut hole in the side of the cliff, about fifty feet above her head. It was an exposed room—part of a room, actually—that had been carved into the rock.

"The church's outer wall collapsed in a rock slide centuries ago," Abdülkerim explained, "taking with it the entrance tunnel and the stair that led up to it."

"So how do we get up there?" Zahed asked.

"This way," the Turk said as he led them to the edge of the cliff and pointed out the footholds that had been chiseled into the smooth wall of tufa.

"Lead the way." Zahed gestured.

Abdülkerim went first, followed by Tess, then Zahed. They clawed their way up the crumbly wall and managed to reach a small ledge. Steep, eroded steps led from there to the three-walled chamber. There was no railing at its edge. Its floor just ended with a drop straight down the cliff.

Tess looked down. The sight made her wince. "I can see why this isn't exactly heaving with tourists."

The Turk shrugged. "This was the vestibule of the church," he explained. "Come. The nave is through here."

He led them through a narrow doorway and switched on his flashlight.

The room they were standing in was surprisingly large, around forty feet deep and half as wide. Aisles ran along either side of it, separated from the nave by columns that were purely decorative as they weren't supporting anything, given that the entire church had been carved out of the soft rock. The nave rose to a soaring, barrel-vaulted ceiling and ended in what looked like a horseshoe-shaped apse.

"The mural's this way," Abdülkerim said, leading them farther into the church, "and the burial chamber's under us."

Tess followed him, her eyes roaming the Byzantine frescoes that covered every inch of the cavernous chamber's walls and ceiling. In the soft, bouncing beam of his flashlight, she glimpsed biblical scenes she was familiar with, such as Christ's Ascension and the Last Supper, as well as more local religious iconography, like a mural of Constantine the Great and his mother, Saint Helen, who was holding the "True Cross," the actual cross on which Jesus was crucified, which she believed she had found on a relic-finding pilgrimage to Jerusalem in A.D. 325.

The walls were also rampantly covered with more disturbing imagery. One fresco showed a monster with three heads and the body of a serpent, devouring the damned. Another showed naked women being attacked by snakes, and another showed a giant locust being warded off by two crosses. Adding to the discomfort was the fact that most of the figures in the murals had their eyes, and sometimes their entire faces, scratched out, defaced by the Muslim invaders who believed that doing so killed the subject in the painting. The frescoes higher up and the ones on the curved ceiling, however, were undamaged, presumably because they were harder to reach. Cold, striking faces with intact almond eyes, black, cordlike eyebrows, and stern, angular mouths stared down at Tess, the smooth paint making it seem as if their skin itself had been plastered onto the wall.

Abdülkerim stopped at the far end of the nave, by the apse. Tess now realized that the darkness had hidden the fact that there were in fact three apses spreading out off the nave. Next to one of them was a doorway, through which Tess could make out a passage.

The Byzantinist shone his light at a mural high up on the half dome of one of the apses. It was a richly detailed work, delicate and finespun, dominated by pale hues of red ocher and green. Crucially, it was also unscathed. It showed a man, on foot, engaged in battle against four warriors. He wore no helmet or chain mail and had no horse. Behind him, several villagers were shown to be hiding in dark openings in a rock face.

The warriors, given that they wore turbans and held scimitars, were clearly Muslim. The figure fighting them was lunging with a broadsword in his right hand. His left hand was held up high, defiantly.

Tess leaned in for a closer look.

The figure's left hand was clearly missing, but it wasn't

due to any paint flaking off. It simply hadn't been painted in. The figure's forearm just ended in a rounded stump.

She saw the inscription on the mural. It was in Greek, written in bold uncial lettering. She concentrated on translating it, drawing on a reasonable familiarity with the language, but one she hadn't put to use in a long time. The Byzantinist stepped in and saved her the trouble.

"'*The one true hand vents his wrath on the heathen raiders*,'" he read out.

Tess glanced at the Iranian. If he was feeling any anticipation, he wasn't showing it. She turned back to the mural. There was another inscription, in smaller letters, above and to the right of the battling figures.

"What does that one say?" she asked.

"'*As for pain, like a hand cut in battle, consider the body a robe you wear. The worried, heroic deeds of a man and a woman are noble to the draper, where the dervishes relish the light breeze of spirit*.' It's from a poem. A Sufi poem, written by none other than Rumi himself."

Which threw Tess. "A Sufi poem? Here? Written in Greek?"

The Byzantinist nodded. "It's unusual, but it's not that surprising. Rumi lived and died in Konya, which is only a couple of hundred mile west of here. Konya was the center of Sufism. Still is, spiritually at least. The Sufis and the Christian of these valley would have been allies of sort, outsiders—followers of an alternative faith living in a sea of Sunni Muslim."

"Let's see the tomb," the Iranian interjected. Some impatience was coloring his tone, for once.

Abdülkerim looked at him with quiet resignation, then shrugged. "This way," he muttered.

The three of them walked in single file, trailing the flashlight's beam down the narrow passage by the side apse. Any natural light from outside was now barely coming through, but the beam was strong enough to light up the ceiling, which was enlivened by an elaborate pattern of crosses that were carved in low relief within a grid of sunken lozenges, before it faded into the shadows.

The passage led to a steep flight of narrow steps that

corkscrewed downward. A small vestibule was at its base and gave onto five rooms. It was too dark to see beyond their doorways. Abdülkerim shone his light into each of them briefly to get his bearings, then said, "It's this one."

He led them into the crypt. It was a long, low-ceilinged room. In its flat floor, Tess noticed two parallel rows of rectangles of hard-packed earth, one row lining each side of the room. They were hard to discern, but they were there, cut into the tufa from which the entire church had been carved. Each patch seemed just big enough to accommodate a human body, and the walls behind them bore inscriptions that were more or less regularly spaced. On closer look, Tess realized they were names.

"They're church elders, and donors," Abdülkerim explained. "These church were expensive to carve and decorate. The paint alone cost a small fortune back then. By paying for this church, these people bought themselves a ticket to Heaven. And a burial spot in here."

Tess surveyed the names and stopped at one of the graves. She recognized the Greek letters. "This is it," she said.

Zahed and Abdülkerim joined her.

"The one true hand," she read.

She looked over at the Iranian, guessing what was in store. Sure enough, he was already unloading the pick-shovel combo, which he handed to her.

"Let's get to work."

Chapter 40

✚

This one was harder to dig out, but at least it was just one grave.

The narrow space felt suffocating, what with the weakening light of the flashlight and the dust that the digging was kicking up. It made Tess work even harder. She just wanted to be out of there as quickly as possible.

The body they found was wrapped in two-foot-wide strips of white linen, like a mummy, and covered with seeds that had long since petrified. Tess and Abdülkerim got down close and carefully peeled back the stiff fabric. The bones within were loose and jumbled up, but one thing soon became clear. There were only enough of them for one hand.

There was something else in there, too.

A prosthetic hand, made out of copper. It was corroded and oxidized, tarnished to a dark brown patina with greenish blue patches all over it. It was startlingly elaborate and well crafted for something that was seven hundred years old.

She held it up to the Iranian. "It's Conrad," she said, then gave him a "what now?" look.

He mulled it over for a beat, then said, "If he had it with him, it's got to be around here somewhere. Maybe even buried with him." He thought about it for a further moment, then said, "Take him out. Let's see if there's anything else down there."

Tess and the Byzantinist lifted the linen cocoon out and set it down in the middle aisle. Tess then stepped back into the shallow pit, got down on her knees, and started digging some more. After only a few strokes, the pick struck something hard, sending a recoil of adrenaline through her. With renewed focus, she started clearing the earth around the hard object with her hands.

"Give me some more light," she told Abdülkerim.

He shone the flashlight at her hands as she scraped the earth back to expose what appeared to be a dark round shape. She cleared more soil from around it to reveal a plain earthenware cooking pot, low and wide, about a foot and a half in diameter and under a foot tall. Her breath caught. She studied it for a beat, then lifted it out carefully and settled it on the flat part of the grave.

She examined it closely. It was plain and unremarkable, lacking any external decoration, and it had some kind of a bowl for a lid that was sealed into place with bitumen.

Abdülkerim's eyes bounced around from the pot to Tess and to the Iranian and back. "What do you think is in it?"

"Only one way to find out," Zahed said.

He snatched the pick from Tess and, before she could stop him, slammed it into the top of the pot. The plate that was sealing it shattered. Zahed then pried off the pieces that were still hanging in place.

He took the flashlight from the Byzantinist and aimed it inside the pot, then turned to Tess, making an inviting gesture with his hand.

"Be my guest," he told her. "After all your hard work, you deserve it."

She looked at him askance, then leaned in for a look. The sight made her heart bolt. She reached in and pulled out the pot's contents: two codices—small, ancient leather-bound books, each roughly the size of a hardcover novel.

She held them with quivering fingers, carefully, as if they were made of the most fragile porcelain, marveling at them. For a blissful instant, all the horrors she'd been through, the Iranian monster standing inches from her—it all faded away. Then she set one down in her lap and examined the other.

"What are they?" Abdülkerim said, his tone a whisper.

Tess gently unfurled the thin leather strap that was rolled around the first codex. The back cover extended into a triangular flap that folded over the front one. She peeled that back, then, slowly, opened the codex.

The golden brown papyrus leaves inside were clearly brittle, their edges crumbled in places. She didn't dare turn a single page, so as not to damage the manuscript, but the lettering on the first page was enough to announce what she was looking at.

"Alexandrian text-type letters," she said. "It's written in Greek."

"What does it say?" the Iranian asked.

Tess read it, then looked up at Abdülkerim and showed it to him. Even in the faint light in the cavern, the astonishment on her face was evident.

The Byzantinist was clearly familiar with Greek writing, his area of expertise. "The Gospel of Perfection." He looked at Tess. "I've never heard of it."

"Me neither. But it's in Greek. *Koine Greek*," Tess said to the Byzantinist, emphasizing the point.

The Byzantinist's expression morphed to mimic Tess's surprise as her point sank in—something the Iranian caught too.

"What about it being in Greek? Why's that such a surprise?" he asked.

"Koine Greek was the lingua franca—the working language—of the Near East during Roman times. It's what any gospels that would have been written around the time of Jesus's life would have been written in. But we don't have any original copies of gospels from back then. The oldest Bibles we have are in Greek, but they're from the fourth or fifth centuries. The older texts we have aren't from the Bible. They're noncanonical, gnostic gospels, like the Gospel of Thomas that was found in Egypt in 1945—and they're Coptic translations of earlier Greek texts." She held up the codex. "This isn't Matthew, Mark, Luke, or John. But it's in

Koine Greek, which means it's an original. Not a translation. It might be the oldest full gospel ever found."

The Byzantinist looked baffled. "Why is it here? How did you know about this?"

"What about the other one?" the Iranian interjected, ignoring Abdülkerim.

Tess set the first codex down and picked up the second book. Again, taking great care, she opened it. Although the two codices were very similar outwardly, this one was different in that it consisted of bound parchment leaves, not papyrus, indicating that it was likely to be more recent than the first. The lettering was the same, though. It was also written in Koine Greek.

"The Gospel of the Hebrews," she read. This was a title she recognized. She looked up from it. "This is one of the 'lost' gospels. Some of the founders of the Church talked about it in their writings, but it's never been found." Her fingers brushed the open leaf with profound reverence. "Until now."

Her heart pounding, she was leafing through its first few pages slowly, her eyes roaming the tiny letters, trying to grasp what they said, when she saw something else. A folded sheet of parchment, inserted between the pages of the book.

She pulled it out and realized it wasn't just one sheet, but four, all folded onto one another. It had to be an official document of some kind, as it was sealed with a dark reddish brown wax seal that had left its impression on the pages of the codex it had been sitting against. She pulled Abdülkerim's light closer for a better look and bent a corner of the top sheet back slightly, but she couldn't see much beyond some of the letters on it. They were different from those in the codices.

"I think it's Latin, but I can't see what's inside without breaking the seal," Tess told Zahed.

"So break it," he replied.

Tess exhaled with frustration. It was pointless to argue with the man. She just fumed in silence and slid her fingers under the upper fold of the sheet. As gently as she could, she popped the seal off the parchment, but still couldn't help cracking it in two. The seal had fulfilled its purpose, even hundreds of years after it had been put in place.

Tess folded the sheets open slightly, making sure she didn't crack them.

The writing on them was indeed different. The words they held were written in Roman literary cursive script—that is, in Latin, not Greek.

"What is it?" Abdülkerim asked.

"It looks like a letter." She squinted as she studied it. "My Latin's not great." She held it up to him. "Can you read it?"

The Byzantinist shook his head. "Greek, no problem. Latin, not my speciality."

She perused the text; then her gaze rushed to the bottom of the last sheet.

"'*Osius ex Hispanis, Egatus Imperatoris et Confessarius Beato Constantino Augusto Caesari,*'" she read out. She paused, her neurons ablaze with the significance of what she could be holding in her hand, which was trembling. Lost in her own world for a brief moment, she mouthed, in a low voice, "Hosius of Spain, imperial commissioner and confessor to the Emperor Constantine."

Zahed's eyebrows rose in a rare display of piqued curiosity.

"Hosius," Abdülkerim observed. "The bishop of Córdoba. One of the Church's founding fathers."

"The man who presided over the Council of Nicaea," Tess added. Something occurred to her as she said it. "Nicaea's near here, isn't it?" she asked.

The Byzantinist nodded, frowning with confusion as he processed the information. "It's close to Istanbul, but yes, I suppose it's not that far from here. It's called Iznik nowadays."

Tess could see that he was bursting to ask her a hundred questions and was just barely managing to hold himself back. Nicaea was an iconic word as far as the early days of Christianity were concerned. There were a lot of unanswered questions as to what had really happened at that historic gathering back in A.D. 325, when Constantine the

Great had summoned the senior bishops from all of Christendom and forced them to settle their disputes and agree on what Christians were supposed to believe in.

Tess looked over at Zahed. "We need to get this translated," she told him.

The Iranian was also lost in his thoughts. "Later," he replied. "Pass them over to me."

Tess took one last look at the document, hesitated, then folded it and placed it back inside the codex as she had found it. She handed both books back to him, and he slipped them into his rucksack.

"Let's see if there's anything else buried with him," he said as he handed the pick back to her.

Tess's mind stumbled. The man didn't seem at all fired up by what they had just unearthed. She thought of questioning it, but decided against it. Instead, she just got back on her knees and dug and prodded around the rest of the grave.

There wasn't anything else buried there.

She looked across at the Iranian.

He seemed dissatisfied. "We're missing something."

Tess couldn't hold back anymore, and her exasperation spilled over. "What are we missing?" She flared up angrily. "This is it. We've done everything we can. I mean, hell, we found his grave. We found these texts, and whatever's in them—that's already one hell of a find. These gospels . . . they're unique. And this man, Hosius . . . he was Constantine's head priest. He was there when Constantine decided to become a Christian. He was at Nicaea, for God's sake. He was there when all the arguments about what Jesus really did and what he really was were thrashed out and when Christianity became what we know it as today. It's where they came up with the Nicene Creed that churchgoers still recite every Sunday. His letter can tell us a hell of a lot about how that really happened. What more do you want? What the hell are we doing here anyway? What more do you think you're going to find?"

The Iranian smiled. "The devil's handiwork, of course. All of it."

"There is no devil's handiwork. They're old gospels."

Just as she said it, she grimaced. An understanding came bursting out of the dust and the darkness.

"You don't get it, do you?" he said, mocking her. "These writings and whatever else the Templars were transporting terrified those monks so much that they were willing to murder to keep them hidden. Then they killed themselves when they lost control of them. They're not just gospels. To them, they *are* the devil's handiwork. They refer to them as something that could devastate their world, their *Christian* world." He paused, then added, pointedly, "Your world."

"And that's why you want them?"

His smile broadened. "Of course. Your world is already crumbling. And my guess is, this could really help you along your downward spiral. Coming on the back of all these pedophile scandals the Vatican has been so helpful in suppressing? The timing couldn't be better."

A nasty chill prickled the back of her neck, but she tried not to show it. "You think you can undermine people's faith that easily?"

"Absolutely." The Iranian shrugged. "I think your people are more deeply religious than you give them credit for. Which makes them all the more vulnerable."

"I know how religious a lot of us are. I just don't think anyone really cares about the fine print."

"Maybe not all of them . . . but a lot of them do. Enough of them to really cause problems. And that's good enough for me. Because that's what it's all about. That's what you people don't understand. This battle, this war, between us . . . this 'clash of civilizations,' as your people like to call it. It's a long-term fight. It's not about who's got the biggest gun. It's not about landing one big killer punch. It's about attrition. It's about killing the body slowly, with lots of well-placed jabs. It's about relentlessly chipping away at the soul of your enemy with every opportunity you get. And right now, your country's in bad shape. Your economy's shot. Your environment's shot. No one trusts your politicians or your bankers. You're losing every war you get into. You're more divided than ever and you're morally bankrupt. You're on your knees on every front. And every jab, every uppercut that can help bring you further down is

worth pursuing. Especially when it comes to religion, because you're all religious. All of you. Not just the churchgoers. You're even more religious than we are."

"I doubt that," Tess scoffed.

"Of course you are. In more ways than you realize." He
thought for a beat, then said, "I'll give you an example. Remember that earthquake that killed tens of thousands of
people in Haiti recently? Did you notice the way your leaders reacted to it?"

Tess didn't get the connection. "They sent money and
troops and—"

"Yes, of course they did," the Iranian interrupted. "But
so did the rest of the world. No, what I'm talking about is
how your leaders really felt about it. One of your most popular preachers went on national television when it hit. You
remember that? He said it had happened because the Hai-
tians had made a pact with the devil. A pact with the devil,"
he laughed, "to help them get rid of the French tyrants who
ruled over them a long time ago. And the amazing thing is,
he wasn't laughed off the stage. Far from it. He's still hugely
respected in your country, even though he just sat there
making the same ridiculous speech preachers have been
making for hundreds of years, whenever an earthquake or
some other disaster strikes. But here's the part I find really telling. He wasn't the only one. Your own president—
your liberal, modern, intellectual president—he makes a
speech about it and he says that 'but for the grace of God,'
a similar earthquake could have hit America. Think about
it. What does that mean, 'but for the grace of God'? Does
he mean God's grace is protecting Americans and that His
grace chose instead to wipe out the people of Haiti? How
different is that from what that preacher was saying? You
really think your president's any less religious, any less superstitious, than that madman?"

"It's just an expression," Tess countered. "People survive something terrible and they think, 'God was watching
over me.' They don't mean it literally."

"Of course they do. Deep down, they really do. They believe it. Your president believes it. You all believe that your
God is the real thing and that, because you are Christ's

chosen people, He will protect you. You're as backward as we are," he chortled. "Which is why all this is important to me. And it's why I won't give up until we've finished what we started."

Tess felt her temples throbbing. The man was never going to give up. And if he ever did, he wasn't going to let her walk away.

The Iranian stared her down in silence, his eyes narrowing to feral slits. "This is a great start. You've done well. But it's not the whole story. Now, we know Conrad came here. From the looks of it, he battled some Muslim fighters. Maybe he died here too. Maybe. What we do know for sure is that when he and his men left the monastery of Mount Argaeus, they had three large trunks with them. Three large trunks that must have had more than just two books in them." He spread his hands out questioningly. "So where's the rest of it?"

Chapter 41

✠

They caught up with them late the next day.

Maysoon knew how to read the terrain well. It helped that she had grown up in the region. What didn't help was that there were six men out there, five of them viciously fit and able, and they were escorting something Conrad was keen to get back without risking any damage to it.

Given their disadvantage, there was only one option. An ambush. It had worked for the Turks. It would have to work for Conrad and Maysoon, if they chose their spot well.

They had to choose it exceedingly well.

They stalked Qassem and his outfit for a few hours, then tracked around them shortly before sunset and rode ahead to size up the ground the Turks would be covering the next day. Maysoon told Conrad they would have to make their move that morning. Any later, and the convoy would reach the wide-open prairies that led to Konya. It would be virtually impossible to take them by surprise there. The landscape was too flat and exposed. They needed to hit them while they were still making their way out of the pockets of trees, the swell of rolling sunbaked hills and valleys.

The problem was, even there, there weren't any great spots to choose from. None at all. The landscape was still too open to present any promising ambush points. There weren't any natural features that they could use. Furthermore, because the area didn't have any narrow trails, bridges, or crossings that the Turks would have no choice but to take, Maysoon couldn't even be absolutely certain of which route they would follow. Which meant that even the most cunning ambush could end up going to waste, with the intended victims not showing up.

They only had one choice. To hit the Turks during the night where they were camped out. Which wasn't a bad option, necessarily. They just needed to plan it right.

Exceedingly right.

One and a half versus six.

It took a while to find them. The Turks were camped out in a sloping thicket of trees, by the base of a winding valley. Conrad and Maysoon left their horses behind and crawled to within twenty yards of them, guided by the amber flicker of a small campfire the Turks had going and assisted by the glow of a bright gibbous moon. They tracked around their perimeter and noted the relative positions of what they saw: the horses, eight of them, tied to some trees off by the lower end of the slope; one man, seated cross-legged with his back to a tree trunk, watching over the animals; the wagon, its two horses still harnessed to it, the telltale silhouette of the trunks visible under a canvas cover; the men, asleep around the fire; another guard, on the opposite side of the small campsite, one they would have missed if it hadn't been for a fortuitous change of position he made that triggered a small rustle.

Conrad nodded to Maysoon. He'd seen all he needed.

They crawled back to safety, and Conrad explained his plan to her. They had a lot of preparing to do, and there wasn't much time to do it. Conrad wanted to hit the Turks just before first light, when the men would be most weary.

By the first hints of dawn, they were ready.

After hiding their horses well out of view from the campsite, Conrad and Maysoon made their way back through the trees and the bushes, carrying the bundles of dried branches and rope that they'd crafted, snaking their way to their staging point overlooking the Turks' mounts. They crouched low and watched. The man guarding the horses was still where they'd left him. He was also still awake. Not ideal, but not a disaster. Conrad had plans for him anyway. Plans that involved sneaking up on him and stuffing his forearm against the man's mouth while slitting his throat with Maysoon's dagger.

Plans that went through without a hitch.

He gave Maysoon a low "all-clear" whistle, and she joined him by the horses.

They worked quickly and quietly, tying one bundle securely to each horse.

Conrad glanced in the direction of the wagon. It was about forty yards away, though Maysoon would have to take a longer, arced trajectory to reach it while steering clear of her father and his men.

Conrad nodded to her. She reached into a leather pouch she had strapped over her shoulder and pulled out the tools she now needed: a fire-steel, a C-shaped piece of hard steel with a straight, sharp midsection; a long, narrow striking stone that had a prominent groove down its center; a small, egg-sized ball of dry grass; and a patch of char cloth made of dried touchwood fungus that had been soaked and boiled in urine.

She crouched low, turning her back to the cluster of sleeping men at the center of the campsite, and spread her tunic wide to shield her hands from any wisp of wind. She then started beating the fire-steel against the flat piece of flint, using short, choppy strokes, holding the touchwood tightly cantilevered over the edge of the striking stone. It didn't take long for a spark to fly up onto the char cloth, and a small patch of red ember lit up within it. With an expert touch, Maysoon then tilted the char into the nest of dry grass and started blowing on it, softly. A moment later, flames licked out of the tinder. She then slid it under a mound of kindling that, almost instantly, caught fire.

The dry grass and branches crackled in the night.

They now had to move fast.

"Go," he whispered. "I'll be close behind."

"You'd better be," she whispered back. She planted a quick, hard kiss on his lips, then slipped away.

He waited until she was about halfway to the wagon; then he eased across to the horses and untied them, quietly, one after another, all but the one that he and Maysoon hadn't lumbered with a special treat. He waited until he saw Maysoon's silhouette climb onto the wagon's bench; then he pulled a cluster of branches out of the kindling and, darting from one horse to the next, he lit up the bundles he and Maysoon had tied to their saddles. One after another, they burst into flame, causing the horses to panic and rear up while whinnying fiercely, with Conrad slapping their rumps and yelling manically to set them off even more.

The night burst to life.

The horses charged off through the trees, galloping furiously, dragging the bundles of flaming branches close behind them like fiery Christmas tree baubles, with flames licking at their tails and their buttocks. Two other bursts of activity snagged Conrad's attention. Through the trees, he glimpsed the wagon lurch forward and thunder away from the campsite, with Maysoon at the reins and cracking a whip, while over by the central bonfire, the Turks were on their feet and scurrying around in apparent confusion.

Manic shouts and panicked neighs echoed around him as the balls of flame disappeared into the forest. It was time for him to get out of there. He sprinted back to the horse he'd left tethered to its tree, the one he would ride out of there. He was ten feet from it when a man sprang into his way, blocking him. It was one of the trader's hired hands. The man drew a big scimitar. Conrad didn't even flinch. Without slowing down, he feigned a left and ducked right instead, avoiding the wild swing of the man's blade and plunging Maysoon's dagger deep into his rib cage. He only stopped long enough to yank it out of him and grab the man's scimitar; then he bolted for the horse, leapt onto it, and spurred it through the trees, hot on the trail of Maysoon and the wagon.

MAYSOON CHARGED THROUGH THE VALLEY without looking back, her sole focus being wrangling more speed out of the two horses that were pulling her and her heavily laden wagon.

Every bone in her body was rattling, every vein throbbing, as the open wagon bounced across the rugged trail. She needed to put as much distance as possible between herself and her father's outfit. They'd be coming after her—of that, she had no doubt, even though there was no reason for them to know who she really was. They'd have a hard time getting their horses back, but at some point, they would. The flaming balls of branches the horses were dragging would die out, and they would stop running. They might even seek out their owners themselves. She needed to give herself as big a buffer as possible and kept on whipping her horses. She knew Conrad would be faster than her. He'd eventually catch up with her. Once he did—assuming he did—they'd veer off onto a southerly heading, toward Christian land, while taking the time to cover their tracks.

So far, so good.

Until a pair of fleshy hands grabbed her from behind and pulled her off her seat.

In the dim predawn light and with the frenetic, jarring pace of the wagon, it took a moment for Maysoon to register who her aggressor was; then her long hair blew off her face and a heart-stopping realization struck them both.

It was her father.

He'd been asleep in the back of the wagon bed, behind the trunks. And right now, he looked even more startled than she was.

"You harlot," he rasped as he tightened his grip around her neck, pressing her down against the trunks. "You traitorous harlot. You steal from your own father?"

He wasn't really giving her much of a chance to answer him. She could barely breathe. She tried pushing his arms off, but he just swatted her hands away and gave her a brutal slap, before digging his fingers back into her neck and choking her again.

"You try to steal from your father?" he blurted again, in a mad rage. "From me?"

Maysoon was gasping for breath. The horses were still charging ahead at full stretch, following the natural bends in the valley, and the old wagon was careening out of control, jerking and shaking violently under her as its thin wooden wheels bounced and flew over the rough terrain. She felt her eyelids droop, felt herself blacking out, felt the world closing in around her and the darkness swallowing her up. Then one of the wheels must have hit a big rock, as the whole wagon bounced violently and swerved left and right, careening out of control before somehow straightening up and resuming its frantic charge. The jolt had knocked the trader off her, tossing him to one side, his hands coming off her neck and freeing up her windpipe. She heaved in some deep, desperate gulps and pushed herself away from him, then spun around to face him, her back turned to the horses.

Mehmet righted himself, keeping one hand on the back of the bench for balance. "I don't know how you thought you would get away with this," he barked as he reached under his sash with his other hand and pulled out a curved dagger. He held it up to her, its blade horizontal and level with her eyes. "But I'll make sure you never think that way again."

He lunged at her, swinging wildly, his face mangled under a furious scowl. Maysoon darted back with each stroke, ducking and bending and just managing to avoid the blade's path. Then he suckered her with another swing and followed it with a punch that caught her on the ear and sent her crashing back down onto the canvas.

THE TRADER SCURRIED ON TOP of her again, pinning her down on top of the canvas that covered the trunks. He had one hand clasped around her throat, choking the life out of her, while the other hand held the dagger right up against her cheek.

"Shame. Such a pretty girl," he grunted as he tightened his grip on her neck—and just then, he saw her eyes flare back to life and widen in shock as they took in something behind him. He'd been so caught up in the moment that it was only then that he became aware of the loud clatter of a horse that was galloping right alongside the wagon. He twisted around in a curious daze, and the sight that greeted him threw every muscle of his into a panicked lock: Conrad, alive and unscathed, on horseback, staring right at him. He held the reins in his mouth, biting down on them through clenched teeth, which only added to the demonic glint in his eyes. Mehmet flicked a glance left to see why that was, but his brain had already anticipated what they would find: a scimitar, swooping down in a big arc, its blade slicing through the bulbous flesh of his neck.

The trader's face twisted with shock as he dropped the dagger and grabbed at his neck. Blood was gushing out of him, his heart still pumping away with abandon, flooding his hands. He held them up to his face and stared at them in disbelief for a moment; then something jarred the wagon again, a ditch or another obstacle that the wheels plowed into at full tilt.

The wagon bounced wildly, bending and pitching heavily to one side, and in his weakened state, the trader lost his balance and flew over the side.

MAYSOON SHRIEKED AS THE WAGON bucked off the ground and came back down with a heavy thud. She couldn't see what it had hit, but whatever it was, it must have done some serious damage, as the wagon's ride had changed dramatically. Something must have happened to its axles or to its wheels, as it was now wobbling and juddering all over the place.

Conrad was still at full gallop, only he'd veered away slightly to avoid the runaway wagon and was now several feet off, though still alongside it. She saw him eyeing its wheels; then he looked up and caught her eye.

"The hub's come off," he shouted. "The wheel's cracked. It's going to come off any second now. Can you grab the reins?" He was gesturing frantically with his bare forearm, indicating the horses. "You need to stop thoses horses."

Maysoon nodded and clambered over the trunks and onto the bench. She looked for the reins, then saw them dragging on the ground, under the drop tongue, between the two horses.

She turned to Conrad and waved negatively. "I can't get to them," she yelled back.

Before she could say another word, the wagon dropped from under her as one of the wheels, the front left one, came off. She hung on as the wagon lurched to one side, then veered violently. Crossbars snapped and pins popped as the rickety conveyance flipped up and toppled over, flinging; Maysoon over its edge. She hung on as it overturned; then she found herself flying off as it crashed onto its side and plowed through the parched ground before the drop tongue sheared off under the tug of the horses. The wagon lurched to a stop as the horses charged away, relishing their release.

Maysoon hit the ground hard, rolling over several times before finally coming to rest on her back. Through groggy eyes, she saw Conrad appear beside her, leap off his horse, and hurry to her side.

"Maysoon," he yelled as he slid to his knees beside her. "Are you all right?"

She wasn't sure. She stayed down for a moment, heavy-headed, her body racked by aches and bruises, her breathing ragged, then tried sitting up, but her hand gave way under her and she toppled back.

"My wrist," she groaned. "I think it's broken."

Conrad helped her sit up and held her hand gently. Trying to move it shot a bolt of pain up her arm. It was badly sprained or broken, but either way, it was out of action.

She held it up to him with a bittersweet smile. "Now we're two halves," she said.

He took her hand, kissed it softly, then leaned in and gave her a long, intense kiss.

He helped her to her feet. The valley was quiet and still. There was no breeze, no movement anywhere. The sun was just creeping over the edge of a steep, bare slope to their right. It would soon get much warmer.

The wagon lay a few yards away, on its side, broken up, a trail of wooden debris behind it. The trunks had fallen out and were scattered around it. They walked over to survey the damage. Two of the trunks were intact, but the third had split open during its fall and its contents were spewed around it.

The horses were nowhere in sight.

"We need to get those horses back," she said.

"They're long gone," Conrad replied, downcast. "No reason for them to come back."

Maysoon was about to answer when she spotted something behind him, about a hundred yards away. A human-shaped lump. She frowned and nodded it to Conrad. He turned and saw it too.

They walked toward it together. It was the trader's corpse, twisted around and covered in dust. They reached it and stood there, with Maysoon just staring at her dead father in silence. After a long moment, she heaved out a long sigh and said, "It's my turn to ask you to help me bury someone."

Conrad put his arm around her. "Of course."

He used his scimitar to dig into the parched soil. Maysoon helped him with her one good hand. He didn't say anything at first. She seemed to need to be left to her thoughts.

After a while, he said, "Earlier, when I asked you about why you were doing this, you said if I knew you better, I'd understand. What did you mean?"

She was still for a moment. "My father, my brother . . . things weren't always like this. When I was a child, in Konya, we had a good life. My parents were good Sufis. My mother especially. She filled our home with caring and love. And I think my father was different back then too. I still have memories of them, together. But after she fell ill and died . . . everything changed. We left Konya. We traveled around. My father became more bitter and nastier by the day. My brother fell under the spell of the Ghazis. He's been wanting to join them, you know. The idea of spreading the faith by the might of the blade holds great appeal to him. And my father was a clever man. He could see the way the wind was turning. He knew they'd end up conquering all these lands, and he wanted to make sure he was on the winners' side."

"And you disagreed with them?"

"You don't know about Rumi. You don't know what it

means to be a Sufi. And for them to turn their backs on something so noble, so sublime ... I couldn't just sit back and watch them turn into these monsters."

Conrad nodded. "They didn't take that well, did they?"

She shook her head, her face flooded with sadness. "No. Not at all."

"Why didn't you leave? Run away, maybe go back to Konya?"

"You don't think I tried?"

He remembered the bruises and nodded, then reached out and gave her face a gentle caress. "I'm sorry it had to come to this."

She shut her eyes and leaned into his hand, enjoying it for a moment. Then she kissed it and pushed it gently away. "Come on. We have work to do."

It wasn't the deepest of graves, but it would have to do. And Maysoon was right. They still had a lot to do.

They had to deal with the trunks and their contents.

They couldn't take them with them. All they had was one horse, the one Conrad had ridden in on. They couldn't just leave them there either. And whatever they were going to do, they had to do it fast. At some point, her brother and his outfit would recover their horses. They'd ride up the valley and find them.

Time was running out.

Then Conrad saw something. In the steep hill that rose up from the valley, now more noticeable under the high sun.

Its face was pockmarked with black holes.

Caves.

Hundreds of them.

They would have to do.

It took hours, but they managed it. Conrad cut up several six-foot-square sections of the canvas cover, then used them as makeshift wraps to ferry loads of the trunks' contents that were light enough for him to carry. Maysoon helped him divide the contents up into manageable loads. He chose one of the upper caves, one that was big enough to crawl through comfortably and tucked out of view, and slung the packs over his shoulder and hauled them up to it, one by one. It took almost nine trips, but by the end of it, the entire contents of the chests were safely nestled in the cave, wrapped in a protective layer of canvas, out of view.

Conrad wasn't comfortable about leaving the wagon behind. If and when Maysoon's brother and his men came across it, they might suspect that the consignment it held was still around somewhere. On the other hand, the Turks had no way of knowing who had attacked them, or how many they were. It had been dark, and no one had seen him or Maysoon close enough to be able to identify them. Provided the trunks were gone, Conrad felt there was a strong chance that the Turks would think whoever had attacked them had brought along enough horses to carry them off.

As long as he got rid of the trunks.

Which he did, using his scimitar to pry the lids off the two that weren't broken, then lugging all three of them up in pieces, to a different cave. Once he'd done that, he used some dried bushes to sweep away his tracks from both caves.

They could finally make a move.

"Will you remember how to get us back here?" he asked her.

Maysoon surveyed the valley, taking note of any landmarks that would help her identify it again. Her eyes settled on the distant mound that was her father's grave. "Don't worry," she said. "I won't forget this place. Not soon enough."

He helped her onto his horse, then climbed up behind her.

"Which way?" he asked.

They needed to find food, shelter, and horses, camels, or mules, any kind of transport that would allow them to recover the trove and complete their intended journey. A journey that, given the deaths of Hector and Miguel, now seemed questionable.

She nodded ahead and said, "North. There are Christian communities there, small villages and monasteries built into cliffs. They'll take us in."

Conrad gave her a doubtful look.

"They don't need to know what you just hid in those caves," she told him.

He shrugged. She was right.

He spurred his mount forward.

They trotted away, leaving behind her father's grave, leaving behind the trove that so many had died for, uncertain about what to do with it from here on.

Chapter 42

✝

Reilly advanced cautiously across the canyon, hugging the shadows.

He'd spotted the dusty Cherokee parked in a small clearing by the side of the road, sitting slightly apart from a handful of other cars. A rusting sign in three languages had told him it was a staging point for hikers setting off to explore the Zelve canyons and that had set his Spidey-sense tingling.

His eyes strained as they monitored the surreal landscape around him. There was too much for them to take in—unusual shapes casting unusual shadows, shapes his eyes weren't accustomed to, the entire target area riddled with ominous dark openings that felt like a thousand eyes tracking his every move. He felt like he'd been sucked into a Dalí painting or teleported into an episode of *Star Trek*, and it was impossible to keep it all under watch. Still, he concentrated on the bigger picture, making sure his peripheral vision was on high alert for any sign of movement.

He navigated his way through a cluster of fairy chimneys and reached a field of massive rock cones that nestled at the base of a tall cliff. Small windows peeked out of every one of them, vestiges of a long-gone community that had lived within. The cliff banked to the right, disappearing out of view behind a thicket of almond trees. The whole valley was eerily quiet now, adding to the sense of unease that Reilly felt with each new step through the ghost town.

He was about to clear the last of the rock cones when he glimpsed movement beyond the trees. He quickly ducked out of view into the doorway of the nearest house. He craned his head out carefully while reaching into his pack for his weapon—and they appeared. The man he didn't know, followed by Tess, then his quarry.

Walking his way.

Unaware of his presence.

Without taking his eyes off the approaching figures, Reilly muffled the gun between his thigh and the rock face and chambered a round, then brought the weapon up. If they were making their way back to the Jeep, they would go past him. Which would give him an opportunity to finish it—for good.

He watched as they rounded the cones, disappearing momentarily behind one of them before reappearing in a gap between two others. He crept carefully from one cone to another, keeping Tess and the others in view, inching closer, his gun ready in a tight, two-fisted grip, until he was about thirty yards from them and had a bead on the Iranian's back.

He debated pulling the trigger right there. Thirty yards, unobstructed view—he wouldn't have too much trouble dropping the bastard there and then. He straightened his arms and took aim, tracking his target with the sight on the automatic's barrel. His chest constricted as he tightened his finger around the trigger. One pull was all it would take. One pull and the motherfucker would be gone.

And none of the questions would be answered.

Not who he really was. Who he was working for. What else he had done. What else he was planning.

The answers would die with him.

Reilly ground his teeth, hard. Wanting to pull that trigger. Wanting it bad. But unable to follow through. And in that moment of indecision, in those fleeting few seconds, the opportunity vanished. The angle of the path meant that the Iranian was now positioned directly between Reilly and Tess, and a bullet from Reilly's gun risked going through him and hitting Tess. He had to find a clear shot again and thought of going for a thigh shot to at least cripple him—

Then he decided he wanted him alive and sprang out from his cover.

"Tess, move away," he yelled, his heart kicking at his rib cage. He was stepping sideways to find a clear angle at the Iranian and keep him off balance while waving Tess to one side before jabbing a finger straight at the Iranian. "You, get your hands up where I can see them. Do it."

They all spun around in surprise. Reilly flicked a quick glance at Tess and registered the relief flooding her face, but he couldn't afford any more than that and yanked his eyes back onto his target.

The Iranian had spread his arms out slightly, low, level with his waist. He had his gaze locked on Reilly and was inching sideways too, clearly thinking the same thing as Reilly and trying to keep Tess in a vulnerable place for a through-shot.

Reilly struck out an open palm at him. "Stop right there and get your hands all the way up. Do it," he growled. "Tess, get the hell away from him—"

And in that instant, everything went wrong.

The Iranian lunged at Tess, too fast and too close to her for Reilly to risk taking a shot, grabbing her and flinging her in front of him to shield himself. He had his right arm tightly clasped around her neck; then he moved his left hand out, just enough to give Reilly a clear view of it. He was holding a phone in it.

"She's wearing a bomb," he shouted back. His right hand went down her front and yanked her shirt up to reveal the canvas belt around her waist. "I'll blow her guts all over this fucking canyon if you don't drop your weapon right now."

Blood flushed into Reilly's temples. "You'll take yourself out too if you do that," he blurted, the realization that he was playing a losing hand flaring through him.

The Iranian grinned. "You think a good Muslim like me would have a problem dying for his cause?" His face tightened. "Put the fucking gun down or she dies," he barked.

Reilly felt his feet riveted to the ground, his arm muscles

taut to their tearing point. He had no choice. He sucked in a deep, slow breath and rotated the gun sideways and up, on display to the Iranian, his other palm open in a calming gesture.

"Put the safety on and throw it away," the Iranian ordered, his hand signaling to Reilly to toss it to his right. "Far."

Without taking his eyes off the bomber, Reilly flicked the safety on. Then he chucked the gun aside and watched it land about ten yards from him, thudding flat against the hard soil, his insides pulverized by the realization that he'd messed up and would probably soon be stone dead.

The Iranian's face relaxed, as did his grip on Tess. He took a step back and away from her, and as he did, his hand dove quietly into his rucksack.

The rucksack dropped to the ground by his feet as his hand came back up. It had a gun in its grip.

"Say hi to the virgins for me," he yelled out as his finger pulled the trigger.

Chapter 43

✟

He's going to kill Sean.

Wild emotions ripped through Tess as her eyes followed the handgun's flight and watched it hit the ground. First he's still alive—not just alive, but here, standing in front of her, unscathed. Not just that, but he's rescuing her. He's got a gun on the son of a bitch—and now he's going to die?

Because of her?

Because of her damn phone call?

No way.

She couldn't let it happen.

No fucking way.

With a ferocious, primal yell, she launched herself at her captor with the unbridled fury of a caged predator. Regardless of the consequences. Regardless of whether or not she was going to get blown apart. If she was going to die, if he was going to hit that button, she was damn well going to take him with her.

She took him by complete surprise.

She hit him hard, slamming into him from his left, the sideways tackle pushing him off his feet and swinging his gun hand wide just as he squeezed the trigger. She didn't see where the round went, didn't have time to see if Reilly was still standing, but her gut told her she'd got there in time and that Reilly had to be okay. What she did see was the Iranian's left hand—the one with the phone. She saw it come up in a defensive reflex just as she rammed him, saw it rising to block her, saw its grasp loosen, saw the phone fly out of it and fall to the ground—and in that millisecond, she felt her breathing cut out, felt the whole world freeze, expecting the explosion, expecting to feel her insides ripped out—but it didn't happen. She didn't explode. She was still there, in one piece, still there to feel the full brunt of the Iranian's elbow that flew up and smashed into the back of her jaw as they both fell to the ground.

REILLY'S HEART BLEW A GASKET as he saw Tess make her move.

It took over, overriding his brain, cutting off any attempt at thought and spurring his legs to just take off.

Which he did—fast, like a sprinter going for gold. Or steel, in this case. The hard, tempered steel of the automatic, ten yards to his right.

He'd seen the phone fly out of the bomber's hand, seen Tess tumble to the ground with him. He didn't have enough time to get to them and intervene. The Iranian would very quickly have the upper hand again. Reilly had to get to his gun, fast, and hope his aim would prove as true as it had been on his best ever day at the firing range. Or better. He'd get one shot, if that. It had to count.

His legs at full gallop, he flicked a quick glance sideways, but couldn't see more than the tangle of both bodies. He flung his eyes back at the ground ahead, at the gun.

Five yards.

Three.

One.

He was there.

TESS FELT HER BRAIN RATTLE under the impact of the Iranian's elbow, but she stayed on him, both hands clamped tight against his gun wrist like the jaws of a rabid wolf.

She had to keep the weapon at bay, just a second or two longer, knowing Reilly had to be on the move, hoping he'd soon be with her, but she only managed to keep the Iranian's gun hand pinned to the ground for a couple of heartbeats before his left hand flew up to her face and shoved her head back. She fell backward, but didn't let go, even as his gun hand rose off the ground and swung toward her.

Instead of recoiling backward, she surprised herself by doing the opposite. She lunged forward and pulled his hand closer to her before biting down into it as hard as she could. She heard the Iranian grunt-curse as her teeth sank into him, and she felt tendons and cartilage snapping under her bite. In the frenzy of the moment, she saw his fingers loosen around the weapon's grip, and her bite went into overdrive. The Iranian shouted angrily and reared up, lifting her up with him as he flung his arm to shake her off. She twisted on herself, felt her neck bending out of shape, but stayed on him, her teeth still digging in—then the gun flew out of his grip.

He lashed out with his other hand again, his fingers digging into her cheeks, looking for her eyes. The pain was too intense—she had to let go. The release unleashed him, and he pushed her off with a hard shove to her chest. She scurried backward, out of his reach, her eyes darting left and right, searching for the gun.

As were his.

Both found it at the same time, a few feet behind him. She met his eyes for a nanosecond, the raw anger blazing out of them more terrifying than the gun itself.

Then he moved, diving for the gun.

REILLY SNATCHED THE GUN off the ground and swung his arms around and up, into position, in a two-fisted stance, ready to take the shot, his eyes taking an instant read of the situation.

The first thing that registered was that the Iranian and Tess were a few feet apart and she was clear of him, which was good. Less good was that the Iranian had the gun in his hand—and was aiming it right at him.

Reilly squeezed off a round and dove to his left just as a volley of bullets whizzed by, so close that he actually heard them cutting the air mere inches from his cheek. He rolled on the ground, heading toward the nearest cone house, pulling the trigger every time he was lying on his front, but he knew full well that he wasn't likely to hit him like that, especially given that the Iranian was also low on the ground and made for a small target. He just had to keep him pinned down long enough to give Tess a chance to make a break for it.

Which, he now saw, she was doing.

THE REPORTS THUNDERED THROUGH TESS'S EARS and froze her in place—then she snapped back and got moving.

She saw Abdülkerim waving to her from behind a cone house and started for him before almost tripping over something: the Iranian's rucksack. She scooped it up by the handle without slowing down and sprinted across to join the Byzantinist.

The man was buzzing with panic. "The phone, that's the trigger to . . . ?" He couldn't even say the word.

"Yes," she fired back, flinching with each gunshot that echoed through the valley.

"Where is it?"

"I don't know," she replied, still breathless. "He dropped it."

"Come," he told her. "Follow me."

He led her through the maze of tightly packed cone houses.

"Where are we going?" she asked.

"In there," he said as he stopped by the doorway of a nondescript dwelling. He pointed inside it. "There's an underground city. Under this village. It's been shut down for years because of the rock slides, but some of it must still be accessible. You need to go down there quickly, you'll be safe in there. There's probably no phone signal, right?"

Tess nodded. He was right. "Okay, but—you're coming with me, aren't you? It's safer for you too."

"No, I—" He hesitated, his eyes twitching left and right. "I'll go get help."

"Listen to me," she insisted, grabbing him by the shoulders, "you'll be safer in there."

He looked at her, his forehead bathed with sweat, then shook his head and said, "I can't. I'll get help. You need to go now. Here," he said, digging into his pack and handing her his flashlight.

Tess took it from him—and just then, his eyes went wild and he pointed behind her.

"He's coming," he blurted.

Tess turned, her mind all jumbled with conflicting impulses—and saw the Iranian charging at her, saw him raise his gun, heard the shot, and felt Abdülkerim's blood splatter across her cheek.

ZAHED KNEW HE HAD to get out of there.

Reilly was rolling his way to cover. Once he got there, the American would be able to get a clearer shot at him. Zahed realized he was too exposed where he was; he had to make a run while he still had the chance.

He'd glimpsed Tess scurrying away with his rucksack—the one with the codices and his handgun's extra magazines in it. He'd brought his gun around to drop her, but the damned American's relentless firing had forced him to duck for cover and given her a chance to slip away.

Now he had to do the same.

He stayed low and let his eyes make a quick scan of the ground around him, searching for the phone. He quickly found it—off in the opposite direction to the cone houses he needed to get to for cover, the ones where Tess had disappeared.

He decided to risk it.

He rolled over to it, firing a couple of shots as he did and reaching it in three spins. He grabbed it, then sucked in a couple of quick breaths to steel himself and spring to his feet. He hurtled to the nearest cone house, peppering Reilly with gunfire as he sprinted across the hard ground, knowing that each bullet counted now that he no longer had the extra ammo clips. Just as he dove into cover, one of the agent's rounds bit into the rock inches from his head, sending tufa shrapnel biting into his cheek, but he was otherwise untouched.

He rushed through the cone houses, on edge, eyes scanning the shifting shadows. Then he saw them, two houses ahead, Tess and the Byzantinist, by the dark doorway.

He had to get to Tess. He needed the books and the ammo clips, and she was all the leverage he needed as far as Reilly was concerned.

The Byzantinist was less crucial right now.

More of a liability, actually.

Which was why Zahed raised his gun and fired.

TESS SCREAMED AS SHE WATCHED Abdülkerim drop to the ground. Blood was spewing out of his mouth, pumped up from the hole that been punched through his chest.

She spun her head back around. The Iranian was charging at her, now only a couple of cone houses away. A crippling fear surged through her. If the Iranian was up and coming for her, maybe he had his phone back.

With chilling synchronicity, he raised his hand—the one with the phone in it—to show her that he did. His scowl had one clear message in it:

Don't move an inch—or else.

Something snapped inside her. A surge of rage pushed her fear aside, fight taking over from flight. Her hands moved to either edge of the rucksack and slid it across her midriff so it was now pressed against the bomb in her canvas belt. Her face hardened as she glared at him defiantly, and she caught a reaction across his face and in his step. It wasn't any more than his eyes widening and his jaw tightening and him faltering for just a split second, but it was there, and it was enough to send a burst of badly needed satisfaction through her.

It didn't change the fact that he was still coming at her.

She had to move.

She cast one last glance at the fallen Byzantinist. The gurgling had stopped, and his eyes were staring out in a dead glaze. She forced herself to accept that there was nothing she could do for him now—then, with the rucksack still clutched against her midriff, she dove through the doorway.

She knew she had to get deep inside, and fast. The cone house was basically a habitable cave. Whatever faint light was seeping in from outside wasn't reaching far in. There was nothing but darkness ahead.

She rushed into it.

REILLY ROLLED INTO COVER BEHIND the cone house and risked a fast peek in time to see the Iranian make a break for it.

He managed to loose a couple of rounds, but had to pull back from the barrage of gunfire the Iranian rained back at him. He cursed inwardly as he rode it out for a couple of seconds; then he peered out again, knowing the Iranian wouldn't be there anymore.

He wasn't.

Fuck.

Reilly bolted out and chased after him, hoping against hope that the bastard hadn't already caught up with Tess.

Chapter 44

✠

Tess gave the cavelike interior a quick scan. The room had been hollowed out of the soft rock, the walls around her riddled with carved-out niches, some small, others big enough to sleep in. Its floor was littered with debris—a broken-up rattan chair, the faded sheets of an old Turkish newspaper, a few discarded water bottles and soda cans. It didn't look like anyone had lived there in years.

She spotted some stairs that spiraled upward in a far corner and stepped toward them, hoping the way down was there too—and her feet stumbled against a wooden hatch that was sunken into the floor. She dropped to her knees and ran her hands across it, brushing the dust off its uneven surface. It was hinged on one side. At its opposite end, her fingers found an old piece of rope that was fashioned into a handle, embedded into the dirt floor around it.

She yanked the hatch open. A cloud of dust billowed up, prickling her eyes and throat. She coughed as she pointed her flashlight into the gaping hole. A very steep flight of steps, also carved out of the tufa, led downward.

A growing rustle from outside, the crush of footfalls drawing near, spurred her to move. With the flashlight clasped tightly in one hand, she clambered down the stairs as fast as she could.

*　　*　　*

ZAHED CAREENED TO A STOP outside the cone house, by the blood-soaked body of the Byzantinist.

There was no one around, but he still didn't like the idea of leaving him lying there, signposting what had happened. He stuffed his gun in his pants and dragged Abdülkerim inside, dumping him just inside the doorway, out of view from anyone walking by.

He saw the open hatch and, in the far corner, the stairs leading up. He drew his gun and looked down through the opening in the floor. There was no sign of movement, no noise coming from there. He thought about it for a second, then crossed over to the stairs and climbed up a few steps, listening intently. He didn't need to go any higher—he could see debris littering the landing. It didn't look like it had been disturbed. His instincts had told him she'd gone through the hatch anyway.

He hurried back down and ducked into the black hole.

TESS WAS BREATHING HARD as she moved through the narrow tunnel.

The batteries in Abdülkerim's flashlight were clearly on their last legs, and the light it was giving off was weakening noticeably. She knew it wouldn't last long, and did her best to save batteries by not keeping it on all the time. She would flick it on and off intermittently, using it to get her bearings before advancing to the next landmark in total darkness. Electric cabling ran along the walls, linking one light fixture to another. There hadn't been any current running through the wiring for years, but it was still a useful trail to follow, and Tess did her best to keep one hand running along its thick, black rubber coating as it led her deeper and deeper into the subterranean maze.

By now, with more than a dozen caverns and tunnels behind her, her sense of direction was completely overwhelmed. She had no idea where she was. The "underground city" may not have been a city exactly, but it was still—literally—mind-boggling: a seemingly endless warren of chambers of all shapes and sizes connected to one another by low-ceilinged tunnels and narrow steps. There wasn't a right angle or a sharp corner to be found. Instead, every edge was rounded, every wall and ceiling curved, and it all had the same numbing color, a chalky off-white tinged with the dirty brown wash of time.

And it was tight. Maddeningly, suffocatingly tight. Even the larger chambers that were used as communal spaces felt unnervingly claustrophobic. The tunnels and stairs were the worst. They were little wider than her shoulders, and she had to stay hunched to get through them. They were that way by design. Invading warriors, if they managed to get past the handful of strategically placed millstones that could be rolled out with the flick of a small stone to block access to the entire underground maze, would have to advance single file after leaving their bulky shields behind. That made them easier to repel. In fact, the entire honeycomb was brilliantly designed as a refuge: There were huge storage spaces for food and animal feed, wineries, wells for water and air shafts for ventilation. Everything was planned defensively; even the chimneys of their fire pits branched out into many small outlets before they emerged aboveground, to spread out the smoke and help avoid detection.

As she advanced farther into the hollowed-out ground, Tess did her best to try to not think about the fact that the entire canyon above her had been condemned because of unstable ground and rock slides. Instead, she tried to remember that there was a saving grace to her being there: The bomb she was carrying around her waist was probably not a threat right now. Still, it wasn't enough to calm her nerves, as her earlier fear was now being replaced by one that was even more terrifying: whether she'd ever find her way back out of that rocky labyrinth and see daylight again.

After going down some steps and banking right through a particularly narrow passage, she found herself in a larger, airier room that had three rough-hewn columns down its center. A stable, perhaps, or an underground church. It didn't really matter. She paused to catch her breath and think. She guessed she was now on either the second or third level, and knew that there could be many more below her. She didn't want to venture too far down—the place was a maze and she ran a real risk of not finding her way back. She couldn't go back out yet, though. Not until she knew the Iranian and his cell phone were no longer a threat.

"Tess!"

The Iranian's yell shook her to her roots as it echoed through the hollow caverns.

"I just want those books," he bellowed. "Give them to me and I'll leave you alone."

She knew what he was doing. Goading her, prodding her to make a move, make a noise, answer back—anything that would reveal her position. Still, he felt dangerously close. So close, in fact, that she now heard scraping along the wall, coming her way.

ZAHED CREPT FORWARD, following the cabling, his trained senses alert for the smallest sign of life.

He figured Tess had to be following the cabling too. Her survival instinct would have told her to do so. Follow it down, and you can follow it back up. She had an advantage, though. The flashlight. He'd seen a faint glimmer of it, flicking on and off for the briefest moments, but it had been enough to draw him in like a homing beacon.

He thought of using his phone to light the way and tried it out. The screen didn't give off much light, and in his situation, it was more of a hindrance than an advantage. It didn't really show him much, but it would announce his presence to Tess. He decided not to use it for the time being. That would also save batteries, and he needed to be able to contact Steyl and other support when he needed it.

He felt himself emerging from a narrower passage into a larger space, and stopped and listened. He couldn't see anything around him, but he sensed her close. He held his breath and froze, concentrating on locking in on her likely position.

A lopsided smile spread across his face as he tightened his grip on the handgun and angled it ahead of him.

Then he fired a single round.

THE DETONATION BOOMED THROUGH THE CAVERN as the round whizzed past Tess and crunched into the wall somewhere beyond her. It took her by complete surprise and she couldn't help but shriek—and in that instant, she heard footsteps charging toward her.

Clutching the rucksack tight, she lunged away from the wall toward the center of the room, cursing at having given herself away like that, summoning her recall of the layout of the chamber and hoping she wasn't about to slam into one of its columns. She felt the Iranian veering toward her, and her whole body tightened in anticipation of his tackle or, worse, another gunshot. Then a different outcome played itself out at hyper–fast forward in her mind's eye, and she instantly adjusted her trajectory accordingly and sped up, hoping she'd gotten it right.

Her splayed fingers found one of the three square columns, and she rounded it and turned slightly, putting it between her and the rapidly approaching stalker—and just as she rounded it, she heard it, skin and bone slamming against stone along with an angry yell of pain.

Gotcha, you bastard.

She'd suckered him right into one of the columns, but there was no time to stick around and gloat. She had to get out of there. She veered back toward an opening she'd spotted in the opposite wall and spread her arms out protectively, looking for the edge of the wall. They found the corner of the rocky surface and she slowed right down and slunk into the passage, moving carefully while running her hand up the wall until it found the cabling. There was no question of using her flashlight anymore. She scuttled ahead, her feet feeling the ground ahead, wary of an unseen step—and then she heard it again.

Movement, more rash, more intense this time.

Angrier.

Chasing after her.

Only this time, it was accompanied by the angry, throaty roar of someone who'd been winded.

ZAHED BOUNCED OFF THE STONE PILLAR and went down like a rag doll. His extended arm had hit it first, which gave him a split second to tilt away and avoid a full-frontal hit.

Still, it hurt like hell. His chest, his shoulder, his hip, his knee, and his cheek—they'd all slammed into the solid rock under full acceleration. He felt a metallic taste in his mouth and wiped it clean with the back of his hand. It was wet with blood.

His mind quickly assessed the damage. Nothing seemed broken, but the heavy bruising would definitely slow him down and limit his agility for a while. He bunkered the pain and focused on the more immediate concern. The gun. He'd dropped it in the collision.

He stayed down and ran quick concentric sweeps of the ground around him. It didn't take long for him to find it. Cursing himself for his mistake, he pushed himself back to his feet, his ears scanning for target acquisition.

He spat some more blood out and screamed her name in rage, and was back after her within seconds.

"TESS! WHERE ARE YOU, BITCH!"

The yell reverberated around her, propelling her forward like wind to a sail. She heard him entering the narrow passage just as she was reaching the chamber at its other end.

This time would be harder. She couldn't use her flashlight, and she couldn't use the cables either. She didn't know what the room looked like—how big it was, its layout, what obstacles or pitfalls it presented. She was as vulnerable in it as he was. Worse, she was the quarry. She had to be quiet; she had to explore it without making a sound. All he had to do was follow the noise, and in the deathly quiet of the subterranean citadel, even the tiniest noise she made was getting amplified way out of proportion. She sounded as discreet as the percussion section of a marching band.

She pushed away from the wall and its cabling and prowled through the darkness blindly, her arms extended defensively like an insect's antennae, groping the air, wary of any obstruction. She found the opposite wall, making the room out to be around fifteen feet wide or so. She ran her fingers up and down its smooth surface as she advanced farther, and then they found something else. A low-level niche in the wall, about four feet wide, starting just above ground level and going up to her waist.

She knew there were all kinds of rooms down there:

wineries, kitchens, food storage chambers, all of which had cavities of various sizes cut into their walls and floors. Before she could think of what this one was, she heard him getting nearer and froze.

She couldn't risk moving ahead, not with him that close. She didn't have much of a choice. She bent down and climbed into the niche, pushing herself into it as far as she could. It was only about a foot and a half deep.

Then she waited.

She'd barely made it in when she heard the soft padding of his feet grow sharper. He'd just entered the room. Spiders scurried wildly through her belly as she shriveled up and pressed back against the wall.

She heard him scuttle along the opposite wall.

So far, so good. Keep going.

He stopped.

She stopped breathing.

He didn't make a sound for what felt like forever. She imagined him there, a few feet away from her, listening intently, like a panther in the dark. She felt every pore on her body pucker up as she made herself as small as she could, her body rigid with tension, her lungs desperate to breathe freely, her mind taut in anticipation of some other jolt—a shout, a bullet, something designed to make her jump.

It didn't take long to come.

"I know you're here, Tess. I can hear you breathing."

She felt her heart contract and freeze as she braced herself for his next move, repeating to herself over and over that she couldn't afford to react. She concentrated intently on her hearing, using her ears as sonar.

She heard a faint scuff.

Then another.

He was moving.

Slowly.

Heading straight for her.

Chapter 45

✛

Tess felt all the blood in her body rush up to her temples. He was only a few feet away. And closing.

She went completely rigid. Every muscle of her body was locked down tight. Forget moving a finger. She wasn't even blinking. It was all channeled into her jaw, which she was biting down, hard. She was expecting him to try to spook her. It was coming; she knew it. And she couldn't allow herself to get caught by it again.

She waited, each second stretching to hours. He was getting closer—so close that she could now hear his breathing. It was subdued, dampened; he knew what he was doing. He had to be breathing through his mouth, she imagined, as she was. It was quieter that way. But it was still there, at the edge of her perception. A bit blocked, wet, gargly. A bit labored. Maybe from slamming into that column, she hoped.

It did little to alleviate her terror.

She could also feel him now. Somehow, even though they weren't touching, she could feel his presence. It was as if she actually did have a sonar within her that had detected him. She heard his fingers land on the wall above the cavity in which she was crouched, the tiniest scrape of nails against porous rock. He was standing right in front of her, feeling the wall, mere inches away now, his waist more or less level with her head.

Her heart was rocketing away, about to burst out of its cage. The pounding in her ears was deafening, and she was amazed he couldn't hear it himself. She knew that if his hand moved downward, even slightly, he'd find the cavity and he'd find her.

She wasn't about to wait for that.

No choice but to act first.

She sprang out from her coiled position, slamming into him at thigh level, thrusting out with as much power as she could muster, her fists clutched tight against the butt end of her flashlight, using it like a mini–battering ram and hoping it caused him some damage. She heard him grunt heavily as she slammed into him and thought she must have hit him where it counted. He lost his balance under the unexpected tackle and fell back, with Tess tumbling over him but managing to stay on her feet. His arms lashed out at her furiously, and one of them struck her across the cheek, but she had the advantage of being on top and pulled back quickly.

She disentangled herself from him and bolted out of the room before he was back on his feet. She had to move as fast as she could, but couldn't risk crashing into anything. She had to use the flashlight, just quick on-off flicks to guide her as she blew through the subterranean maze, keeping an eye on the cabling and following its trail, flying from one chamber to another, hunched through the narrow tunnels, her chest heaving with panic. She was making too much noise to be able to hear him coming up behind her, but she didn't care. All she was focused on was covering as much ground as fast as possible and putting as much distance as possible between him and her.

She was charging out of a stepped passageway when two arms grabbed her and pulled her in. She let off the beginning of a shriek before one of the hands pressed hard against her mouth and muffled her scream.

"Shh, pipe down," he hissed, low and urgent. "It's me."

Her heart soared.

Reilly.

REILLY PULLED HER TIGHTLY AGAINST HIM, away from the opening she'd just burst through.

He kept one hand clasped against her mouth and trained his hearing in the direction she'd come from. He heard nothing, but he knew it wouldn't be long before the Iranian caught up with them.

"How'd you find me?" she whispered.

"My BlackBerry's screen and those cables," he told her. "I followed them down and saw the light flickering. You have a flashlight?"

"Yes," she mouthed. "He's right behind me. And he's pissed off."

Reilly thought hard and fast. "Okay. Keep going. I'll stay here. He can't be far behind. Draw him out. Let him follow you. I'll get him when he comes through here."

"Are you su—"

"Just go, do it," he insisted, herding her away.

She darted back in and her hand found his face. She planted a quick kiss on his lips before setting off.

He tucked his handgun into the small of his back and sank back against the wall by the opening, feeling the coolness of the perspiration along his spine as it came into contact with the volcanic rock. There was no point wasting ammo in the dark, and besides, he would prefer to get the Iranian alive. He thought he'd be more nimble with two free hands; he'd be able to inflict more damage. Which right now was a very appealing prospect.

He saw the flickering of Tess's flashlight, getting dimmer as she disappeared farther into the bowels of the citadel.

Then he heard him.

Frantic movement, closing in.

Reilly tensed up.

The scrapes grew louder, the breathing more intense. The Iranian was plowing ahead now, like a steamroller. Reilly could almost smell his fury.

He waited, his body stiffening up for the brawl, his hands tightening into fists, his mind's eye converting every sound into a visual and projecting it into the impenetrable darkness around him—then he heard him emerge from the passageway and pounced.

He hit him full-on and rammed him, slamming him against the wall. He knew the Iranian had a gun, and his hands dove straight for where he guessed the bomber's gun hand would be. He quickly found his opponent's right wrist just as the Iranian squeezed off a thunderous round that lit up the chamber in a cold white flash. Reilly kept his left grip clamped around the bomber's gun hand, pinning it back against the wall and pounding it repeatedly against the tufa while his other fist flicked fierce jabs at the Iranian's head. He connected hard, once, twice, hearing the cartilage snap and the blood gurgle, waiting to feel the man's gun tumble out of his hand, but the Iranian was hanging on to it stubbornly. Reilly was looking to land a third punch when he got something he hadn't counted on: a knee to the kidneys, quickly followed by a battering ram of an uppercut straight to his chin. The first impact winded him, and the second rattled his brain and caused him to lose his grip for a moment—which was just enough for the Iranian to shove him off with a scream of rage.

The gun was still in the man's hand.

Reilly dove and rolled over himself just as the bullets drilled into the ground around him. Shards of tufa splintered off and cut into him as he yanked out his own gun and loosed off several rounds of his own, but none of them seemed to connect. His ears ringing from the deafening gunfire, he thought he heard his opponent scampering out of the chamber and he chased him out with a couple of rounds, but he didn't hear the telltale sound of a round punching through human skin and bone and the accompanying outburst of pain.

Worse, the Iranian was now heading toward Tess.

Reilly found the cabling and felt his way forward, moving frantically now, one hand on the wiring, the other clutching the gun tightly, his ears attuned to make sure the Iranian hadn't stopped and wasn't about to ambush him.

He stopped at the mouth of another tunnel. "I wouldn't go out there if I were you," he shouted into the darkness, hoping to get a handle on the man's position and to distract him from finding Tess. "The Jandarma should be all over this canyon by now and they're not going to let you walk out of here alive." He waited for an answer, then added, "If you want to live, your best bet's walking out with me. The things you know can be of great value to us."

Nothing.

He crept through the tunnel, through another cavern, and up to the entrance of another passageway. "You want to die, asshole? Is that it?"

Still nothing. The Iranian wasn't a lightweight. But then, Reilly had known that already.

He pressed ahead, through a curving stairwell and across another chamber, and was about to go up what felt like a tight tunnel when he heard her.

"Over here," Tess whispered, from his right.

She reached out and pulled him to her.

"He pass you?"

"Yes," she replied. "When you were calling out to him. He stopped to listen to you, but didn't see me."

"Any idea where we are?"

"No. But we've come up a bit. I'd guess we're maybe a couple of levels underground?"

"There's no point trying to get him in here. It's too dangerous," he said. "We've got to get out of here."

"We need to get this belt off me first," she told him. "There's no signal in here. I can't go back outside, not while I'm wearing it."

Reilly's insides knotted. "How's it locked into place?"

"There's a padlock. On the back." She took his hand and guided it around her back.

He felt it. It seemed heavy and solid. He gave it a tug to test it, more out of frustration than with any expectation that it would give. "Can you turn it around so the padlock's on your side?"

"Sure, it's not on that tight. Why?"

"I can try to shoot the padlock off. But I need light."

Tess exhaled heavily. "You sure?"

"If you stand right up against the corner of the opening of the tunnel, I'll angle the shot away from you and into the tunnel. Even if it bounces off the metal, it's not going to hit you."

"You sure?" she repeated. She didn't sound convinced.

"I want it off you," Reilly insisted. "Trust me. But I'll need you to flick the light on. Just for a second. On and off, that's all. Okay?"

He'd rarely, if ever, heard her scared. Hadn't really known her to fear much.

She was scared now.

He helped her position herself right against the edge of the opening into the next tunnel. She tilted her waist out as much as she could and tucked her arms behind her back, out of view. Reilly held the padlock out so it was peeking out from the corner of the doorway. He brought the barrel of his gun right up against its body, pushing it even farther away from Tess.

"Ready?" he asked.

"You ever done this before?"

"Not really."

She shrugged. "Not the answer I was hoping for."

"On three. One. Two."

She flicked the light on at three and Reilly pulled the trigger. The padlock exploded with an earsplitting crack and a flurry of sparks—and just then, several rounds punched the tufa around them.

"Back," Reilly hollered, pulling Tess away from the tunnel opening as rock shrapnel flew wildly around them.

Then he heard it—the dead snap of the handgun's slide locking back after it had belched out its last round.

"He's out of ammo," Reilly yelled as he pulled the belt off Tess and flung it into a far corner, then grabbed the flashlight and charged out after him. "Come on."

He raked the beam ahead of him and spotted the Iranian ducking out of the tunnel and crossing another cavernous room.

He chased after him, his legs flying now, closing in on his prey, the taste of the imminent catch coursing through him.

ZAHED GROUND HIS TEETH as he hurtled through the honeycomb.

He cursed the American woman—cursed her for luring him down here, cursed her for taking his rucksack, cursed her for leaving him out of ammo.

It was time to cut his losses and get the hell out, assuming he'd be able to. He didn't know what was waiting for him aboveground. He knew Reilly had to be bluffing about there being any troops there, but he couldn't be sure of that. Even though the canyon hadn't been swarming with tourists, someone was bound to have heard their earlier gunfight. They might have called the cops. The area could soon be seriously hostile, and slipping away from it wouldn't be easy, given the limited number of ways in and out of the canyon.

He had to make it out first.

He stormed through a large communal room and dove into a sweeping passageway, the chasing light flickering in and out of view. It was helping him, bouncing off the walls, lighting up passages, giving him glimpses of clarity, but as long as it was there, he was the deer in the headlights. He had to get out of its range. He was moving frantically, as fast as he could, and didn't know where he was going. It didn't matter right now. All he could do was follow the cabling, hoping it led back to the entrance.

He could hear Reilly keeping pace, not far behind. He needed to lose him. He glimpsed a narrow stairwell and took the stairs, two at a time. They led both left and right. He chose right and hunched through the passageway, moving quieter now, hoping to confuse his pursuer and buy himself some time.

He had to do something. Delay him somehow.

And then he saw it.

At the mouth of the tight tunnel, a rounded edge, sticking out from the side of its wall. He'd spotted it on the way in.

It was a millstonelike trapdoor. A circular, one-ton piece of rock, with a diameter of around four feet. It was designed to keep invaders out and could be rolled into place quickly just by releasing a couple of timber wedges that held it back.

"Freeze, asshole."

Zahed turned.

Reilly was there, at the other end of the tunnel. The American had both gun and flashlight aimed at him, the beam making him squint.

He glimpsed Tess appearing behind the agent. His eyes looked for her belt, but it didn't seem to be there, and from the defiant glare in her eyes, he gathered she was no longer wearing it.

"I should have killed you back in Rome," Zahed called out to Reilly, buying time.

"Too late now, dickhead. Put the gun down."

Zahed's eyes darted across to the base of the millstone and back. The timber wedges that would have been used by the early villagers were long gone. Instead, a rusted piece of iron bar, a far more recent addition, stuck out from the side wall and held the stone in place. It looked like a crude fitting that had been put in decades ago, before the canyons had been condemned and evacuated. There were hardly any tourists visiting Cappadocia then, so safety hadn't been a paramount issue for the local, self-appointed custodians of the underground cities.

Which was just as well.

"I can't walk out of here with you, you know that," he yelled out as he flicked quick glances at the iron rod, processing his options, evaluating his chances.

"It's your choice, pal. Walk out with me, or be carried out in a black zip bag," Reilly shot back. "I'm easy, either way."

"On second thought, you know what?" He paused for a second, then shouted out, "Fuck you," briefly enjoying the confused look on the agent's face—and moved like lightning. He darted to his right, the edge of the millstone shielding him from harm, and flipped the gun around in his right hand so he could use its grip like a hammer.

And slammed it against the base of the iron rod.

The angle was perfect.

The bar moved, crumbling the soft rock it was sitting in. A second strike jarred it further.

Tess yelled something out, and Reilly was already rushing toward him, firing.

The third strike did the trick, loosening the bar—just as a round from Reilly's gun exploded straight through his exposed hand.

*　　*　　*

REILLY SAW THE IRANIAN LUNGE sideways and raise his gun like a hammer.

He didn't understand what he was up to—but he knew it wasn't good. He couldn't get a clean shot at him, not with that protruding disc of stone blocking him. All he could see of him was his hand, gripping the empty weapon.

"The millstone," Tess yelled. "It's a trapdoor."

Reilly charged through the tunnel like he'd been shot out of a cannon, firing as he moved. He heard Zahed's right hand hammering away at something, each strike echoing back at him, his heart pounding inside him at triple speed. He saw the eruption of blood from his opponent's left hand and heard him grunt heavily from the hit, and was just a few feet away from reaching him when the huge stone disc suddenly rolled out of the wall. The ground under his feet shook as the millstone slammed into the opposite side of the tunnel just as he got to it, his fingers instinctively reaching out to stop it before pulling back at the futility of his move.

The tunnel was blocked. Completely, utterly blocked.

Reilly tried to push the millstone back, but it wouldn't budge. It was designed to roll into position on an incline, and was too heavy for him to move back on his own. Reilly cursed aloud and ran his fingers all over it in desperation. It had a small opening at its center, about three inches square. He peered through it, a sinking feeling choking his throat. He couldn't see anything on the other side. It was shrouded in darkness.

Then he heard him. Groaning, cursing, agonizing over his injury. Which was nice to hear. The Iranian seemed to be in serious pain.

After a few drawn-out seconds, the wounded man's voice rang out from behind the trapdoor. "You comfy in there, Reilly?"

Reilly brought the barrel of his weapon up to the hole and replied, "How's the hand, jerk-off? I hope I didn't put too big a dent in your love life," before stuffing the gun through the opening and firing off four rounds. Their reports bounced through the tunnels and died out; then he heard the Iranian again.

"Stop wasting your bullets and start looking for a way out of there." His voice was loud, but not loud enough to mask the agony the man was clearly suffering. "It's not going to be easy. I think it might be impossible. But try. Do it for me. Make the impossible happen. And if you do, know this. This isn't over. Somewhere, somehow, I'll find you. Wherever you are. I'll come find you, and Tess . . . and then we'll end this properly, all right?"

Reilly shoved his gun through the hole again and emptied his clip feverishly, yelling out in frustration, hoping one of the rounds would find flesh and bone. And when the echoes of the detonations died down, all that was left was the furious mutterings and the distant footfalls of the Iranian, which receded until there was nothing left but a drowning silence.

Chapter 46

✠

"What about moles? They don't have moles down here, do they?"

"Moles?"

"You know," Tess rambled on. She was finding it hard to keep quiet in the oppressive darkness. "Moles. Or any other kind of nasty critters with big teeth and claws." She fell silent for a moment, then added, "What about bats? You think they have bats in here? We're not that far from Transylvania. Maybe they have vampire bats out here. What do you think?"

"Tess, listen to me," Reilly said calmly. "If you lose it, I'm going to have to shoot you. You do realize that?"

Tess laughed. It was a hearty laugh, borne more out of fear and nervousness than out of her thinking his words were particularly funny. The reality of their situation—being stuck down there, in a condemned underground labyrinth, several levels below the surface—was getting to her. She usually prided herself on not being the kind of person to panic. She'd lived through a few harrowing situations, and she'd done all right and gotten through them. Adrenaline usually kicked in and fueled her drive for survival.

This was different.

This was looking like a slow, agonizing, and frustrating

end. Like being marooned in space without the relatively quick release of a limited supply of oxygen.

It was enough to drive one mad.

She'd lost track of how long they'd been down there. Hours, certainly. How many, though, she couldn't say.

They'd tried moving the millstone back, but it was impossible. It had been designed to be rolled back from the inside, but they lacked the timber levers to do so. They'd then looked everywhere for another way out, following the cobweb of electrical cabling in all kinds of directions. They'd used the flashlight sparingly, but it had eventally died out. They'd then resorted to the faint light from the screen of Reilly's BlackBerry, but that had died out too.

Tess knew these subterranean citadels were huge. Estimates for the number of people that could shelter in the larger ones that had been uncovered varied wildly, ranging from a few thousand to as many as twenty thousand. Which was a lot of space to cover. A lot of tunnels. And a lot of dead ends.

She knew they weren't going anywhere anytime soon.

"What if we're trapped here forever?"

Reilly held her tight, his arm coiled around her. "We won't be."

"Yeah, but what if?" she pressed, tucking into him even closer. "Seriously? What happens to us? Do we starve to death? Do we die of thirst first? Do we lose it and go nuts? Tell me. You must have had some training in this stuff."

"Not really," Reilly told her. "It's not exactly the kind of thing they expect you to go through in the New York field office."

The darkness was absolute now, so dark it was actually blinding. There wasn't even the faintest glimmer of light. Tess couldn't see anything of Reilly, not even the ghost of a reflection coming from his eyes. She could only hear him breathing, feel his chest rise and fall and his fingers tighten around her. Her mind wandered to the not-so-distant past, to an earlier time, curled up with Reilly in the dark, not that far away from where they now were.

"You remember that first night?" she asked him. "In the tent, before we got to the lake?"

She sensed his face broaden into a smile. "Yup."

"That was nice."

"It was pretty amazing."

"More than amazing." She thought about it, reliving it. It stirred up a comforting warmth inside her. "I've always wanted to relive that first kiss," she told him. "Nothing ever compares to it, does it?"

"Let's test that theory." He cupped her face in his hands and drew her near and kissed her long and hard, a desperate, hungry kiss that said more than any word could ever express.

"I could be wrong," she finally said, dreamily. "Or maybe there's something about this Turkish air. What do you think?"

"This air? In here? Not exactly doing it for me, but hey, don't let me spoil your party."

Darker thoughts pushed their way through. "I don't want to die here, Sean."

"You're not going to die here," he told her. "We're going to make it out."

"Promise?"

"Abso-fucking-lutely."

She smiled—then it all came back. What she'd been through the last few days, how they'd gotten here. A gaggle of disparate thoughts, swooping in and out of her mind.

"The guy," she remembered, "the bomber. He told me something. A couple of things he said I ought to look up. He said it was important."

"What?"

"He asked me if I'd ever heard of Operation Ajax."

Tess couldn't see Reilly's features in the darkness, but she didn't need to. His pause, and his breathing, told her all she needed to know. He knew what it was.

"What was the other thing?" Reilly asked her, his voice still subdued.

"He said I needed to find out what happened on the morning of July third, 1988."

Reilly paused again, inhaling and exhaling deeply this time.

"What?" Tess asked.

After a moment, Reilly said, "I'd say our guy is telling us he's Iranian. And that he's got some serious anger management issues."

"Tell me something I don't know."

Reilly let out a slight chortle. "Operation Ajax is the code name of an old screwup of ours. A major one. In Iran, back in the fifties."

Tess winced. "Ouch."

Reilly nodded. "Yeah. Not our finest hour."

"What happened?"

"Around the time of World War One, the British controlled Iran's oil production," he told her. "Back when they were an empire. And they were basically raping the country. They were taking all the oil revenues and throwing back crumbs to the locals. The Iranian people—rightly—got really pissed off about that, but the British government didn't give a rat's ass and kept refusing to renegotiate terms. This went on for thirty, forty years until the Iranians elected a guy called Mohamed Mosaddegh to become their prime minister. We're talking about Iran's first democratically elected government here. Mosaddegh won by a landslide and immediately started the process of taking back Iran's oil production and nationalizing it, which was why he was elected."

"I bet the Brits must have loved that," Tess remarked.

"Absolutely. Mosaddegh had to go. And guess who stepped in to help them overthrow him?"

Tess grimaced. "CIA?"

"Of course. They went all out for him, and they pulled it off. They bribed and blackmailed scores of people in the Iranian government, in the press, in the army, and in the clergy. They smeared the guy and everyone close to him; then they got mobs of paid thugs to march down the streets and demand his arrest. The poor bastard, who was basically a selfless patriot, spent the rest of his life in prison. His foreign minister got the firing squad."

Tess sighed. "And we put the Shah in his place."

"Yep. Our friendly puppet dictator who we could count on to sell us cheap oil and buy our weapons by the shipload. Our guy rules his country with an iron fist for the next twenty-five years, with the help of a secret police that we trained and that made the KGB look like pussies. And that went on until 1979, when Ayatollah Khomeini channeled the Iranian people's anger and got them to rise up and kick the Shah's ass out of the country."

"And we got ourselves an Islamic revolution that hates us."

"With a passion," Reilly added.

Tess's face tightened with frustration; then a realization flourished in her mind. "Mosaddegh wasn't a religious leader, was he?"

"No. Not at all. He was a career diplomat, a sophisticated, modern man. The guy had a PhD in law from some Swiss university. The mullahs running the country today never mention him when the coup comes up, like on its anniversary. He was way too secular for their liking." He paused, then said, "There was no Islamic Republic back then. *We caused it.* Before we screwed that pooch, Iran was a democracy."

"A democracy that didn't suit us."

"It's not the first time that's happened, and it won't be the last. It's all about cheap oil . . . Still . . . just imagine how different the world would be right now if we hadn't done that back then," he lamented.

She let the information sink in for a beat, then said, "I'm not sure I want to ask about the third of July."

"Another stellar moment for Uncle Sam," Reilly grumbled.

"Tell me."

Even in the pitch-black cavern, Tess felt Reilly's face darken.

"Iran Air, flight six-five-five," he told her. "Takes off from Iran on a half-hour hop across the gulf to Dubai. Two hundred and ninety passengers and crew on board, including sixty-six kids."

Tess felt a stab of horror. "The one we shot down."

"Yep."

"Why? How did it happen?"

"It's complicated. The plane's transponder was working and it was sending out the right code. The pilot was in his

assigned flight airway and he was in touch with air traffic control and speaking in English. All routine, all by the
book. But for a bunch of reasons, our guys thought it was
an F-14 attacking them and they lobbed a couple of missiles at it."

"They knew it was a civilian plane?"

"No. Not until it was too late. The ship had a list of all
local civilian flights, but they screwed up their time zones.
The ship was running on Bahrain time while the flight list
showed Iranian local time, which is half an hour off."

"You're kidding me."

"Nope. And it's not the first time something like that's
happened either. Remember Cuba and the Bay of Pigs?
One of the main reasons that failed was a time zone
screwup. The bombers that flew out of Nicaragua were
meant to get air cover from fighter jets coming off one of
our carriers. The bombers were under CIA control and
working on Central Time. The fighters were controlled
by the Pentagon, which was on Eastern Time. They never
hooked up, and the bombers were all shot down."

"Jesus."

Reilly shrugged. "Simple mistakes, but ones that
shouldn't happen. With the Iranian plane, it was a combination of a lot of them. Our ships have systems that as-
sign codes to potential targets. For some reason, the code
the airliner was given was changed after they'd logged it
in, and then it was given to another plane, which was another mistake. So the radar operator looks down at his
screen, sees it in one place, looks away, looks down again,
sees it's somewhere else, it looks like it's moved incredibly
fast, and he panics, thinking it's got to be a fighter jet. Plus
the arrows that show whether a plane is climbing or coming down are really hard to read. The ship's radar operator
panicked and thought the plane was diving and attacking
them. So he sounded the alarm and the captain fired his
missiles. The guy was apparently a hothead who liked to
pick fights. Shoot first and ask questions later. The CO of a
frigate that was there alongside them that day singled the
guy out as being way too aggressive. But it was a major
fuckup, a tragic one. Both our ship and the airliner were in

Iranian water and airspace. A lot of people died. A lot of kids. It deserved an apology. A huge one."

"Which they never got."

"Not a word. We never admitted any wrongdoing. We cut the relatives of the victims a few checks, but we never accepted responsibility, never apologized. Even worse, the guys on that ship got medals. Medals. For exceptional conduct. How's that for a slap in the face? Bush Senior, who was vice president at the time under Reagan, actually said, 'I'll never apologize for the United States of America. Ever. I don't care what the facts are.'"

"The noble, measured words of a true statesman," Tess said wryly.

"And we wonder why whack jobs like their current president get so much traction when they tear into us and call us the 'Great Satan,'" Reilly added. "They got their revenge, though."

"When?"

"The Pan Am jumbo that got blown out of the sky over Lockerbie," Reilly told her.

"I thought the Libyans were behind that. Didn't they try two of their agents for it, and one of them's now dying of cancer or something?"

"He's not dying. And you can forget what you've read. The Iranians were behind it."

Tess went quiet for a long second. "So, do they give you history lessons at Quantico, or what?" she finally asked.

Reilly breathed out a dry laugh. "Some. But not about that. It's not a great idea to lay out your dirty laundry for impressionable agents during basic training, is it? Hardly the best motivator."

"What then?"

"Come on. Give me some credit here. Iran's a hot button right now. Priority one. And I need to know the whole backstory of who we're dealing with, especially when they're trying to get their hands on nukes."

Tess nodded, processing what he'd told her. After a moment, she asked, "So how does it feel? Knowing the bad guys you're after might be the result of something we did?"

Reilly shrugged. "History's one long series of one country messing with another. We're as guilty of it as anyone else, and it goes on. So a lot of what I do has to do with dealing with blowback from the fuckups of others—usually the geniuses running our foreign policy. But it doesn't change the fact that assholes like our Iranian friend need to be taken out. It has to be done, and I have no problem doing it. I mean, sure, maybe the guy has grievances that stack up. Maybe we're the ones who triggered whatever turned him into this bad motherfucker . . . It doesn't change what he is now, or justify what he's done."

Tess frowned, deep in thought. "You think he might have lost some family on that plane?"

"Sounds like it. It happened in 1988. That's twenty-two years ago. Say he's in his midthirties now. That puts him in his early teens at the time. Not a great age to lose your parents, if that's what happened. It's easy to see a lot of hate coming out of that."

"God, yes." She pictured the Iranian, as a boy, being told that his parents or his siblings had been killed. Her mind drifted to Kim, and for a brief instant, she imagined her in the same situation. Then an idea dropped into her head and rescued her from that grim picture. "You guys must have a passenger manifest of that flight? A list of the victims?"

"There is a list. The one they used to pay the survivors' relatives. But figuring out which one of them left behind a son, in a country we have zero diplomatic relations with, ain't gonna be easy."

"So even knowing that won't help figure out who he is?"

"Probably not."

"You don't sound too hopeful."

Reilly shrugged again, remembering his thoughts in the car, when Ertugrul had picked them up at the airport. "Ever since Ajax, every time we've gone head-to-head with the Iranians . . . we've lost. The embassy in Tehran. The choppers in the desert. The hostages in Beirut. Iran-Contra. The insurgents in Iraq. Even the goddamn World Cup, back in 1998. We've lost every time."

"Not this time though," she said, trying to believe it.

"Damn right," he said, hugging her close to him.

She snuggled up against his chest, listening to his breathing, and something inside her stirred. An anger, a resolve, a hunger. She righted herself and turned to face him, then moved in and planted her mouth on his, lifting her leg to sit astride him.

"Hey," he mumbled.

"Shut up," she mouthed back.

"What are you doing?"

"What do you think?"

Her fingers were working on loosening his belt.

"We're supposed to conserve energy," he managed in between hungry mouthfuls of her.

"Stop talking then." She was now tugging down her own pants.

"Tess," he started to say, but she interrupted him, squeezing his face in her hands.

"If we're going to die here," she whispered into his ear, lowering herself onto him as she tasted the saltiness of a lone tear that slid down her cheek and trickled onto her lip, "I want to die knowing there's a big smile on your face. Even if I can't see it."

Chapter 47

✠

Reilly was the first to stir.

The silence around him was surreal, and it took him a moment to process where he was. He sensed Tess, asleep beside him on the hard ground, her breathing shallow and calm. He didn't know how much time had passed since they'd fallen asleep in each other's arms and didn't have a clue as to what time of day or night it was.

He sat up, slowly, twisting his head around to stretch the stiffness out of his neck, conscious that every movement he made—the brushing of cloth against cloth, the tiniest scrape of his shoe against the hard ground—was getting amplified out of all proportion. It made the natural isolation chamber he was in feel even more unnerving. He rubbed his eyes, then looked around, more out of instinct than out of necessity, given the stygian darkness around him—and something registered. Something he hadn't first noticed.

There was an odd shimmer in the air, a kind of phosphorescence, floating across the walls of the cavern. It was barely visible, faint and ghostly. At first, he wasn't sure it was actually there, or if it was just some kind of reaction in his retinas, maybe due to being deprived of any kind of light. He tried blinking the tiredness away and focused on the wall again.

It was there.

A spectral glow of light, filtering through.

From outside.

Hope swelled inside him. He got up and, his arms outstretched to keep him from hitting anything, he advanced slowly across the cavern. The glimmer wasn't enough to light his way, but he felt marginally more comfortable moving around with it there than without it. It seemed to be coming from a tunnel that led away from the cavern, one he and Tess had, he thought, checked out. He crouched and crept through the passageway, his splayed fingers feeling the walls around him.

They found an opening in the tunnel wall. It was waist-high, a round hole around three feet in diameter. The light seemed to be gliding in from there. Reilly ran his hands along its ledge, letting his touch do the exploring. The ledge was only about a foot and a half deep. Beyond it was a void. A void that dropped down—and rose up.

A shaft.

Reilly leaned right into it for a closer look. Light—daylight—was definitely seeping in from above. But there was something else. Noise, from below. The gentle murmur of water. Not a gush. More of a slow meander.

He backed out of the hole and got down on his haunches, his fingers searching the ground. He found a plum-sized piece of loose rock and picked it up. He leaned back into the opening, extended his arm over the hole, and dropped the stone. After about two seconds, and without bouncing against any bends in the shaft, it struck water with a clean splash that echoed up to him.

He knew he'd found a well that culminated in some kind of ventilation shaft. He guessed that the sun was possibly at an angle where its rays were coming through the shaft with enough strength to find their way down to the tunnel he was in, but if that was the case, it meant that the light wouldn't necessarily be there for long. He started drawing a mental picture of how the well could be laid out. During their fruitless exploration the night before, Tess had told him about the underground cities' elaborate water-collection and ventilation systems, designed to allow the escaping villagers to bunker down for extended periods of time while hiding out from invading forces. The ventilation shafts extended all the way to the bottom of the complex and were barely narrow enough for a human adult to crawl through. They had gates and spikes built into them to block any uninvited guests. The design also catered to a safe supply of drinking water, one that couldn't be cut off or tampered with from the outside. The villagers had dug wells that allowed access to subterranean streams, and carved out other shafts that collected rainwater from the surface. Both systems had to be well hidden to block enemies aboveground from either crawling in or pouring poison into them.

Reilly thought it over. He doubted he could make it up to the surface through a ventilation shaft. On the other hand, Tess had told him that the handful of wells in the underground settlements were usually connected to one another through a system of channels. Given that it was the height of summer, he thought there was a chance that the water level down there was manageable. Which meant that maybe, just maybe, he could use the well to reach another part of the complex—one that wasn't blocked to the outside world.

He roused Tess from her sleep and showed her what he'd found. The glimmer was fading, no doubt from the sun's shifting position. They had to move fast.

"I'll go first," he told her. "Keep an ear out in case any help shows up from the tunnels."

Her hand reached out and grabbed his arm, stilling him. "Don't. There's water down there. What if you can't get back up?"

"We don't have a choice," he said. He dredged up a smile, though it was barely visible. "It's summer. The levels can't be that high."

"I'd buy that—if it weren't for the melting snow, doofus."

"I'll be fine," he assured her with a slight chuckle.

She frowned. "The codices," she said. "If there's water . . . they might get damaged. Beyond repair."

"So leave them behind."

"We might never find them again."

Reilly reached up and cupped her cheek in his hand. "What's more important? Your life, or these books?"

She didn't answer, but he felt her nod slightly. Then her tone went dead serious again. "What if you don't find your way back?"

Reilly could just about see the reflection in her eyes. That comment was harder to deflect. She was right. Then he remembered something, and glimpsed a possible solution on the wall behind her.

"The electrical cabling. Help me rip it off the walls."

They went around the passageways and caverns in the darkness, feeling their way around and yanking as much electrical cabling as they could. They managed to gather a couple of hundred yards of it and tied the various sections together to make it one continuous length.

Reilly took one end of it and tied it onto the fixings of one of the wall lights. He tugged at it, hard. It didn't budge. The fixing itself seemed solid enough to hold his weight, and the cable was strong. The weak link was the soft rock the fixture was anchored into. He had no way of knowing if it would hold, or if it would just crumble off. Regardless, he dumped the big roll of cable down the well; then Tess handed him the pick-shovel combo tool from the Iranian's rucksack.

"You've got the gun. Use it if you have to," he said.

Tess nodded, still clearly uncomfortable with the idea of his leaving. She gave him a deep kiss; then he climbed into the hole.

"I'll be back," he told her.

"You'd better be," Tess replied, her hand holding on to his tightly for a few seconds more before finally letting go.

THE CLIMB DOWN WAS, as Reilly's drill instructor back at Quantico liked to say, character-building. Character-building, and slow. He made his way down one small, pre-carious move at a time, his back pressed against the wall of the tunnel, his arms and legs sprung out against the opposite face of the narrow passage, his taut muscles clamping him into place.

The way back up, if there was one, wasn't going to be much fun either.

The tunnel didn't widen, which allowed him to make it all the way down until his foot felt water, after what he estimated was a descent of not far from a hundred feet. He held there for a moment and caught his breath, hesitating. He had no way of knowing how deep the channel was. If he let go and allowed himself to fall into it, and if it was too deep for him to stand in, he risked getting carried away by the current—and drowning, if the canal didn't have an air gap above it.

He didn't have much choice.

He took hold of the cable and, slowly, eased himself off the wall and onto it, his legs the last to let go of the tunnel. The cable held. He breathed out with relief and, one hand at a time, lowered himself down into the water. The stream was, surprisingly, freezing. Surprisingly, because of the intense heat aboveground. Tess's comment about the melting snow brought a small smile to his face. He kept going until the water was up to his armpits—then his feet felt something and landed on solid ground.

"I'm down," he yelled up. "I can stand in it."

"Can you see anything?" she shouted back.

He looked downstream. The pale shimmer on the water's surface disappeared into blackness. He turned the opposite way. It was just as dark.

His heart sank.

"No," he shouted, trying to keep his voice even.

Tess went quiet. "What do you want to do?" she finally asked.

He moved away from under the shaft and took a couple of steps upstream, his hands holding on to the cable tightly. There was an air gap between the surface of the water and the roof of the channel. If he bent his knees and crouched through, he'd be able to walk upstream—for a while, anyway. He couldn't see how far it stayed that way. He tried the same downstream. The roof was lower there, and after barely a half dozen steps, it disappeared underwater.

He called up to her. "I'm going to see if there's another shaft out of this place. Upstream looks doable."

Tess went quiet again. After a beat, she said, "Good luck, tiger."

"I love you," he hollered back.

"I'm almost thinking it was worth getting into this mess just to hear you say it," she laughed.

He reeled in the cable and tied its end around his waist, then started hiking up the channel.

The bottom was smooth and slippery, the soft tufa buffed and polished by eons of water. He had to move slowly and with extreme care, and even though the flow of the stream wasn't too overpowering, it was still there. The difficulty was in having to use his arms to keep feeling the roof of the channel in search of another shaft. He narrowly lost his footing twice from the awkward stance, but before long it became a moot point as the roof dropped down and disappeared underwater.

The air gap was gone.

Reilly stood there for a beat, frozen, exhausted, his fingers and toes aching from the constant exertion. He stared into the blackness, contemplating what it meant if he had to make his way back to Tess without having found a way out. He cursed inwardly, wanting to yell out his rage and pound his fists against the damn tunnel walls, but he held back and sucked in some deep breaths and tried to calm himself down.

He refused to give up.

There had to be a way out.

He couldn't fail Tess. Nor could he let the Iranian win.

He had to keep going.

He filled his lungs with air and exhaled twice, then sucked in a deep breath and held it and crouched underwater. The water chilled his eyes as he strained to look ahead; then he kicked forward and started swimming upstream. He struggled to make any headway as his arms and feet pushed the water back furiously, and he kept darting one hand upward, over his head, running it against the roof of the tunnel, hoping it would find an opening and present him with another air gap. He felt his lungs about to explode, and turned and headed back, counting the number of strokes he took, and with a greedy gulp burst out into the air pocket he had left.

He stood there, letting his breathing settle, and mulled it over. He thought he'd felt the roof rising slightly before he'd had to give up and turn back. The problem was, there was a point of no return in venturing up that tunnel, and he needed to know what it was. At some point, he'd have to decide whether to turn back or keep going—knowing that if he did the latter, he would run out of oxygen before he made it back to the air pocket. He decided to test it and see how long he could stay under. He took in as deep a breath as he could, then ducked under the surface, staying in place but imagining himself swimming, and counted how many strokes he could make before he had to come up for air.

He managed sixteen. Which would be less if he were actually doing it and pushing against water, so he factored it down to fourteen. Which meant that after seven strokes underwater—or possibly eight or nine, given that the way back would be faster as he'd be swimming with the current—he'd need to decide whether to keep going, and possibly drown, or head back. He thought he'd managed about five or six strokes on his earlier attempt, and he'd barely made it back, so that sounded about right.

He moved back upstream and got right up to the point where the roof of the tunnel hit the water. With his knees splayed wide and bent, he crouched right down and craned his head back and sideways until his forehead was literally scraping the roof. He paused for a short rest to allow his muscles to regroup; then he took the three breaths, kept the third in, and went under.

This time, he tried moving faster, his feet kicking harder, his arms staying down and not looking for an air pocket he knew they wouldn't yet find. As he fought the streaming water, still in utter darkness, he counted down each stroke in his mind.

His heartbeat rocketed ahead as he took his sixth stroke.

Then his seventh.

Then his eighth.

His hand rose up, but it was still submerged. There was still no air above him.

He had to decide. Right there and then. He had to decide whether to keep going or turn back. He thought he'd sensed the roof rising the last time around, but right now, he wasn't sure anymore. Too many variables were clouding his mind.

Nine.

Ten.

He kept going.

Chapter 48

✠

His lungs were on fire.

Maybe clear air was only five or six strokes ahead of him. Maybe he could make it there—if he calmed down. But the awareness of the impending drowning, the awareness of the finite amount of time he had left, was making it worse. It was flooding his body with adrenaline and stoking his heartbeat to a point where his lungs were ready to explode outward.

For a split second, Reilly imagined what drowning would be like, but he quickly quashed the thought and pushed harder, moving even faster now. His hand was still sliding against the smooth roof of the tunnel, desperately seeking out his salvation. For an instant there, it did feel like the roof was sloping upward, barely perceptibly, but enough to give him hope, enough to make him fight the water even harder—then something pulled against him, yanking him back.

The cable, the one around his waist. He'd run out.

His hands went into a frenzy, working feverishly at the knot, pulling and tugging ferociously until he broke free from its grip. He flung it aside and started again, but the reality of it all was flooding in, the realization that he had to die now, that his willpower was fighting a losing battle to contain his lungs' need to let something in, anything, even if it was freezing cold water.

He felt a surge of blood in his forehead, a panic that raced through every neuron in his body and choked his very soul, and although he wasn't ready to give up, although he absolutely did not want to die, the need to breathe in was stronger than him, stronger than he could now overcome— and in that moment of pure terror, in that instant when his life seemed like it was about to get flushed away in a surge of molten snow, something broke through, a signal, coming from the tips of his fingers, fighting off the dread with a stab of hope.

A coolness.

The coolness of air slipping past damp skin.

His fingers were in open air.

It sent an electric shock through his body and spurred him forward even faster. He planted his feet against the bottom and took a couple of steps forward, his hand groping the roof of the tunnel frantically, the water splashing against it and confusing his senses, his face turned up and staring desperately into the inky blackness above him— then he rose. He couldn't last another second. He just burst up, his face tilted sideways, hoping his face wasn't about to collide with solid rock.

He found air. The clearance was no more than a couple of inches, but it was enough. He inhaled furiously, letting the air howl into his lungs, coughing and sputtering from the water that was also trickling in, dizzy with oxygen and elation.

He didn't move, not for a minute or so. He just let his heart calm down, let his lungs gorge themselves with air, let the tension seep out of his muscles. When he felt settled again, he took a couple of steps farther upstream, checking the roof as he did. It was rising again, slowly but surely. And in the distance, as if congratulating him on passing some kind of sadistic test, a wraithlike halo of light was beckoning him from the roof of the channel, maybe thirty or so yards upstream.

GETTING INTO THE SHAFT was the hardest part of the ordeal.

Reilly used the pick to hoist himself up into it, the move all the more arduous due to the added weight of his drenched clothes. His first few attempts ended in defeat as the soft tufa he'd planted the pick into crumbled under his weight and sent him splashing back into the stream, but he finally managed to hook it into a more solid patch and lift himself into the vertical shaft.

Like a moth drawn to the light, he climbed up and found himself in a similar passageway to the one he had left Tess in. He found the cabling on the wall and followed it first in one direction, then in the other until he found some steps that led upward.

Upward.

He found his way back to the mouth of the shaft and pulled the cabling off the wall beside it as a marker for his return trip, then followed the cabling through a seemingly endless series of chambers and passageways, smashing the light fixtures wherever he encountered them to lead him back to the shaft. And then it appeared, first as a hint of its presence, then quickly growing so it brought back the caves around him into view: sunlight, bright, glorious, and inviting.

He emerged in a canyon he didn't recognize. There was no one around either, just a bare, desolate landscape. It was similar to the one that had led into the underground city—more rock formations of what looked like huge, upside-down incisors, more meringue-like hills—but it was a different canyon—of that, he was certain. He used his pick to gouge a big X by the entrance of the cave dwelling he had emerged from; then, making sure he made a mental note of every turn he took and using his pick to leave markers behind at every bend, he staggered ahead, looking for help.

A lone mule, tied to a stake in the ground, interrupted his aimless wander. Then the rasp of a throat that had endured decades of nicotine damage added to his confusion.

"*Merhaba, oradaki.*"

He stopped and scanned his surroundings. There was no one around.

"*İşte burada. Buradayım,*" the voice called out.

He followed it upward and saw an old man just sitting there, in the middle of nowhere, perched on a rickety wooden chair in a small, exposed chapel that had been carved into the rock face. The man was waving at him with a slow, frail arm. A small table next to him displayed a few cans of soft drinks, while a tin kettle stood ready on a small camping gas burner.

The man flashed him a mostly toothless smile. "*İçmek için birşey ister misiniz, efendi?*" he asked, pointing at the cans on the table.

Reilly shook his head and looked at him for a curious second, making sure the man was actually there and not some figment of his battered mind. Then he hurried over to him.

IT WAS ANOTHER THREE HOURS before he made it back to Tess. He'd brought help with him, in the form of the old man's son and two grandsons, along with plenty of rope and a few flashlights.

He hadn't been able to explain where he'd left her, not that he knew himself. The surest way to get back to her was to retrace his steps. With the aid of the locals, it was an easier journey than his solo trek. The submerged part of the channel was the only real challenge they faced; a bucket, held upside down like a diving bell, was the only available solution, but it did the trick. Reilly had also taken along the one thing he knew Tess would be happier to see than his own face: a plastic bag, one that was big enough to seal shut. To keep the codices, and Hosius's document, dry.

The grin on her face when she saw it told him he was right.

That was the good news.

The bad news was confirmed once they finally got back to the entrance of the subterranean citadel that they had gone through on the way in.

Abdülkerim was still dead. And the Iranian had, it seemed, vanished.

Chapter 49

✠

It didn't take long for the canyon to be swarming with cops.

The Jandarma had been on alert in the area, and the old man's call to his local cop had brought them storming in. There was little they could do. The roadblocks they'd set up hadn't netted the Iranian. The cavalry had ridden in too late.

The procession of grim news—confirmations, really—continued. Ertugrul hadn't survived his head wound. Keskin, the captain of the Özel Tim unit, was also dead, along with several of his men. The troops scurrying across the canyon were clearly enraged by the bloodbath up the mountain and desperate for payback, but there was none to be found. All they could do was cart off Abdülkerim's body and seal off the handful of entrances to the underground settlement while awaiting the arrival of a bomb disposal expert who would disarm the detonator in the rigged belt Tess had been wearing—assuming they ever found it.

An urgent alert was sent out to local cops to contact all doctors and medical facilities in the region. From what Reilly had seen, the Iranian's gunshot wound hadn't seemed trivial. He wasn't sure where the bullet had struck, but he knew enough about gunshots to know that a hand injury like that was never an easy wound to fix. Without the proper debridement, fracture stabilization, and antibiotics, the likelihood of the Iranian's being able to keep all five fingers and not lose significant usage of his hand was far from certain. He'd need a good trauma center and a skilled surgeon to avoid an irreversible disability.

One thing the Turkish authorities wouldn't be doing was analyzing the codices Tess had found. Tess hadn't mentioned going into the rock church to them. She insisted on keeping that little segment of her misadventure out of the debrief, and Reilly had agreed.

Once the formalities had been dealt with, they were driven to a nearby hotel, pending further instructions. The hotel, a fifteen-room warren built into a cliff overlooking a small stream, had been fashioned from the remains of a monastery. Stables and dormitories had been turned into guest rooms, and niches in its passageways had been fitted with glass fronts and used to display archaeological curiosities from the monastery's past. Reilly and Tess were given a room that was a converted chapel. Pale sunlight from a small, solitary window suffused the dark space with a timeless glow and hinted at the remains of thousand-year-old frescoes that adorned its decoratively carved walls. Tess had initially balked at the idea of spending any more time in any cavelike surroundings, but the hotel owner's soothing demeanor and the smell of his wife's white bean, lamb and tomato stew soon quelled her unease.

FUELED BY A CONSTANT SUPPLY OF THICK, sweet Turkish coffee, Reilly spent the better part of an hour in the owner's office, on the phone with Jansson, Aparo, and a handful of other agents who were all huddled into a conference room back at Federal Plaza in lower Manhattan.

The news wasn't good, but then again, Reilly hadn't expected much from their end. This was way outside their playground. If the Iranian was going to be found, it was going to happen because of the efforts of the Turkish authorities, not the FBI. They had no significant intel that was relevant to share with Reilly regarding the Vatican bombing or the attack on the Patriarchate in Istanbul, and there was no point in calling in another drone, not until they had some kind of lead on Zahed's whereabouts.

They had one new piece of info, though. A body had been recovered in Italy, close to a summer resort, in the mountains. It was identified as that of an administrator from a small airfield about an hour and a half east of Rome. The man's corpse was unlike anything the authorities there had seen. Extreme body trauma didn't even begin to describe it. Every bone in his body had been pulverized. They'd concluded that the man must have fallen from a great height, either from a helicopter or from a plane. Fallen, or thrown out, more likely. And given the proximity of the airport to Rome, they'd flagged it as potentially linked to the Vatican bombing. Which, Reilly thought, was probably on the money.

He filled them in on what the Iranian had told Tess about Operation Ajax and the airliner. He wasn't surprised at having to explain what they were to most of the personnel on the call. Jansson told him they'd go through whatever intel they had on the downed flight's passenger manifest.

"You should get back here now," Jansson concluded. "It looks like our guy's gone dark. Who knows where he'll resurface. In the meantime, there's nothing more you can do out there. Let the Turks and Interpol take it from here and do their job."

"Sure," Reilly grunted. He was too tired to argue, and as much as he hated to give up the hunt, he knew Jansson was probably right. Unless something new came up, there was little he could do to justify sticking around.

"Get back to Istanbul," the assistant director in charge of the New York field office told him. "We'll get the embassy to sort out some transportation for you."

"Make sure they factor Tess in," Reilly said.

"Okay. I'll see you when you get back. We've got a few things to talk about," Jansson added somewhat stiffly before ending the call.

Reilly didn't like the sound of that. Jansson obviously wasn't going to let Reilly's solo adventure slide. He'd be getting his ass handed to him, no question.

He went back to the room and found Tess coming out of

the bathroom, freshly showered, wrapped in a thick white towel. A radiant smile lit up her face when she saw him, the same smile that reached deep into his very core and never failed to ignite him like a blowtorch. Despite everything that was swirling around in his head, he craved her more than ever before and felt like pulling her into his arms and spending a few days in bed with her. He drew her over and gave her a long, deep kiss, enjoying the smooth feel of her shoulders under his fingers, but it didn't go further. There was too much bouncing around inside him.

Tess must have sensed it. "What's the scoop?"

Reilly grabbed a can of Coke from the minibar and settled himself on the bed.

"Not much. Our guy's gone. That's about it."

Tess puffed up her cheeks and exhaled slowly. "So what do we do now?"

"We go home."

Her face sank. "When?"

"I'm waiting to hear back. They're going to send a plane to fly us back to Istanbul."

Tess nodded. Then she dropped her towel and, instead of joining him on the bed, reached for her clothes.

"Where are you going?"

Tess picked up Hosius's letter and held it up. "I want to know what's in here before we leave."

Reilly shot her a look. "Tess, come on."

"Relax. I'm just going to see if they've got a computer I can use. Maybe a scanner too. I could use some help translating this."

Reilly studied her for a beat, then shook his head. "What is it with you and these books?" He sighed with exasperation. "I ever tell you about my friend Cotton Malone?"

"No."

He leaned back against the pillows. "Great agent. One of the best. A few years back, he decides he's had enough intrigue for one lifetime. Looking for some peace and quiet. So he leaves the service and moves to Copenhagen and opens an antique bookshop."

Tess gave him a look that said she knew where this was going. "And . . . ?"

338 ‡ RAYMOND KHOURY

"His days as a gun-toting government agent? Much more peaceful."

Tess grinned. "I bet. I should meet him sometime. Sounds like he might have some good stories to tell, starting with where he got that name. In the meantime," she said as she held up the document and crossed to the door, "I've got some translating to do."

Reilly shrugged and slid down the bed. "Knock yourself out," he told her as he curled up with a pillow, deciding his mind and body could use a break.

"Sean, wake up."

He sprang up at her voice, his eyes stinging in protest. He hadn't realized he'd fallen asleep.

"What time is it?" he asked groggily.

"Doesn't matter." Her voice was alive with excitement as she bounced onto the bed next to him and held up the ancient sheets to his face. "I got this translated. It reads like Hosius wrote it in his own hand. In A.D. 325. In Nicaea. At the end of the council." Her eyes were dancing left and right, scrutinizing every reaction on Reilly's groggy face. "He wrote it himself, Sean. Right after the big meeting."

Reilly's mind was still booting up. "Okay, so—"

Her enthusiasm blew over his words. "I think I know what Conrad had in those trunks."

Chapter 50

✝

The imperial palace was quiet.

The long, drawn-out council was now over. Weeks and months of heated debate had finally ended with grudging compromise. All present had signed off on what had been agreed and were now heading back to their dioceses, to the east and to the west, all over the emperor's dominion.

Constantine was pleased.

Resplendent in his imperial purple robes, festooned with a dizzying array of gold and jewels—the same as he wore on the first day of the proceedings, when he'd addressed the assembled clergymen, fully conscious of the awe his glittering outfit would instill in them—he looked out the window at the sleeping city and smiled.

"I'm pleased, Hosius," he told his guest. "We have accomplished a lot here. And I couldn't have done it without you."

Hosius, the bishop of Córdoba, nodded graciously from his seat by the large, roaring fireplace. Mild and conciliatory by nature, the priest was in his seventh decade. It had been a hard few months for him, and they had taken their toll on his mind as well as his body. Like virtually all who held high office in the Church, Hosius had suffered under the persecutions of the Roman emperors. His wrinkled skin still bore the traces of it. Then everything had changed with Constantine. The rising general had embraced the Christian faith, and as he consolidated his hold on the throne, he'd ordered an end to its suppression. Hosius's reputation had gotten him invited to the emperor's court, and eventually, he'd become the new emperor's chief theologian and spiritual advisor.

They'd come a long way since then.

"These disputes," Constantine said. "Arius, Athanasius, Sabellius, and the rest of them, and all their petty contentions . . . Was Christ divine, or was he a created being? Are the Son and the Father of one substance, or not? Was Jesus the son of God or not?" He shook his head, angered by the reports—he hadn't seen them with his own eyes—of mosaics in Arian churches in which Jesus Christ was depicted as a man who aged to a ripe old age, white hair and all. "You know what the real problem is? These men have too much time on their hands," he said, his tone quietly angry. "They don't realize that besides being unanswerable, the questions they keep asking are dangerous. Which is why they had to be stopped before they ruined everything."

Constantine understood power.

He had already done what no emperor had done before him: He had unified the empire. Before his ascendancy, the Roman Empire had been divided into eastern and western parts, each ruled by its own emperor. Betrayals and territorial wars were commonplace. Constantine changed all that. He took power through cunning political maneuvering and a series of brilliant military campaigns, defeating both emperors and proclaiming himself the sole emperor of east and west in the year 324.

But his people were still divided.

Beyond east and west, he had major religious chasms to bridge: pagan versus Christian and, even more troublesome, Christian versus Christian. For there were many different interpretations of the legacy of the preacher they called Jesus Christ, and the disputes between the various groups of converts were turning violent. Accusations of heresy were hurled and counterhurled. Incidents of torture grew more gruesome. One victim—Thomas, the bishop of Marash—was particularly frightful to look at. He'd had his eyes, nose, and lips cut out. His teeth had been pulled, and he'd had his arms and legs chopped off. He'd been kept prisoner by his Christian tormentors in Armenia for more than twenty years, suffering an additional mutilation on each anniversary of his captivity.

It had to stop.

Which was why Constantine had called all the bishops and senior church dignitaries from across his empire to the city, to attend the first general council of the Church. Over three hundred prelates, accompanied by many more priests, deacons, and presbyters, had heeded the call of his strongly worded epistles. Only the bishop of Rome, Pope Sylvester I, wasn't in attendance. He'd sent two of his most senior legates to represent him. Constantine didn't mind his absence. The emperor already had enough to contend with, what with the presence of the more authoritative bishops of the east. He was happy to preside over matters himself and wave his big stick to get them to sit down, have their debates, argue over who and what Christ really was and what he did, tangle over how they were going to share in the jurisdiction of his bountiful legacy—and agree.

On everything.

Constantine had long been aware of the unstoppable popularity of the Christian faith. His mother was a fervent Christian. Twenty years earlier, he'd witnessed Diocletian's Great Persecution, when the emperor had ordered churches across his empire to be destroyed, their treasures plundered, their scriptural writings burned, acting on the advice of the oracle of Apollo—and he'd seen it fail. He'd seen the wide appeal of Christianity's inclusive and hopeful message, and its relentless spread across the empire. He knew that painting himself as the faith's great defender, rather than emulating his predecessors as its great persecutor, would buy him a lot of followers. Furthermore, the distant lands he'd conquered held diverse tribes of barbarians, from the Allemani to the Picts and the Visigoths. He needed to find a way to unite them all.

One religion, common to all, would achieve that in spades.

Christianity, he knew, was that religion.

And, as he'd discovered, not even he was immune to it.

He thought back to the Battle of the Milvian Bridge more than a decade earlier, where his army had defeated that of his brother-in-law, the emperor Maxentius. He'd seen something in the lead-up to the big battle. In the sky. He was certain of it. A sign. The *Chi-Rho*, a monogram comprised of two superimposed Greek letters—the first letters of the word *Christ*. That night, he'd dreamed of victory and had a vision of a man—was it Christ himself?—telling him to go out and conquer in the name of that sign. He'd ended up having the Christogram painted on the standards carried by his troops, and he'd been blessed with a stunning victory that had given him one half of the empire he coveted.

The sign had kept on bringing him victories.

Constantine understood power, but he also understood the power of myth. He was deeply steeped in religion, having been brought up around pagan and Christian thinkers in Nicomedia, in the Eastern Empire. Like all his peers, he sought out the advice of oracles and believed in the rewards of religious piety. After that fateful battle, and throughout his campaigns, Constantine claimed that a divine hand had helped him achieve his victories. And inspired by ancient scripture, he came to see himself as a messiah—a warrior-king, anointed by God to rule over the people he had united and lead them to a golden age of peace and prosperity.

In hoc signo vinces indeed, he thought. "In this sign, conquer." But the power of the message wasn't just effective in conquering an enemy; it was also effective in conquering the hearts and minds of the people. And for that, it was a work of genius.

"We have to protect this faith, Hosius," he told the bishop. "We have to safeguard it and smother any challenges to it before they can grow. Because this faith is truly divinely inspired." He paced around the room, his face alive with zeal, his arms sweeping the air with unbridled enthusiasm. "It welcomes all and it's easy to join. Converts don't need to turn their lives upside down to be part of it. They don't need to become celibate or worry about what they can and can't eat or chop off parts of their manhood to be allowed in. And the organization . . . the hierarchy in the clergy, the churches, the discipline—it's all hugely effective at bringing in converts and keeping them in line. But most of all, its divine inspiration is in its message." He smiled at his seated guest, a smile of deep satisfaction. "Good and evil, Heaven and Hell, eternal paradise and eternal damnation? Rewards in the next life to give hope to those who have nothing in this one and keep them from rebelling? Sin and the need to keep temptation at bay, the lot of it administered by men with divine authority and seared into the consciousness of every child from the day the child is born?" He chortled. "It's so brilliantly conceived and brutally effective it could only have been dreamt up through divine intervention. I mean, imagine . . . these people out there, these Christians . . . my predecessors and my rivals have been hounding them and killing them just as they killed Jesus three hundred years ago. They've been persecuted, humiliated, shackled and spat upon, and left to rot in dungeons because they wouldn't worship our pagan gods and perform the sacrifices required of them. They've been blamed for everything from famine to flooding, they've had their women raped and their property confiscated . . . and yet they still cling to their faith. They still soldier on." He paused, marveling at the very concept he was describing. "That's power. That's real power. And we need to protect it if we're going to harness its full potential."

The Spanish bishop cleared his throat and said, "You've achieved a lot, Your Majesty. You put an end to their persecution. You showered them with donations and tax breaks and gave them a chance to be part of the ruling class and prosper and spread their message."

"Yes," the emperor agreed, "and it's going to turn this empire into the greatest empire in the history of mankind. Which is why I can't let this message—this vision—be compromised. That gentle revolutionary from three hundred years ago is my enabler. He's the instrument that allowed me to unify this empire and rule over its people with a mandate from God himself. And I can't let anything threaten that. It would be most unwise—and dangerous for us all."

Much as the pragmatic ruler within him was concerned about the disputes, the superstitious part of Constantine was just as worried. He feared that schisms within the Church were the work of the devil, and that a divided Church could offend God and incur his wrath. Constantine had to thwart the devil's ambitions. He saw himself as a successor to the original evangelists, a man whose God-given mission was to protect Christianity and spread the word of God to the far reaches of his empire and beyond.

A thirteenth apostle.

He had to put an end to the infighting.

All of which was why he'd invited the bishops of his empire to come to Nicaea and told them, in no uncertain terms, that they wouldn't be leaving the imperial palace until they'd settled their disputes and agreed on what story they'd be preaching from their pulpits.

One story.

One dogma.

No divergence.

After many weeks of fierce debate, they'd finally reached a consensus. They'd agreed.

They had their story.

Hosius sat there in silence for a long moment, watching the emperor. Then, hesitant, he asked, "There is one last matter to be discussed, Your Majesty."

Constantine turned to him, curious. "Yes?"

"The texts," Hosius asked. "What would you like done with them?"

Constantine frowned. The texts . . . the infernal works that had caused so much discord. Ancient writings, gospels and ruminations from the very dawn of the faith, opening up all kinds of questions.

Unwelcome questions.

"We have settled on one orthodoxy," the emperor said. "We've agreed on what the gospel truth shall be from here on. I see no need to cloud the issue further."

"What are you saying, Your Majesty?"

Constantine thought about it for a moment, a shiver of doubt scuttling down his spine.

"Burn them," he told his trusted advisor. "Burn them all."

HOSIUS THOUGHT BACK to the emperor's words as he watched his two acolytes load up the carriage in the dimly lit coach house.

He understood the emperor's decision, even sympathized with it at many levels. It was the wise thing to do. The texts were, indeed, dangerous.

Hosius was intimately familiar with the debates that had been raging at the heart of the faith. He'd witnessed, first-hand, the zeal with which the various Christian movements argued their views. In the last year alone, the emperor had sent him to Antioch twice to mediate such theological disputes. They hadn't been pleasant trips.

But he also had his doubts.

Yes, the faith needed to be unified under one vision. Yes, a unified faith would bring about an era of unparalleled peace and prosperity.

But at what cost?

Hosius knew that once Constantine was done with it, Christianity would far more resemble the pagan beliefs that it was superseding, particularly Mithraism and the cult of Sol Invictus, than its own Judaic origins. By necessity. Most of the emperor's subjects were pagan. To win them over, they needed to move them over gently to the new faith. They couldn't force them to drop all their previous rituals and beliefs, ones they had been prepared to die for. Even the emperor himself, Hosius knew, still harbored doubts and, deep down, didn't want to risk displeasing the gods of his past.

Hosius could also see another danger in what was happening. He was fully aware that the Church had been effectively giving its blessing to Constantine's supplanting of Jesus Christ as the Messiah. The emperor was now the godsend, not Christ. He was the warrior-king with divine backing, the man who would achieve with the sword what Christ had failed to do with his words. He was the polar opposite of the peace-loving, gentle savior, and he still had the backing of all the priests, deacons, and bishops across his empire.

Dangerous indeed.

But if the Church was going to survive, it needed a champion.

Constantine had embraced the faith, stopped the persecutions, and was making Christianity the newly unified empire's official religion. He would bring about a new golden age. And, as part of that plan, he was turning the old city of Byzantium into his new capital, his New Rome. A capital that was home to great avenues, magnificent palaces, and sublime buildings. Buildings like the new Imperial Library, where a small army of calligraphers and librarians would toil at transcribing ancient texts from the fragile papyrus they'd been written on onto more durable parchment and keep the flame of knowledge alive.

The library would also keep something else alive.

Something Hosius felt a need to conserve.

He watched his acolytes put the third of the chests onto the wagon bed and cover it with a tight canvas cover. He tensed up with anticipation. They would soon set off, protected by a small detail of guards, under cover of the night.

He hoped his betrayal would never be uncovered. Even if it were, he was prepared to die to protect it.

He couldn't burn them.

Even if they threatened the orthodoxy. Even if they threw up dangerous questions.

They had to be kept. They had to be protected.

They were sacred.

And if not now, if not during his lifetime or the lifetimes of many of his descendants, there would come a time when they would be read and studied openly. A time when they would enrich man's understanding of his past.

He would see to that.

Chapter 51

✝

"So Hosius decides these writings shouldn't be destroyed and stashes them away somewhere safe. How did they end up in the Templars' hands?"

"I don't know," Tess replied, her mind hurtling down many avenues at the same time. "But somehow, the first Templars to show up at the monastery, the ones led by Everard—"

"The ones the monks poisoned," Reilly interjected.

"Yes, somehow, they got hold of them." A beacon lit up somewhere in the maze and drew her toward it. "That was in 1203. Just before the sack of Constantinople," she told Reilly, her eyes flaring with the thrill of a newly established connection. "What if that's where they'd been kept all along, in Constantinople? What if whoever Hosius had entrusted to look after them figured they had to get them out of there and moved to somewhere safe before the city was overrun by the crusaders?"

"The crusaders—in other words, the pope's army."

Tess felt her skin light up. "The pope's army had the city under siege. They'd just pillaged Zara, a Catholic city. The people of Constantinople could expect even worse, given that it was the capital of Orthodox Christianity. The Orthodox patriarchs and the popes had spent the last couple of hundred years trading insults and excommunicating each other. It didn't take a soothsayer to know what the crusaders would do to them once they got inside the city walls. Whether the pope knew the documents were there or not, they were still at risk."

"So they ask the Templars to take them somewhere safe? Why the Templars?"

Tess processed the timeline. Another beacon flared up, dazzlingly bright and irresistible. "What if the Templars were in on it from the beginning?"

"What do you mean?"

"Three years ago, at the Vatican, the first time you met Brugnone, he told you the Templars had found Jesus's journal in Jerusalem. He confirmed what Vance had suspected—that they'd used it to blackmail the pope and that that was how they got so rich and powerful so quickly. Well . . . where did that journal really come from?"

"Didn't they find it buried somewhere in the remains of the old Temple of Solomon in Jerusalem? I thought the story was that they spent their first few years out there digging around, and then when they found it, it allowed them to blackmail the Vatican into backing them and that's when all the donations of money and land started pouring in."

"That's what we've always assumed. But what if we were wrong?" She thought back to the origin of the Templars that was common lore—nine knights from across Europe who all showed up in Jerusalem one day back in 1118, out of the blue, and told the king they wanted to protect the Christian pilgrims who were streaming in to see the newly conquered holy city. The king gave them huge premises to use as their base, the site of the old Temple of Solomon—hence, Knights of the Temple, or Templars—premises they didn't apparently leave for nine years, years that they supposedly spent digging around, looking for something that, when they found it, gave them great wealth and power. Something that Tess believed she and Reilly had uncovered three years earlier.

"Did the first Templars really find it after digging around those ruins?" she asked. "Or was that just their cover story? What if it had been part of the trove of Nicaea from day one?"

"So they lied to the pope to sex it up? To make it sound more mysterious, more mythical?"

"Partly," Tess speculated. "It would also keep the rest of the trove safe. There was no reason for them to alert the pope and his cronies to the fact that there were all these other gospels and writings out there. Why put it all at risk?"

"But that would mean the founding Templars knew about the trove from day one," Reilly observed.

"Which begs the question," Tess jumped in, "who were they really, and why did they choose to make their move and blackmail the pope when they did?" She was having trouble keeping up with the implications of every new realization. Everything she'd thought she knew about the origins of the Templars—who they really were, where they came from, why they appeared when they did, what they were really trying to achieve—it was all suddenly thrown into question.

"When did they first show up on the map?"

"In 1118. A pretty revolutionary time," she thought aloud, her mind on fire now. "It was the first time that any pope, the leader of the Catholic Church and Jesus's representative on earth, wasn't spreading His message of love and peace. Instead, he was telling his flock to go out and kill in the name of Christ, telling them all their sins would be forgiven and Heaven would be theirs if they went out and butchered the heathen in the name of the Cross. And at that point, his holy army was winning. They had taken over Jerusalem—the Muslims were on the ropes. The pope was the leader of the only superpower around, and the world was his for the taking."

Reilly processed her words. "Maybe someone, somewhere decided to create a counterpoint?" he put in. "A force that could check Rome's supremacy and maybe put the brakes on before it all got out of hand?"

Tess nodded, her eyes distant. "Maybe everything we thought we knew about the Templars is wrong."

A silence fell over them, allowing their ideas to find some purchase. Then Tess's expression lost its inspired lightness and sank, heavy with trepidation. "I can see why our Iranian friend wanted to get his hands on Hosius's stash. We've got to find it, Sean. If it's out there, we've got to find it first. We can't let some bastards in Tehran dump it on an unprepared world."

"You really think it can still cause trouble?" he questioned. "Even in today's world? People out there are pretty cynical."

"Not about this. Not about the Bible. There are two billion Christians out there, Sean, and a lot of them think of the Bible as God's words. *His actual words*. They think the twenty-seven texts that make up the New Testament were handed down to us by God himself, to help us lead better lives and achieve eternal salvation. They don't realize that nothing could be farther from the truth and that what we call the Bible was actually put together a few hundred years after Jesus's crucifixion. But we know different. We know for a fact that early Christianity was very diverse in its beliefs and in its writings. It was made up of scattered communities of people who had competing interpretations of what Jesus was and what he preached and what he did, communities that based their faiths on very different ideas. And before too long, they started squabbling about whose version was right. Ultimately, one of these groups won by gaining more converts than the others. And the winners decided which of these early writings were the ones their converts should follow, they changed them to fit the story they settled on, and they branded all the others blasphemous and heretical and suppressed them. They buried the competition, along with their beliefs and practices, and then they rewrote the history of the whole struggle. My point is, they decided what would be considered genuine, sacred scripture, and what wouldn't. And they did a great job. There's hardly anything left of the texts they didn't like. The only reason we know they even existed is that they're occasionally mentioned by early Church writers, and the handful of copies we have of any of these competing versions are down to the occasional fluke, like the discovery of that stash of gnostic gospels at Nag Hammadi back in the 1940s."

"Until now," Reilly put in.

"Absolutely. And imagine for a second what would have

happened if one of the other groups of Christians had won that struggle. We could have ended up with a very different religion, one that doesn't have much in common with what we call Christianity today. And that's *if* it would have made it this far in the first place. 'Cause it's possible, even likely, that if Christianity hadn't taken on the form it did take, the all-welcoming, supernatural story of death and resurrection and eternal salvation that cobbled together elements from all the empire's existing religions into a new, one-size-fits-all package—Mithraism, Sol Invictus, a virgin birth, a resurrection three days later, the day of the sun and 'Sunday,' the twenty-fifth of December—and allowed it to grow in an organized way and become the official religion of the Roman Empire . . . Constantine might not have embraced it. He might not have been able to convince his pagan populace to accept it, and our world would be very different today. Without Christianity as its bedrock, Western civilization would've developed in ways you and I can't even begin to imagine. *And it's all down to the sacred texts the founders chose to build their Church on.* 'Cause that's what any religion boils down to, isn't it? Scripture. Sacred texts. A story, a fable, a mythical tale that someone wrote down a hell of a long time ago.

"But those early, competing Christianities were very, very different. And their gospels, their scripture, described a very different set of events and a very different set of beliefs from those in the New Testament. Some described Jesus as a Buddha-like preacher whose secrets would only be revealed to a few lucky initiates. Others talk about him as a revolutionary leader who would liberate the poor from their Roman oppressors by force. Some of them describe Jesus as a divinely inspired guide to spiritual enlightenment who went around saying very New Agey things like *'You saw the Spirit, you became Spirit. You saw the Christ, you became Christ. You saw the Father, you shall become Father.'* They have radically different takes on the whole human-divine debate about Jesus and on how we can achieve salvation—though it usually boils down to understanding the true meaning of Jesus's words and discovering the truth about our own divine selves without the need for priests or churches or weird cannibalistic rituals like eating the body of Christ and drinking his blood. And fans of these noncanonical gospels will tell you they predate the four that are in the Bible. They'll claim—and there's a lot of evidence to support this—that the four gospels in the canon were heavily edited and massaged to support the setting up of an organized Church in His name and to justify having a hierarchy of bishops, priests, and deacons and give them power over their followers as the legitimate heirs of the apostles and—and this is the key part—the exclusive providers of eternal salvation. Which is what they achieved. Exclusivity. Remember, before Christianity, people in the Roman Empire worshipped all kinds of gods. No one had a problem with that. There was huge tolerance and respect, and the concept of heresy and of believing in 'the right god'—orthodoxy—didn't exist. There was no sin we needed to be saved from, either. It was only with Christianity that the idea of what a person believed in started to matter, and matter a lot, because his or her eternal life suddenly depended on it.

"Purists and staunch Bible defenders, on the other hand, will tell you anything that doesn't conform to the four gospels in the canon is of dubious origin. They'll say they had to be written *after* the four gospels that are in the Bible, and they'll tell you their authors were 'corrupted' by gnostic influences. They label them 'heretic.' You know what the word means? *Choice.* Literally. That's the root of the word. It just means someone who chooses to believe something else. That's all. But the winners chose what we should believe in. They chose which writings were sacred and which ones were 'heretical.'

"The thing is, right now, we don't know for a fact which one of the two sides is right. We don't know which writings are the 'corrupted' ones. It's all theory and conjecture—because there's so little that survives from back then. We don't know for a fact when Matthew, Mark, Luke, and John were written, or in what order. We don't. We don't really know who wrote them, but we know it wasn't any of them—they're not written in the first person, for starters, and we know they were written long after they were dead.

But we're told they're the real deal. We're told they're the ones that tell the true story of Jesus and his preaching and that anything that deviates from them is bogus. But there's no proof of that. And there's a hell of a lot of material to support questioning it. The world's top biblical scholars have documented references to many other writings, other gospels that have never been found but that could predate the ones in the Bible—close to fifty of them, at last count. That's fifty other gospels that we've never had a chance to read, and those are just the ones we know about. And yet we still take the book we've been handed down for granted as being the real thing, and that's the book that rules almost every aspect of our lives. It's the book they quote in the Senate when they're deciding whether or not to go to war, or if a woman can have an abortion or not. It's the book that people believe contains the words of God. Literally. Without having the first clue about where it came from or how it was really put together."

"And this trove could change all that," Reilly noted.

Tess nodded. "Are you kidding me? We're not talking about postage stamp fragments like the Dead Sea Scrolls or even a few random codices like the ones from Nag Hammadi. We're talking about an entire library of gospels and early Christian writings here, Sean. Dated, documented, complete, and original, not translations of translations of translations—a full, authentic, unadulterated picture of all the different takes on Jesus's life and words. It could revolutionize our understanding of the man and the myth—in fact, I'm sure it would. 'Cause I don't doubt for a second that Jesus's words were very different from what we've been sold since Nicaea. I mean, how else could His message of possession-free selflessness, a message that was aimed at lifting up the poor and the oppressed, have ended up as a religion of the rich and powerful in Rome without being corrupted to fit its new agenda?"

"The religion of the emperor," Reilly said, recalling Hosius's letter.

"Exactly. Think about what really happened at the Council of Nicaea. An emperor—not a pope—brought together the most influential priests and bishops from all over his empire, sat them in a room, and told them to work out their differences and come up with one doctrine that would become the official, accepted version of Christianity. An emperor, not a pope. A warrior-king, a ruler, *a messiah*, really, if you want to use the real meaning of that word—a man who had just defeated his opponents and taken control of a divided land and who needed something incredibly powerful to unify all the different parts of his empire. We have a chance to discover the texts that didn't make the cut, the other versions of what Jesus said and did—the ones Constantine and the founders of the Church decided we shouldn't know about."

Her eyes blazed into him. "We've got to find it," she insisted. "It's an incredible, crucial key to our history, but it can also be devastating. We've got to find it and make sure it's handled the right way. These writings could answer a lot of questions for those who can handle the truth, but they'll also kick up one hell of a crisis for those who can't, and there are a whole lot more of those out there. A few years ago, one line, just one line from some fragments of a supposedly earlier version of the Gospel of Mark, was enough to whip up a storm of controversy because it insinuated that Jesus had spent a whole night teaching 'the secrets of his kingdom' to another man who was only wearing a 'linen garment,' with all the connotations that entails. Imagine what a truckload of alternate gospels might do."

Reilly studied her thoughtfully, absorbing her words, but even before she was done, he already knew he couldn't head home. Not yet. Not before doing everything he could to try to find those chests. In the wrong hands, they were potentially a weapon—a weapon of mass despair, if you considered that a third of the planet's inhabitants were Christian, and that a lot of them considered every word in the Bible to be sacred and inerrant. The problem was, he didn't want to involve the Bureau and, by association, the Vatican. Things hadn't turned out too well on that front the last time around. And he certainly didn't want the Turks involved either. Historic artifacts, especially religious ones, would get confiscated before they'd even had a chance to look at them.

No, if he and Tess were going to do this, they were going to have to do it on their own. Below the radar. Way below. Subterranean below.

"I'm with you," he finally agreed. "But how? What more can we do? You hit a wall, didn't you? You said the trail went cold."

Tess was up now, pacing around, a bundle of nervous enthusiasm. "It did, but . . . we're missing something. Conrad must have left us a clue, even in death. He must have." A realization ignited her eyes. "It's got to be in that church, where he's buried."

"You were just there. You said there was nothing else buried with him."

"There's got to be something else," she insisted. "Something we missed. We have to go back there."

Chapter 52

✝

Tess cloaked her unease as she watched Reilly go into no-nonsense, steamroller mode to get past the two Jandarma soldiers who were posted outside the hotel.

He told them he'd lost his BlackBerry somewhere in the canyon during the shoot-out, and insisted in no uncertain terms that he absolutely had to go back there to try to recover it since it held confidential FBI material. At the first balk, he ratcheted his tone up a notch and made it sound like a full-bore diplomatic incident was in the offing if any delay resulted in his not getting the device back and that, if he didn't get there soon, the area would be swarming with American troops in order to secure the missing cache of state secrets.

The snow job worked. Twenty minutes later, the hotel's van deposited them in the clearing at the mouth of the canyon. A Jandarma Humvee was still stationed there. The only other car in the lot was the dead Byzantinist's dusty Cherokee, a grim reminder of the blood-soaked trail that had claimed its owner.

They were soon trudging past the cone house where the man had been gunned down. The blood spatter had soaked into the soft, porous rock by the doorway, its faded appearance already making it look like a remnant from the distant past. There were no cops cordoning off the area, no yellow tape, no crime scene investigators poring over every indentation in the tufa. There was no need for any of it. It was all pretty cut and dried, and if the Iranian were to be caught, he wasn't going to face a trial by jury.

As she went by, Tess found herself shivering and couldn't shake the image of Abdülkerim's face bursting with anguish the moment the bullets ripped through him. She'd barely met the man, barely gotten to know him. She realized she knew nothing about him, whether or not he was married or had kids. And now he was dead. All within hours of her meeting him.

They climbed up to the church. Using flashlights borrowed from the hotel, Tess pointed out the mural in the apse's half dome to Reilly before leading him down to the crypt. She was still shivering as they entered the burial chamber, which was just as they'd left it. Being there was making her relive the scene. It was as if she were watching herself in a 3-D holographic diorama, a haunting replay with Abdülkerim's worried face front and center.

Reilly must have sensed it. "You okay?" he asked.

She shook the disturbing images away and nodded, then showed him Conrad's open grave. The broken pieces of the cooking pot were lying beside it. Nothing had been moved.

Reilly glanced around the room. "What about these other graves?"

She raked the beam across the markings on the walls. "Church dignitaries and benefactors."

"They could be hiding something else."

"Maybe," Tess told him, her tone skeptical. "Short of digging them all up, it's impossible to tell. The thing is, if that's where Hosius's stash is buried, I think they would have left something behind, some clue to point to it. Otherwise, it could be lost forever. But they're just names, and none of them stand out as being out of place."

"Okay. So there's the mural and this crypt. Anything else?"

Tess shook her head. "We looked around the rest of the church before we left. That's it." As she said it, she remembered something—something that had occurred to her back when she was online and getting Hosius's letter translated, at the hotel. She went back to what he said. "The mural."

Almost in a trance, she led him back up to the apse. She studied the mural again, aiming her light at the Greek lettering above the painting.

"It's just weird," she said, almost under her breath, "having lines from a Sufi poem here, in a church."

"Sufi being . . . ?"

"It's a mystical form of Islam," she explained. "Very popular in Turkey. It was, anyway, before it was outlawed in the 1920s."

"Hang on, a Muslim saying in a church?"

"Not exactly Muslim. Sufism is different. It's so different that hard-core Muslims like our Saudi friends and the Taliban consider its followers dangerous heretics and have totally banned them. They're terrified of them because Sufism is very pacifist and tolerant and liberal—and it's not about worship. It's a personal experience. It's about seeking one's own path to God and trying to reach spiritual ecstasy. Rumi, the mystic who wrote this poem, was one of Sufism's founding fathers. He preached that Sufism was open to people of all religions and that music, poetry, and dancing were the way to open the gates of paradise and reach God—a god who's not the god of punishment or the god of revenge, but the god of love."

"Sounds groovy." Reilly smirked.

"It is. Which is why Rumi's really popular back home. Massively popular. I even read somewhere that Sarah Jessica Parker does her aerobics to rock 'n' roll versions of his poems. He's been turned into this New Age guru, which doesn't really do justice to the intensity and depth of his writing, but it's understandable given that he wrote things like, '*My religion is to live through love*,' which, you've got to admit, is pretty radical for a thirteenth-century Muslim preacher."

"I can see why the Saudis don't want his message to spread."

"It's sad, really. Tragic. It's a message that could do a lot of good out there right now."

Reilly stared at the fresco again. "Okay, but heretic or not, we still have a Muslim-lite line of poetry on a thousand-year-old church wall. Which, like you said, is pretty weird. What does it say anyway?"

"Abdülkerim read it out for us." She highlighted the Greek writing above the wall painting and translated it aloud, remembering the Byzantinist's words. "*As for pain, like a hand cut in battle, consider the body a robe you wear. The worried, heroic deeds of a man and a woman are noble to the draper, where the dervishes relish the light breeze of spirit.*"

Reilly shrugged. "*A hand cut in battle.*' There's your reason. Can't be that many poems with that line in them."

"Sure. But Rumi died in 1273. He had to have written it long before Conrad lost his hand."

Reilly reflected on the lines. "What does it mean anyway?"

"I'm not sure. I've got the rest of the poem here. I pulled it up online." She fished a bunch of printouts from her rucksack and found the right sheet. "Here we go. The poem is called 'Light Breeze.' It says, '*As for pain, like a hand cut in battle, consider the body a robe you wear. The worried, heroic deeds of men and women seem weary and futile to dervishes enjoying the light breeze of spirit . . .*'" She stopped. Her face crumpled up with confusion. "Wait a sec. This is different from what's on the wall."

"Read it out again?"

Tess concentrated on the Greek letters, comparing them to what was on her printout. "The mural says the heroic deeds are 'noble,' not 'weary and futile.' And it's the deeds of 'a man and a woman,' not of 'men and women,' plural. The rest of it's very different too." She paused for a beat, concentrating on the parallel sentences. "Whoever put that inscription up there must have been trying to tell us something." Her breathing quickened. "Maybe it's telling us where the rest of the chests are."

"The result of Conrad's 'worried, heroic deeds'?" Reilly asked.

"Not just Conrad's. It says the deeds of 'a man and a woman.' Could that mean Conrad and some woman?" She frowned, deep in thought. "Was there a woman with him? And if there was, who was she?"

"Hang on, weren't the Templars monks? Like with vows of chastity and all that?"

"You mean celibacy, and yes, they were celibate. No women allowed in their world."

"And they did this voluntarily? At a time when there was no ESPN?"

She ignored him and brooded over it for a few seconds, then pulled out a pen from her sack and scribbled down the version from the mural on the sheet of paper, next to the printout of the original.

She compared them again. "Okay. Let's assume the changes were made for a reason. To point us somewhere. So whoever wrote this changed the deeds from being 'weary and futile' to being 'noble.' What if that refers to recovering the stash of Nicaea and keeping it safe?"

"Keep going."

A wave of heightened awareness flooded through her. It was a sensation she loved, the feeling of being in the zone and knowing it. "The deeds aren't weary and futile. They're noble. To 'the draper.' 'Where' the dervishes relish the light breeze of spirit."

"I'm all ears, Yoda," Reilly said.

"What if it's telling us who was looking after them?"

"The 'draper'?"

"A draper where the dervishes live."

"Which is . . ."

"In Konya, of course."

Reilly shrugged. "I knew that."

"Shut up. You don't even know what a dervish is."

His expression turned mock-sheepish. "It's not something I'm proud of."

"A dervish is a member of a Sufi brotherhood, you Neanderthal—a Sufi order. Rumi's followers are the most famous of them. They're known as 'whirling dervishes' because of the prayer ritual that they do where they whirl around like spinning tops, which they do to reach a kind of trancelike state that lets them focus on the god within them."

"'The god within them,'" Reilly noted, serious now. "Sounds kind of gnostic, doesn't it?"

Tess raised an eyebrow. "True." She flashed him an impressed look and said, "Maybe not so Neanderthal after all," then mulled the idea over for a beat. The spiritual message was indeed similar. She parked the thought for the time being and said, "Rumi and his brotherhood were based in Konya. He's buried there. His tomb is now a big museum." Her mind was already two steps ahead of her mouth. "Konya. It's got to be in Konya."

"Conrad died here. Konya's—how far is it from here?"

Tess tried to remember what Abdülkerim had said. "A couple of hundred miles west of here."

"Not a small distance to cover in those days. So how did it get there? Who took it there?"

"Maybe the same person who wrote this," she said, gesturing at the Greek lettering on the mural. Her mind was still leapfrogging ahead in search of answers. "But Konya was Sufi territory back then. Still is. If Hosius's stash was taken there, whoever did it must have been close to the Sufis—or been a Sufi himself."

"Him- or herself," Reilly corrected her. "Remember, a man and a woman. Could our mystery woman be this Sufi?"

"Could be. Men and women are considered equal in Sufism, and many Sufi saints were mentored by women." She thought about it for a long second, then said, "We've got to go there. We've got to go to Konya."

Reilly gave her a deeply dubious look. "Come on, you don't really think that—"

"These changes were made for a reason, Sean. And I really think there's a strong chance it's telling us that Hosius's trove was handed over for safekeeping to some Sufi draper in Konya," she insisted. "That's where we'll start."

"How?"

"Professions are often handed down from generation to generation in this part of the world. We need to find a draper whose ancestor was in one of Rumi's lodges."

Reilly seemed far from convinced. "You really think you're going to find a family of drapers that goes back seven hundred years?"

"I know I'm going to try," she taunted him. "You got a better idea?"

Chapter 53

✝

KONYA, TURKEY

A few precocious stars were ushering out the setting sun as a taxi dropped Reilly and Tess off in the heart of one of the oldest settlements on the planet.

Every stone in the city was soaked in history. Legend had it that it was the first town to emerge from the great flood, and archaeological evidence showed people living there continuously since Neolithic tribes settled in the area more than ten thousand years ago. St. Paul was said to have preached there three times from as early as A.D. 53, setting the city onto a stellar path that reached its peak when it became the capital of the Seljuk Sultanate in the thirteenth century—the same time that it was home to Rumi and his brotherhood of dervishes. The city had declined precipitously since its glory days under the sultans, but it was still home to the second-most-visited attraction in Turkey, with more than two million visitors streaming in every year to pay homage to the great mystic. His mausoleum, the Yeşil Türbe—the Green Tomb—was the spiritual epicenter of the Sufi faith.

It was also where Tess decided they'd start their search.

She knew it wouldn't be easy. Sufism was still banned in Turkey. There were no lodges to poke around in, no elders to ask. At least, not out in the open. Sufi spiritual gatherings were only conducted in strict privacy, away from uninvited eyes. The threat of prison sentences still loomed large for potential offenders.

Sufism had been outlawed in 1925, soon after the father of modern Turkey, Kemal Atatürk, founded his republic out of the ashes of the religion-driven Ottoman Empire. Desperate to demonstrate how Westernized his new country would be, he strove to ensure that his new state was strictly secular and put up an impermeable wall between religion and government. The Sufis, whose lodges wielded influence at the highest levels of Ottoman society and government, had to go. The lodges were all shut down, with most turned into mosques. Public rituals, which were perceived by Atatürk and his government as too backward and a drag on the Western-inspired modernity they aspired to, were banned, as was any teaching of the tradition. In fact, the only visible manifestation of Sufism in the country left today was in the folkloric dance performances of the *sema*, the whirling prayer ceremony of Rumi's followers that had, ironically, now become one of the main touristic emblems of the country. And that was only after they had been grudgingly reallowed in the 1950s, following an inquiry by the curious wife of a visiting American diplomat who was keen to actually see one. And so the bighearted faith ended up being banned by both the fundamentalist regimes farther east in countries like Saudi Arabia and Afghanistan, for being heretically liberal, and by the progressive Turks, for the opposite reason.

From the sea of austere beards and tight head scarves all around them, it was clear that Konya was a very pious and conservative place. Contrastingly, Westerners in casual summer clothing were also out in abundance, both groups mingling and mixing casually. Tess and Reilly joined the flow of pilgrims, dozens of men and women, young and old, from all corners of the globe, heading toward the shrine. It loomed up ahead, unmissable with its squat, pointed, turquoise-tiled tower. The big, gray medieval building had been Rumi's *tekke*, the lodge where he and his followers lived and meditated. The lodge was now a museum built around his tomb and those of his father and other Sufi saints.

They followed the procession through the large arched portal and into the heart of the mausoleum. Dioramas of mannequins in traditional Sufi settings filled most of the rooms, lifeless re-creations of now outlawed practices, an eerie reminder of a not so distant tradition that had been stopped in its tracks.

Tess found a stall with pamphlets in various languages and picked up an English one, then perused it as they meandered past the various displays. Something in it made her nod to herself, which Reilly caught.

"What?" he asked.

"Rumi's writings. Listen to this. '*I searched for God among the Christians and on the Cross and therein I found Him not. I went into the ancient temples of idolatry; no trace of Him was there. I entered the mountain cave of Hira and then went very far but God I found not. Then I directed my search to the Kaaba, the resort of old and young; God was not there. Finally, I looked into my own heart and there I saw Him; He was nowhere else.*'"

"Brave guy," Reilly commented. "I'm amazed they didn't lop his head off."

"The Seljuk Sultan actually invited him to live here. He didn't have a problem with Rumi's ideas, just like he didn't have a problem with the Christians in Cappadocia."

"I miss those Seljuks."

Tess nodded, her mind floating across the imagined landscapes of alternate worlds. "You know, the more I think about it, the more I see how much common ground there was between what the Sufis believed and what I think the Templars were going for. They both saw religion as something that should bring us all closer together, not a divisive force."

"At least these guys didn't get burned at the stake."

Tess shrugged. "They didn't have a king lusting after the gold in their coffers."

They stepped through a doorway that led into the grand room where Mawlana Jelaluddin Rumi, the *mevlana* himself—the master—was buried. The cavernous space around them was breathtaking, its walls masterpieces of ornate gold calligraphy carvings, its ceilings dazzling kalei- doscopes of arabesques. At its center was his tomb. It was oversized and stately, swathed by a huge, gold-embroidered cloth and topped by an enormous turban.

They stood back and watched as teary-eyed pilgrims rubbed their foreheads on a silver step at the base of the tomb before kissing it. Others stood around the room, reading the poet's words to themselves or sharing them in small groups, their faces alive with felicity. A great hush suffused the space, and the mood in the shrine was gently reverent, more akin to fans visiting the tomb of a great poet than to any kind of fervent religious pilgrimage. Which was what Tess had feared. There was nothing there that looked like it was going to help her locate her elusive family of drapers, assuming they'd ever existed at all. She needed to ask around but didn't know whom to ask.

They left the shrine and wandered down a broad bou- levard that led deep into the old city. Shops, cafés, and res- taurants teemed with locals and visitors, while kids played freely on grassy knolls. The city exuded a tranquillity that Tess and Reilly had both sorely missed.

"Maybe we can find a town hall," Tess said, her gait slow and ponderous, her arms folded with frustration. "Some- place where they keep civic records."

"Maybe there's a drapers section in their yellow pages?" Reilly added.

Tess wasn't in the mood.

"What? I'm serious." He gave her an empathetic grin, then said, "Problem is, we've got a slight language barrier here."

"The only dervishes around seem to be the ones doing the big shows for the tourists. They deal with foreigners. We should be able to find someone who understands us there. Maybe we can convince one of them to introduce us to a Sufi elder."

Reilly pointed a finger down the road. "Let's ask them."

Tess turned. A sign announced "Iconium Tours," and be- low, in smaller letters, "Travel Agency."

*　　　*　　　*

"I CAN GET YOU IN to see a *sema* tonight," the owner of the agency, a gregarious man in his early fifties by the name of Levant, told them with infectious enthusiasm. "It's a wonderful show. You'll love it. You like Rumi's poetry, yes?"

"Very much." Tess smiled uncomfortably. "But would this be a real prayer ceremony or a more"—she wavered—"touristic show?"

Levant gave her a curious look. He seemed slightly offended. "Any *sema* is a real prayer ceremony. The dervishes who will be whirling there take what they do very seriously."

Tess flashed him a disarming smile. "Of course. That's not what I meant." She took a deep breath, looking for the right words. "It's just ... see, I'm an archaeologist, and I'm trying to understand something I found. An old book. And it talks about a draper—this is going back quite some time, a few centuries ago." She paused, hastily pulling out a crumpled piece of paper from her pocket. "A *kazzaz*, or a *bezzaz*, or a *derzi*, or a *çukacı*," she said, stumbling over the different ways of referring to a cloth maker that the taxi driver had given her. She wasn't sure how to pronounce that last one and showed the agent what the driver had written down for her—in letters she could read, since another of Atatürk's momentous reforms was to abandon the Arabic alphabet and make Latin letters the norm for writing in Turkish. "A draper who was a dervish here in Konya. Probably a senior one, an elder, that kind of thing. I know it's a bit tricky to talk about it, but ... you don't know anyone who might know a lot about that, an expert on your local dervish history?"

Levant pulled back slightly, and his expression retreated into more guarded territory.

"Look, I'm not here in any kind of official capacity," Tess added by way of comforting him. "This is just a personal quest. I'm just trying to understand something about an old book I found, that's all."

The travel agent massaged his mouth and his chin with his hand, then ran it up his face and all the way across his balding pate. He glanced at Reilly, studying him too. Reilly said nothing and just stood there, trying to appear as sheepish and unthreatening as he could. The bald man's eyes settled back on Tess; then he leaned in and his expression went all conspiratorial.

"I can take you to a private *dhikr* this evening," he told them, referring to a Sufi remembrance ceremony. "It's a very private affair, you understand. Informal. Just friends getting together to"—he paused—"celebrate life." He held her gaze, waiting to see if she got his gist.

She nodded. "And you think there'll be someone there who can help me?"

Levant shrugged, like, *Maybe*. But his "maybe" was definitely skewed positive.

Tess smiled. "When?"

THE ELDER WASN'T MUCH HELP.

The prayer ceremony itself had been spellbinding. It was held in the grand living room of a large old house. The dervishes, a dozen or so men and women, lost themselves in their trances and spun around endlessly, arms spread out, right hands opened upward to receive the blessings of Heaven, left hands pointing down to channel it to the earth, moving to the tender, mesmerizing music of a reed flute—Rumi's beloved *ney*, the divine breath that bestows life on everything—and a drum. From a seated position, an old man, their master, accompanied them by reciting the name of God repeatedly, the part of the ceremony that was most strictly forbidden. But no one stormed the house and no one was arrested. The times were, it seemed, a-changing.

But the elder wasn't much help—in fact, he wasn't any help at all. With his grandson to translate, he told Tess he didn't know of any drapers or cloth makers who had been notable dervishes, and didn't know of any who were currently, either. Tess and Reilly thanked their hosts for their hospitality and wandered off in search of the hotel the travel agent had booked them into.

"I shouldn't have let myself get carried away like that," Tess grumbled, feeling exhausted and crestfallen. "There were plenty of lodges in Konya, even back then. The odds of stumbling onto the right one . . . it wasn't likely, was it?" She sighed. "This could take a while."

"We can't stay here any longer," Reilly said. "They want me back in New York. And we don't even have a change of clothes or a toothbrush between us. Seriously. This is nuts. We don't even know it's here."

"I'm not giving up. We just got here. I need to go to more of these ceremonies, talk to more elders." She glanced at Reilly. "I've got to do this, Sean. We're close. I can feel it. And I can't walk away from it. I've got to see it through. You go. I'll stay."

Reilly shook his head. "It's too dangerous. That son of a bitch is still out there somewhere. I'm not leaving you here alone."

The comment soured Tess's face. Reilly's concern wasn't unfounded.

"You're right, I know," she said, nodding slowly to herself, unsure about what to do.

Reilly put his arm around her. "Come on. Let's find that hotel. I'm beat."

They reached the bazaar district, where they asked for directions before cutting through a galleried market hall the size of an aircraft hangar. Despite the late hour, it was still buzzing. All kinds of smells accosted them from colorful piles of fruit and vegetables, bucket loads of freshly made *domates salçasi* tomato sauce, and huge sacks of sugar beet and spices of every color, the whole succulent tapestry manned by old men in patterned hats, old women in multicolored head scarves, and *çay* boys hawking syrupy-sweet tea. A pit stop of doner kebabs and minty yogurt drinks was hard to resist. They hadn't eaten much all day.

"Can't you stick around a couple more days?" Tess pleaded, the idea of heading home and giving up the search sitting as heavily in her stomach as the thought of staying there alone.

"I doubt it." He chucked his empty sandwich wrapper into an overflowing garbage bin and downed the last of his drink. "I still have a lot of explaining to do over Rome."

"Rome." Tess shrugged, her tone distant. It felt like a lifetime ago.

"They don't even know we're here. I need to call in and find out when we're being picked up and see if they can pick us up from here. Besides, I want to get back. There isn't much I can do from here. I need to be back at my desk to coordinate the intel and make sure all the alerts are properly in place so we don't miss him the next time he pops up." He put his hands on Tess's shoulders and pulled her closer to him. "Look, it doesn't mean you have to give up on this. We've got a contact here now, that travel agent. You can call him from New York. Let him do your legwork. He's better placed to do it anyway. We can pay him for it— he seems like a helpful guy. And if he comes up with something, we'll fly back."

Tess didn't answer him. Her expression had gone all curious and she was staring at something beyond him. Reilly eyed her for a beat, then turned and saw what she was staring at. It was a carpet shop. A bald, chubby man was carrying in an advertising sandwich board from the sidewalk. It looked like they were closing up for the night.

"You've gone into shopping mode now?" Reilly asked. "With everything else that's going on?"

Tess shot him a reproachful grimace and pointed a sly finger at the sign above the shop. It read, "Kismet Carpets and Kilims," and below that, "Traditional Handicraft Workshop."

Reilly didn't get it.

Tess pointed again and made a face like, *Look again.*

He looked again. Then he saw it.

In smaller letters, at the bottom of the sign. Next to the shop's phone number. A name. The name of the owner, presumably. Hakan Kazzazoğlu.

Kazzaz-oğlu.

Reilly recognized the first part of the word, but it didn't gel with what he expected to see. There wasn't a fabric in sight. "It's a carpet shop," he noted, his tone confused. "And what's with the 'oğlu'?"

"It's very common suffix in Turkish family names," Tess replied. "It means 'sons of,' or 'descendants of.'"

She was already heading into the store.

Chapter 54

✝

As Tess had deduced, the carpet seller was indeed the descendant of a draper. In her desperation, Tess had been more forthcoming with him than she had been with the Sufi master, telling him that she had come across some old biblical manuscripts and was trying to find out more about their provenance. After a bit of hesitation, she'd even reached into her rucksack and shown him one of them. Sadly, he didn't turn out to be any more helpful than the elder.

It wasn't that he was being evasive or difficult in any way. The man just genuinely seemed not to know what Tess was talking about, despite being very candid about his family history and about being a practicing Sufi himself.

It didn't deter Tess. She felt sure that they were on to something. It wasn't necessarily a draper and his fabric store they were looking for. It was a name. A family name, one that could be associated with any profession or any kind of shop. And in that sense, the carpet seller had been helpful. He wrote down a list of all the other Kazzazoğlus he was aware of and where their places of business were. There were more than a dozen of them, everything from other carpet sellers to potters and even a dentist. He also listed several other possibilities where the family names were also derived from the other ways of saying "draper" in Turkish, using the same words the taxi driver had given Tess.

They thanked the man and left him to close down his shop.

Tess felt rekindled. "We can't leave," she told Reilly, holding the list up to him. "Come on. One more day. Just buy us one more day. Give them some line about a lead concerning the Iranian. You can come up with something."

He rubbed the weariness from his face and looked at her. Her infectious drive was hard to resist at the best of times. Given what he'd been through the last few days, he didn't stand a chance.

"You're bad," he said.

"The worst." She smiled, and led him back to the hotel.

REILLY GAVE APARO THE LOWDOWN on what they were going to do and set up a vague lead story for his partner to give their boss. He and Tess then left the hotel bright and early the next day and spent it scouring the shops the carpet seller had listed for them.

The people they met were overwhelmingly kind and welcoming. With each inquiry, Tess found it easier to be more open and felt no qualms about showing around the two codices. But it was ultimately pointless. No one knew anything about a stash of ancient books, and if they did, they weren't saying and were hiding it well.

She and Reilly closed out the day with the last name on the list. It was a ceramics and earthenware shop with an astounding variety of multicolored and intricately decorated tiles, plates, and vases in its front window, run by a chubby, soft-spoken, and easygoing fortysomething-year-old with intensely dark eyelashes that would have made him the perfect plus-size model for Maybelline if they ever chose to market mascara for men. They spoke openly for ten minutes or so, helped by the fact that there was no one else in the store apart from the owner's teen daughter, who shared her father's eyelashes but not his corpulent physique and was a much better Maybelline bet, as well as a shrunken elderly woman the owner introduced as his mother, who was equally clueless about Tess's inquiries.

Despite their not being able to help Tess, the sight of the rare book had piqued a surge of interest in both the shop-keeper and his mother, as it had with many of the others. The old woman shuffled over and, softly, asked if she could take a closer look at the codex. Tess handed it to her. The woman opened it gently, glancing at the inside page and turning over a couple more.

"It's beautiful," the woman said as she perused its contents. "How old do you think it is?"

"About two thousand years old," Tess replied.

The woman's eyes widened with surprise. She nodded slowly to herself, then closed the codex and gave its brittle leather cover a soft pat. "This must be worth a lot of money, no?"

"I suppose so," Tess answered. "I never really thought about that."

Which seemed to surprise the old woman. "Isn't that what you're after? You're not hoping to sell this?"

"No. Not at all."

"What then?"

"I'm not sure," Tess said, thinking aloud. "This gospel—and any others that might be out there—they're part of our history. They need to be studied, translated, dated. And then, whatever's in them needs to be shared with whoever's interested in learning more about what took place in the Holy Land back then."

"You could still do that by selling it to a museum," the woman pressed, her eyes now alive with a hint of mischief.

Tess half-smiled. "I'm sure I could. But that's not what I'm looking for. It never was. And these books . . ." Her expression darkened as she reached out and took the codex back from the woman. "A lot of people got hurt on the way to finding them. The least I can do is make sure their pain and suffering wasn't entirely in vain. These books are their legacy as much as anyone's."

The woman tilted her head with a kind of "too bad" shrug. "I'm sorry we couldn't help you," she offered.

Tess nodded and tucked the ancient book back into her rucksack. "That's okay," she replied. "Thanks for your time."

With nothing more to discuss, all that was left for her and Reilly was to politely extricate themselves from the shop once the conversation turned to the fine ceramics the family produced and the bargain prices that were on offer.

They left the three generations of Kazzazoğlus to close up their store and stepped out into the still night. The hotel wasn't too far, a ten-minute walk from the shop. It was a simple, medium-sized place. Modern, three stories high, the kind of hotel one usually associated with a secondary airport. Long on functionality, short on charm. Then again, Reilly and Tess weren't exactly on their honeymoon. Their room, which overlooked the main street from the top floor, provided them with a decent shower and a clean bed, and that was all the charm they needed right now. It had been a long day, the latest in a string of long days and longer nights.

Tess felt glum. She knew she was out of time. They'd be heading home the next day, empty-handed. There was no way around that. They kissed and held each other quietly for a long minute in the cocoon of their unlit room; then Reilly pulled out his phone and dialed Aparo's cell. Tess crossed over to the window and stared out, lost in thought. The city had settled into sleep mode, and the street below her was deserted. A lone streetlamp stood sentinel to the left of the hotel entrance, bathing the cracked sidewalk with its jaundiced light. The only movement came from a trio of stray cats that slipped in and out from under some parked cars as they hunted for scraps.

As her eyes tracked them absentmindedly, she thought back to the last time she'd noticed any, outside the Patriarchate in Istanbul, just after she'd been told they were revered in Turkey as bringers of good fortune. The memory made her shiver. They hadn't been particularly auspicious on that occasion. She looked out across the canopy of trees and rooftops and, for a moment, pictured herself out there, on her own, roaming the town, without Reilly close by. The thought gave her little comfort. The Iranian was still out there, somewhere. Out there and pissed off. No, Reilly was right. She couldn't stay. It wasn't the sensible thing to do, and right now, with a daughter and a mother waiting for her back home, sensible was definitely the way to go.

She turned to join Reilly, and her gaze swept downward, finding the cats again. They skirted the edge of a storefront before slipping into a darkened alleyway—past a lone figure that was standing at the alley's mouth.

A lone figure that was looking up in Tess's direction.

Tess stiffened. There was something familiar about its silhouette. Her eyes locked in on the sight, her retinas straining to sharpen the image bouncing off them.

It was a teenage girl.

Not just any teenage girl.

The girl from the ceramics shop.

She didn't move. She was just standing there, in the shadows, watching the hotel. And despite the darkness, Tess could make out the whites of her eyes, tiny twin beacons of light in the desolate nightscape.

Their eyes met. Tess felt a jolt at the base of her neck. It seemed mirrored in the girl, who turned abruptly and scampered into the alley.

Tess bolted for the door, screaming to Reilly, "It's the girl from the shop. She's outside watching us," before rushing out.

She flew down the stairs and out the hotel doors and tore down the alleyway, with Reilly close behind. There was no sign of the girl. Tess kept going until she reached an intersection with a narrow street. She looked left and right. The street was lifeless.

"Where the hell did she go? She couldn't have gone that far that fast," she blurted.

"You sure it was her?"

"Definitely. She was looking right up at me, Sean. She must have followed us back. Why would she do that?" Then she remembered something. "Shit. The gospels. They're in my rucksack."

She moved to head back to the hotel, but Reilly stilled her with an arm and brought around her rucksack, which was slung over his shoulder, with the other. "Calm down. It's here." The bag was all they'd brought with them to

Konya. In addition to the two codices, it also held Reilly's handgun.

Tess exhaled heavily with relief. "You think this is what they're after? You think she was scoping us out to try and grab them?"

"I don't know. Maybe." Reilly glanced around and got his bearings. He gestured right. "Their shop's in that direction. Maybe that's where she's headed."

Tess thought about it for a quick second, then nodded. "Makes sense. Let's go there."

"Why?"

"I want to know what the hell she was doing here."

Chapter 55

✠

Finding the shop was easier said than done.

The old district's narrow streets and alleyways were a confusing maze, even more so at night, with very few streetlamps around. And when they finally reached it, it was all dark and locked up for the night.

Tess marched right up to it and started slamming her palm against its aluminium shutters. "Hey," she yelled out. "Open up. I know you're in there."

Reilly stepped in and stopped her. "You're going to wake up the whole neighborhood."

"I don't care," she blurted back. "Maybe their neighbors need to know about what kind of scams these people are running." She pounded the shutters again, shouting, "Open this door. I'm not leaving."

Reilly was about to interfere again when a light came on behind the louvered wooden shutter of a window above the store. Seconds later, it squealed open, and the head of the shopkeeper poked out.

"What are you doing here?" he asked. "What do you want?"

"I want to talk to your daughter," Tess said.

"My daughter?" The shopkeeper was clearly dumbfounded. "Now? Why?"

"Just tell her I'm here," Tess insisted. "She'll know."

"Look, I don't know what you think you're—"

A voice coming from a narrow alley that ran down the side of the store interrupted him.

"*Yatağına dön.*"

The old woman stepped out of the shadows, addressing her son sternly and waving him back inside with both hands. "*Yatağına dön,*" she repeated. "*Bunu halledebiliriz.*" She watched as he nodded; then he reluctantly closed the shutters and disappeared behind them.

The woman turned to Tess and just eyed her without saying a word, though the tension in her face was evident, even in the dim light of a lone streetlamp farther down the road. When she moved aside, the teen girl was there, behind her.

"What was she doing outside our hotel?" Tess asked, her whole body buzzing with anticipation.

"Lower your voice," the woman hissed. "You're going to wake everyone up." She rattled off a quick sentence in Turkish, and the girl slipped away.

"Hey," Tess blurted, stepping forward. "Where's she going?"

"The girl did nothing wrong," the woman countered. "You should leave."

"Leave? I'm not leaving. I want to know why she followed us back to the hotel. Or maybe we should just report it to the police and see if she'd like to tell them instead."

This made the old woman flinch. "No. No police."

Tess opened out her palms questioningly and gave her a "well then?" look.

The woman frowned, visibly tormented by something. "Please go."

Something in the way she said it lit up a different pathway in Tess's mind. She'd been so protective of the codices she'd failed to consider the other possibility.

Her tone softened and she inched closer to the old woman. "Do you know something about these books?"

"No, of course not."

Her rapid-fire denial was far from convincing.

"Please," Tess insisted. "If you do . . . you need to know this. There are others looking for these books. Murderers.

They've killed many people while trying to find them. And just like we found you, they could find you too. If you know anything about them, you should tell us. It's not safe for you right now."

The woman studied Tess, her mouth a tight line, her brow knotted, her hands shivering perceptibly despite the balmy weather, her eyes betraying some intense debate going on deep within her.

"I'm telling you the truth," Tess added. "Please. You've got to trust me."

The seconds stretched interminably; then a verdict seemed to scrape through with the thinnest of majorities, and the woman grudgingly said, "Come with me," before turning and heading down the side alley.

The shop was a small, detached stone structure, two stories high—the shop itself and the apartment above. Tess and Reilly followed the old woman past a freestanding flight of stairs that led up to the shopkeeper's living quarters and stopped outside an old oak door at the back of the building. After some fussing with some keys, the old woman snapped its lock open and led them inside.

They followed her through a small hallway and into a larger room, where the woman switched on a floor-mounted lamp. They were standing in a living room that had a set of French doors giving onto some kind of backyard. It was also cluttered with the memorabilia of a long, full life. Overcrowded shelves strained under the weight of books, picture frames, and vases. A couch and two armchairs were arrayed around a low coffee table and were barely visible under a camouflage of kilim throws and needlepoint cushions, while the walls were a patchwork of small paintings and old black-and-white family photos.

"I'll make some coffee," the old woman grumbled. "I know I'm going to need it."

She padded out of the room. Moments later, the audible fumblings of a pot and a tap were quickly followed by the sound of a struck match and the soft hiss of a gas burner. Tess edged across to take a closer look at the framed photographs. She recognized younger versions of their reluctant hostess alongside various people, records of another era.

A couple of dozen frames into the slide show, she stopped in front of one that reached out from the wall and grabbed her by the throat. It showed a young girl standing alongside an older man, a proud father-and-daughter pose. Behind them was a large wooden contraption from a bygone age, a semiautomatic loom of some kind.

A loom used to manufacture cloth.

A piece of machinery used by a draper.

"That's my mother, and her father," the old woman said as she returned from the kitchen with a small tray and settled down on the couch. "It was our family business for as long as anyone can remember."

Tess's skin was twitching. "What happened?"

"My grandfather lost all his money. He spent it all on a modern loom that was supposed to come from England, but the middleman he bought it from took all his money and disappeared." She poured thick coffee into small, shot-sized cups and gestured for Tess and Reilly to join her. "He died heartbroken not long after that. My grandmother had to do something to make a living. She knew how to fire clay. It was her father's business. And this"—she waved her hands around her—"is the result."

"You sell some beautiful things," Tess remarked with a smile as she sat down on the couch by the woman. Reilly joined them, settling into the armchair and putting the rucksack down by his feet.

The old woman casually waved away Tess's comment. "We take pride in what we do, whatever it is. It's not worth doing otherwise." She took a sip from her coffee, decided it was too hot, and set it back down. She sat quietly for a moment, then let out a long sigh and raised her eyes to Tess. "So tell me . . . who are you, exactly? And how did you end up here, in this lost corner of the world, with these old books you're carrying?"

Tess glanced at Reilly, unsure about what to say. A moment ago, she was seething with indignation, thinking the old woman was out to steal the codices. And yet here they were now, comfortably ensconced in the woman's living room, sipping coffee and having a courteous little chat.

Reilly nodded her a go-ahead, mirroring her own feelings.

So she told her. Everything. The whole story, from Sharafi's appearance in Jordan to the shoot-out in the underground city, although she skirted around the gorier parts of it, not wanting to shock her host. Throughout, the old woman listened intently, surprise and fear playing on her face, her eyes roaming Tess's face and glancing away to Reilly every now and then, only asking for additional clarification a time or two. By the end of it, her hands were shivering. And once Tess was done, she sat quietly for a long moment, working the story over in silence, clearly racked by indecision and worry.

Tess hesitated to wade in. After giving her what she felt was enough time to process it all, she asked, "Why did your granddaughter follow us to our hotel? You asked her to, didn't you?"

It seemed like the woman didn't hear her. She just kept staring into her coffee cup, lost in thought, back in the grips of some momentous struggle. After another lengthy deliberation, her words came out slow and soft.

"They didn't know what to do with them, you know," she told Tess, barely able to look at her. "We've never known what to do with them." She shut her eyes with remorse, then turned to face Tess. It was as if she'd just crossed a line from which there was no return.

Tess stared at her blankly for a second, making sure she'd heard her right; then a searing charge of elation burst out of her heart and swept through her. "You have them? You have the other books?" She was now on the very edge of the couch, every pore in her body brimming with anticipation.

The old woman studied her, then nodded slowly.

"How many?"

"Many." She was surprisingly casual about it, as if she were confirming the most trivial of comments. "The woman, Maysoon. She brought them here, for safekeeping. After Conrad died."

Tess couldn't believe what she was hearing. Her face

felt like it was on fire. Her eyes flicked across to Reilly and were met with a broad, supportive grin. She turned back to the old woman. "So Conrad did have a woman with him?"

"They met in Constantinople, where they both lived."

"She was a Sufi?" Reilly asked.

"Yes."

Tess asked, "So what happened to them? Conrad did die in Zelve, didn't he?"

Chapter 56

✠

The villagers received them with a warm, if tentative, welcome.

Conrad and Maysoon found the small settlement in a narrow canyon, tucked away from the outside world, a cluster of rock cones set around a church that had been carved into a cliff face. Their arrival was an unusual occurrence. The villagers didn't get many visitors and were wary of them at first. Still, they brought with them news of the outside world and a sense of event that was rarely seen in the isolated, canyon-based community, and the locals soon relaxed. The priest who tended the rock church also ended up grudgingly giving them his approval, despite his obvious wariness at the sight of a knight of the Cross traveling with a heathen companion. The fact that Conrad had fought to free the Holy Land and lost his hand doing so forced the man to overcome some of his prejudice. Maysoon also helped win him over when, much to his surprise, she quoted lines of scripture that she had learned as a child while studying tolerance under her Sufi master.

The local midwife who doubled as the town's physician helped Conrad splint and dress Maysoon's wrist, and they were offered food and drink. By nightfall, the two of them were huddled together by a window high in a carved-out cone of rock whose sole occupier had recently passed away, watching the sky above the rim of the canyon run the gamut of imaginable pinks and purples before settling into a crisp, uniform blackness.

Conrad hadn't said much all evening, and he hadn't said a word for the last half hour. Every breath he exhaled was swirling with despair.

Maysoon pulled back from his chest and scrutinized his face.

"What is it?" she asked.

He didn't answer or meet her eyes at first, seemingly lost in his melancholy. After a long moment, he said, "This. What I'm doing. It's pointless."

"Why do you say that?"

"It's pointless. Hector, Miguel . . . they're gone. God knows what's waiting for me in Cyprus." He sighed heavily. "I can't do this alone."

"You're not alone."

He looked at her, and his face brightened a touch. "You've been magnificent. But it's still pointless. Even to-gether, we can't do this. I was a fool to think I'd ever be able to make a difference."

She edged closer. "No, you weren't. You were right to go after it. You were right to find those books and get them back. But if you can't achieve what you set out to do . . . it doesn't mean you still can't change the world."

"What do you mean?"

"You wanted to use these writings, this knowledge, the same way it's been used for the last couple of hundred years. You wanted to blackmail the pope with it and get him to free your friends and reinstate your Order. Which is a noble goal, of course. You had to try and make that happen. But if you'd succeeded . . . the knowledge in these books would have stayed locked away and hidden from the rest of the world."

Conrad's face crinkled with confusion. "Keeping it se-cret was why the popes gave us anything we wanted. It's what allowed us to build up our strength and our standing while waiting for the right time to share it all with everyone out there."

"Was there ever going to be a right time? Or is it always the right time?" She shook her head. "People have kept these texts hidden for a thousand years. You and the Templars who came before you have been using them as a weapon for centuries, and if Hector and Miguel were still alive, you'd still be trying to use them that way. Maybe the time has come to look at things differently. Maybe it's time you started thinking about how to bring these writings to light instead of keeping them locked away."

"It's not possible," Conrad countered. "Not now. Not when the pope is as strong as he is. Look at what happened to the Cathars. The Vatican has inquisitors everywhere. Nothing heretical can ever be allowed to make itself heard."

"There's always a way. Look at Rumi. His preachings were all about love and looking inside ourselves for enlightenment. His words would have been considered blasphemous by any conservative cleric, but they caught the heart of the sultan himself, who invited him to live and preach in his capital and became his protector."

"I'm not a preacher."

She smiled. "No, but maybe it's time you started thinking like one." She drew nearer and kissed him before slipping her tunic off her shoulders. "But not in every sense of the word."

THEY SPENT THE NEXT DAYS working the wheat fields with the villagers by day and debating their options by night. How to transport the texts was still a central problem. They only had one horse to their name, and—not that they had the means to pay for it—there was only one open wagon in the settlement, one the villagers couldn't do without.

Conrad couldn't see a way out of their quandary, and with each passing day, his anger and frustration grew. The thought of his brethren rotting away in French jails and his impotence at doing anything to help them was eating away at him. A week earlier, he believed he could make a difference. All that had changed with the ambush in the canyon.

Then, on the morning of the ninth day, everything changed again when half a dozen pairs of hooves and a familiar voice echoed through the village.

"Maysoon," the man bellowed. "Conrad. Show yourselves if you don't want every man, woman, and child in this village to perish."

Conrad hurried to the window, closely followed by Maysoon. They looked out to see Qassem and the two surviving hired hands trotting slowly down the central alley of the cone houses. Her brother had a woman with him, sitting sidesaddle on his horse. He held a dagger to her throat. They recognized her from the fields. She was the sister of the midwife who had tended to Maysoon's wrist.

"How did they know it was us?" Maysoon asked.

"The woman," Conrad said, indicating the hostage with a nod. "She knows our names."

"But how did they find us?"

"Greed and revenge," he said. "There are no better motivators."

"What are we going we do?"

Conrad glared at the three men, men who had killed his friends, men who had scuttled his plans and sealed his brethren's fate.

Men who had to pay.

"End this," he replied. He then leaned out and shouted, "Let the woman go. I'm coming out."

Qassem looked up, saw Conrad, and said nothing. He just threw the woman to the ground and glared at him.

Conrad spotted his prosthetic hand, dangling from the side of the Turk's saddle. It only made him angrier. He pulled back from the window and strode across to a wall niche and reached for his scimitar.

"You're not going down there alone," Maysoon told him, finding her crossbow, but as she grabbed it, her wrist gave way under its weight. She winced with pain as the crossbow clattered to the floor.

"No," he flared. "Not with your wrist like that. I need you to stay here. This is my fight."

"I want to help," she insisted.

"You've done more than enough, more than I ever had

the right to ask for," he said, his eyes burning with determination. "I need to do this alone."

His tone made it clear he wasn't open to negotiation.

She breathed long and hard, then nodded grudgingly.

He picked up the crossbow, set it down in the niche, and picked up her dagger. "Help me with this," he said, placing it against his left forearm. "Tie it to my arm."

"Conrad . . ."

"Do it, please."

She found some leather straps and used them to attach the dagger's handle to the stump of his left arm.

"Tighter," he said.

She tightened the straps to a solid, tourniquet-level pinch. The blade was now an extension of his arm.

He picked up the scimitar with his right hand. Felt his veins swell with fury. Looked at her. Moved in and swept her up in a long, feverish kiss.

And stepped out into the sun.

"Where's my whore of a sister?" Qassem barked.

"Inside," Conrad replied, sidestepping, moving into wider, open ground. "But you'll need to get through me first."

Qassem's eyes flattened to narrow slits, and he smiled. "That was my plan."

The Turk nodded to his men. The two riders drew their scimitars, spurred their mounts, and charged.

Conrad watched them hurtle toward him, side by side, and put himself into a defensive crouch, knees bent, shoulders tight, the blade of his sword held straight up in front of his face. Old instincts flared back to life and slowed down time, putting every detail of his approaching opponents into hard focus, allowing him time to read them and plan his blows with deadly accuracy. He spotted a vulnerability in the stance of the rider to his left, who was right-handed, and decided to take him out first. With the riders less than ten yards away, he charged them, bolting at an angle, beelining for the man to his left. The move startled his opponents, who had to yank on their horses' reins viciously to adjust course. Conrad timed it perfectly and got right up to the horseman to his left before the one to his right could correct course fast enough. His target was also struggling to control his mount, opening him up to Conrad's blade that struck him across his midsection and sliced right through his side. The Turk flinched sideways and fell off his mount. Just as he hit the ground, Conrad was on him and finished him off with a dagger to the heart.

The second rider pulled his horse around and, angered by the knight's counterattack, came storming back. Conrad didn't move. He stood his ground, giving his mind the time it needed to find an opening in the man's reckless charge, coiling his muscles for the next assault.

He saw it and made his move, darting sideways, putting the dead Turk's body between himself and the horseman to confuse his advance. The rider made the same mistake his crony had and allowed Conrad to get onto the wrong side of his blade, giving the knight the advantage of going for his undefended flank. Conrad let his sword rip, swinging with ferocious strength and opening up a wide gash right through the man's thigh, virtually chopping it off. The rider instinctively pulled on his reins, shocked by the sight of his exposed muscle and flesh. Conrad didn't give him any breathing space. He charged after him and was on him before the rider even realized he was there, striking him from the right, ripping his back open before shoving him off his saddle and finishing him off with another blow.

And that's when the bolt struck his shoulder.

It rammed into him from behind with a violent, silent impact.

Conrad staggered forward a couple of steps under the momentum of the hit, then turned around, heavy-footed. Qassem had dismounted. He was standing by his horse, staring at Conrad, the spent crossbow in his hand. He threw it to the ground, drew his scimitar, and strode toward Conrad, his brow gnarled in an infernal scowl.

Conrad knew it was bad. It had hit him in the right shoulder. His good arm. His only good one. The one he needed to work the sword. The arrow was lodged firmly in his shoulder blade, unleashing a cascade of pain with the slightest movement of his right arm.

A cascade he would have to ignore if he was going to defend himself.

Qassem didn't break step, his eyes locked on Conrad, his sword held low to his side. Then his stride turned to a trot, then a sprint, and with a loud howl, he raised his sword and, with a running leap, brought it crashing down onto Conrad.

Conrad lunged sideways, putting his body out of reach and blocking the blow with his own sword. The blades clanged heavily into each other, the strike reverberating through Conrad and shooting a spasm of white-hot pain across his shoulder. He felt his knees buckle, but he couldn't let them fail him now, couldn't let the pain cripple him. Qassem spun around and swung again, his blade flying through a full loop before crashing back down against Conrad's sword.

The third strike flung the scimitar out of Conrad's hand, his fingers unable to ignore the agony in his shoulder.

Qassem stood still, breathing in deep snorts, and smiled. His eyes dropped to the dagger strapped to Conrad's forearm and his smile turned into a mocking grin.

"I don't know whether to kill you, or just take your other hand off—maybe your feet too—and let you live on like a pathetic, crippled maggot," he chortled. "Maybe I should do that to you both."

Conrad's feet faltered. He was having trouble breathing, and he felt a taste of blood in his mouth. His heart spasmed at the realization. The arrow hadn't just lodged in his shoulder. It had punctured his lung.

He knew how that would end.

He'd seen it enough times.

He looked up at Qassem, and saw a reflection of his realization in the Turk's face. The man held his gaze for a moment, then raised his scimitar like an executioner and held it there.

"What the hell. Maybe I'd better do it now before you rob me of the pleasure—"

And his face froze in a tight clench just as something thumped into him from behind and crunched its way out of his chest.

A bolt.

He stared down at the arrowhead that was sticking out of his rib cage and dripping with blood, and surprise flooded his face. He turned around, slowly, Conrad following his gaze.

Maysoon was standing in the clearing, by his horse.

A crossbow in her hands.

Pain visibly etched into her face.

The woman from the fields, the one the Turk had taken hostage, was there, beside her. A clutch of bolts in her hand.

Qassem moved to head toward them, but Conrad wasn't about to give him that chance. He pushed hard on his legs and rose up, using his body's momentum to tackle the Turk and plunge his dagger deep into his back, twisting and turning and grinding it in, making sure he cut through as many organs and ducts and arteries as possible.

The two men tumbled to the ground in a bloody, dusty heap.

The Turk spasmed and gurgled for a few seconds, his eyes wide and locked on to Conrad with silent rage, before he gave out a final shudder and his body went limp.

Conrad let his head drop back onto the hard, dry soil. He stared at the sky; then Maysoon was right with him, cradling his head, running her fingers through his hair, tears streaking down her face.

"Don't leave me," she sobbed.

"Never," he replied, but he knew he was lying. Blood was bubbling out of the edge of his mouth and his breathing was getting more ragged. The air he was fighting to take in was escaping before getting a chance to do its job.

"Keep it safe," he mumbled. "Find a way. Keep it safe. And maybe, one day, someone will be able to do what we couldn't."

"I will. I promise . . . I will."

With startling speed, his lips began to turn blue and his skin took on a dusky pallor. His mouth felt heavier, and as his brain grew starved of oxygen, his words became more slurred.

And then he was gone.

Chapter 57

✝

"They buried him there, in the church. Then she came to Konya and settled here," the old woman continued. "She joined a *tekke*. And for the next several months, she went back to that cave many times, alone, taking an extra horse with her, and brought back the texts, one small load at a time. She kept them hidden and didn't tell anyone about them. And then, years later, she met someone."

"A draper," Tess guessed. She was utterly spellbound, hanging on the woman's every word.

"Yes. He was also part of the same lodge. She confided in him. Told him her secret. Eventually, they got married. Started a new life together, here, in Konya." Her face softened into a bittersweet smile. "They were my ancestors."

"So the mural, the lines from the poem . . . that came after?" Tess asked.

The woman nodded. "Yes. She went back and had it added much later. In the church where Conrad was buried, as you saw."

Reilly asked, "How do you know all this?"

The woman pushed herself to her feet and crossed to an old desk. She rummaged through it and recovered a small key, which she used to open one of its drawers. She pulled out a folded document and brought it over to show Tess.

It was composed of several handwritten pages, old and

yellowed. Tess couldn't read them, as they were covered in a tight Arabic script, the alphabet used in Turkey before 1928.

"This tells the whole story," the old woman said. "It's everything Conrad told Maysoon. It's been handed down from generation to generation. Has been for close to seven hundred years."

"And all this time, the texts stayed hidden," Tess said.

"Maysoon had promised Conrad to keep them safe and to try and share them with the world. But there was no way for her to do that. Not back then. East and West were fiercely divided. In this land, the Seljuks were on the way out and the Ottomans and their hordes of 'warriors of the faith' were taking over. They were out to create an Islamic empire, and the last thing Maysoon wanted was for these writings to be used as a weapon to discredit an enemy faith."

Tess glanced at Reilly. He'd also caught the echo in the woman's words and gave Tess a discreet, cognizant nod that caused a small flutter in her belly.

The old woman caught their drift and half-smiled wistfully; then her mouth folded with despair. "She didn't know who to turn to in the West either. The Templars were gone, of course. And the Church was hugely powerful back then. No one, not even a king, would have dared to champion something that threatened its dominance."

"So they kept them tucked away . . . here?"

"Yes," the woman said. "Safely stored, waiting for the right day."

Tess's throat tightened up like a pinched straw. She had to ask again. "*Here* here?"

The old woman nodded.

Tess swallowed an invisible golf ball. "Can we see it?"

The woman didn't answer at first. Then she got up from the couch and stepped across to the desk, where she retrieved some keys. She turned to face them and said, "Come."

She led them across the living room and through a dark, narrow hallway that had the kitchen off one side and looked like it gave onto a bedroom at its far end. It had a lower ceiling than the living room and was lined with cupboard doors on one side. A kilim carpet hung from a brass rail on the opposite wall. The old woman opened a cupboard door and brought out a flashlight, then went up to the kilim and pulled it to one side. Cut into the wall behind it and barely visible in the darkness was a narrow, winding staircase, not much wider than a man's shoulders.

The old woman entered the niche and climbed down, taking each of the tall risers with care, steadying herself against the curving wall, the light of her flashlight playing against its rough, pockmarked surface. Tess and Reilly followed. The stairs wound down twice before ending in a tunnel, also narrow and rough. It all had a similar feel to the underground city they'd been trapped in, and Tess wondered if it was of the same vintage.

The old woman led them past a series of old wooden doors lining one side of the tunnel, over a length of about thirty yards, until she reached the last door, one that faced down the tunnel. She then unlocked it, stepped inside, and ushered them in behind her.

They were standing in a small room. More of a walk-in cupboard, really. It was windowless and low-ceilinged and, like the chambers in the underground city, had a pleasant temperature despite the heat aboveground, and none of the humidity.

Tess looked around, and every last molecule of air in her lungs gushed out.

All of the small room's walls, apart from the one with the door in it, were lined with shelves. The shelves, in turn, were lined with books. Old books. Small, leather-bound, positively ancient codices. The oldest books on the planet: two-thousand-year-old gospels, from the earliest days of the Church.

Dozens of them.

Tess couldn't believe it.

Her mouth managed to ask, "May I?" as she pointed at one of them.

The old woman gave her a resigned "help yourself" gesture.

Tess reached out and picked up one of the books. It was

very similar to the two codices she'd found in Conrad's grave. Same kind of leather binding, same folded back, same strap wrapped around it. It seemed in equally good condition. She hesitated, then peeled back the fold and opened the book and looked inside. It had similar lettering, Koine Greek.

She translated its title page aloud: "The Gospel of Eve."

Tess wasn't familiar with it. The old woman watched her with slight bemusement, then said, "I was curious about that one too. But it's not the Eve you think."

Tess gave her a curious look. "You know what's in these books? You've read them?"

"Not entirely. I've just taught myself a little bit of Coptic and some old Greek here and there and managed to understand some of what's inside them."

A particular question was clawing away inside Tess, desperate to get out. "If I ask you about a particular text, would you know if it's here or not?"

The old woman shrugged. "Probably."

Tess inhaled nervously. "A few years ago, I held in my hands something I believed was the journal of Jesus. His own writings. His diary."

The woman's eyes widened. "You saw it?"

"Yes, but I couldn't tell if it was real or if it was a forgery. And I never got a chance to put it through any lab tests to find out. Do you know anything about it? Do you know if it was the real thing?"

The woman smiled, then shook her head. "It wasn't. It was a forgery."

The finality of her answer stunned Tess. "How do you know that?"

"Maysoon's letter. Conrad told her all about it." She ordered her thoughts, then added, "They were only able to make it because they had all this to work with," gesturing at the shelves of ancient texts.

"Wait a sec. You're saying the Templars knew about this trove all along?"

"Knew about it? They wouldn't have existed without it. That's how it all started. With the original Keepers of this trove, the men who looked after it and kept it safely hidden at the Imperial Library in Constantinople. It was all their plan."

"You're saying the Templars were dreamt up in Constantinople?"

The old woman nodded. "The Keepers had been guarding the trove of Nicaea for centuries, ever since Hosius had saved it from burning and smuggled it off to safety in Constantinople. The Keepers guarded it, waiting for the right time to make it public and share it with the rest of the world. But that moment never seemed to come . . . and by the end of the first millennium, the world took a darker turn. The pope was out of control. And when he came up with the notion of a holy crusade and ordered Christians to go to war and kill in the name of Christ, they knew he had lost it completely. Jesus's message had been completely obliterated. But the crusaders were winning their battles and giving the pope more and more power. With control over the Holy Land and all the monarchs of Europe kissing his feet, the pope would have supreme power over most of the known world. The Keepers were horrified by what was happening and felt they had to do something. They needed to find a way to rein him in. And they came up with a radical idea. They decided to create a counterforce. A military organization that could challenge Rome's supremacy and keep its influence in check. They had all this to work with," she said, waving at the astounding collection of writings around her. "The threat of making it public would have probably been enough to scare the pope into giving them what they wanted, but they felt they needed more. They needed to be sure. They needed one more book. One hugely powerful text that would terrify Rome into submission. So they decided to create the ultimate gospel."

"The personal journal of Jesus," Tess said.

"Exactly." The old woman nodded.

Tess looked at Reilly, and that fateful moment of years earlier came rushing back. The two of them, standing on that cliff. Watching the vellum pages glide down and get swallowed up by the churning sea. The answer they never got—until now.

The old woman pressed on. "They had all this to base

their work on, to create their forged masterpiece, to get it right. It would also make the find seem unquestionably believable. After all, all these books are the real thing. It was only natural for Jesus's own journal to be part of this collection. So once it was ready, they acted. They sought out others who shared their concerns. Knights, learned and enlightened men from across Europe who they had met over the years, at the library. Nine of them."

"The first nine Templars. Hughes de Payens and his men," Tess said.

The old woman nodded again. "The knights went to Jerusalem, where they approached the king. They told him they were there to protect the pilgrims coming to the holy city, and got him to give them the ruins of the old temple to use as their base. And after years of supposedly digging around, they sent a message to Rome, saying they'd found something. Something . . . disturbing. The pope sent his envoys. The knights showed them some of the gospels that you see here. Then they showed them the real prize. The pope's men were horrified. They went back to Rome and confirmed the find. The pope gave the Templars everything they wanted in exchange for keeping it quiet."

Tess's head was spinning. It was a lot to take in. "And after that, the Templars sent the gospels back here—or rather, back to Constantinople?"

"They'd been safe there for many centuries. The Holy Land was a war zone. The Keepers wanted to make sure the gospels were safe."

"But not Jesus's diary?"

"No," the old woman said. "That stayed with the Templars, at Acre. It was the source of their strength. They wanted to keep it close, under their guard. Which was a mistake. But remember, it was also a forgery. As far as the Keepers were concerned, its value was strategic, not historic."

Tess was completing the puzzle in her mind. "So then in 1203, the pope's army is at the gates of Constantinople. The Keepers are worried about losing their trove. They send out a distress signal."

"Yes. The Templars send out a few men to smuggle it out

to safety. But they lose it until Conrad and Maysoon manage to get it back . . . a hundred years later."

"But by then, it's too late to do anything with it. The Holy Land is back in Muslim hands, the forged diary of Christ is lost, and the Templar Order's been wiped out by the King of France, with the help of his puppet pope." Tess frowned, remembering the unfortunate tale of the last survivors of the Falcon Temple that she and Reilly had uncovered three years ago. "Imagine . . . If Conrad had managed to get his hands on this just a few years sooner . . . it could have changed everything."

The old woman shook her head. "There was no chance of that happening. Conrad only heard about it because he was living in Constantinople. And the only reason he was there was because the Templars were wanted men."

Tess nodded. The cruel machinations of fate had loaded the dice against him right from the beginning. "These Keepers," Tess asked. "What happened to them? Did Maysoon try to find them?"

"She did," the old woman said. "But there was no trace of them. They were probably killed during the sacking of the city, maybe by agents of the pope who were looking for the trove."

"And so Maysoon and her descendants—your family— became the new Keepers," Tess observed.

The old woman nodded. "Come," she said. "Let's go back up. I'll make another pot of coffee."

They filed back down the passage and up to the kitchen and stood there while the old woman refilled the tin pot, fired up one of the gas rings on her cooker, and settled the pot on it. A loaded silence smothered the room. After a long moment, Tess broke it.

"So what do we do now?"

The woman weighed her words, then looked at Tess and said, "I don't know." She paused for a beat, then asked, "These killers. They're still out there?"

Tess nodded.

"Then it has to be moved, doesn't it?" the old woman said. "It can't stay here." She sighed heavily. "Can you get it somewhere safe?"

Tess had been mulling over various soft approaches to try to propose the very same thing, but for the old woman to offer it like that took her by complete surprise.

"Of course."

The old woman's shoulders hunched slightly under the weight of her decision. "I don't have much choice, do I? And maybe that's not a bad thing. You have to understand. This . . ." She waved her hands expansively, taking in the ground under their feet and the secret it held. "It's much bigger than us. It always has been. It's a burden that's been handed down, generation after generation . . ." She shook her head ruefully. "I didn't ask for this. I didn't have a choice in the matter, just like my ancestors didn't. But I did what was expected of me, as many others did before. And no doubt, if and when the day comes, my son will do the same. But to what end? What can we possibly do with it, from here? We're a simple people, Miss Chaykin. We live simple lives. And this . . . this deserves some serious attention. The kind of attention someone like you can bring to it. You would be doing me and my descendants a favor. You'd be relieving us of this enormous weight—especially now that you're telling me there are people out there willing to kill for it." She put her hands on Tess's arms. "It needs to be moved to safety. You need to take it from here and do what you think is best with it. Will you do that?"

"It would be a privilege."

"And don't worry," Reilly added. "I'll make sure you're well protected until this thing's over."

The old woman's face softened with a hint of relief, then knotted with a question. "What will you do with it?"

"It'll need to be properly photographed and catalogued," Tess said. "Then translated. Then we'll need to figure out who to share it with and how to do that without stirring up too much of a fuss."

The old woman didn't seem convinced. "The Dead Sea Scrolls are still shrouded with suspicion. The Nag Hammadi gospels are barely known . . . What makes you think these will be received differently?"

"We have to try. These writings . . . they're part of our evolution, as a civilization. They'll help us gain in maturity and enlightenment. But it needs to be done slowly, carefully. It has to be timed right. And not everyone will be convinced, or even interested. Those who want to believe, those who really need to believe ... none of this will matter to them. It's not going to change things for them. They'll always believe, no matter what. That's what the word 'faith' means to them. It's all about maintaining a solid, unwavering belief regardless of any proof that says otherwise. But for those who are more open-minded and who'd like to make up their own minds ... they deserve to have all the necessary information at hand to help them make that decision. We owe it to them."

The old woman nodded, seeming somewhat more at peace with her momentous decision—then a creak from the living room area caught her attention and made her frown. Reilly and Tess tensed up and went rigid. Reilly brought his hand up to his mouth in a stilling and silencing gesture.

He crept over to the edge of the kitchen and listened. Heard nothing. Kept his ear turned for a moment, just to be sure. Still heard nothing. Despite that, he wasn't comfortable with just ignoring what they'd heard. He gestured again for the women to stay still, and his other hand reached instinctively to seek out his handgun—then he realized he didn't have it on him. It was in the rucksack, in the living room.

He glanced around and spotted a large kitchen knife on the draining board by the sink. He grabbed it, then crept to the doorway and flicked off the kitchen's overhead light, plunging the small space into darkness and casting them in the cold and flickering orange-blue glow of the gas flame.

The old woman sucked in a short and sharp intake of breath.

Tess tensed up even more.

She watched the shadowy contours of Reilly's silhouette skulk out the door and disappear from view. She held her breath, waiting, listening, the euphoria of the last half hour now vaporized. For a few strung-out seconds, she heard nothing but the frantic bongo solo in her eardrums—then she heard a sharp snap followed by a grunt of pain, a clatter of something metallic, and a loud thump, like a hefty mass hitting the floor.

A fleshy, hefty mass.

The abrupt noise froze her solid. Then she heard it. The voice she had hoped never to hear again, the one she had planned to expunge from her memory with extreme prejudice. The one with the annoyingly smug tinge to it.

"Come on out, ladies," the Iranian said before appearing at the kitchen door and flicking the light on. He smiled and casually waved them out of the room with his handgun. "Join us. The party's just getting started."

Chapter 58

✠

R eilly's vision was blurred and his skull was flooded with pain as he writhed on the floor of the living room. The hit had come in fast and hard, a rifle butt to the jaw that cut his legs out from under him and dropped him before he even saw who'd hit him.

He could see them now. Men he didn't recognize, three of them, armed and efficient, slipping past him. Then he saw one he did recognize. The Iranian was herding Tess and the old woman into the living room, at gunpoint. Reilly's angle of vision, low and oblique given that he was still down and had his head twisted to one side, made the sight look even more disturbing.

"Sit down," the Iranian said as he nudged Tess with his silencer and prodded her toward the couch.

The two women set themselves down on the edge of the seat cushions, side by side. The Iranian then spat out some orders to his men in a language Reilly couldn't understand and waved them off. The three men scurried out of the room, presumably to check out the rest of the house.

Reilly caught Tess's eye. He gave her a slow blink and a tiny nod to try to reassure her. It didn't do much to alleviate the fear in her eyes, but she still managed a slight nod back. Reilly then gave the rest of the room a quick sweep, from his low vantage point. He spotted Tess's rucksack. The one with the gun in it. It was still where he'd left it, leaning against the side of the armchair, by the side of the couch. About eight feet away from him. A paltry distance to cover in a sprint, but a significant one given his current stance.

Reilly inhaled deeply and tried to flush the grogginess out of his head. He peered up at the Iranian. The Iranian, as if sensing him, looked down at him. He didn't look great. His face was more sallow than Reilly remembered it, and he had a sheen of sweat across his forehead. More noticeable, though, was the rage that was seething in his glare. It seemed to Reilly that the man could barely contain the fury that was raging inside him. Reilly decided to keep quiet. The situation was too precarious, his position too weak to risk provoking the man any further. He decided to bide his time and play it submissive, and broke off eye contact and lowered his gaze.

He was surprised to find that the wound to the Iranian's left hand looked like it had been properly tended to. The dressing was neat and tidy, though there were traces of blood seepage on it. Reilly ran a quick mental assessment of what was going on and who he was dealing with and decided the Iranian's men were probably PKK—militant Kurdish separatists that Iran had funded and armed over the years. They undoubtedly had doctors on tap who had a wealth of experience in dealing with war injuries. They could also travel unchallenged throughout Turkey—being Turks—to lend a friendly fist to someone like the Iranian bomber when needed.

Which wasn't great news.

Reilly didn't know how many men the Iranian had co-opted. He'd seen three of them. There had to be more outside.

Not great at all.

"So what's going on?" the Iranian asked, spreading his arms out theatrically and looking around the room. "One minute you're settling into your room for a nice, cozy night. Then you're running around the city's backstreets like headless chickens. What could have possibly triggered this urgent late-night get-together?"

A holler came from deep inside the house. The Iranian

turned, acknowledged it with a curt reply, then turned to Tess and smiled. A moment later, one of his men appeared through the doorway. He had an AK-47 slung over his shoulder and in his hands were a few of the old books.

The Iranian took them from him and studied them for a moment; then he glanced up at Tess, his mouth arced with glee. "More gospels?" He held her gaze for a moment, then asked the man a question. The man's reply seemed to really impress the Iranian. "A whole room of them?" he said to Tess. His grin broadened. "It sounds to me like your persistence has paid off handsomely."

Tess didn't reply.

The Iranian shrugged, rattled off some instructions to the man who'd brought him the books, threw one last glare at Reilly, then left the room. The man raised his Kalashnikov machine gun and held it firmly. He kept oscillating it slowly back and forth from Reilly to the two women while keeping an unblinking watch over them.

Reilly's instincts flared. He knew this might well be his last opportunity to do something.

One man guarding them.

A gun in the rucksack.

A chance.

He waited until the man's gaze swung away from him and made his move, pushing himself forward on his hands and knees toward the rucksack.

The move was clumsy.

The guard saw it. He freaked out and yelled at Reilly while charging to intercept him. Reilly saw the man's booted legs hurtling toward him and heard Tess shriek as he reached out for the rucksack, but he couldn't get to it fast enough—the guard cut him off with a massive kick to his left midsection. Reilly's kidneys lit up as he flew back from the impact and rolled over, grunting with pain. The man kept pace with him, crab-stepping after him in a tense crouch while shouting out a torrent of warnings and curses, his gun barrel swinging from Reilly's face and across to the two women and back.

Reilly came to a stop right by a side table across from the armchair. He was hunched over, groaning with pain, breathing hard. He peered up and, from the corner of his eye, glimpsed the guard looming over him. The man was all wild-eyed and jittery and standing less than two feet from him. Reilly caught his breath for a beat while his hand slithered silently under the side table. He knew he'd only get one chance to get it right, and the downside of getting it wrong was too horrific to imagine.

His fingers groped the floor tiles and found the fallen kitchen knife, the one he'd dropped when he'd been knocked down, the one he'd spotted when he was sprawled on the floor.

The fingers tightened around its handle.

The Iranian's voice bellowed out questioningly from deep in the house.

The guard turned his attention to the doorway to answer him.

Reilly pounced.

He flipped over with lightning agility, raising his arm and plunging the knife straight down into the man's booted foot. The blade cleaved right through leather, skin, and bone with a sickening sound, a combination of ripping and suction, and the man howled with pain, the pain that Reilly knew would distract him for a second, maybe two—either way, long enough for Reilly to launch himself at him.

He sprung up and clasped his left hand around the gun's wood foregrip while swinging a ferocious right elbow straight into the man's face. Bone and muscle trumped skin and cartilage easily as the guard's nose imploded in a geyser of blood and the machine gun spat out a wild triple burst that bit through the old carpet and hammered the floor. Reilly pushed harder to make sure he kept the AK-47's barrel aimed away from the women while he spun around, driving his other elbow into the man's chest and putting his back to him, using the momentum to try to wrestle the gun out of his grasp just as another one of the Iranian's men burst through the front door.

The damaged guard wasn't letting go. He was hanging on to his gun tenaciously, his fingers clasped around it. Reilly saw the second gunman raise his weapon and did two things in quick succession. He flicked his head back, ramming the back of his skull into the guard's already battered face, and he wrenched the guard around so he was now facing the man in the doorway, pulling his machine gun up as he did. The AK-47's barrel lined up with the second man a split second before the gun facing back came up far enough, and Reilly squeezed the guard's fingers against the trigger. Another triple-tap rang out and the man in the doorway staggered backward, dark red puffs erupting from his chest and shoulder.

Reilly saw Tess and the old woman, crouched low on the sofa, Tess with her arm around the woman. His eyes locked with hers.

"Get out," he yelled to her as he fought with the guard, who still wasn't letting go of his weapon. "Get out, that way," he rasped, motioning with his head toward the glass doors that gave onto the backyard.

Tess didn't move at first—then loud footfalls and shouts echoed from the hallway that led back from the kitchen.

"Go," Reilly barked again as he struggled against the guard's viselike grip. "Move."

He saw Tess and the old woman get up and make for the French doors just as a third gunman emerged from the hall. The Iranian was right behind him. They both had their weapons raised.

The gunman turned and spotted Tess and the old woman just as they reached the garden doors and started fiddling with the doorknob. Reilly saw him shout something and spin his weapon around to face them. With one savage pull, Reilly yanked the Kalashnikov out of the guard's grip and flung it at the gunman. The machine gun flew across the room, twirling around itself horizontally like a boomerang and clearing the couch before slamming into the gunman's chest and deflecting the rounds his weapon was spitting out.

Reilly was now running on hyperdrive. There wasn't a nanosecond to lose if he was going to buy Tess and the old woman enough time to get away. He was no longer thinking or moving consciously. Instincts hewn out of years of training and fieldwork had taken over and were ordering his muscles to move. He felt himself twirl around as if caught in a sudden invisible vortex, felt his fist tighten up and watched it plow into the cheek of the man he was grappling with; then he was already following the flying machine gun across the room before his opponent hit the ground. He saw his legs take two long strides, vault over the couch, and leap at the gunman by the doorway, tackling both him and the Iranian and sending them crashing back against the doorframe.

He heard the Iranian shriek with pain as his wounded hand hit the ground, and managed a couple of solid hits on the downed gunman, hurting him badly before the Iranian's knee came out of the tangle of limbs and pummeled Reilly in the groin. It punched the air out of him. He staggered backward and his head snapped back against the floor. Through jarred vision, he caught a vague glimpse of Tess and the old woman. They had finally managed to pry open the French doors and were rushing out—

—but the Iranian had recovered his weapon and was now scrambling to his feet.

Reilly needed to buy the women a last reprieve.

He lunged forward and intercepted the Iranian, clasping both hands on to the man's machine gun and shoving against it to slam him into the wall. The Iranian grunted hard as he plowed into it. Reilly had the advantage of two usable hands and pried the AK-47 out of the Iranian's grip, twisting the machine gun upward as he did and ramming his opponent's jaw with the butt of its folded metal stock. A spurt of blood spewed out of the Iranian's mouth and splattered the wall behind him as his wounded hand came up to block another hit.

It was like a red rag to Reilly.

He turned the machine gun on its end and, using the gun's folding metal stock as a battering ram, hammered the Iranian's hand to the wall.

The Iranian let out an elemental howl as the gun's metal stock pulverized the bones and tore apart the tendons in his hand. The excruciating pain caused his knees to buckle and he just rag-dolled to the floor, his eyes shut tight. Reilly felt his veins popping with bloodlust. He brought the gun back up, lining it up to pound the Iranian's head this time,

knowing the blow would crush the man's skull and possibly
end his life there and then—

—but before he could bring it down, something hard hit
him from behind, battering him at the base of his neck and
cutting off the power supply to his arms.

One of the other gunmen was back on his feet.

As Reilly tumbled to the ground, he saw that it was
actually worse than that. Two of them were back up, the
guard whose face he'd wrecked and the gunman who'd appeared with the Iranian.

The rest was a blur of fists, elbows, and kicks, raining
down on him from all sides. With every blow, he felt his
strength seep away, felt the blood from his cuts cloud his
vision and choke his throat, felt the breath fighting to find
its way into his lungs, felt his fingers and hands go numb
from the lack of circulation. The last thing he saw was the
Iranian's face, glaring down at him fiercely through a fog
of rabid sneers, his entire face just dripping with venom—
then a final kick to the face cut out all the light and dumped
him into a painless sleep.

Chapter 59

✠

RHODES, GREECE

"*E*ndaxi, tower. Clear takeoff, runway two five, wilco. Request maintain fifteen hundred feet to alpha to take a good look at your beautiful island, Niner Mike Alpha."

"Fifteen hundred feet to alpha is approved. Enjoy the view."

Steyl smiled and throttled forward. "Roger. *Efharisto poli.*"

He nursed the Cessna Conquest off the runway and into the early-morning sky. It felt good to be airborne again. He had been getting antsy, sitting idle at Rhodes's Diagoras International Airport, refueled and ready, unable to venture far from his aircraft while he waited for Zahed's signal. He'd been fast asleep when the call had finally come in, late into the night. Then he'd gone back to sleep for a few hours before setting off at first light.

He was flying southwest, headed for another island—a much smaller one this time, the island of Kassos, his official destination. It was in the opposite direction to where he needed to end up, but it was the most suitable foil, given that its tiny airport didn't have a control tower and that procedures had to be followed rigorously if he didn't want to raise anyone's suspicion. Which he wouldn't. Finding holes in the procedures, no matter how rigorous, was second nature to Steyl. He knew what he was doing, probably better than anyone in the business.

He reached the approved altitude in less than a minute and radioed the tower again, and was instructed to switch over to the approach controller's frequency. He did so, got cleared to stay at fifteen hundred feet all the way to Kassos, and was told to switch over again, this time to Athens Information, for the rest of his journey. Which he did. But he also did something else. He switched off his transponder. Without it, the plane's transponder code, altitude, and registration wouldn't appear on the tower's radar. It would only show an anonymous blip.

He kept up the pretense and stayed on his announced heading for another minute while gently descending to an altitude of five hundred feet. He contacted the tower again, but got nothing back. Which made him smile. They couldn't hear him. He was out of radio contact—which also meant he was outside the radar's sweep.

He could now go anywhere he liked, undisturbed.

He banked left to head south and passed the southwestern tip of Rhodes. He maintained that heading for another ten kilometers over open water, then pulled the plane sharply around to a northeasterly heading, toward his real destination: a remote location just under three hundred miles away, deep inside Turkey.

The visibility that low was lousy. A light wind and high barometric pressure had generated a light mist that squatted ominously over the water. Steyl couldn't see Rhodes anymore because of it, which was good. It meant no one could see him from land. His only remaining risk was being spotted by a ship. So he switched on his weather radar, which would show any vessels ahead of him. He'd have plenty of time to skirt around any that happened to crop up and continue on his stealthy voyage.

At low altitude, he'd get there in a little over an hour. He didn't plan on spending more than a few minutes on the ground, so the round-trip would take around two and a half hours, total. Which was fine for a low-altitude, sightseeing trip to a small island that didn't have a control tower. He wouldn't be missed.

He checked his watch, then pulled out his satphone and called Zahed. He informed him of his progress, then settled back and took in the view as the Conquest's twin turboprops reeled in the Turkish coast. If all went well, he anticipated parting company with the Iranian by the end of the day. He'd then head back to his villa in Malta, where he would lie on his sundeck with a cold beer in his hand and figure out how to spend his latest chunk of easy money.

ZAHED WAITED ON THE EDGE of the salt lake and watched as the sun tore itself from the far side of the water's pristine, flat surface.

By midmorning, it would look like an infinite expanse of white under a radiant blue dome. Right now, the low sun was bathing it with a crisp, bronzelike wash. It looked like a dull metal sheet that stretched out from right under his feet all the way to the horizon. *Another insane landscape*, he thought. He'd seen more of them in the last few days than he thought possible. The entire cursed region seemed to him like it had been cut and pasted from another planet. He took comfort from the thought that he'd soon be out of it. Back into comfortable, familiar, earthly settings. Back home. Where he'd be feted for achieving the impossible.

For bringing back his prize.

The early-morning air was still and cool and reeked of salt. It helped with his dizziness, but not with his throat, which felt as parched as the dry lands that were spread out before him. He was also shivering. He'd lost a lot of blood, and despite the painkillers, he was still hurting badly. The shakes were also getting worse. He needed medical attention, and soon. He knew his hand was bad. He knew it might never work properly again, knew he might lose it altogether. Either way, it would have to wait. He had to get out of there, fast. The American woman had managed to escape. She would have alerted the Turks. His hand was a huge price to pay, but it was still cheap when compared to his freedom and, quite probably, his life.

His phone beeped. He reached for it and turned to face the opposite direction and concentrate on the horizon. It wasn't long before he spotted the tiny dot, streaking in low and fast, the low sun glinting off its windshield. He confirmed to Steyl that everything was clear, then gave his men a nod and took a step back for a wider view. The engines of two SUVs, which were parked a hundred meters apart, one behind the other, rumbled to life. Then their lights and their flashers came on, two distinct sets of red and yellow beacons against a perfectly flat copper backdrop.

Zahed watched the plane line up along the axis made by the two SUVs and studied the makeshift runway beyond them. It looked perfect. Dry and hard, flat as a football field, not a ripple as far as the eye could see. The lake's name, Tuz Gölü, simply meant "salt lake." Which is what it was. A massive, six-hundred-square-mile pool of shallow, saline water that dried up and turned into a gargantuan bed of salt every summer. Two-thirds of the salt that ended up on dining tables across Turkey came from there, but the mines and processing plants that made it happen were farther north or on the other side of the lake. The area Steyl had chosen was, as the pilot had predicted, deserted. It was also less than an hour's drive from Konya. Yet more feathers in the pilot's peacock tail of a cap. And yet more confirmation for Zahed that he had chosen well.

Moments later, the faint buzz of the aircraft cut through the silence. It was barely audible at first; then it turned into an earsplitting roar as the plane swept low over the parked cars, its inertial separators open to direct any salt powder away from its engines. Its undercarriage virtually skimmed the front car's roof before touching down flawlessly. Zahed was already moving, clambering into the lead car as Steyl engaged the engines' reverse thrust and braked hard up ahead.

The two SUVs accelerated heavily and chased after the aircraft. Less than seven hundred meters later, they were parked alongside it.

The transfer didn't take long. With the plane's turboprops still beating the air, the boxes of codices were loaded up first, stacked behind the backs of the two rear seats. Then it was the human cargo's turn.

Reilly.

He was hustled up to the plane and dumped behind a partition at the very back of the cabin.

Still unconscious. But alive.

Which was how the Iranian wanted him.

Less than four minutes after touching down, the Cessna was airborne again. An hour and eleven minutes later, it was back on the ground at Diagoras. It didn't spend more than twenty minutes on the tarmac. The handling agent who drove up to the plane was the same man that Steyl had dealt with when he'd first landed in Rhodes. He didn't need to check the plane again. Zahed sat out the formalities, silently huddled behind the partition, alongside the inert Reilly. Steyl filed his flight plan and signed the forms, got the all clear, and took off again.

Iranian airspace was less than three hours away.

Chapter 60

✟

Sitting in the back of the Jandarma Humvee, Tess felt pulverized.

After what had felt like an interminable run of horrors, she'd finally found something to feel good about. A crack of light had somehow found its way through the dark shroud that had been suffocating her since that fateful day in Jordan, but just as quickly as it had appeared, it was now gone again. All the elation, relief, and excitement—wiped out in a few minutes and replaced just as quickly with more foreboding and gloom.

She hated the helplessness, the sense of defeat, the fact that yet again, she and Reilly had been bested. Most of all, she dreaded finding out what had happened to him and couldn't help but imagine the worst. The Iranian now had what he wanted. There was no reason for him to hang around. There was also no reason for him to show any restraint in whatever it was he had planned for Reilly.

The thought made her stomach turn.

The local police had shown up soon after the shootout, alerted by the gunshots. The Jandarma had swooped in shortly afterward. The Iranian and his thugs had taken away their dead crony's body, but there was still plenty of evidence of the bloody shoot-out in the old woman's house, all of which had only made the Jandarma officer angrier. Tess had sat there passively as he'd bawled her out for having left the hotel in Zelve without authorization, and she'd played dumb, saying she'd only been following Reilly's lead. She also concentrated on keeping the old woman's role in all this under wraps and made sure the woman understood to follow her lead and not mention the gospels the Iranian was after or the stash of troves in the underground crypt.

It seemed to be working. They were taking her and the old woman to the local police station for their own safety, as well as, undoubtedly, more questions. It hadn't been a comfortable lie, since she knew that her only hope was with these local cops, but she didn't think that added level of disclosure was relevant to their efforts. All she could do now was wait—and hope. Maybe they'd manage to lock down the country before the Iranian made it out. Maybe they'd get lucky and stop him at some roadblock. Maybe they'd catch him at some border crossing or at some local airfield.

She rubbed her eyes and tried to massage the worry out of her temples. The thoughts weren't offering her much solace, not when all they were doing was conjuring up harrowing images of a bloody confrontation that ended in disaster for the man she loved.

"I'm sorry," the old woman said, her soft-spoken words pulling Tess out of her swamp of despair.

"For what?"

"If I hadn't sent my granddaughter . . . if I had stayed hidden . . . none of this would have happened."

Tess shrugged. Of course, there was truth in her words. She and Reilly could well have been flying back to New York right now. But, she also knew, life didn't work that way. Unintended consequences were part of its fabric, and there was little point in wallowing in regret.

"It's not over yet," Tess told her, trying to believe her own words.

The old woman brightened. "You think . . . ?"

"There's always a chance. And Sean's usually pretty good at spotting them."

The old woman smiled. "I hope you're right."

Tess managed to give her back a half smile and tried to block out the gruesome worst-case scenarios that, she knew, were not only possible, but probable.

Chapter 61

✠

Reilly woke with a start, flinching backward with a sudden intake of breath. An acrid smell was spearing his
nostrils, an intensely vile odor that reminded him of rotting
corpses. His eyes flared wide, and his vision snapped to attention and broke through the tarlike mire inside his skull.

The Iranian was right there, up close and personal, mere
inches away from his face. His hand was hovering under
Reilly's nose, holding the small ampule there far longer
than was necessary. The man was sweating and was blinking with nervous energy, and he seemed to be visibly enjoying the discomfort he was causing. Then he flicked the
ammonia tab away and pulled back, giving Reilly a fuller
view of his captor.

"You're back," the Iranian said. "Good. I really didn't
want you to miss this."

Reilly didn't know what he was talking about. There was
a distinct lag between the words coming out of the Iranian's
mouth and his absorbing their meaning. They didn't sound
promising. His thoughts spun off to Tess and he looked
around, worried he'd find her there too. He couldn't see
her anywhere.

"No, she's not here," the Iranian told him, as if reading
his thoughts. "We didn't have the time to go looking for

her. But I'm sure I'll bump into her again sometime. I'd like that."

Reilly felt his blood boil, but he kept it hidden. There was no point in giving the Iranian the satisfaction of seeing him unsettled. Instead, he grinned and tried to say something, but felt his lips crack. He moistened them with his tongue, then said, "You know, that's not a bad idea. She doesn't have any gay friends."

The Iranian's hand flew up and punched Reilly across the cheek.

Reilly kept his head turned away for a moment to let the pain settle, then faced the Iranian again and managed a slight, lopsided grin. "My bad. Guess you haven't come out of the closet yet, huh? Not to worry. It'll be our little secret."

The Iranian raised his hand again for another strike, then pulled back and smiled. "Maybe she can convert me. What do you think?"

Reilly felt heavy-headed and decided there was no point in riling the man up any further. He focused on taking stock of his surroundings and saw that he was in a small aircraft, one with a cabin he wouldn't be able to stand upright in. A prop plane, judging by the engine noise.

One that was airborne.

That last point struck home and goosed his blood pressure. It didn't help his condition, which was pretty damn awful. His head was pounding from the inside with what felt like a polonium-level hangover. His breathing was hard and painful. Blood had caked inside his nostrils, blocking most of the airflow to his lungs, which were also hurting from the battering his rib cage had suffered. He could also taste a foul mix of mucus and blood that was sitting in his throat. The sensation was soon replaced by the pain that was being telegraphed from every corner of his body as his neurons came back online. His eyelids felt heavy, and one of his eyes, he now realized, was half-shut, no doubt from swelling. His lips also felt swollen and had scabbed cuts in several places. He knew he had to have busted ribs and had probably lost a tooth or two as well. Weirdly, his socks and shoes were also missing.

He was laid out on some kind of cushioned seating at the very back of the cabin, an L-shaped banquette that abutted a wood-paneled partition that separated the small niche from the rest of the cabin. He tried to move and realized that his hands and feet were tied. His hands were behind his back, so he couldn't see what was holding them together, but his ankles were bound together with some white string. All four joints were already hurting from the strain, and he could see the swelling and bruising where the string was biting into his flesh. An odd thought glided into his mind, the notion that it might have been pulled from the curtains at the old woman's house. It wasn't particularly thick, but it was strong and there had been enough of it to go around his ankles many times.

He didn't think he was going to be wriggling his way out of it anytime soon.

He glanced out of the small oval window on the cabin wall facing him. He couldn't see any clouds. There was nothing out there but endless blue sky, clear and unblemished. He tried to figure out what direction they were flying in. The sun seemed to be streaming into the cabin from the front of the aircraft, slightly to the right and at about a forty-five-degree angle. It had the bright intensity of a morning sun. It seemed to indicate that they were flying east. East, from somewhere in central Turkey.

He pictured the map. Nothing good was east, not for him. Syria. Iraq. Iran. Not the friendliest of places for an American FBI agent.

His blood pressure spiked further.

He looked at the Iranian. "We're heading east."

The Iranian didn't respond.

Reilly said, "What, your visa run out?"

The Iranian smiled thinly and said, "I miss the food."

Reilly glanced down at the man's hand. It didn't look great. Its dressing was loose and messy, and it was heavily stained with blood.

Reilly nodded in its direction. "You might need some help cutting up your steaks."

The Iranian's smile disappeared. He smoldered quietly for a beat; then his right hand flew up and punched Reilly again. He breathed in deeply and said, "Hang on to that thought. You'll need it on your way down."

A flood of unpleasant images cascaded through Reilly's mind. Images of hostages held for years in grimy cells deep inside hostile territory, chained to walls, beaten and abused and forgotten until some nasty illness finally liberated them from their torment. He was about to say something; then he remembered something else and his blood pressure shot further into the red zone.

The report. The one he'd been given back in Istanbul.

The one about the Italian airport official with the pulverized bones. The one they thought had been tossed out of a helicopter or a plane.

Alive.

He flushed the fear away and snared the Iranian's smug look. "I don't even know your fucking name."

The Iranian debated answering for a beat, then seemed to decide there was no harm in it and said, "It's Zahed. Mansoor Zahed."

"Good to know. Wouldn't want you buried in an anonymous grave. That's just not right, is it?"

Zahed gave him a thin smile. "Like I said. Hang on to that one too. You'll have plenty of time to savor it."

THE IRANIAN EYED REILLY CURIOUSLY.

Although he thought he'd decided what to do with him, he was still of two minds about it. Both options were very attractive.

He could still take Reilly back to Iran. Lock him up in some isolated hellhole in one of the country's prisons. Have fun with him for years to come. The agent would be a great source of intel. They'd break him, without a doubt. Then he'd tell them everything he knew about FBI and Homeland Security procedures and protocols. On top of recovering the trove of Nicaea, capturing and bringing back the head of the Counterterrorism Unit of the FBI's New York City field office—and without leaving a trail of bread crumbs at that—would be a spectacular coup for Zahed.

It all sounded rosy—until reality crept back in. Zahed was a pragmatist and knew how it could actually play out.

He knew he'd probably end up losing control of Reilly's fate. Even if Zahed tried to keep his presence quiet, the American agent was such a prize that word would get out. He'd stir a lot of interest. Others would get involved. Others who might have other ideas about how best to make use of such an asset. At some point, they might even decide to use Reilly as a bargaining chip for something they wanted badly. If and when that happened, he would be freed. At which time, Zahed knew, the man would make Zahed's life hell, even from several thousand miles away.

That possibility made the option unacceptable.

No, he thought again. He'd made the right decision. He couldn't take Reilly back to Iran with him. Besides, the option he'd chosen would give him immense pleasure. It would be a moment he'd never forget, one he'd savor for the rest of his days. It was just a shame he wouldn't be able to see Reilly's mangled body after he had hit the surface of the water, which, to someone traveling at that speed, would feel just as hard as concrete. The agent would be dead before he even got a taste of the salt water.

Zahed enjoyed letting the image play out for a moment in his mind's eye, then plucked an internal handset off the wall and hit two keys.

Steyl, in the cockpit, picked up instantly. "Is he up?"

"Yes. Where are we?"

"We just entered Cyprus airspace. About half an hour from landfall."

"Let's do it," Zahed said.

"Okay," Steyl replied.

Zahed hung up and smiled at Reilly. "I'm really, really going to enjoy this."

Then he punched him again.

Chapter 62

☩

"Niner Mike Alpha, we have a problem. Unable to maintain cabin pressure. Request descent flight level one two zero."

The controller was quick to respond. "Niner Mike Alpha, are you declaring an emergency?"

Steyl kept his tone even. "Negative, not at this time, Mike Alpha. We suspect an unlocked door. We need to depressurize, lock it, and repressurize. It's happened before."

"Roger, Mike Alpha. Descend at your convenience. No known traffic below you. Base of controlled airspace at eight thousand feet. Good luck."

Steyl thanked the tower, then adjusted the autopilot pitch control wheel upward, causing the plane's nose to tilt downward, and throttled back, dramatically reducing power from both engines. This made the aircraft think it was landing and triggered the landing gear alarm to remind its pilot to drop the gear. Steyl had anticipated the loud, continuous beep that wailed briefly through the cabin and hit a button by his right knee to kill it.

With its nose pitched down by fifteen degrees, the Conquest started a sharp descent from its cruising altitude of twenty-five thousand feet down to twelve thousand. It was the maximum cabin altitude the aircraft's systems would allow Steyl to request, given that the cabin was already pressurized. Accordingly, Steyl turned the pressurization control knob clockwise to its maximum position, getting the compressors to raise the cabin altitude from its cruising setting of eight thousand feet to the less comfortable, reduced-oxygen equivalent of twelve thousand feet. At a rate of change of five hundred feet per minute, it would take eight minutes for the pressure to get there. Then, once inside and outside pressures were equalized, Zahed would be able to open the cabin door. The Iranian had told Steyl he wanted Reilly to have the longest fall possible, and although Steyl knew it was possible to open the door from a couple of thousand feet higher, twelve thousand was a safer bet. From that height, Reilly's drop would last a little over a minute. Steyl knew that as far as Zahed was concerned, longer would have been better, but a minute was still long enough. It would still feel like an eternity to anyone, especially when that person was aware of what was lying in wait at the end of it.

REILLY HEARD THE ENGINES WHINE DOWN, felt the cabin pitch forward and the plane start to drop, and knew what was happening.

A spasm of fear rocked him, but instead of paralyzing him, it jump-started his mind and threw it into survival mode. There wasn't much he could do, given how he was tied up, but he had to try something.

He glanced around. He view was limited by the partition to his right. He could only see the very back of the cabin. He saw a stack of cardboard boxes piled up behind the Iranian, and glimpsed the leather binding of an old codex poking out from the uppermost box. His mood darkened as he remembered that Zahed and his men were now in possession of the trove of Nicaea. He pulled his gaze away from the boxes and surveyed the rest of the space. He spotted a drawer with a green cross symbol on it, under one of the rear seats. The first aid kit. He imagined he'd find a small pair of scissors in there, scissors that could cut through his binds. There was a slight obstacle blocking his way to the kit, in the form of the Iranian, who was watching him like a falcon and caught Reilly's wandering eyes.

Zahed didn't say anything. Just brought up his good hand and did a small *tsk-tsk* wave of his forefinger while giving him a chiding look.

Reilly's eyes stayed locked on the Iranian, and he managed a wry, relaxed smile. Which caused Zahed's expression to tighten.

Reilly let out a small chuckle. It might not have been much, but right there and then, unsettling the Iranian, even just a little, felt really good.

CLOSE TO SIX MINUTES AFTER starting its descent, the Conquest leveled at twelve thousand feet. Steyl checked the cabin altitude reading. It was still working its way up to its target.

It was time to get Reilly into position.

He climbed out of his seat and joined Zahed at the back of the cabin.

"Which end do you want?" he asked Zahed.

"Take the legs."

Steyl nodded.

He grabbed Reilly's legs firmly and locked an arm around his ankles to keep him in place; then he stepped back, hunched in the low clearance of the cabin, and pulled him off the bench and onto the carpeted floor.

Then he started dragging him toward the cabin door.

Chapter 63

✠

Reilly hit the carpet with a muffled thud and went ballistic.

He was bucking and writhing furiously to free himself from the grasp of the South African, twisting his body left and right while alternating bent knees with sudden kicks despite having both ankles tightly anchored together. Each twist and each kick sent pain ricocheting through him, but he just ignored it and kept fighting. Then from somewhere behind him, the Iranian moved in. Using his good arm, he put Reilly in a choke hold. Reilly was now restrained from both ends and had to fight even harder. The choke was vise-tight, but after several manic twists and lunges, he managed to slip out of the South African's grip. Using his palms to balance himself, he lashed out at the man with big, two-legged kicks, keeping him at bay while flicking backward head butts to try to hurt Zahed.

"Christ, I thought you were going to sedate the fucker," the South African blurted as he tried to wrest control of Reilly's legs.

"No," the Iranian said, struggling to keep Reilly's neck tied down with his elbow, "I want him fully awake. I want him to feel every second of it with a clear mind."

This only spurred Reilly further as he swung his legs wildly, aiming for the South African's face. His position was too awkward to really put much sting in the kicks, and the man kept blocking them before they connected. Then Reilly decided to double his efforts on the Iranian's front. The Iranian was the weaker of the two. One decent hit there could be a game-changer.

He had to land it first.

He snapped his head furiously from side to side, like a marlin fighting off a heavy line, trying to shake the Iranian's grip, widening the strike zone Zahed needed to keep clear of—then he sensed the man within reach and bucked back, arcing his head backward as suddenly and as viciously as he could. The back of his skull connected with some part of the Iranian's face. He couldn't tell where it hit, but it was hard enough for him to hear the splatter and feel Zahed's grip falter. Reilly moved quickly and squirmed his head under the man's elbow. The Iranian tried to recover, but Reilly's head had already slipped partially through the man's bent elbow.

He bit into it like a rabid dog.

Zahed cursed with pain and flicked his arm up, but Reilly wouldn't let go, sinking his teeth even deeper into the man's forearm. But focusing on the Iranian made him lose focus on the other man, who moved in and managed to hook his arms around Reilly's ankles, reining him in again. Then Zahed freed his elbow and drove it back down into the base of Reilly's ear, rattling his head again and allowing the Iranian to put his choke hold back on.

Reilly kept twisting and bucking, but they had him solidly locked in as they wrangled him past the hoard of ancient texts and through the tight space between the two forward-facing club seats, before dumping him face-first onto the small clearing between those and the two rear-facing ones. The floor of the cabin was way too narrow for him to fit across it. They twisted him around so he was lying diagonally, his feet by the front right seat, his head only inches from the base of the cabin door.

"You gonna be able to hold him?" the South African asked.

"Just do what you have to do," Zahed said, breathing hard as he straddled Reilly's back, his weight driving Reilly's tied arms into his back and Zahed's right forearm—the good one—pressing across the base of his neck, barely allowing Reilly to breathe. "I've got him."

STEYL HELD THERE FOR A BEAT, making sure Zahed did have Reilly pinned down solidly; then he pulled back off him, slowly, ready for any sudden frenzy from the FBI agent.

None came.

"I'll radio in and slow us down," he told Zahed. "Give me a minute."

"Go."

Steyl got back in his seat.

He radioed Nicosia control to inform them he was level at flight level one two zero and asked for permission to slow down to one hundred knots. His request was promptly approved. With his engine power already reduced, the plane was slowing down. Steyl increased propeller pitch to change the angle of the blades. This was like downshifting a car from fifth gear to second. The props shot up to almost nineteen hundred rpm, and the noise inside the cabin went from a low-frequency rumble to a high-pitched whine.

Steyl watched the airspeed drop to the target level.

It got to a hundred.

They were ready.

"Open the door," he called out to Zahed. "I'll join you as soon as it's fully open." He had to stay in his seat while both sections of the door were being opened, to make sure he could deal with any unexpected complications during the unorthodox maneuver.

He turned around and watched as Zahed, still straddling Reilly, reached up and twisted the latch to unlock the upper section of the door.

The Iranian nudged it out.

The wind caught it instantly and flung it open.

A gale of cold air blasted into the cabin with a deafening howl.

Then came the frenzy.

Chapter 64

✠

R eilly felt the seconds ticking away inside him like he'd swallowed a time bomb. His face was pressed down against the rough nylon carpet, jamming his right eye shut and making it hard to breathe.

He couldn't move. The Iranian had him locked down solid. But at least the man was now alone. If Reilly was going to do something, he had to do it before the pilot came back. Tied up as he was, he'd be pretty helpless against the two of them.

Which meant he had to make his move real soon.

Then he heard the pilot give the Iranian the go-ahead, felt the Iranian lift up slightly off him, heard the latch click open.

He knew the Iranian's good hand was busy working the door. Knew the man couldn't use his other hand to counter Reilly's move.

Decided it was now or never.

Coiled his strength, concentrating it where he needed it most.

Heard the door whip open, felt the air roar in, felt the bracing cold slap the urgency into him.

Banished never to oblivion and went for now.

He lashed out, twisting sideways against his left shoulder and lifting off the ground with as much force as he could muster, turning his back away from the rear of the cabin and from the Iranian. At the same time, he threaded his fingers together and swung his right elbow back as hard as he could while bending his knees right back and unleashing a furious back kick. Elbow and feet connected with flesh and bone and generated faceless pained grunts, but they weren't game changers in and of themselves. Reilly knew he wouldn't really hurt the Iranian with the moves. He just needed to destabilize him and get him off his back—literally—for a couple of seconds.

Which he did.

The Iranian lost his balance and faltered off him for not much more than a couple of precious seconds, but it was long enough to allow Reilly to complete his move.

With ice-cold air whipping around him like a tornado, Reilly followed through with his flip until he was fully on his back and did two things in quick succession. He pulled his legs in and let loose with a massive, two-footed kick that caught the Iranian right in the chest and shoved him back against the bulkhead. Then Reilly rocked back and brought his knees right up into a fetal position and arced his back to shorten the distance from his shoulders to his hips and allow his hands to slip out from under him in one fluid swing.

They were still tied together. But at least they weren't behind him anymore.

Zahed straightened up just as Reilly rose to his feet. The Iranian was in front of the half-opened cabin door and sidestepped away from it, toward the middle of the cabin. They squared off for a beat under the five-foot clearance, hunched over under the cabin's low ceiling, eyeing each other, gauging their next moves. Then Reilly caught a slight twitch in the Iranian's eye and realized he was about to get ambushed.

He spun around as swiftly as he could, given that his ankles were tied together, and lunged at the South African through the narrow space between the two rear-facing seats, with his arms extended forward. He couldn't use them to land any decent strike, not with them tied together and not with his precarious footing. Instead, he used them to grab the pilot by the neck and just pulled him in toward him, while angling his forehead slightly down a nanosecond before it struck the bridge of the pilot's nose. It was as savage a head butt as Reilly had ever delivered, its crack audible despite the gale force wind spinning around the cabin. The South African staggered back through the tight space between the two seats, bounced against their sides like a pinball before cracking his head against the wood-paneled vertical partition that separated the cockpit from the cabin and crashing through its narrow opening.

Reilly knew Zahed would be moving on him, but he still didn't manage to turn in time to fully deflect the strike. The Iranian had his gun out and brought it down on Reilly with a vicious right-handed swing, catching him on the edge of his jaw. It wasn't a clean hit, but it still caused serious damage, shooting pain across Reilly's face and blacking out his vision for an instant.

Reilly flew sideways, to his right, in the direction of the swing, slamming into the left rear-facing club seat, the one that backed up against the pilot's seat. He turned his head in time to glimpse Zahed moving in for another blow, arm raised, anthracite metal glinting under the cabin's down lighters, and he managed a desperate lunge off his seat in time to slam into Zahed and send him reeling back a few feet.

Reilly bounced back into the chair, his head spinning, his feet wobbly, pain searing every inch of his body. In his daze, he saw Zahed recover and come at him again, saw him raise his handgun like a hammer, felt his strength ebbing away and his arms unwilling to rise again to deflect another blow. He darted his eyes around unconsciously, looking for a weapon, something, anything to use to block the attack. The only thing his eyes snagged was a fluorescent yellow nylon case with two black handles. It was about two feet long, a foot high, and half a foot wide, sitting innocuously behind the right-hand club seat, glinting at Reilly.

He reached out and grabbed it. It was heavy—twenty-five pounds, maybe thirty. Which felt like a hundred, given Reilly's state.

He didn't have time to think. Didn't even know what he was doing. He was just flying on instinct, his limbic system running the show while his consciousness rebooted. He just yanked the case out and swung it at Zahed, battering him in the chest and sending him flying back against the left, forward-facing club seat, the one directly behind the half-open cabin door. Reilly lost his grip on one of the handles at the end of the swing and the case's Velcro fittings flew open under the momentum of its heavy load, which was another fluorescent yellow nylon boxlike bundle, only this one had a couple of differently shaped handles sticking out of it.

A bolt of understanding rocked Reilly.

It was the plane's life raft. Stowed within easy reach and clearly visible in case of an emergency.

Which, as far as he was concerned, this sure as hell was.

He saw Zahed rise out of the seat and reached for the bundle's handles. Reilly's fingers clamped around them, and he pulled, hard, and ducked away, toward the opposite side of the cabin, away from Zahed and the cabin door.

The life raft started inflating instantly, unfolding itself with a loud, violent hiss and spreading out with startling speed. Given that it was seven feet wide, the cabin's five-foot diameter blocked it from fully inflating upward, downward, or sideways. The only place for it to go was along the axis of the cabin, squashed into an upright oval ring. The tight space was also making it expand much more violently than it would under normal, unconstrained conditions. After four seconds, it was already big enough to act as a barrier between Reilly and Zahed. After eight seconds, it was fully inflated, its underside facing Reilly, its topside facing Zahed, its leading edge bursting through the partition behind the front row of seats. As it crowded into the cockpit, the engine whine rose noticeably, turning it into a higher-pitched scream. The plane accelerated noticeably, its propeller blades now spinning even faster. Not only that, but the cabin also pitched forward by about ten degrees. The life raft had pushed forward the power levers, prop levers, and autopilot pitch control wheel, all of which sat side by side in the cockpit's central console.

The plane was dropping.

Reilly caught his breath and steadied himself against the seat nearest to him. He heard the wind wrench the open door panel off its hinges and watched it get sheared off the plane. His eyes wide with alarm, he scanned left and right, looking for direction while trying to calm his mind, fighting the primal fear from the surge of chemicals that his amygdala was flooding his brain with and trying to reinstate some kind of rational control.

Gunshots interfered with the process.

On the other side of the life raft, Zahed was firing furiously, obviously trying to deflate the raft or kill Reilly.

Or both.

Bullets were ripping through the life raft's nylon skin, and there was nowhere for Reilly to take cover.

He ducked down and moved forward as several objects fell to the cabin floor and rolled forward, the contents of the life raft's emergency pack that had fallen out of it as it twisted in the confined space.

Reilly's eyes danced over the cascade of items, processing their value. He saw an expandable paddle. A sea mirror. A jug with a handle for bailing. Rescue line. Hand flares.

And a knife.

Not huge. Not a carbon-steel combat knife that could gut an alligator. Just a safety knife with a floating orange handle and a tame-looking, five-inch serrated blade.

It was just lying there, resting against the base of the club chair.

Calling out to him.

Stabbing him with hope.

He reached down and grabbed it. Five seconds later, his hands and feet were free. A round penetrated the seat behind him, drilling into its thick leather padding; then another nicked his left shoulder and plowed into the bulkhead. The life raft was made up of separate compartments and, despite the holes cutting through it, it was still fully inflated, but it wouldn't be long before it started to sag and give Zahed the opportunity to get out from behind it.

Reilly had to take him out before that happened.

He also had to move fast. The plane was still dropping.

He crouched low and bolted toward the back of the cabin, away from where the bullets were landing. He stopped at the edge of the life raft, took a deep breath to steady himself, and pounced, pulling the raft's edge away with his right arm while lunging with the knife in his left arm.

He caught Zahed by surprise and cut him across his right wrist.

The Iranian's handgun fell from his hand and a fountain of blood erupted from his arteries. He just stood there, frozen in place, staring at Reilly in utter shock, still pinned against the cabin door by the life raft's self-erecting canopy.

Reilly's eyes lasered into him. He would have liked to savor the sight for longer, but he couldn't afford to loiter. The plane was still dropping, smooth and unfussed, without banking left or right, just heading down to the sea in a straight line, the autopilot clearly still engaged.

Reilly scowled at the Iranian.

Reached behind the man and popped open the lower section of the cabin door.

Consigned every pixel of Mansoor Zahed's wide-eyed, livid expression to his memory.

Shouted, "I guess you won't be needing that tombstone after all."

And shoved him out with a heel kick to the groin.

Chapter 65

✝

The Iranian dropped out of view instantly and without a sound.

Reilly stood in the freezing gale and watched the rising sea through the open doorway. For a moment, he wondered if, of the two of them, the Iranian wasn't the luckier one. Then he turned his attention to the massive nylon bumper blocking his route to the plane's controls, stepped around it to where it was jammed through the cockpit's doorway, and started hacking away at it with his blade.

He shredded, pulled, peeled, and ripped away at the yellow nylon wall like a psychopath on a rampage.

He couldn't feel any pain anymore.

His training was paying off, adjusting and optimizing his bodily functions for the one task they needed to ensure right now: survival. Everything was working toward that end. His adrenal glands had flooded his system with adrenaline, heightening his brain's ability to process information and making it more alert to a barrage of sensorial inputs. Endorphins were flooding through him to dampen any pain he felt and stop it from distracting him. His brain had unleashed a flood of dopamine, causing his heartbeat to speed up and his blood pressure to rise. His bronchial passageways had dilated, allowing more oxygen into his lungs to fuel his bloodstream faster. His liver was secreting a rush of glucose to boost his energy. Even his pupils had widened, for better vision.

A synchronized piece of machinery, dedicated to its own longevity.

He pulled apart enough of the life raft to clear a path into the cockpit. Pages from Steyl's information ring binder were flying all over the place, ripped out by the hurricane that was swirling inside the cabin. He swatted a couple of them away as he stepped over the fallen pilot's prone body and climbed into his seat.

He tucked the knife under his belt, strapped himself in quickly, and looked out. The sea level was looking worryingly close and getting closer by the second. Worse, the aircraft was vibrating heavily, its airspeed dangerously high.

Reilly's eyes scrutinized the instrument panel. He had never flown an aircraft before, but he'd been in enough cockpits of small aircraft in the course of his work to know broadly what the controls did and what the main gauges meant. He saw one that told him the plane was dropping at close to fifteen hundred feet per minute. Various other dials had their needles well beyond their red lines. One of them, the airspeed indicator, had a needle that was pushing against its stop pin, off the scale and way beyond the red-and-white "Maximum Operating Speed" barber pole. He knew he needed to throttle back to try to slow the plane down, but before his hand reached the twin levers, he heard a mechanical splutter over the high-pitched scream of the engines. It was coming from his right. He flicked a glance out the side window in time to see the starboard engine's exhaust pipe belch out a trail of black smoke and flames.

Within seconds, the port engine did the same.

Full power at low altitude was beyond the engines' design limits, and smoke started pouring into the cabin through the air vents in the ceiling. A bunch of warning lights lit up at the top of the instrument panel. Reilly leaned in for a closer look. The most prominent pair among them had "FIRE—BLEED AIR SHUTOFF PUSH" marked on each of them. His heart pounding, he flicked up the safety flaps on them and pressed the square buttons, which killed the air intake from the engines and cleared the smoke from the cabin. Just then, two other buttons lit up. They were marked "BOT ARMED PUSH." He wasn't sure what they were, but figured they were also related to the fire and hit them too. Those must have triggered the extinguishers, as the fire and the black smoke that were gushing out of the engines stopped. But then, so did the engines. They shut down, cutting out the noise and slowing down the plane's descent. Within seconds, the props stopped turning altogether. Reilly saw that they had feathered, their blades now angled parallel to the airflow and perpendicular to the wings. On cue, two green autofeather lights within the warning lights clusters started blinking.

He'd succeeded in putting out the fire, but in doing so, he'd also killed the engines.

The Conquest was now hurtling toward the sea. Disconcertingly, it was still doing that in a controlled manner, the autopilot maintaining it in a clean, linear glide slope.

A heading Reilly needed to overcome.

He tightened his grip on the wheel and pulled it hard toward him. He felt the plane's nose edge up a touch, but it was too hard to maintain the pull on it, and the second he relaxed his grip, even barely, the nose went right down to its diving stance, rushing toward a watery grave. He was fighting a losing battle. Something was blocking his efforts and keeping the plane stubbornly glued to its trajectory.

Then he spotted it. The small, red switch on the pilot wheel marked "A/P DISCONNECT."

Autopilot disconnect.

He had nothing to lose. If the autopilot was running the show, it was the enemy. It needed to be eliminated.

He hit the switch and heard something that sounded disconcertingly like a loud doorbell. The wheel immediately went looser in his hands. He hauled it back again, making sure he kept it and the pedals centered to keep the wings level. This time, he felt a change. The nose was edging up. Not much, but enough to be noticeable. It fueled him to try even harder. He kept pulling, as much as he could. He saw the water level rising up dizzyingly to meet him and pulled even more. It felt like he was trying to physically lift the plane up himself, which, in a way, he was.

With each concerted pull, the Conquest's nose came up some more, and as it did, the plane's airspeed decreased. But then if Reilly relaxed his grip, even marginally, to regroup for a new pull, the nose fought him and went back down. It was like trying to reel in a monster marlin. By the time he could see the texture of the individual ripples in the sea's surface, the indicator was telling him he was traveling at a little over a hundred knots. Water was rushing past below him now, an endless dark blue conveyor belt that was whizzing by, tantalizingly close and welcoming and yet easily deadly if the ditching went wrong.

Reilly tried to steady his breathing and kept the plane straight and almost level, avoiding any banking and bringing it down ever so gently. He was in no rush to hit the water. Unless a tanker appeared in his flight path, he felt safe where he was. As long as he didn't try to land, he didn't run the risk of plowing into the sea and getting shredded in the process.

Still, he had to land at some point. And he had to do it before he hit landfall, which was out there somewhere.

He concentrated hard, and kept massaging the wheel to keep the nose more or less level and control the glide. Then a continuous horn blared—the stall warning.

He had to bring it down now.

He nursed the wheel forward by a fraction of a millimeter. The plane drifted lower, one foot at a time, slowly, gracefully. It skimmed the tips of the small swells in a veil of spray; then it touched down. The sea was pretty calm, and although the Conquest's fuselage skittered across the white tips, it didn't flip over or break up. The feathered props helped keep the ditching smooth, and the small aircraft kept bouncing along until the weight of the water finally overwhelmed its forward momentum and it plowed to a sudden stop in a cloud of white foam.

The deceleration was brutal, ninety knots to zero in under a second. Reilly was thrown forward against his shoulder harness, but it did its job and kept him from slamming into the controls or flying out the windshield.

Water started rushing into the cabin instantly.

Reilly knew he didn't have long to get out. Not with the

cabin doors sheared off. He yanked his harness off, got out of his seat, and scrambled out of the cockpit and through the narrow gap between the two front seats, over the dead pilot's body. Several inches of water were already sloshing around in the cabin, with more flooding in every second. His eyes darted around, searching for a life jacket. They found something better, another bright yellow pouch, this one tucked away behind the other front club seat and smaller than the life raft's valise. Big blue letters across it told him it was the "Emergency Grab Bag," which sounded just right to him.

He grabbed it and bolted to the cabin door; then he stopped in his tracks and cast his eye toward the back of the cabin, to the crates that were stacked between the rear seats and the partition behind which he'd been stowed.

The texts.

The ones that had survived since the dawn of Christianity.

The two-thousand-year-old legacy that Tess had brought to light.

His chest constricted at the thought of losing them, of letting Tess down, after everything that had happened.

He had to do something.

He had to try to save them.

He stormed up to the crates, scanning the cabin around him, looking for something he could use to save them, something he could put them in that was watertight. Anything. A bag, some plastic sheeting—part of the life raft. It was there, ripped apart, big chunks of yellow plastic sloshing around in the rising water.

It would have to do.

He grabbed hold of a big chunk of it and pulled it toward him, looking for a decent piece that would be large enough to do the job. He found a section that might work, part of the tubular ring of the raft. He pulled out his knife and sawed away at it, cutting out a duffel bag–shaped section that was open at one end and sealed at the other.

The water was now at his knees and rising fast.

He stomped across to the crates, pulled the top one open, and started loading up the leather-bound codices into the nylon tube, one by one. He knew he wasn't handling them with anything near the care they deserved, but he didn't have a choice. He knew he wouldn't be able to save them all—he knew that—but even saving some of them, a few of them, was still something.

The water reached his thighs.

He kept going. Popped the top off the second chest, started loading books from it too.

The water was now at his waist. Which meant the third chest was now submerged.

He had to go. He had to try to seal the top of the nylon tube and get out of there. If he didn't move fast, he'd be trapped in the cabin.

He twisted the top of the tube around on itself, tightening it as much as he could. It wouldn't be watertight; he knew that. But it was the best he could do. He grabbed its neck and fought the torrent of water all the way back to the cabin door.

It was like trying to climb into a storm pipe during a monsoon.

He took a deep breath, ducked underwater, and pushed himself through the narrow opening, pulling the nylon tube with one hand, the grab bag with the other.

He came out on the other side with the plane partially submerged, and stepped onto the wing. He scuttled across to the port engine and sat on its cowling, which was still just above water. He rummaged through the grab bag and pulled out a life jacket, which he slipped on and inflated, and a personal locator beacon, which he clipped onto the jacket and activated.

He rode the cowling down as it slipped below the surface. The Conquest's tail followed and went under less than a minute later, leaving him floating around with the eerily serene white silhouette of the plane disappearing into the darkness below him.

He hung on to the nylon tube, gripping its neck as tightly as he could with both hands, fighting to keep the water out of it. But he knew it was hopeless. He could see water seeping in through the folds in its neck. The nylon it was made of wasn't designed to be easily folded. It was designed to be tough, to withstand punctures and heavy seas. And much as he tried, Reilly knew he was fighting a losing battle.

With every passing minute, more water seeped in. And the more it seeped in, the heavier the tube became. After about half an hour, having expended every last micron of energy that he possessed, Reilly couldn't keep it afloat any longer. It was simply too heavy. He also knew it was probably pointless. The texts were soaking with water by now. They were no doubt already ruined, the trove of information in them lost forever. And if he kept hanging on to them, they'd soon take him with them.

With a long, soul-wrenching howl, he let go.

They drifted away, then went under, a yellow nylon tube of inestimable value, leaving him floating around aimlessly, one lone speck of life in an unforgiving sea.

Chapter 66

✝

Reilly felt himself slip in and out of consciousness several times, the cool water lapping against his head and nudging him awake each time his mind and body tried to shut down.

The sea was being kind to him, with nothing more than a gentle swell that made staying awake even harder. But he knew it would get colder, and possibly rougher, as nightfall approached. The vest could keep him afloat, but it wouldn't keep him alive if the water got choppier and his body decided to surrender to exhaustion.

He found himself thinking of Tess, thinking that she was most probably safe, which was good, but that he'd let her down in losing the trove of Nicaea, which would be a big blow. He tried focusing on that disappointment, using it to stay afloat, thinking that at least if he kept himself alive, he wouldn't cause her another loss, and he'd be able to tell her exactly what had happened, which would at least do away with the burden of uncertainty that would otherwise gnaw away at her for the rest of her days.

After a while, he just let himself go, relying on the life jacket and its personal locator beacon to do its job. He just drifted along the deep water, drained beyond words, waiting for a rescue he hoped would eventually show up.

*   *   *

ONE HUNDRED AND EIGHTY MILES due east of his position, the air traffic controller who had been tracking the Conquest's progress after Steyl had radioed in for permission knew something was wrong as soon as he saw the plane drop below twelve thousand feet and accelerate.

After three no-response calls and less than a minute after he'd first noticed the plane's unusual behavior, the controller activated the emergency SAR plan. A British Royal Navy Sea King HAR3 Search-and-Rescue chopper took to the air from its base at Akrotiri in Cyprus just as Reilly's plane was hitting the water.

The signal from Reilly's PLB, giving his location, was forwarded to the chopper's pilot while it was speeding to the Conquest's last known position. And just over an hour after he'd found himself floating in the Mediterranean, a frogman was riding a harness down to pull him to safety.

HE WAS FLOWN BACK TO AKROTIRI, where he had his injuries looked at and dressed by military medical personnel at the Sovereign Base Area's Princess Mary's hospital.

Even though the plane had ditched in international waters, there was a whole bunch of questions that Reilly needed to answer regarding who was on it, what had happened, and why it had happened. The British were asking. Before long, officials from the Cypriot Directorate of Civil Aviation and the National Guard showed up, and they were asking too.

For a while, Reilly was on his own. He fielded the questions with as much restraint as he could muster, but he was tired and he was hurting and his patience was running thin. He put a call in to New York, got through to Aparo and asked him to help get him out of there, but he knew it would take time. The American Embassy was an hour's drive away, in Nicosia, and the FBI didn't keep a legat there. Still, calls were made, and at around midday, the embassy's defense attaché showed up, took control and whisked Reilly out of there. More important, he was able to help Reilly with the question he had been desperate to have answered from the very moment he'd been winched aboard the Sea King.

It wasn't an easy question to answer. With all that had happened and with Ertugrul dead, there was rampant confusion at the consulate in Istanbul and it was hard to pin down the person who was best suited to find her. It took many phone calls and several frustrating waits, but they were finally able to track her down to a police station in Konya.

Hearing her voice did more to soothe his aches and pains than all the painkillers they'd given him. She was safe and well. But she also needed help.

She was also caught up in a similar bureaucratic web. A whole different bunch of questions needed to be answered, and they weren't about to let her go until they got their answers.

"Hang tight," he told Tess. "I'm coming to get you."

THE JET ARRIVED LATE IN THE NIGHT, a spotless white knight bearing the discreet emblem of the Gulfstream Aerospace Corporation. Reilly watched with mounting impatience as it taxied to the private hangar and its engines whined down. Then its cabin door snapped open and the Vatican's secretary of state, Cardinal Mauro Brugnone, stepped out.

His furrowed face cringed with surprise and sympathy as he took notice of the bruising and cuts littering Reilly's face and hands. He spread his arms wide and embraced the agent before pulling away and saying, "So . . . it's gone? It's definitely gone?"

He already knew it was. Reilly had told him so when he'd called him, but he hadn't told him the whole story.

"I'm afraid so," Reilly replied.

"Tell me," the cardinal said, inviting Reilly on board.

While the pilot hurried to complete the requisite paperwork that would allow them to take off again, Reilly filled in his host on what had happened. By the end of it, the cardinal's back was hunched forward, the skin under his eyes and skin weighed down by the distressing revelations.

They sat in silence for a moment; then the pilot reappeared and confirmed they'd have wheels up within minutes. Brugnone didn't say anything. He just nodded, still stewing over what Reilly had told him.

"Maybe we can recover them," Reilly offered. "It can't be that deep out there. I'm sure it's within reach. And if we did, maybe we can still read what was on them. Forensics labs can do amazing things these days."

Brugnone looked at him with a shrug and raised eyebrows. Evidently, he didn't put any more stock in Reilly's words than Reilly did himself.

"This suits you, doesn't it?" Reilly asked. "I mean, if they're gone for good. No questions asked. No damaging revelations . . . no headaches?"

Brugnone frowned, then said, "Of course, I prefer that whatever was in them should never come out. I wouldn't want everyone to know what they said. But *I* would have liked to know. Very much so."

He held Reilly's gaze for a long beat, then turned and stared out into the darkness, looking like a man in deep mourning.

Chapter 67

✠

They were met at the small, mostly military airport by Rich Burston, the legat from the FBI's office in Ankara. Burston had flown down from the Turkish capital in a military helicopter. He had been Ertugrul's boss, and as they drove through the deserted, dark flatlands on their way into the city, Reilly was able to tell him firsthand about how his agent had been killed.

The legat was anxious. "We need to be in and out as quickly as we can," he told Reilly. "I don't want these guys figuring out who you really are. Unless you want to spend the next few days answering their questions."

Reilly understood what the legat was talking about. The plane had gone down in international waters. It had taken off from a Greek island. There was only so much the Cypriot authorities could demand to know.

This was different.

Reilly had been directly involved in events that had led to the deaths of several Turkish soldiers, including, Reilly knew, a senior and well-respected officer. The Turkish authorities would want to know exactly how and why that had happened.

"I'd rather talk them through it over the phone from Federal Plaza," Reilly told him.

"Yeah, I don't blame you. Just leave the talking to me and follow my lead."

Reilly said he would, then turned to the cardinal. Brugnone just nodded his agreement.

IN THE END, it all went down reasonably smoothly. They were able to get Tess and the old woman out of custody without too much aggravation. The late hour helped, as did the fact that the brass of the Jandarma weren't based in Konya.

A local police detail was assigned to keep an eye on the old woman and her family business for a few days, although Reilly didn't think she was in any more danger, not with Zahed dead and the stash of codices gone. Still, it was better to be safe than sorry, and he was happy to know that she'd be protected until things died down.

The pale glimmer of dawn welcomed them as they walked out of the police station. The street was deserted. The city was still well settled into its habitual nightly slumber, with only the hum of scattered air-conditioning condensers detracting from its serenity.

Tess held Reilly's hand in hers as they walked to the waiting cars. She was exhausted, physically and mentally. She was also deeply disappointed. In a few words, whispered in a snatched, private moment, Reilly had told her and the old woman that the texts had been lost, swallowed up by the sea.

The news had gutted her. The codices had survived close to two thousand years of intrigue. They'd made it through the Crusades, the fall of an expansionist empire, and a couple of world wars, but they hadn't survived the savagery of the twenty-first century.

They stopped outside the police car, the one that was taking the old woman back to her son's apartment above the shop. Tess let go of Reilly's hand and gave the old woman a hug.

The old woman held on to her for a long moment, then pulled back. "Will I see you tomorrow?" she asked. She had Tess's hand tightly cupped in both of hers.

Tess hesitated, and turned to Reilly. He was still dosed up on painkillers and looked a mess. She knew he was keen to get out of there as soon as possible. Brugnone's jet was waiting to fly them out of the country and back to Rome, and they'd take a commercial flight back to New York from there. She also wanted to get home to try to put the madness behind her. But standing there, looking into the old woman's delicate eyes, she realized she couldn't leave her like that. She wanted to spend more time with her. In little more than twenty-four hours, they'd been through a lot together, and she felt it would be rude to just disappear from her life like that, even if it wasn't forever. But she didn't think she had a choice.

Reilly's grim expression confirmed it. "I'm sorry," he told her. "We can't stay. There's a plane waiting for us."

The woman's expression sagged. "Not even for a few hours in the morning? I was hoping you would come over for breakfast at my son's place. Over the shop." She tried to give him a smile, but it barely made it past the melancholy that was weighing her down.

Reilly glanced across at the legat. The man shook his head softly, his expression telegraphing a genuine sense of regret.

"I'm sorry," Reilly told the woman.

She nodded slowly with resignation. One of the cops opened the car door for her. She stood still for a moment, then turned to Tess and said, "Can you follow me to the shop? On your way to the airport?"

Her words surprised Tess. "What, now?"

She tightened her hold around Tess's hand. "Yes. I'd like to give you something. A souvenir. Give me the chance to leave you with a nicer memory of Konya than what you've seen so far."

Tess held the woman's gaze. There was something more there, something unsaid. Something the woman really needed Tess to respond to.

Trying not to telegraph her suspicions and suddenly wary of the cardinal's presence, she looked a question at Reilly and the legat.

The legat shrugged. "I suppose we could. As long as it's

just a quick stop. And I do mean a quick stop. I don't want either of you here a minute longer than you need to be."

THE LEGAT AND THE CARDINAL WAITED in the comfort of the air-conditioned car while Tess and Reilly joined the old woman outside the storefront.

She woke her son up and got him to come down and unlock its entrance for them, then shooed him away and sent him back up to bed before inviting them in.

Tess hadn't really noticed how gorgeous some of their ceramics were. There were vases, bowls, and plates of all sizes, elegantly shaped and exquisitely painted.

"Choose anything you like, please," the old woman told them. "I'll be right back."

Tess watched her step away to the back of the store and disappear down some stairs that must have led to a basement.

She glanced at Reilly. He looked rough and weary, like being there was the last thing in the world he needed. Which, in fairness, it probably was.

She was hoping it would prove different.

She was about to confide her suspicions to him when the woman reappeared. Two things immediately signaled to her that she was right, and she felt a flutter in the pit of her belly. One was the way the old woman glanced furtively beyond her and Reilly and out the shop window, as if she were checking to see if anyone was watching. The other was what she was carrying.

It was an old shoebox.

The old woman cast another look out front, then presented the box to Tess. "These are for you."

Tess's heart jumped a couple of gears as she looked at her quizzically. She wanted to ask the obvious question, but the words died out in her throat. She just took the box and opened it.

It was filled with dozens of plastic sleeves.

Tess took one out and opened it up. It was about six inches wide and was all folded up on itself, like an accordion-style wallet sleeve that people used to hold family photos in the pre-iPhone era.

She opened it up.

It was made up of a couple dozen pockets, each one about an inch and a half tall. Inside each pocket was a six-inch strip. On each strip were four 35mm negatives.

Tess knew what they were before she held the sleeve up to the light. Although the image was dark and reversed, she could see the distinct silhouette of a rectangular object against a neutral background. Some of them showed the backflaps and the leather ties clearly. The image on each negative was reversed, so the object in the photographs looked dark, its background light. Inside the dark rectangles were rows of tiny, light characters, as if written in white ink on a black page.

The writings on the codices.

They were there. Lots and lots of them.

"You took these?" she asked the woman.

"My husband did. Many years ago, long before he died. We thought we had to keep some kind of record of them, in case they were ever destroyed in a fire or something. They were so fragile, we had to be very careful, but we managed it. I have prints of all the pictures in storage, but they're too heavy for you to carry without anyone noticing."

Tess's fingers skipped deeper into the box. "Are they all in here?"

The old woman nodded. "Every page of every book." She shrugged, a pall of resignation darkening her face. "I know they won't convince anyone. People will easily say these pictures are fakes. But it's the best I can do."

Tess considered her words for a beat, then shook her head. "It doesn't matter." She gave the woman a warm, comforting smile. "This isn't about convincing anyone of anything. It never was. It's about knowledge. It's about history, and truth. Those who believe every word in the Bible was dictated by God himself—they were never going to be swayed anyway. We know that. Even seeing and examining the codices with their own eyes wouldn't have made a difference to them. But for those of us who are looking to understand the roots of faith better, for those of us who are curious about our history and about how we got to be the way we are . . . these are plenty. Believe me. Plenty."

The old woman seemed pleased with Tess's words and nodded her agreement. "Be careful with them."

"Oh, trust me, I'll make sure they're safe." She looked at Reilly, her face all luminous and giddy and brimming with an almost childlike glee. "We'll make sure of that, right?"

Reilly studied her for a beat, amusement playing across his bruised face, and raised an eyebrow. "I'm guessing you have your ending now?"

"You bet." She smiled. "Come on. Let's go home."

ACKNOWLEDGMENTS

My thanks to all the friends and colleagues—Bashar, Nic, Carlos, Ben, Jon, Brian, Claire, Susan, Eugenie, Jay, Raffaella, and everyone at Dutton, NAL, and Orion—without whom my efforts would be nothing more than pixels on the screen of my laptop. Thanks also to the Burstons, Joorises, and Chalabis for lending me their secluded homes (and sailboat), where said efforts could flourish without too many distractions.

Bigger thanks, though, this time around, are due to all the friends and family who helped us through this less than memorable time. There are far too many of you to mention, but you all know who you are and we're very fortunate to have you in our lives. Your friendship, help, and support has been phenomenal, and if anyone deserves to be thanked for making this book possible, it's you.

ABOUT THE AUTHOR

Raymond Khoury is the *New York Times* bestselling author of *The Last Templar*, *The Sanctuary*, and *The Sign*. An acclaimed screenwriter and producer for both television an film, Khoury lives in London with his wife and two children. For more information on the author's books, visit his Web site at www.raymondkhoury.com and join his Official Page on Facebook.